Explosive Disorder

A novel

Pan Telare

Explosive Disorder

Oak Lee Publishing
P.O. Box 5039
Bozeman, MT 59715

2015945243
978-0-9862262-4-3

First Edition, First Printing, 2015

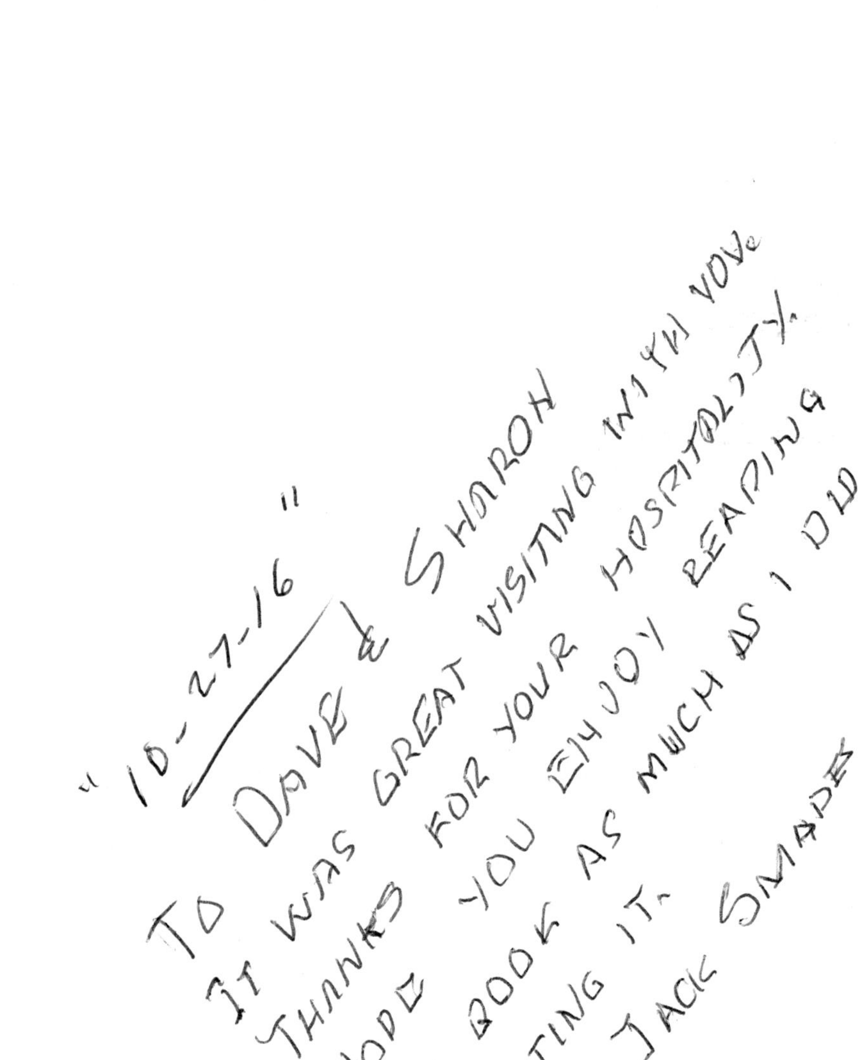

"10-27-16"

TO DAVE & SHARON

IT WAS GREAT VISITING WITH YOU.
THANKS FOR YOUR HOSPITALITY.
HOPE YOU ENJOY READING
MY BOOK AS MUCH AS I DID
WRITING IT.

JACK SMADER

This is a book of fiction. Some things in this book are fictitious.

Fiction

Sometimes invented by the imagination: an invented story: a factual description of something that is not a fact: a description of events that are not real.

Fictitious

Of, relating to, or characteristic of fiction, a falsely assumed concept.

Some things aren't.

Acknowledgements

Thank you all. Without your help I would have been plooouh.

Doctor Lisa Gray Whitaker and Jerry Montgomery for reading editing correcting and fixing.

Bob Neberman for your support and your technical knowledge about the transportation, shipping, customs and handling of freight.

Bud Mellor for your superior knowledge about how ships are made, how they are operated, and what can happen if things go wrong.

Leonard Bleininger for all your knowledge about aircraft, their capabilities, and the airplane business in general.

Jerry Montgomery. Thanks for everything, buddy.

Cast of significant people

Sargent Pizzametski LAPD
Doctor Make Caston. MD
Georgia, Make's secretary at DHS
John Walker, Make's immediate boss
Laura Caston. Make's Wife
Lon Dove, Make's boss's boss. John Walker's boss
Frank Fox, the director of the FBI.
Doctor Curt Delk, authority on Yemen Al-Asiri PETN progress
Isabell Franks, Deputy Secretary of Homeland Security
General Richard Johnson, Joint Chiefs
Mal Thorp, gunrunner and twin brother of Ishe Thorp
John Standard, Yemen Police Chief
Don T. Park, Private Investigator in KC
Ishe Thorp, Boat Captain and twin brother of Mal Thorp
Colonel Wright, works for NRO
Air Marshal Halt, TSA
Al-Absent, resident of Rukob, Yemen
Al-Abeb, Arab, ground man, worked for Make
Al-Asin, Yemen explosives maker
Al-HAmi, Arab, got Makes Iridium
Al-Kabob, a giant Irishman living in Yemen

Glossary:

AGRFM = Air to Ground Radiation Focused Missile

AQQAP = Arabian Peninsula

Banbury mixer = Compounding. The workhorse mixer of the plastics and rubber industries

CAA = Civil Aeronautics Administration

CAB = Civil Aeronautics Board

CADOHS = California Department of Homeland Security

DHS = Department of Homeland Security

Dogs (navy slang) = handles, that when turned, sealed the door water tight

DP10 = Deep penetration attachment for warheads

FAA = Federal Aviation Agency – air traffic control

HE = high explosive

Iridium = Motorola developed world wide satellite cell phone

Nishtun = a coastal town in southeastern Yemen. It is located at around. 15° 49' 26" N, 52 ° 11' 3" E

NRO = National Reconnaissance Office

PETN = Pentaerythritol tetra nitrate, an explosive, 35,500 feet per second gas expansion rate.

RPG = rocket propelled grenade

RTV = room temperature vulcanized. A caulking compound commonly used on metal

Sana'a = the capital city of Yemen

Tivars. Military rifle, Semi auto, full auto, 3 shot grenade launcher, scope w/ laser range finder, and folding stock and bipod. Made in Europe, fires 7.62 military ammo.

TSA, Transport Security Administration - guards on planes

VFR = visual flight rules

Zodiac =An Inflatable Boat with an outboard motor

Introduction

Some books of fiction contain events, technologies, or equipment that just couldn't be. This isn't that kind of book. There are other novels that contain only things that could actually happen. This is that kind of a book - with a twist.

I have a friend, a good friend who, after I had known him for 3 or 4 years, revealed to me some part (as it turned out, only a facet) of his life that amazed me. I had never thought of him as being the kind of person that had ever been involved in the activity he described. As time went on, he told me of other events that were equally amazing. He has done, seen, been involved in things that only a very, very few people in the whole world have ever experienced. I have never doubted him and I occasionally think about some of the things he has told me. After a while, I realized that his activities could be the basis of a book.

The real Doctor Make Caston was shocked when his parents died. It was very difficult for him because he was an only child, young and alone. But he got through it. Later, he entered medical school. He did it because he thought it would be a wonderful thing to help people and because his dad had wanted him to be a surgeon. Med school was also very difficult for him but he got through that too. And he got good grades. All this because he has always been a very tenacious guy. He gets things done because he finishes what he starts regardless of the obstacles. He now lives in the Southwest.

And I learned by writing this story that sometimes, when you are out with the boys, things happen that you can't tell anybody about. Not your closest friends, not even your wife.

This book is about international terrorism, SEX, and some other fun stuff.

Pan Telare
Prescott, Arizona
2015

Chapter 1

Thursday, 10:15—10:50 AM

I am very comfortable. I gradually become aware of a distant humming sound. As I listen it becomes louder and sharper. It sounds like an engine running. There is light in front and above me. I squint my eyes and look. There is no definite horizontal line: just dark below, and gradually it gets very bright with a white light as I look up higher. Up above, the light is bluer. My vision is so blurred that I can't see anything clearly, but I don't really care. I close my eyes.

The noise is getting louder. There is a constant ringing in my ears but the low pitched sound is very loud now. I think it's the sound of a loud un-muffled engine. It's almost deafening. My God, the wind is blowing every which way. I open my eyes again to find a bright but still blurred world. There are vertical dark things, probably supports for the top-if that is a top. I seem to be moving gently up and down and there is a lot of vibration. I blink my eyes trying to improve my sight. I wish I could see better.

Gradually my vision clears. Eventually, it gets good enough that can see shapes and forms. I believe I'm in the pilot's seat of an airplane. And now the noise is almost overpowering. I'm confused. I don't think I've ever seen this plane before. I don't remember how I got here. It's a small, single engine aircraft and it looks dirty inside. The seat next to me is split or some of the fabric is ragged. I am restrained in the seat somehow. It's a lap belt and a shoulder harness. How did I get in here? I don't remember what I have been doing. My God, I've got to get out of here. I try to turn around but I can't move much. I have got to get this harness off. I panic. I can't get it off of my shoulders.

I'm so tired. That just wears me out pulling on that harness.

Now I can see the instruments in front of me. When I look at things up close they are still blurry. And I can see my harness more clearly now. I can see the buckles. I unlatch the shoulder harness and turn to see where the pilot is and who else is in this airplane. More panic. There is no one else in the plane. Oh my God, what am I going to do? I'm alone in a strange airplane and I've no idea of where I am or how I got here. I was in Tucson just a little while ago. I can see pretty good now. I think I'm over the water. It looks like water. I can't see any other planes in the sky, or boats on the water below me. But my vision's a long way from perfect. This is just about as lonesome and scared as a person can get. How will I ever get home?

My head feels strange or I feel strange. It is hard to describe, but something isn't right with my body. There's still lots of ringing in my head.

How can this be? My last recollection is of being in an auditorium. I remember now, it was the Tucson Convention Center. I was attending a symposium that had to do with robots. Yes, the interface of robotics with surgery. I remember; I'm a surgeon and I had decided to attend this meeting because of the rapid invasion of robots into the surgery business. I remember it now. But, how did I get here? I've got to find land so I can get this plane down. I remember now, I'm Make Caston.

I wish I could stay awake.

I'd acquired a private pilot's license years ago while I was in school but had not flown much in the last ten years. But a year or so ago I had rented a 172 and flew around town, just to keep my flying skills up. Now I'm glad I did.

I can see the instruments clearly, what's left of them. The ones that are still in place are mostly round and black colored as are the holes where other instruments once were. The instruments and the holes are about the same color. What's left is a fuel gage surrounded by three black holes, an altimeter, attitude indicator, airspeed indicator, and a magnetic compass. And on my right there is a vertical hole where the com stack was. Now it has only one item in there, a nav. Com, your basic radio. The rest of the stack has been removed as have the rest of the instruments. Someone has cannibalized this airplane. They have left just enough instrumentation in it to fly VFR. Looking through some of the holes I can see wiring that has been cut. Someone has taken off the panels, removed most of the instruments and put the panels back. Christ. They even took the tachometer. At least the clock is still there.

My heading is 282 degrees, my airspeed is 110 MPH, and I've about half of a tank of gas left. I'm too close to the water for comfort though – about 1000 feet. However, I think the plane's on some kind of autopilot that I'm not familiar with so, probably, I should leave things alone until I decide what to do and how to do it.

I am so sleepy.

When I consider all my options, it seems best to turn 180 degrees and go back in the direction I came from. I check my heading again before I start my turn and, to my horror, find my heading is now 286 degrees. I've swung right four degrees while worrying about my future. I'm not flying in a straight line; I've been flying a circular path! Now my whole plan's worthless. I have no idea which way is home! How can that be? I can't have been on autopilot. There is no autopilot. Somebody took it out. What's going on? There's no rudder trim on any 172 that I've seen. I put my hands on the yoke for the first time and find that I'm flying in a plane that just likes to fly in a great circle. I straighten it out but then, when I let go of the yoke, it starts turning again.

My God, I'm in an airplane. How'd I get here? . What am I going to do?

Oh, that's right. This plane doesn't have an autopilot. They took that when they took the com stack. I crank the yoke and swing the plane around to the right until my heading's a little bit south of due east, about 105 degrees. I hope that will get me to land somewhere. I start a very gentle climb. A higher altitude will enable me to see farther ahead. I open the throttle a little bit more. Oh, Christ they took the tach! That's right. I remember now. I hope I don't over speed the engine. I'm probably over the pacific and not very far out. What time is it? I take my watch off. I look at it for a long time before I can see what time it is. It says 12:51 but when I check the clock on the plane it says 2:52. How can that be? Nothing makes any sense. How did I get in this plane, where am I, why doesn't my watch agree with the clock on the plane? How did I get over the ocean this quick? I was in a meeting an hour ago.

I remembered now that at 11:30 there was a lunch break in the meeting and I walked out of the auditorium with a couple of guys I met there. I don't remember getting to the lunch room though. How did I get here?

Where am I? Oh yeah, I'm in an airplane, a 172. I remember, the plane keeps turning to the right. I should correct my course back the 105 degrees. Then I thought, why bother, I don't know which way home is anyway, but then I decide my original plan was the best thing so I, again, correct my course to 105 degrees. At the very least, I should stop going in circles. This plane just likes to turn right. I will have to continually put a little left turn on the yoke to stay on 105 degrees.

Next I try the radio. There's a frequency that's for guys like me that don't know which frequency they should use. I wish I could remember that frequency. I start calling different frequencies and saying something like, “If you can hear me please reply”. I don’t get a response. Fuck!

I pull out the papers that are in the side pocket. One blew around the cabin then finally got stuck under the other seat. There are several aerial maps. My vision isn’t good enough to read much, but I can tell they’re all for Arizona, New Mexico or Utah. Another paper blows out the open window before I can grab it. In the bunch of papers I had there’s a sheet of paper torn from a spiral notebook. Someone had written in big letters, “*1200=VFR transponder*”

and “*121.5 guard frequency*”.

That’s it; I have trouble setting 121.5 for the “emergency” guard frequency but finally get it dialed in. I start calling for help but I get no response. I’m probably too low and too far out. About three minutes later I hear a voice. I can tell it’s a woman’s voice talking but it’s continually breaking up then reconnecting. I just can’t understand what she was saying. Finally, I ask the woman to listen for me again in a couple of minutes. Then I notice directly ahead of me on the instrument panel there’s an embossed metal tag, 913 R, this is the plane’s ‘N’ number.

Chapter 2

Thursday 11:00 AM

"Yes, I got the tickets--Hold on, I got another call. I'll get back with you." The Desk Sargent at LAPD headquarters jabs button three and answers, "Sargent Blackwell."

"Officer Blackwell, this is John Corrigan at ATC4."

"Hold it, hold it. This is Sargent Blackwell and what is ATC4?"

"I'm the supervisor at Air Traffic Control, station 4. We are located in Ogden, Utah."

"Ok, so what have you got?"

"This is a new thing for us. We have a plane coming in that was reported stolen a couple of weeks ago. It was taken from Kirkland in Albuquerque. It is pure luck that we still had a hot sheet with this plane on it, it's so old. I was told that if they are gone more than a day or two, we never get them back. Anyway, I talked to Homeland Security, I talked to LAX emergency, and I talked to someone in the airport police. They are the ones that told me to call you. They said you would be able to verify everything and make things happen. I mean verify that the plane is actually stolen and get somebody to find it. It got handed off to us from OC, that's Orange County control tower. That's very unusual."

"So you mean the plane is coming here?"

"Yeah, I talked to the guy flying the plane. He said he thinks he can get to LAX. He should be there in 51 minutes"

Shit. "I'll take it from here. How do I identify the plane and what's your number?" *He sighs and dials.* "Hi honey. Hey, I've got a hot one here. I will probably not be able to go with you tonight. I'll leave the tickets with the desk Sargent. Take one of your girlfriends with you and you can pick up the tickets on the way. I'll see you when this is over."

Blackwell's honey said, "Bullshit, it's never over." Disconnect. "That bastard. He's got something on the side, I know it."

Blackwell jabbed another button.

"This is the La Brea precinct, Sargent Louise Bone."

"Hi Louise, this is Jerry Blackwell. How're you doing?"

"Great Jerry, it's good to hear from you. I haven't talked to you since, oh about 9:30. What's going on? Anything exciting?"

"No, my social life is pretty dull, I'm sorry to say. However, this is business now; I got a guy comin in in a stolen plane. They need a detective at the airport so I thought I'd give you a call."

"Jerry, I gotta go. I got another call. I'll get somebody out there."

"Hey wait. Louise, before you go, tell them it's plane number 913 Romeo. Call me if you get a chance, ok Louise?"

Chapter 3

Thursday 10:35 AM

The Deputy Secretary of Homeland Security, Isabell Franks is 40 years old and she commands a position in the United States Government that, at this time, with the exception of the President, is the most significant, most powerful office in the country. While in her midterm as Governor of Arizona, she had been called to the Whitehouse. When the President asked her if she would take the job, she immediately said no, she didn't think she could handle it. She could barely keep her head above water governing her home state. But President Fred O'Clare did a superb job of schmoozing and she finally agreed to accept. Her hair that used to be a beautiful auburn color now has lots of gray. Well, at least there's some good news; she had lost 8 pounds.

When the outside line in the deputy secretary's outer office rang, her receptionist, Tim answered, "This is the office of the Deputy Secretary of Homeland Security. How can I help you?" Moments later he reported: "Ms. Franks, John Corrigan, Air Traffic Control Supervisor, Ogden, Utah on line 2."

Two minutes later Isabell said, "Tim, we have an emergency. Get me all appropriate offices you can find and put them on a common line so I can talk to them."

Twenty five seconds later, "I've got someone from five of the six departments on line two."

The Deputy Secretary said, "Ladies and gentlemen, we have a single engine aircraft seventy miles out, about fifty minutes away. The plane was reported stolen two weeks ago. The pilot seems confused. The plane is owned by a Mr. Thorp who the FBI is watching. Inputs?"

"U S Customs, We need to secure him when he gets here."

"Emergency Management here. I'd say, get somebody out there to look him over. What's he got? We don't know."

"Military Advisor, We've got F/A18's in the air. We can make contact in twelve minutes max."

Franks asked, "What's the threat level? Anyone?"

"Holmes at Transportation security, At this point I'd say he's a level two. If he wasn't confused and had a destination in mind he would be a one."

"Mansfield, Secret Service, I agree. A level two. Send the Black Hawk with full compliment. They can handle anything in the air and when he gets on the ground too."

"I'm Don at Intelligence and Analysis. I'd agree with level 2 and I think the Blackhawk is a good idea."

The Deputy Secretary said, "Level two and Blackhawk it is. Thank you people. Back to work. Tim get that Blackhawk in the air with a full compliment. When he gets there let me talk to him."

Thirty minutes later, "This is the Deputy Secretary, tell me what you see."

"Mam, I believe it is a Cessna 172 but it is a beater. The right window behind the door is out and part of the aircraft skin at the back of the window is bent out somehow. The whole right side is covered with something black or gray. Probably oil. I've talked to the pilot. I don't think he knows his name and he seems to think he is or was just in Tucson. I've been friendly to him and telling him I'm here to help him get home. So far he's followed my instructions. He said the plane is a little hard to control. The only problem I see is his fuel level. He's been looking at the fuel level gage for a half hour and it always said the same thing, half full."

"Ok. Change of plans. He's a threat level 2. He's not going to LAX. Is there an airfield that you think he can reach that is away from a populated area?"

After brief pause, "Mam, there is a small air park called Compton/Woodley County Airport. He is about the same distance from that as he is from LAX. I can't guarantee he can get anywhere, mam. He may run out of fuel."

"Ok airman. Try to get him to Compton/Woodley. And thank you, air man. What's your name?"

"Dusty Rhodes, Mam."

"Dusty, if we talk again you can call me Isabell."

"Mam, I mean Isabell. Do you think it would be a good idea to have the Coast Guard on alert? Maybe a boat headed out from Long Beach?"

"I think it is an excellent idea, Dusty. Thank you." She punched in Tim. "Tim, first call LAPD and tell them the plane has been diverted to Compton/Woodley County Airport. Suggest they should have a detective and a CSI team there. Explain to them that we have a visual on him and we don't see any bomb threat, but we can't be sure so they should keep the bomb squad on alert. Compton/Woodley's only twenty miles away. The detective can decide when he gets there. And tell them about the Blackhawk too. Then, call LAX emergency and LAX police and tell them the plane is being diverted to Compton/Woodley county airport and they should stand down. And get the coast guard alerted too. Tell them what we've got." *Oh, I forgot something*, "And Tim. Get hold of the Department of Transportation. Tell them what we've decided about 913Romeo and what we are doing about him. Ask them to advise the FAA that we'll rescue 931Romeo, and suggest that the West Coast FAA might work with Dusty Rhodes."

Isabell tapped her ball point on the desk as she wondered about the security level. She was doing things, making decisions that could get someone killed. *Dusty Rhodes doesn't have any way of knowing the Cessna pilot's intentions. That guy could be a terrorist willing to give up his life to kill Americans. He could land at Compton/Woodley with a hundred pounds of HE and a hundred pounds of shrapnel and kill the helicopter crew and everyone else around there. And destroy the helicopter too. Or he could dive his plane into downtown LA in a big mall. He could…I've got to get to work. This could make a person nuts.* She walked to the window wondering. *And my security section is the easy part. Politicking is a hundred time more dangerous. Why'd the President pick me? He told me that the border crossing situation would get worse and he wanted someone familiar with that area. And an even more curious question is, why did I accept? I love my state. And the zinger is, for every hundred sincere Mexicans that cross the border, there is a smuggler with a bag of pot or worse, on his back. Shit. This is nonproductive thinking. I've got to stop it and get back to work.* She punched in her assistant again: "Tim is that situation still going ok?"

"I haven't heard any bad news so he's probably ten minutes out by now. At least he's over dry land."

It wouldn't surprise me if, in a few years, the President was named 'humanitarian of the year' or of the century. What he did probably saved thousands of Mexicans from starving to death.

What would it take to fix Mexico? How can they be so different from us, for Christ sakes? They are right next door. Christ, I've got to stop this and get to work.

Chapter 4

10:45 AM

I maintained my 105 degree course and checked out the rest of the aircraft. This wasn't your average Cessna. Someone beat it up pretty bad. Behind the copilot door the window's missing. Part of the edge around the open window is beat up. Some of the metal is bent outward. That's where all the wind is coming from. That's where a map and some papers went. Maybe that's why the plane keep's trying to turn right.

I'm afraid I'll go to sleep again and the plane will turn. I've got to stay awake.

On the radio I repeat my call for help and am rewarded with the same voice but the signal is stronger. I think she's asking who I am. Using the planes identification that I've found, I say "913 Romeo". Now I can hear her. I am told I've got the control tower at Orange County and I should switch to frequency 124.3 LAX for further directions.

OC: "913R, Orange County, say intentions."

913R: "I'm lost. I'm over water. I can't see any land. I don't know where I am. I need directions to Orange County, I guess."

OC: "Call SOCAL approach on 124.3"

Make had difficulty dialing 124.3 then, finally got the frequency dialed in and said, "SOCAL approach this is 913R, I'm lost I need directions."

On a landline, "SOCAL, this is OC. 913Romeo is lost over water. We gave him your frequency."

"Thanks OC, we got 913R now."

SOCAL: "Squawk 7700 and say your intentions."

913R: “Landing. I want to land at the nearest airport.”

SOCAL: “Squawk 7700”

No signal on 7700

SOCAL: “Squawk 7700”

No signal on 7700

SOCAL: “Change your transponder frequency to 7700.”

No signal on 7700

SOCAL: “913Romeo. You should change your transponder frequency to 7700.”

Make has been asleep, ”What?”

SOCAL: “913Romeo. You should change your transponder frequency to 7700. Change the setting on your transponder to 7700 then push the transmit button.”

913R: ”What? Oh, no. There’s no autopilot. Oh, transponder. That’s right somebody took some of the instruments. I think somebody got the transponder.”

The Blackhawk interrupts, Blackhawk 1: “SOCAL, I’ve got a visual on 913R?”

SOCAL: “Squawk 7700 and say your intentions. Are you military?”

Blackhawk 1: “Not military. I’m with Homeland Security [illegible] ’aking him to Compton/Woodley county airport.”

SOCAL: “Good. That’s what is needed. 913R se[illegible] confused.”

Chapter 5

Thursday, 11:25 AM

The helicopter pilot was good. He stayed right beside me and gave me instructions. With his help, I made a successful landing. But I still feel different. Something is wrong with me. Anyway, I'm at a small out of town airport.

Once the plane stopped I noticed two men with assault weapons in front and two to the sides of me. When I cut the engine other men opened both doors and ordered me out. As soon as my feet hit the tarmac I was grabbed by two guys and patted down by a third. When they'd determined I was safe I heard one of the guys in back of me say, "You did a good job, buddy. Nice landing." When I turned I recognized him as the helicopter pilot. I thanked him profusely.

I was having trouble walking. The walk to a metal building wore me out. It couldn't have been more than fifty feet. It made me feel dizzy. I was wobbling and had difficulty going in a straight line. Two of the military men assisted me down the hall of what might be called the administration building. They helped me into a chair. Now I'm not so dizzy. I think walking helps. One of the more friendly men stayed with me. I ask him a lot of questions but get no acceptable answers. He apologizes for his lack of answers but ended up saying some form of, "Someone will be along directly to answer all your questions."

I keep getting sleepy.

Someone woke me up. It was a policeman. He identified himself as Sargent Pizzametski, of the Los Angeles police department. He immediately started asking me a lot of questions. I ...ve him all the information I had given the air traffic controllers but ...'t satisfied. I told him that I was a surgeon who lived and ...Phoenix area. I told him all about my life and my family. I told him of this morning's meeting in Tucson. I told him everything I knew about the situation. During the next half hour I was asked the same questions over and over and I gave the same answers each time. But the plain fact is, I have no idea how I got from my lunch break to the Cessna, or why, or why I was out over the Pacific. There was another mystery he hadn't asked me about. The plane's clock's on Central Standard Time?" How can that be? Have I been in a different time zone? I told him about that too.

Pizzametski abruptly stopped his questioning and advised me that he had arranged for a doctor to check me out. Then he started giving me answers to some of my questions. They shocked me. It was Thursday, not Tuesday. My God, there is something seriously wrong here. What's happened to me? Actually, I didn't believe him. "That can't be."

Pizzametski said, "It is true. I'm telling you the truth. It is Thursday." He pointed first to his desk calendar then to the date on his iPhone.

"My God, where have I been for two days? What's going on? If it's really Thursday, my wife will be frantic. I've got to call her and let her know what's happening. She'll be worried sick". Pizzametski produced a phone and left me to call home.

Chapter 6

North Scottsdale, AZ

Laura wasn't too surprised when she got a call from Make. It was about noon. It sounded like he was still a little drunk. But he was often gone. She thought this was just another one of his...problem times.

She was able to get a flight to Los Angeles at 3:10 that afternoon. She had been to her yoga class, and was outside tending to her flower garden when he had called. She had just enough time to shower, wash her hair and pack a few things for her carryon. She had arranged for a taxi to take her to the airport.

After her shower, Laura blow dried her hair. It was slightly curly, brown, and very thick. She had it cut shoulder length. It was "easy Care" hair. Getting ready was quick and easy for Laura. Her Mediterranean skin only needed a little moisturizer and her makeup was just a little lipstick and some mascara. She decided to wear a simple, knee length, fitted dress and some comfortable shoes. And, of course, some jewelry. Make always bought her jewelry. He had good taste and knew what she liked.

As soon as she deplaned she took a taxi to Los Angeles Police Department, La Brea Division.

Chapter 7

Compton/Woodley County Airport

The conversation with Laura was difficult for both of us because she asked me many of the same questions Pizzametski had asked, and I still didn't know many of the answers. I told her I loved her and would get home as quick as I could but reminded her that I was not free to go. Pizzametski had not even given me a hint about how long I would be here.

Suddenly, I realized I'm very tired. I may have dozed off momentarily. I'm weary actually, and so I disconnect without satisfactorily answering her. *She is such a good person and I have deceived her and lied to her a lot the last couple of years. I feel so bad about that. But it had to be done. And I'm so sleepy. I could really nod off again right now.*

Then, when Pizzametski came and said, "Stand up Doctor Caston", I thought, *my God. Is he going to cuff me*? But he didn't. Instead he assisted me while he maneuvered us down the hall, through the door and into his police car. At least I got to sit in the front seat. Walking tended to revive me but when I sat for very long I got sleepy.

As we drove, Pizzametski gave me another surprise. The plane that I had been in had been reported stolen two weeks ago. At first, just for a moment, when he told me this, I didn't remember I'd been in a plane. Then I did remember it. I'm really screwed up.

He said the LAPD had found that, until I showed up on the radar today, the only other sighting of the Cessna had been in Monet, Missouri, last Monday. It was fueling stop.

Monet, Missouri. That's the Midwest. That's the time zone the airplane's clock was set for. Was I in Monet, Missouri? What in the world is going on here? My God, have I been gone nine days instead of two days? Which Thursday is it?

Sargent Pizzametski interrupted my thoughts saying, "I'm taking you to 'Family Hospital'. It's a small facility in south LA. We keep a doctor on call there all the time. It's standard procedure. I just want to make sure you're ok. Look doctor, I know you may feel like you're being jerked around but there are certain steps we have to take when we have someone that doesn't answer our questions – and you don't. But I really think you want to, you just can't remember, that's all. Doctor, I am doing what I think is best for you at this time."

Pizzametski changed the subject, "I used to live around here. We'll go past my old house. I bought it ten years ago when it was a better neighborhood. It's kind of gone to the dogs, now but it was pretty when we first moved in. My wife loved the house and the neighbors but she didn't like being married to a policeman." *But I loved her. My God I miss her.*

It sounds like the sergeant is trying to put me at ease or maybe he just gets lonesome and melancholy every time he drives through his old neighborhood. "It sounds like you are telling me you and your wife have split. I'm sorry Sargent; I know that must be tough. How long were you married?"

"Three years. Seven years ago seems like forever. God I hate this. Let's talk about something else. How long have you been married, doctor? And have you got any kids?"

I think Sargent Pizzametski is a lonely guy. That's too bad. "It's my first and only marriage. I've been married to the same girl six years. I love her and she loves me but it's been kind of rocky lately."

"Yeah, I know about that last part. Well, here we are. Let's go in. This doctor's name is Cox."

Chapter 8

Family Hospital

I was able to get the seat belt off by myself. I seemed to be getting a little more coordinated, but Pizzametski opened my door for me and watched as I got out. He probably thought I was going to fall on my head or something but this time I succeeded in staying upright.

Inside, after Pizzametski introduced me to the police doctor, they took me into one of the examining rooms and sat me on the end of the exam table. The first thing the doctor did was look at my eyes. "Do you use recreational drugs or do you take prescription drugs?" When I answered no he asked me if I knew what year it was and who the President was. I must have gotten the answers right because next he said, "I suspect you've been given some kind of drug. There's some of it still in your body. We'll do a tox screen and find out what's going on with you."

I'm a doctor and I have never said any of that to any of my patients. But I liked Doctor Cox. I thought he was a good doctor and he had a good bedside manner. He's just used to a different kind of clientele than mine. When I told him I was a surgeon in Phoenix, he said he knew that. Pizzametski had told him. He asked lots of questions about soreness: did I hurt here, did it hurt when he pressed there, etc. Finally, he led me into the lavatory and stood me in front of the mirror. As he shined his flashlight in my eyes I could see my eyes were slightly dilated. Then he held a small hand mirror so that I could see the back left side of my neck. There was a puncture wound there.

Doctor Cox told Pizzametski and me that he thought that I was physically exhausted but, otherwise I was ok. He suggested that I should get a lot of rest. He thought the drugs would wear off by tomorrow and I would probably be a lot better. The Sargent and I both thanked the doctor.

When we left the office it was a little after noon. The Sargent said, “Let’s get some lunch. You should be starved by now.” I should have been hungry but I really wasn’t. I knew I should eat something so I said, “Sure.”

At a diner on Florence Avenue, we sat in a booth by a front window. Pizzametski said, “I have to keep an eye on my car. Kids like to steal police cars.”

“How old are you Sargent?”

“Thirty. I’m thirty years old as of last week. I joined the police academy when I was twenty one. When I graduated from the academy I was paired up with a lady cop driving a car. She was a tough girl but I learned a lot about being a policeman from her. I think that‘s what ruined our marriage, Rose and I.”

“How did it ruin it? What happened?”

“Nothing happened. I’d only been married for a year, for Christ sake. You don’t screw around when you’re a newlywed. But Rose got more and more convinced. Part of the problem was after we had been on first shift for about four months we got rotated to night shift duty. I’d leave home about four. By five PM my partner and I, her name was Maryanne, would hit the road. We’d patrol around our assigned area, answer a few calls, then when the shift was over, go back and write our report. Sometimes after that we’d go have a beer at a little place where cops hang out. So I’d get home at one thirty or maybe two AM. Rose just couldn’t handle it. We didn’t have any kids and so one day she just walked out. She filed the next day. I tried to talk her out of it but she said she was through. That’s the ‘end of story’. I was depressed for a while but I got over it.”

I couldn't think of anything much to say except, "Sorry Sargent. That's got to have been rough." *I don't think he's over it yet.*

On the way back to Pizzametski's office I asked the Sargent about his name. "It's Polish. My parents came to the United States right after the Second World War. They lived in the Polish quarter of New York but moved to LA when I was a one year old."

"You got any brothers o\r sisters Sargent?"

"Yeah, I've got two brothers older than me and a younger brother. No sisters. God we had fun when we were kids. We lived in LA but there were lots of fields to play in. LA was a lot smaller then. I learned to shoot with my dad's 22 rifle. We use to take cans out to a plowed field and shoot them. Later I graduated to my dad's Colt 45.

"So how'd you come to be a cop?"

"I went to Sierra Vista High School. A cop came out during my senior year and I guess he was recruiting. He sounded pretty good, but I didn't apply right away. I worked construction for a while but I could see that that was going nowhere so I started at the academy. I really like being a cop but I'm not sure I want to do it for the rest of my life".

Pizzametski was about 5' 10" tall, 180 pounds and when he drove the police car, he appeared to handle it like it was some felon he'd just caught. I could tell he was thinking about something, probably about what he was going to do with me.

Once inside the police department I climbed the stairs without difficulty. I seemed to be getting steadier by the minute. Pizzametski put me in interrogation room four and said, "I'll be back shortly."

I fell asleep in the chair. I was dreaming of Laura. I was in my office one morning when she came in. My God she was beautiful. It seemed like the office lit up the moment she came through the door. There was a couple in my waiting room, and I believe they sensed the same thing. She said she wanted to apply for a job, and I hired her immediately. After I had explained her duties as receptionist, I looked over her application form. That even looked good. She had a BS degree in marketing. She was twenty eight years old.

We were married eight months later. I am a lucky man.

Pizzametski woke me up. I don't think I slept very long. He had a young lady with him. "Doctor Caston, this is Frida. She's with Homeland Security." Frida was about thirty five and a little over weight but she had a beautiful face. She smiled as we shook hands. "It's nice to meet you Dr. Caston. The Sargent has told me a little bit about your adventure and it sure is an amazing story."

"Yeah, I know. It's just a guess, but I bet you're about to tell me that it's so amazing that you don't believe it, right." *I'm feeling a lot peppier. That food must have picked me up.*

She sat across the table from me and took out a notebook. "Well, the Sargent said I should consider believing you but it is a tough tale to swallow because of the brevity of it. You don't have much to say about what has happened to you. There is so much that must be missing that I bet it bothers you more than anybody. I just thought that if I talked to you in person you might remember some more."

Pizzametski started to leave then turned at the door and said, "Frida get back with me before you leave, and Caston, you are not free to go. Stay right here till I get back."

"Am I under arrest?"

"Not yet." Sargent Pizzametski smiled as he said that.

"God, I hope he is kidding."

"Dr. Caston, have you remembered anything more since the last guy questioned you?" Frida ask.

"No, not really. I sort of have flashes of something but they are so short that I can't tell you much about them. I've been kind of tired and I've had trouble thinking straight. But I'm feeling a little better now."

"I need to make sure your stats are correct. Then I'll get out of here. You are Doctor Make Caston. Right?"

I nodded yes. "You are married, no children, right?"

"Correct."

"You are an orthopedic doctor specializing in foot surgery, and you and your wife live in Phoenix.

"Well, we live in Scottsdale. And my wife's name is Laura."

"Both parents deceased?"

"Yes."

When I was a teenager my father told me that being a doctor was a good thing, and a noble profession. I hadn't thought about it much. When you are fourteen, boys think mostly about football and girls in that order. One day my mom had dropped me off in his office. She had a lot of shopping to do and I knew I would be bored going with her. It was my choice. My dad's outer office had really great magazines. INTERAVIA was my first choice: it was almost all in French and it was about planes and military things, and the advertisements usually involved young girls with very few clothes on. It was my first year in high school. I was taking French and it was a great magazine for a teenager. My dad had said that his customers were high class and they wanted high class magazines to look at.

One time, while concentrating on my French, I became aware of a woman talking in a rather strident voice. I looked up and saw she was with a blond haired man that I had seen in the movies a few years ago. When he turned so I could get a good view of his face, I was shocked. He looked so old and wrinkled. The woman was talking to my dad, describing her husband's reason for being there. She concluded by saying his face looked like forty miles of bad road. I thought that was a funny way to describe his face but I felt sorry for him because it was an apt description. A year or so later I saw him in a TV sitcom. My dad had made him young again. I was so impressed; I decided that very moment that I wanted to do facial reconstruction. "Dad, I'm going to be a surgeon just like you." Turned out, I work on the other end instead.

Sitting with Frida and reminiscing was very relaxing. I felt a little better. Interrogation room four was about six by eight with the one way mirror on the end and the camera above it. The walls were dirty green. *God, I'd hate to be a suspect in here.*

"Are you being treated fairly here?"

"What? Oh, I'm sorry. I was a hundred miles away, thinking about my dad. I guess I was dreaming or something. What did you say?"

"I said, are you being treated fairly here? If you say you are being threatened or in some kind of danger, I can pull you out of here, you know."

"Yeah, I thought you probably could. But I'm ok. Pizzametski is younger and probably stronger than I am. He looks really healthy--and he has a gun. But he has never threatened me. He is a tough guy but he isn't hostile. He is just doing his job, I guess.

I'm really not concerned for my wellbeing. I think he's on my side but I know he's bothered because I don't know the answers to a lot of his questions. At first, I think he thought I was holding something back because I didn't want him to know, but I think he believes me now. I saw him in that glass office talking to another guy and it looked like the guy was giving him a bad time. I couldn't hear what was being said but the guy pointed to me a couple of times during the conversation."

"That was probably Watson, his boss. He wants to put you in lockup."

"Christ." *I'm in this mess just because I can't remember where I've been What in the world is going to happen to me? Will I ever get over this?*

Frida asked, "What was the first thing you remembered this morning?"

"I was in the pilot's seat, the left seat, of an airplane and it was dirty and unkempt. I remember thinking how filthy it was. I just now remembered, remembering this stuff. I don't know whether you know what I mean or not but that's the way it is. I don't remember the event but I remember that I remembered it. Anyway, I remember having some papers that were really important to me and I couldn't control them. Couldn't hold on to them. They kept getting away from me. I guess they were blowing all around. I know now the window behind the copilot's seat was out and that's why everything was blowing around." Just for an instant, Make thought he could hear the helicopter. "I just now realized. It is the first thing I really remember clearly. The helicopter. It was the noise; whop, whop, whop, whop. All of a sudden, it was loud. It scared me for a minute. I couldn't think what it was. I couldn't see it but I heard it. Then the next thing I heard was 'hey there buddy I'm in a chopper behind you. They sent me out here to see if you needed anything. If you come right to eighty two degrees you will be heading toward LA. If that's where you want to go'. I think I cried then and laughed at the same time. 'If that's where you want to go'. My God it was the first time I thought I might survive the day. And then when that thing came up into view out ahead of me, it was huge. I've never seen a helicopter that big. The Sargent said it was a Blackhawk. I'd never seen a Blackhawk."

Freda said, "Hearing you say that makes me want to cry too. So, I understand you were in a Cessna. You seemed to land it ok. When did you learn to fly?"

"Soon as I got out of school. I'm a licensed pilot. But I think it's been about ten years since I've done a lot of flying. I rented a 172 a couple of years ago with an instructor and took a check ride. But that was only for forty five minutes or so. I just wanted to keep my hand in. That's all"

"That must have been a creepy feeling, to wake up all alone over the ocean and not know where you were"

"I don't remember much about it. I just know it was absolutely terrifying. I didn't know where I was or which direction I should go. And there was no one to talk to. Oh yeah, I remember, when I finally got someone on the radio. Then it was still terrifying till the helicopter showed up. I've never been as frightened as I was when I first realized that I had no idea where I was and had no way of finding out. I'm beginning to remember some things now."

"Good." She seemed to be studying me. "What do you remember about last Tuesday? You said you were in Tucson at a seminar. What's the last thing you remember?"

"It was almost noon and we broke for lunch. I think I remember walking out with a couple of guys but I don't know their names."

"Actually, you had lunch with three other people. We have you on a security camera walking toward the hotel restaurant then again at a table in the restaurant. One of the men you were with is Bob Rogers. I've talked to him on the phone. He remembers you but he doesn't know the other two. Do you remember either of them?"

"I don't remember any of that. What did he say? Where did we go?"

I thought I saw some sympathy in her eyes. "I'm sorry. He left you with the two other men. He doesn't know what happened to you after he left the restaurant. One of our people in Tucson talked to him too. He doesn't remember seeing you the rest of the seminar but that doesn't mean anything. There were seventy seven people in that room."

Freda then took her IPad from her purse and showed me a part of the security camera feed. There I was with three other men. I didn't recognize any of them.

"I really, really wish I knew what happened to me but I just don't. Once, just a minute ago, while we were talking, just for an instant, I think I had a flash of being in a cold white room like a surgery. But I'm not sure."

"Wonderful. I talked to Doctor Cox. He said that might happen. He said you have Retrograde Amnesia. We will have a specialist talk to you. This guy is good. He's a psychiatrist who has handled other memory loss problems just like yours."

"My God, I'm not nuts. I don't want any shrink."

"No, no. It's ok. You'll like him. Really. He's Oriental. His name is Doctor Zhang Wei. After a long pause I said. "Ok, I'll see him, but look, I'm really beat. Can't we make it tomorrow? I'd just like to get some rest. And I've got to call my wife again. I think I hung up on her. She's probably pissed and worried too".

Freda said OK. She said Doctor Zhang Wei would see me tomorrow. I really didn't want see anyone right now. I just wanted to lie down, rest up and maybe figure out what was really going on. How did I get from a Tuesday meeting in Tucson to a Cessna, 150 miles out over the Pacific on Thursday?

I thought Freda was OK. She was definitely on my side.

Pizzametski came back. He returned my billfold, and keys. *I have no way of knowing if I had anything else in my pockets. Did the guys that put me in the plane keep some of my stuff?* He said he believed my story, but there were a lot of the pieces missing. I would have to stay in town for a few days. He said that if I agreed to do that he would put me up in a hotel. If not, they would just keep me here at the police station. Does he have anything more comfortable than a cell or would he keep me in his lockup? I wondered what "a few days" was. I didn't know and I didn't want to ask. *I'm so fucking tired, I just want to rest. What's wrong with me? I hope it's just the drugs.*

Getting out of the police station and into Sargent Pizzametski's car was a difficult task for me. I couldn't walk straight. I bumped my shoulder going out through the door. I'd been setting too long. Pizzametski helped me get to his car and then get into it. I'm a mess. *Am I getting worse instead of better?*

Finally we got to the hotel. Pizzametski's idea of a nice place was different from mine. My room was clean, and that's the best I can say for it. The view was of an air shaft. I thanked Pizzametski for bringing me here then I sat down and thought about what I should do next. I took off all my clothes, filled out a laundry ticket and left the whole thing outside my door. Then I flopped back on the bed. *God it feels good to lie down*. The next thing I knew, it was dark outside. I had slept thirteen hours. It was 3 AM and I felt a lot better. It's amazing what a few of hours of sleep can do. I knew I had to call Laura again, late as it was. And I thought I would probably have to apologize to her occasionally during the conversation, but as it turned out, she didn't answer. I left a message. I knew she was pissed off at me and I understand why too. When I had talked to her earlier I probably sounded like I was drunk. And, of course, I didn't know where I had been for the last two days. She probably didn't believe that either. I had better get home before my marriage goes the same way the sergeant's marriage went.

But there was a good thing that happened while I was worrying about Laura. I don't know why but I began to have some recollection of the last two days. I actually remembered someone fastening my seat belt-or trying to. I was resisting his efforts and it was causing him to have a lot of trouble reaching across me to fasten the clip. I think he hit me. I have a little soreness on my left cheek bone. Who was that guy?

Chapter 9

Thursday, 5:00 PM

Pizzametski's squad room, LAPD

The Sargent wrote up part of his daily report, then a young officer approached, "Pizz, you got a visitor."

Pizzametski examined the young officer's I.D., "Officer Clanton. Am I pronouncing that right?"

"Yeah, that's my name, Clanton."

"I haven't seen you before. How long have you been a police officer?"

"Today's my first day. I just got out of the academy."

"Well, officer Clanton. We are on a first name basis around here and my first name is Sargent Pizzametski. You got that?"

"Yes sir, Sargent Pizzametski. I just didn't know we were that formal around here."

"*We* are not that formal around here. *You* are that formal around here until you get to know who the hell you're talking to. OK?"

"OK, Sargent Pizzametski."

"Now, Officer Clanton, who is the visitor, what does he want, and how did he get my name in the first place?"

"Sargent Pizzametski, It's not a he, it's a she. She's about thirty, and very nice looking. Hot actually. That's just my opinion, sir. What she wants is to talk to you. And she said her husband had called her and told her to talk to you."

“Fine. Please go out there and tell her that I’ll see her in 5 minutes.

Pizzametski finished writing on his report, hit “enter” and walked to the desk sergeant’s area. *Wow, she is a knock out. Officer Clanton may not know much about squad room protocol but he sure has a good eye for girls.* “Hello, I’m Sargent Pizzametski. Can I help you?”

“Oh thank you. I’m Laura, Make Caston’s wife. I’d like to see him, please. He called me and said he was in jail and that I should call you, but I came instead. What’s he done? I’m so worried about him. Can you please let me see him?”

Pizzametski sympathized with the young lady and, besides that; he thought he was probably in love. Her auburn colored hair was trimmed just above her shoulders, just the way Pizzametski liked it, and she had a great body. Tiny waste and nice boobs, also just the way he liked it. He said in a consoling voice, “Please come in to the office and don’t worry about him. When I explain everything I’m sure you’ll see that it’s going to be ok.”

As they passed Pizzametski’s desk he said to his partner, whose desk was setting adjacent to Pizzametski’s, “We’ll be in four.”

“Lucky you.”

As he pushed open the door to interrogation room 4, Pizzametski ask Laura to sit down. He watched her walk in and sit. She was wearing a snug blue dress that came to just above the knees and had little slits up each side. Her black shoes had low heels and she was carrying a large printed satchel. She smelled good, looked good and had a beautiful smile. She was one sexy babe. He thought to himself, that Caston is a lucky bastard. “I want to apologize for the accommodations here. But this is the best we've got." She had beautiful, slightly dark skin. *She is fucking beautiful.*

* * * *

Laura had liked Make from the first time she had seen him and it had been obvious he liked her too. She had wanted to live in the Phoenix area and thought Scottsdale was the part of town she should be in. And she decided that she had the best opportunity for employment at a doctor's office. As soon as she stepped into Make's front office she felt comfortable. It seemed like a nice place and Make made her feel wanted. It was so nice to be met with such enthusiasm. When he hired her after a very brief interview she suspected he may have wanted a little more than a receptionist. But she was used to that. And besides, he was good looking. He was about five foot eleven, with a well-built 175 pound body with a nice tan. She thought, *that's the best looking doctor I've ever seen.*

Laura was sitting in a padded chair in front of a small table. Pizzametski sat on the other side, the side with the metal ring. He said, "OK, let me first explain, your husband in not in jail, he's staying at a hotel near here. I put him there. It's at our expense. Mr. Caston showed up here today with an amazing story. We interviewed him briefly and decided that he probably hadn't committed any crime. The only thing we might possibly hold him on would be criminal possession, and that would be a stretch. Besides, to me, he just didn't seem like the type."

Laura said, "Please tell me where he is. I'd like to go see him now. I'm very worried about him."

"He is in the Hotel Maple, room 345. It is only 2 blocks south of here on the same side of the street. But I wish you'd let me tell you a little bit about what happened to him before you go." The Sargent ran his finger around the steel cuff ring attached to the metal table. “You see, when Mr. Caston came in here this morning he was very stressed out. Very tired out. I had an LAPD doctor examine him to make sure he was all right. And considering that he may have been drugged and was under a great deal of stress, the doctor thought he would be a lot better tomorrow. But the doctor pointed out that Mr. Caston should get some rest, lots of rest. The doctor thinks he’s been drugged. They did draw blood but the tox screen results won’t be available till tomorrow or the next day. It’s because of that that I put him in the hotel and promised him he wouldn’t be disturbed until tomorrow morning – 9 AM to be exact. Sooo, I’d like to suggest that you postpone visiting or even contacting your husband today. I’m sure he is asleep by now. And tomorrow I’ll take you to hm. There are lots of good hotels around here and I’d be glad to help you find one.”

Laura hesitated. She was worried about Make but finally agreed to Pizzametski’s suggestion. It seemed like that was the best thing for Make. On the way to the detective’s car she asked, “Why don’t I stay at the hotel Make is staying at? That way you wouldn’t have to cart me around so much.”

“I thought you might ask that. Our precinct keeps a hotel room reserved for situations like your husband’s. But frankly, it isn’t the best place in town. I think you would be happier in a slightly different part of LA.” Actually, Pizzametski was smitten. She was beautiful. She seemed nice, and she was obviously stressed too. He wanted to hold her and comfort her. He closed his eyes...hold her and touch her.

Laura said, “That sounds good. And I really appreciate you taking the time to help me. I don’t know LA at all. But I do feel bad about taking you away from your family.” He seemed unusually helpful. *I hope he isn’t just trying to get in my pants.*

As he drove, Pizzametski said. “It’s no problem at all. I’m divorced and right now my only family is my cat. So don’t fret about that. On rare occasions, when I have to be real late or even be away for a few days, I have a neighbor who is a cat lover too. I just give her a call and she’s happy to take care of Spot.” To Laura it seemed that Pizzametski was protesting too much. *I think he missed his wife and family.*

“Would you please tell me why my husband is involved with the police? I don’t understand. If he hasn’t done anything, if he is not under arrest, why are you holding him?”

“That’s a fair question. He was in a plane headed for LA and air traffic control recognized the plane’s ID. Your husband was in an airplane that was listed as a stolen aircraft. This got a lot of people interested including Homeland Security, the airport police, and finally our department. The interesting part was that your husband couldn’t answer most of our questions. He didn’t say where he’d been for the last two days, how he got out over the Pacific, why he was in a stolen plane, where he got the plane, or who owned it. He didn’t answer a lot of our questions. At first we thought, actually most everyone that talked to him thought, that he was holding something back from us. Our doctor contacted a shrink and told him about Mr. Caston’s condition. They decided that he really doesn’t know the answers to our questions. The shrink said Mr. Caston has retrograde amnesia. He may remember more later but how much more, they don’t know. They said it’s really important that he gets some rest now. We don’t want to cause him any more concern. That’s why we put him in a hotel. He probably thought he was losing his mind. The shrink thinks that if Mr. Caston doesn’t get his memory back by next week he’ll probably not remember a whole lot more. The shrink is going to see him tomorrow.”

Chapter 10

Thursday 5:50 PM

The L. A. Hotel Downtown

They arrived at the hotel and Pizzametski stopped in the check-in parking space. “Why don’t we go in and get you a room. Then, if you like, we can continue this conversation.”

After she had checked in, Laura seemed a little less anxious. Pizzametski said, “I would like to talk to you more about your husband and the situation he’s in. Why don’t we sit in the lobby and chat? Maybe you could fill in some of the blanks.”

When they found a quiet corner, Laura said, “When I talked to Make on the phone he didn’t seemed to know where he had been, how he got there, or why the police had him. So I can understand why you suspected he was up to something. What did he tell you? He must have told you something”

Pizzametski tried to be more assuring. “He didn’t tell me much. He probably told you about the same thing he told me. By the time I got to him he looked so tired and exhausted that I also thought it best for him to get some rest. And he had a lot of anxiety about his phone calls to you. He’s afraid that his story, or lack of it, had made you think he had done something wrong. And I suppose maybe he thinks that possibly he has. I know almost nothing about him. What’s your husband like, what does he do? Has he ever had problems like this before?”

“I suppose you’ll learn soon enough. You said the doctors drew blood to test him for drugs?”

“Right. We ordered a full tox screen. It’s a thing we normally do in a situation where we’re not sure who we’re talking to.

We also took his fingerprints and his picture and we did a facial recognition scan. But I would still like you to tell me about him. There is so much more you could tell me that would help me understand what has happened to him. How did he come to be in a stolen aircraft and how did he learn to fly that particular plane? He said he had a pilot's license. What has he been doing the last two days? He doesn't know anything about any of that. I've got lots of questions here. I hope you can help me out."

"Well, first off, he has a drinking problem. Sometimes he's sober for a long time, maybe a year. Then the next thing I know he doesn't show up. Then in a few days--maybe a week--he calls me or he comes home. He is usually a mess for a day or two days. After that he is all cleaned up and he goes back to being a regular husband. My husband is a foot surgeon. He has an office with a hand surgeon and a physical therapist. It's called Hand and Foot Medicine. It's in Scottsdale. When he is around, he's good to me. He has a good income. We have no financial problems. I pay the bills and Make keeps money in our bank accounts so I know he has a good income. Most of the time Make is either in his office or on call at the hospital, so I have lots of spare time. I do volunteer work, usually at Bright Horizons. And, sometimes I help out at his office if the receptionist goes away. By the way, that happens a lot. I suspect my husband hits on them. He always hires really great looking girls. He does have a pilot's license and used to fly occasionally. But he hasn't done that recently, not that I know about. He's done lots of crazy things but never in a plane. Actually, I shouldn't say that. I really don't know what he does. He makes me nuts sometimes."

"Ms. Caston, I want to make sure you're comfortable. I want to assure you that your husband is not suspected of committing any crimes. We are trying to help him and we want to know where he's been so maybe we can find who stole that plane. And, if he really has been drugged, we want to know who drugged him."

Laura was feeling a little less tense. “Thank you Sargent. I appreciate your spending time with me. I know that’s not part of your job, but it is comforting.”

“Look, it is getting late. My shift is over. Would you like to have dinner? They say eating is a very soothing thing.” *I know I would like to do some soothing.*

I’ve got to watch out for this guy. But he is nice. “Sargent, thank you. That’s a nice offer. Are you sure I am not putting you out. I am a little hungry.”

* * * *

From the first day she had worked for Hand and Foot Medicine, Make had pursued her. It was obvious. But she liked it and besides he was a good looking man, unmarried and his prospects for the future seemed excellent. Make Caston seemed just right for her.

* * * *

By the end of the shift, Sargent Pizzametski was back in the squad room trying to catch up on the day’s happenings and finish his report. The lieutenant liked the reports to be finished by early evening. *Well, he won’t see this till tomorrow morning. He reads them all before the beginning of the next shift. He’s going to have a ball with this one. ‘…John Corrigan at ATC4, Utah air traffic controller. He said orange county airport tower had picked up a call for help from 913 Romeo and they handed it off to him. In response, Corrigan called Homeland Security; it was taken from Kirkland in Albuquerque. LAX emergency, and LAX airport police,* John Corrigan *called LAPD. And that is how Officer Blackwell got on to it. Blackwell called me and…Good lord, I’ll never s get this written in time.*

She is really cute. She is probably 29 or maybe 30. She's married to a doctor. Is he ok? He's a foot surgeon for Christ sake. He's got a drinking problem? That doesn't make any sense.

I have got to get this written. *Homeland Security got a chopper to guide him in. They landed right beside him and…*

I'd like to be right beside her now. My God she was pretty, and nice. I wonder, what she does, she volunteers. What kind of people does she know, probably lots of doctors? What's her social life like?

Chapter 11

Friday Morning

Make's L.A. Hotel Maple, room 234

Pizzametski knocked lightly at first, then after a few seconds, he used a little more vigor. Looking at his watch, he turned to Laura, "What does your watch say?"

"8:52."

"Yeah, that's about what mine said too. He ought to be here. I told him 9 o'clock."

"Maybe he's down stairs having breakfast."

"Maybe. I peaked in there as we came in, but I didn't see him."

A hotel cleaning lady was approaching with her cart loaded with supplies. "Sir, I think he's not in there."

Pizzametski asked, "Did you see him leave?"

"No sir, but this is the second room I cleaned. Three four five was an early checkout." She pulled her check sheet from the rack on her cart. "See, I finished this room at 7:40." She held the list for Pizzametski to see. "I've been up here since about 7:10 and I haven't seen anyone go in or out of that room."

Pizzametski showed her his ID card, "LAPD, would you let us in please?"

The maid stood back after opening the door but moved to watch as Pizzametski and Laura looked briefly inside the room. "Well, looks like she did a nice job."

Turning to the maid, Pizzametski said, “Do you remember, was there anything unusual about the room, I mean like a sign of a struggle or any blood, maybe?”

Smiling she replied, “Sir, I've been cleaning hotel rooms for a long time. After the first month, there was no such thing as unusual. If the walls were covered with blood that wouldn't be unusual.”

“OK, was there any blood?”

“No sir.”

Turning to Laura he said, “Let's go down stairs. Hopefully he's waiting for us. Damn, I told him to stay in the room.”

The lobby and dining room were sparsely occupied. There were two couples in the dining room and that was all. At the counter Pizzametski asked about Mr. Caston, room 345.

Before answering, the young man behind the desk scrolled the monitor screen. “Sir, he checked out at 4:13 AM. His laundry was delivered at 12:20 AM.”

Pizzametski said, “His laundry. Shit. Did he say where he was headed?”

“I don't know sir. I just came on at nine. Most everyone in the front came in around nine.”

Pizzametski ask the concierge but got the same answer. “OK, we've got to check the airlines, the bus lines, taxies. We've got to locate him. I'll call it in.”

Pizzametski jabbed at his cell, then started to give instructions. He abruptly stopped, looked at Laura, said, “Oh you wouldn't know. You haven't seen him in a week.” Turning back to his cell he said, “I don’t know what he was wearing. Shit, I don’t even know how tall he was. He didn’t have a hat...”

Laura was five foot five inches tall. She put her hand on Pizzametski’s wrist and pulled his cell down to her level, “Five foot, eleven inches, 175 pounds, dark complexion and brown eyes, brown hair, age thirty six.”

She touched me. Pizz was momentarily taken back, then, “Yeah, and no facial hair except he hadn’t shaved in a couple of days. His hair was brown. He’s Caucasian. Get back to me quick.” Turning to Laura, Sargent Pizzametski said, “Thanks for the help. Let’s go out in front. Maybe a cabbie will remember something.”

There were two cabs. The first one remembered a 4:21 pick up to LAX. “Yes sir, I remember the guy. Tall, probably six foot, and good lookin. He had to stop at the bank first. He said he was going, I think, to the Midwest somewhere. I let him off at Southwest Air.”

“How long would it take you to get us to Southwest Air?”

“About twenty minutes if traffic doesn’t screw us up.”

Pizzametski opened the cab door and urged Laura to get in. To the driver he said, “I guess there’s no rush. He’s probably gone by now. Fuck. Why didn’t he stay in his room?”

Laura liked Sargent Pizzametski. He seemed ok. She said, “Look, you don’t know anything about him. He’s not apt to stay anywhere he’s supposed to stay. He’s a loose cannon. He’s wild. The things he does used to make me nuts but now I just don’t care. He always does stuff like this.” Laura had tears on her cheeks. “I might as well tell you. We’re getting a divorce. It is just because of this kind of stuff. He’s getting worse. I knew he drank a little when

I first met him but I liked him anyway. He didn't drink a lot and he never got drunk and he was fun to be around. We had a good time. He made a lot of money and we had fun spending it. We traveled a lot. At first he was just a little bit wild. Now he's not in touch with reality. You know, when you first heard that he woke up alone in a plane, over the Pacific, I'll bet you'd never heard of anything like that. Well, I hadn't either but I wasn't surprised at all. If anybody would do that it would be Make."

When Pizzametski said, "I'm Sorry" he really felt that way. He hated to see Laura so unhappy that she cried. "Look, I know it's none of my business but I have to tell you, my wife divorced me for the wrong reason. Please don't divorce your husband until you are absolutely sure you have good reason. A divorce is a terrible thing."

"Thank you for telling me that, Sargent. It must have been terrible for you. I guess I shouldn't have said 'divorce'. It's just that our life has been so difficult the last year or so. When we were first married, we talked about being married a lot. And there was one thing that we both said was the most important thing: we'd always be truthful to each other. We agreed that we'd never lie to one another; we wouldn't play games with each other. We'd always be straight and above board, and look at us now! Half the time I don't know where he is, what he is doing, or who he's with. I've never fooled around on him and I don't do crazy things. My life is just plain, normal living. I can't imagine what happened to Make. Well, anyway, things were sure great for about four years."

"I wish I could help but I really can't. My marriage only lasted for three years, and it ended because I had a job that kept me away from home too much. And Laura, I did some pretty dumb things too and I regret them every day" Pizzametski was bothered by what Laura said. He was momentarily annoyed and angry with Make Caston. *That bastard.* Then he realized he had to stop worrying about someone else's problems. *Why am I this involved?*

This is not my job. "Laura, when we get to the airport I'll probably go on the next flight that heads to where your husband went. I want you to go back to your hotel and wait. I'll keep in touch with you by phone." Then Pizzametski said to the driver, "When I get out take this lady back to her hotel."

"No, driver, that won't be necessary. I'm getting out here."

"No, you're not Laura. Please. This is my business, not yours. Do not follow me."

"Sargent, I just want to look in the airport for Make. And besides, you underestimate me. I decide where I want to go and when I want to go there. As long as I don't interfere, you can't stop me."

"You and I both know that if you follow me, when and if I find your husband, you will interfere, so won't you please not follow me?"

"Neither of us knows exactly what we'll do but, unless I am under arrest, I get to do what I want to. Are you going to arrest me Sargent Pizzametski?"

"I'm not going to arrest you unless you do interfere with police business."

"Thank you Sargent." Laura stepped out of the cab smiling. "And it would be very nice of you if you would keep me informed when you find my husband. Good bye Sargent Pizzametski."

After Laura walked away, the cab driver said, "Wow."

To the cabbie, the Sargent looked exasperated. As he headed toward the terminal entrance, Pizzametski said, mostly to himself, "Wow is right. But I like it. She knows what she wants to do and she does it."

Entering the terminal, Laura realized how she missed Make. *Yes I love you. At least the old Make. But the last couple of years - I don't know. You do such outlandish things. Are you a hopeless alcoholic?* "My God what am I going to do?" After walking around through some of the shops she knew that Pizzametski was right about one thing--she had no business being here. There was zero chance she would find Make. She went back outside and got a cab back to the hotel. She spent the rest of the day worrying about her future. *Will we still be together this time next year?*

Chapter 12

Friday, 10 AM

Laura's Hotel

In the hotel restaurant, Laura finished a breakfast she really wasn't real hungry for. *My God, I've lost my appetite, I can't even think straight. I don't know what to do?* Her gloomy thoughts were interrupted when her cell rang, the caller ID indicating Phoenix, "Hello."

"Hi sweetheart. How are you doing?"

"Make, what are you doing in Phoenix? You're supposed to be in LA. The whole world is looking for you. You can't just leave like that, Make, I don't know you anymore. I'm worried about you, and you piss me off all at the same time. I don't know what to do."

A brief silence. Then Make replied, "I can understand that. Look, meet me in Phoenix at the airport. Get a ticket then call me back and let me know your arrival time. I'll be there when you step off the plane."

"That's probably bullshit. I can't believe you anymore, Make...What are we going to do? I can't keep going on like this. This is ridiculous."

"Laura, please don't talk like that. Meet me at Sky Harbor, PHX. I promise I will be there. OK? Please, Laura"

"I'll think about it." Laura hangs up. In a few seconds Laura's cell rang again, "Honey please, please. I absolutely promise we can fix this."

"I'll get the ticket. The monitor said there's a plane that leaves here at 10:40 AM, Southwest Air flight 745, arrives, PHX at

1:14 am. Make, just so you know, if you are not there, we're through. Do you understand what I'm saying?"

* * * *

1:15 PM

LAX

When Laura stepped out of the airway ramp into the gate area she saw Make. He looked grim. "Laura, I know the last few years have been a bother to you. But--"

"Bother? Are you serious? Make, you are completely unreliable. I really didn't think you would be here. I don't know why I came actually." She started to cry.

"I'm really sorry Laura. I'm sorry I've acted the way I have, but there's an explanation for it."

"Yes, I know. You are an alcoholic and you can't change. That's the explanation."

Make started walking Laura down the hall, "There's a way that everything can be explained and, once you hear it, you'll understand. Please try to trust me for just a little longer and--"

She interrupted again, "Do we have to keep walking? Let's sit. It's been a long day already."

"Yes, sorry but we do need to walk. What I'm going to tell you is something I don't want anyone else to hear. It'll sound unbelievable to you but there is a way I can prove it's the truth."

"What does that have to do with walking? Why do we have to keep walking? This whole thing sounds dumb to me."

"OK, we will sit for a little while but I can't tell you what I have to tell you while we're sitting. I can only tell you while we're walking. The walls have ears and eyes."

"Make, I think you've lost your mind."

"Please. All right, let's just go outside. There's a bench we can sit on out there that's OK. I know it's hot out there but I'll explain everything."

Make held the door for her. Once seated, he said, "Promise you won't jump up and leave until you hear the whole story."

Laura forced a smile but only for a moment, "Alright, let's hear it." *God, I hope he's not going nuts.*

"Here goes. Don't go away, OK?"

"I won't go away."

"I have two jobs. The one you don't know about is, I work for Homeland Security."

"What are you talking about?"

"You said you would listen. You promised you would listen."

"All right. I'll listen. I'll listen but I don't believe this. I'll tell you right up front. I'm not going to believe any part of this one."

"And I am not an alcoholic either."

"Right."

"Here's the next step." He took a small 'Post-It pack' out of his pocket. "I'm going to write five numbers on this and I want you to remember them. And, if someone comes by here while you are looking at them, hold that paper close to you so no one else can see them."

"This is incredible."

Make quickly wrote on the top sheet, pulled it off the pack, and handed it to Laura, "Will you remember those numbers in that order?"

"Yes, I'll remember them in that order," she said sarcastically.

"Good." He retrieved the paper and quickly marked out the numbers. "Now here's what you have to do next. I want you to find a number for Homeland Security and call them at 2 PM. Ask them for Paul Riley. This is how I can prove that what I am going to tell you is the truth."

"Make, you're scaring me. I almost hope this is more of your bull."

"Well, at least, you didn't get up and leave." Make looked at her longingly, "So will you really make the call just the way I said to do it?"

"Yes. I said I would. But if you do work where you said, that secret place, why don't you just tell me the number and I'll call them right now. And why all this cloak and dagger thing? What's going on with you anyway? Why don't we just go home and make that call?"

"This is serious and it's important that it's done the way I said. You'll see why."

"OK, I'll do it. But only because, at least this isn't as stupid as most of your explanations."

"Have you remembered those numbers?"

"Yes."

"Are you sure?"

"Let me see them again." Make rewrote the numbers.

When the numbers are memorized, Make took the Post-it pack and put it in his pocket. He put the two wadded up pages in the other pocket. Then he stood and said he didn't want to be with her when she made the call. He wanted her to do it without any coaching from him. He then told her he had business to do and he would be back by 2:15.

As soon as Make left, Laura's cell rang. *My God, I'd better write those numbers down before I forget them.*

"Laura, this is Pizzametski. I've been in Page, Arizona. Your husband's not there but he was. Mr. Caston talked to the guy at the airport who pumps gas. The gas pump guy said that the guy flying the plane, 913 Romeo, the plane that your husband was in, was at that airport last Saturday, The man asked the pilot where he had come from and where he was going. The pilot told him two different things. First the pilot said he had come from the Midwest. Later, after the plane had been serviced, he said he was on his way to Chicago. Now that doesn't make any sense. You don't go from the Midwest to Page, Arizona, on the way to Chicago. Actually, the gas pump guy said the pilot was 'a flakey son of a bitch.' And I agree with the gas pump guy. There is something wrong here. I'd sure like to talk to that pilot. Either he was stoned or he was trying to avoid telling anyone where he was really going, and he got his lies confused. I think someone told that pilot to get that plane to Tucson and don't let anyone know about it, and he was just trying to avoid answering any questions. I don't know for sure that he was headed to Tucson, but I'm sure he was not on his way to Chicago."

"Maybe the pilot said he came from Chicago?"

"Yeah, and maybe he didn't want anybody to know where he was going."

Laura decided against telling him she was with Make in Phoenix, “So what are you going to do?”

“I don’t know, but you sit tight. I’ll keep you posted. And what are you doing?”

Pizzametski sounds awfully friendly. Is he interested in me? “I’m sitting in the bar having a Make special.”

“What the hell is that?”

“Vodka martini. What’s your special?”

Is she trying to hit on me? “Bud lite. I’m not complicated. I’m just a cop.”

This conversation is headed in the wrong direction, Laura thought. *I’ve got to end it now before he asks what I am wearing.* “Thank you for keeping me informed, Sargent. Maybe I’ll talk to you tomorrow.” *Well, that was a flirtatious bit. Why did I lead him on? I’m still married. I miss Make – the fucking bastard. Now, I’ve got to get back to Make’s mystery numbers. Where did I put that pad?*

Laura was skeptical but she did as Make had told her to do. First Laura used her cell to Google the number for Homeland Security. There were four different numbers listed in the Phoenix area. He had told her to call any one of them. After the usual, “Dial one for our hours, dial two for…” she told the person that answered that she wanted to talk to Paul Riley. “Please stay on the line and I’ll transfer you. This may take a minute or two.” Seconds later, “This is Paul Riley.”

Laura thought, *my God. This is getting scary.* "I was told to tell you, "two eight five one six"."

“You can believe him.” Then the call dropped.

Laura was shocked. As she considered the enormity of what had just happened, she realized that this had to be real. *Is Make really not a drunk? Oh my god, he's not.* If Make had told her what number to call, it could have been just another of his attempted con jobs, but she had gotten the phone number from Google. *That really was Homeland Security I just talked to. Oh my God.* She knew Make was not going to lie to her now. *I can hardly believe all this but it has to be true. How could I have not known about this for the last two years? Maybe Make's ok after all. I feel better already. I sure hope this is for real. It has to be. Holy shit. I can't get use to this.*

Chapter 13

Morning

Scottsdale AZ, Caston's home

Laura and Make were lying face to face. Laure woke up first. It was 5:42 AM and the sun was just starting to come in the high windows. It was going to be a beautiful day. Laura moved closer so that her forehead just touched Make's. He looked at her and smiled, "I love you Laura."

"I love you too Make."

Make moved his head so that their lips barely touched, light little kisses. More little kisses then Make pulled back slightly, paused, then said, "Laura, do you know what day this is?"

She couldn't think of any significant day, "You've got your period?"

Make thought this was very funny and laughed, "You dip; no I haven't got my period. It's the twelfth. In ten days, a week after next Saturday, I will be thirty-fucking-six years old."

"Oh, I like the fucking part."

* * * *

After they made love. Make smiled.

Laura smiled, "You know I never stopped loving you. Even when I thought you were doing foolish, crazy things. Even when I thought you might be having an affair. Even when I thought you were a hopeless drunk, I never stopped loving you. Well, maybe that last one is a stretch. By the way, the sex is better now that I understand that you're not…what I thought you were…" She rolled over and lay on top of Make.

Make said, "I was so worried. Pizzametski told me how his marriage broke up. It was because his job kept him out late at night and his wife thought he was fooling around when he really wasn't. I know it's been terrible for you. That's why you had to be bought in. I told my boss it had to be done and he agreed. He took it up to the Hardware Review Group and they agreed too."

"The Hardware Review Group is making decisions about our marriage? How do they have time to review the hardware and control our marriage at the same time? Do they control other people's lives or just ours? That all sounds crazy to me."

"Honey, I'm so sorry that you have to live with a guy that works where I do. I know it sound like I work with a bunch of crazies, but they are really ok. That's just a title, the 'Hardware Review Group'. It's intended to avoid having people know what they really do. And they are certainly not crazy."

"So what do they do, when they are not doing crazy stuff, I mean?"

"They make high level decisions. That is all I can tell you."

"And what do you do?"

"I'm a manager. I have a group of people who gather information. I just put it all together. That's all."

Laura was beginning to see serious possibilities here, "Make, do you kill people?"

"No, I don't kill people."

"So when you manage your group and you get information, what do you do with that information?"

"I pass the information up to a higher level."

“And, I assume they pass it up to a next higher level, etc., etc.”

“Sometimes.”

“And maybe at one of those really high up levels, they decide to kill somebody?”

“Laura, just drop it.”

* * * *

Later, when Make and Laura were out on the veranda, Pizzametski called Laura, “Sargent Pizzametski, what’s up?” she asked.

“Hello Laura. I think your husband is in Phoenix. Where are you?”

“I’m in Phoenix. Where are you?”

A slight pause, “Laura, I wish you hadn’t followed me here. I don’t want you to get hurt. Your husband may be in danger and there’s no point in you getting involved.”

“I got here yesterday. When did you arrive, Sargent?”

There was a pause again, then Pizzametski said, “You are with your husband right now, aren’t you Ms. Caston?”

“Yes Sargent. He called me yesterday morning from our house and I caught a plane as soon as I could. I’m here with him now. Won’t you please come join us?”

* * * *

They sat at a table in the outside eating area. When Pizzametski showed up he started to apologize, but Laura put him at ease, “It’s OK Sargent. There was no way of you knowing that I got a call from Make yesterday. When you called it sounded like you had some news."

Make interrupted, "Sargent would you like something? Maybe a beer or some food?"

"Thanks. A Bud Lite would taste good right now. I'm not use to this heat."

Laura said, "So, what's new Sargent? You did a lot of traveling around."

"First, the tox screen results are in. Everything was completed last night. And I mean everything. They can get an awful lot of information out of a few drops of blood. That's why I just got here about three hours ago."

"It's OK Sargent. Were there any drugs in my husband's blood?" Make came back with three beers.

"Yes there were five different drugs. The report used the word "cocktail" to describe them. Someone must have really known what they were doing. The tech who did all this said that it would have put your husband in a twilight sleep. In his report he listed Neurontin, Keppra, Trileptal, Topamax, and Versed. You probably know what all those would do to you, don't you Doctor. The tech said you probably would be able to walk if told to do so but wouldn't have remembered much of it. Someone may have put you in that plane and told you to fly west, and you did it until the drugs began to wear off. The tech thinks you may remember more as time goes on. Doctor Caston, do you have any idea who would want to drug you…and put you on a plane headed for the middle of the Pacific? Doctor, someone was trying to kill you. Why would anyone want to do that?"

"I have no idea. I'm not a detective." *Mal put me on that plane, I know it. He was trying to get rid of me.*

"Have you ever damaged a patient or been sued by a patient or anything like that? You must have pissed off someone at some time."

"Not that I know of Sargent. By the way, there's a medical review board that handles all complaints and makes sure all disagreements are resolved."

"I know. I checked with them already. I just thought there might be some new problem that hasn't gotten to the review board yet."

"Sargent, I just don't know why anyone would do that because of my practice. I've got to be honest with you, though. I haven't told you, but I have a drinking problem. I do well most of the time. I go to AA meetings even when I have to be out of town. And they really help me. Actually, I am going to a meeting tonight." *What can I do to get rid of this guy? I guess he has to clean up this case. I hate lying to people but that's kind of what you have to do in this business. I am sure glad I don't have to lie to Laura any more. I can't think of any reason where I'd have to. Anyway, I think she and I are fine now.*

Chapter 14

Monday morning

Fort Huachuca, Sierra Vista, AZ

"Come in Make. Glad you could make it." Lon Dove said. "Gentlemen, this is Doctor Make Caston. Make, this is General Richard Johnston, Joint Chiefs".

Make shook hands. "Nice to meet you General."

"I think you know Jake James."

"Nice to see you again, Jake."

"This is Wisconsin Congressman, Richard Jaradie."

"Pleasure to meet you, Congressman." Make joined the group standing at the conference room table.

"Gentlemen, this is Doctor Curt Delk. The Doctor knows a lot about Yemen. Doctor, please tell us the details of what you have briefed me on."

Everyone but doctor Delk took a seat. Make thought Doctor Delk was probably forty years old. He looked authoritative. The doctor said, "The information I am about to give you is three days old. One of our men in Yemen has knowledge of what they are doing with PETN. They have found that if it's coated with three thin layers of a cheap kind of RTV it becomes completely invisible to all known scanning techniques. The RTV is diluted to make it thin and paintable. They brush it on and let each layer vulcanize before the next layer is applied. That way they have a thin, about a third of a millimeter thick, layer of RTV. During this process, dilute acetic acid is a byproduct of the vulcanization. It smells like vinegar. The odor completely masks the PETN. As you probably know, PETN is difficult to detect anyway. This RTV coating guarantees that it will not be detected at the airport. So, what they are doing now is, they are making “turds”. The Doctor used a laser pointer to direct their attention to a PowerPoint view of a beautiful, round, white stone structure. The blue sea could be seen in the background. “At 345 Mukalla St. in Mesoo Star, Yemen, there are about twenty men and boys’ working two shifts, all night and all day, trying to mold PETN into the shape of what comes out of your butt. They’re having production problems but they will get them solved.

Each turd will weigh about 8 grams. They will then be coated with RTV as I have described. We think they are going to make a large number of them, probably more than 20,000, then send them all over the world. They will be doled out to followers who are willing to give their lives for jihad. They will be held until an opportune time then detonated. The holder of one of these devices can store it anywhere until he is ready to use it. At that time he might literally, shove it up his butt, get on a plane, go into the toilet, poop out his turd and blow the tail end off of a Boing 777. The detonation process is essentially the same as before except the RTV skin has to be penetrated with the catalyst. He can inject the catalyst if he has a syringe or he can simply break the turd in two and apply the catalyst. The newest version of the catalyst compound is highly oxygenated so that only 4 cubic millimeters need to be placed in contact with the PETN to cause complete detonation. That is four one thousands of one cubic centimeter of catalyst.

There was an Egyptian in Mesoo Star, who had been seen talking to one of the PETN group. He told our man he had just negotiated a deal for the sale of pickle jars. It all makes perfect sense; RTV smells like vinegar, pickles are packaged in jars of vinegar; they plan to call their molded PETN ‘pickles’. If they can ever get this production going good they are going to ship PETN pickles all over the world.”

"Thank you doctor," Dove said. "Make, this is the hardware review group you are sitting in on. You were invited so that you might have time to clear your people out of that area. We have authorized a drone air strike on Mesoo Star. It was planned for Monday but there's a logistics problem. Mesoo Star is full of tourists and to minimize collateral damage, we will utilize an AGRFM weapon. That device won't be in place until about noon Wednesday. It will be delivered to the target at 3:15 AM Thursday, Yemen time. I hope you will be able to get your people away in time. Assuming a successful strike, the place will remain pretty much intact but the people in there will all be gone. Also, you will need to look at your old nemeses, Thorp. Doctor Delk thinks that it's possible that a quantity of "turds" or pickles have already been delivered to the dock to be shipped. Since Thorp is the appropriate shipper he will bear close surveillance."

"Thank you for the 'heads-up'," Make said. "That's all good information. Just the kind of thing I need to know." *I've got to find out what AGRFM is.* Make knew PETN was an extremely powerful explosive but he didn't know it could be transported undetected. *I've got to get a handle on shipments of that stuff.*

* * * *

Later that day, back in Scottsdale at Make's DHS office, Make had just dropped in to pick up his mail.

On paper, Make worked for the research section of the Technical Documents Division of the US Government Printing Office, an obscure group which sometimes had to travel. They spent a minimal amount of money and were frequently out of the office. In reality, a great deal of money was funded directly to this office. This was set up through congress in a way that it didn't show up on any books.

But the secretary was always there. She was very efficient. If you were to look in the office she might be seen using a normal phone system. However, in her boss's office, there was a more sophisticated source of communication which she used as needed. At this very moment she was communicating with one of Make's men using a device associated with Iridium. She told him that it was imperative that none of his people be in or even close to Mesoo Star, a location in Yemen. 345 Mukalla St. was very near the seashore.

"Get your people away from that area and don't get near it for at least a week."

Chapter 15

Monday noon

Maelstrom Air Force Base, Montana, Weapons Depot, Nuclear

The phone rang, "Airman Wiggins."

"Airman, this is Colonel Potts. Let me speak to the officer in charge."

"I am sorry sir, but Captain Miles is not here. He was just called to a meeting and he said he wouldn't be back until after lunch."

"What's your name, son?"

"Airman Wiggins, sir."

"Airman, Wiggins, I'm Colonel Potts. Do you know and understand what you have in your supply room?"

"Yes sir, I know all the equipment here, sir."

"There is a round stone building that has a thirty-five-foot high ceiling that is two foot thick, marble, and they are making bombs in there. I want something that will penetrate that ceiling and kill everybody in there and not blow up the building. "

"The LXE is the lowest yield AGRFM we've got sir. That's thirty five thousand REMS per square centimeter at ten feet, sir. That will fry a cow clear through…sir."

"Holy shirt."

"Yes Sir. Colonel Potts sir. I can't guarantee the building though. Ninety five percent of the yield is radiation but the other five percent is blast. It's about like one stick of dynamite. What's the building like, sir?"

"As I said, it's stone, probably two feet thick marble. It's about thirty feet across and it's got windows high, right up where the domed ceiling starts. And there is probably a door someplace."

"Sir, if the building doesn't collapse I believe anyone outside the structure will be ok from the AGRFM radiation coming out of the windows because they are so high up. And radiation won't come through the walls. But people standing outside the door won't survive unless they are a long way outside the door."

"OK, what about penetrating the ceiling? Is that going to blow the ceiling off?"

"You'll probably want a DP sir. I don't think it will blow the ceiling off, but I can't guarantee that, sir."

"What about collateral damage?"

"When the DP burns through, there may be some bits of hot marble rain down on anyone outside, sir. Sir, I can't guarantee any of that, sir."

"I know there's not any guarantees in this business. I'm not expecting that. Tell me about the DP."

"DP stands for deep penetration, sir." Airman Wiggins looked at a chart he got out of the file cabinet. "Sir, I would suggest a DP10. It will burn a hole through the ceiling plenty big enough for your LXE to go through. Subtracting the kick from the DP, that will put the yield at twenty-two feet below your two-foot ceiling, sir."

"OK that sounds good. Airman, you keep saying that the DP burns a hole through the ceiling. Does it really burn its way through the ceiling?"

"Oh, no sir. That's just a figure of speech, sir. That big part on the front end of the DP is a shaped charge. That blows a ten-inch diameter hole through the ceiling, then the long-stemmed part that comes through next will widen the hole out to, oh I'd say two feet, but it's just a powerful explosive."

"Ok, Wiggins, I want to make absolutely sure you have this equipment before I present it. I'm going to wait on the phone until you go and locate both these items to make sure we can make the assembly. I don't want to recommend something that we can't produce. You see what I mean?"

"I understand, sir. I'll go check right now sir. Colonel, sir, DP's are about a quarter mile away from here in the small parts storage building. It's going to take me twenty minutes to locate both items. I could just call you, sir."

"Ok, but make it quick. By the way, how long will it take you to assemble that?"

"DP's are quick, no assembly required. Installing the thermal batteries in the AGRFM's takes about an hour and forty five minutes. Attaching the DP takes about an hour and cradling the assembly ready for in a C130 is a half hour. We can have the whole assembly ready to go in four hours from now, sir."

"Barney, grab a tow and come with me. We're going to get a DP."

* * * *

"Myers."

"General Myers, this is Colonel Potts. We can have a system ready to fly in five hours. Using a C130J with stops at New Brunswick, Iceland, Germany, then a carrier in the Red Sea, we can be ready to deliver in forty hours."

“What else you got on that CJ?”

“Nothing sir. Just the arming crew.”

“God we waste so much. I hate waste. But we have to do it. We are sending a big airplane half way around the world with a four hundred pound package. Christ. That plane is capable of carrying a 70,000 pound load. I hate it. I just hate it. Colonel Potts, you have a few hours before takeoff. Look around. See if you can’t find somebody or something that needs to go in that direction.”

Chapter 16

Monday night

Tempe, AZ Motel

North of Broadway and east of Hayden in Tempe, Arizona, sitting back from the street, was an old motel. Built in the fifties when that was bare ground, it was a nice, medium-priced business named 'The Dolison'. Now, other buildings lined the streets making it almost invisible. Make was meeting with his group there tonight. In separate rooms, each of the four men sat on a chair facing the bed where Make had placed his communication equipment. The eight-by-eight rooms were barely big enough for a chair and the bed. Make sat in his car in front of one of the rooms.

Make told his Yemen group about the possible shipment of PETN, and then asked Marvin for a report.

"Nothing new on PETN production. Al-Asin is out of town. They made a few pickles before he left but I know they had fewer than fifty. Their first run was twenty or so but they threw some in the sea because they were defective. Now that Al-Asin is gone the rest of his bunch is doing nothing. They only made product while he was there and he left almost as soon as he got his group together. I know they didn't make any product after he left. They seem to be pretty disorganized and nobody in that group knows anything about PETN. It is my opinion that they don't know how to use the stuff and they're all afraid of it."

Make asked, "What do you mean 'out of town'? How does a guy like that just up and go out of town?"

"Whoever is running him gave him a ticket to a meeting somewhere. I don't think he told his guys where he was going or when he would be back. And I sure don't know."

"Try to keep track of them," Make said. "If someone takes leadership and gets them organized they might become a threat again. They'll be lucky if they find someone as good as the Al-Asin. Just keep track of them and him if he ever comes back. And if you think they are getting together again signal us immediately. Can you put one of your guys in their group?"

"Not really," Marvin answered. "It is such a small group that everybody knows everybody. Half of them are related. But I've got an idea. What if we get a PETN expert and get him an introduction to the group. They might take him in. Do you think he would be accepted because he knows PETN? If he worked it right he might get them to blow themselves up."

"That's a lot of ifs," Make said. "I don't know how we could do that. And it might backfire. Just keep a close watch on them for now. Have you got a good handle on your people?"

"Yeah we are good. We are pretty tight right now."

"Good. About your idea about adding a PETN expert to the group though. It certainly is interesting. I am going to tell the boss about it and see if he thinks it's practical. Since we are on the PETN subject, the test experts now think they know how to make a sniffer that will detect the stuff. They haven't got it working yet but they think they will have a viable device in 90 days. Who's next?

"Ralph."

"Ok Ralph. You're up"

"I've got a guy near Wadi Doan. It is in the south part of Yemen. It's in the Hadramaui Mountains, very remote. He went to a group of tribesmen and told them he was with al-Qaeda. He told them that any AQAP men or other supporters should meet in Casa Bugshan, the mosque, in the first week in July. He's going around in that general area with the same story. If he can generate enough interest to get a bunch together it might be worth a strike."

"Why is he doing that?" Make asked. "We didn't authorize that. Is somebody else trying to run a game?"

Ralph replied, "I didn't tell him to do it. Either someone else has gotten to him or he decided on his own. He may have thought it might help. He hasn't had any work from me in a while. Maybe he thought if he did something on his own we would think he was more qualified to work for us."

"We can't have that," Make said. "Can you get him stopped? If he does get a group together we wouldn't know who is in there. I don't think a strike would be authorized unless there was a serious bad guy in the group. We'd probably just kill off a bunch of innocent people and get some bad press among the natives. Ralph, your job for now is to find out if it can be stopped and if so, stop it. Does he know who's in the group he's getting together? And finally who told him to do that? Could al-Qaeda be running him for some reason? That's a worry."

"Who's next...anybody?" Make asked.

"I've got a bad problem."

"Who's talking and describe your problem."

Tony leaned close to his mike, "I'm Tony and one of my guys on the ground is missing."

"Oh shit. How long?"

"He missed a pickup four days ago. He is my best guy. He's the one that put us on to the bomb maker in Abubaker Ahladi. The one that blew himself up. Remember that? He's been with me eight months and now he's gone. His body hasn't shown up so the theory is that he was kidnapped."

"What have you done?"

"I put my handler in a safe house. My ground guy's family is going crazy. They're looking all over for him and at the same time, of course, they're worried that they might be next. I plan on just being quiet for a while."

"That's good. That's the thing to do. Anybody else?"

No one said anything, so Make said, "Ok guys don't leave for a couple of minutes then start out." Make switched his system so that only Marvin could hear him, "Marvin, I want to talk to you again. I don't like that whole thing about Al-Asin going to a meeting. I am afraid something bad's going to happen. I wish he would go away and stay away."

"Make, are you saying you want him killed?"

"No. I am not saying that. I'm not saying I want him killed. I'm not authorized to do that. I'm saying I am afraid that with his being there with his group, trying to make PETN, and now being called away to a meeting, there must something big going on. And something big and high explosives are a bad combination for the civilized world."

"Make, I do want him killed," Marvin said. "He's really bad. But I can't kill anybody either. However, if anyone does get killed it sure would be nice if it was Asin. Christ, half the people in Rukob want him killed. If they hadn't all been afraid of him he would've been dead ages ago. He's a mean son of a bitch, Make. Remember he killed two of his own people last month and one of them was his cousin. It's a bad management tactic I know, but while he is around, it sure keeps the rest of the flock on track."

"Marvin, do you think the people in Rukob know he's making PETN?"

"When he was here, I'm sure no one in his group told anyone but now that he is gone someone might tell. I don't know."

"What if it became general knowledge what twenty men and boys were doing every day at 345 Mukalla St. in Mesoo Star?"

"If that happened I'm sure the problem would go away one way or the other."

"How would you suggest it might be done?" Make asked.

"It's really difficult. If he comes back and finds who told, he'll kill them and their relatives too. And everybody knows that."

"I've got a plan. Have two dozen flyers printed up. Very brief wording in big letters so they can be read at a distance. Something like, 'They are making explosives in Mesoo Star'. Something like that. Then hire a guy that lives far away to deliver them at night by boat. He has to be someone that's a total stranger to everyone in Mesoo Star so if anybody sees him; they won't know who he is. He spreads the flyers around, gets in his boat and leaves. And it would be good if this happens before Asin gets back."

"I like the flyers idea. That's good. The delivery is crucial. I'm not crazy about that part. What's wrong is we need somebody that lives at least a hundred miles away for it to be somebody that no one knows. The sea around there is tricky. To go that far takes a pretty good boat, not just a row boat. And he has to be someone that knows the sea. How about if we get someone with a car to just drive through town late at night and spread the fliers as he goes?"

"Yeah, I like that better. He could live two hundred miles away and do that. How far is Sana'a?" Make asked.

"No, Sana'a too far," Marvin said. "That's a ten hour drive each way. Let me take it from here. I'll get somebody in a car to do it and it will be somebody that no one in that area knows. I'll take care of it, ok?"

"Do it. I like it. By the way, what's the difference between this and telling somebody to kill him?"

"I just feel better this way. Besides, we are not ordering anybody to kill anybody. We are just distributing flyers."

"Right, so half the town will kill somebody. Anyway, you're right. Just do it." Make drove away from the motel area back to North Scottsdale. *My god, I've just sentenced a man to death. But somehow, it doesn't seem so bad.*

* * * *

Make was not mechanically or electrically technical but he had made up a communication system that was probably impossible to bug. Sometimes he talked to his people over scrambled phone systems and sometimes he spoke to his people using the iridium phone. He felt that both of these systems probably would not be compromised. Local group meetings were different. When he needed to talk to his people locally, he arranged for a meet at an out of the way motel. He would rent the right number of rooms ahead of time. He would arrive early and install his system, which consisted of a lot of wires, microphones, head phones, a wire-wound pot and some toggle switches and a car battery. He'd made a switch box so that he could talk to all of his people and he could control whether or not they could hear each other. He would rent enough rooms for each of his people, next to one another if possible. In each of the rooms, he would place a mike and earphones and run wires back to his car. Each of his people would park directly in front of the room he was to occupy and go in. Most of his guys had never seen one other and some of them, Make had never met. False names were used by each man and after the meeting each left at a different time.

Once, when he was meeting with his group, they had discussed his communication system. Some thought it was archaic, and one said it was 'low tech in a high tech world' but Make said that if someone knew anything that would be better he would really like to hear about it. After a brief period with no comments, all had to agree with its salient feature; none of them could think of any way it could be compromised. Land lines broadcast, cell phones broadcast, hand held devices broadcast, and all other kinds of communication broadcast. Twelve volt, DC with no carrier wave does not broadcast. And Make always parked his car where he could see all the wires.

Chapter 17

9 AM Tuesday

The Office of the President

"Alright George, what's next on the agenda?

"Nothing until ten, Mr. President. You have about 28 minutes to think sweet thoughts."

"And at ten?"

"A photo shoot is scheduled from 10 until 10:30. You will present the Silver Star medal to Lieutenant Walter J. Cahn. He was wounded in action in Afghanistan. He will show up at ten. You'll have a few minutes to get acquainted with him while the camera people are setting up. From 10:30 until 11:30 you have Omar Al-Phaki. He wants to talk you about OPEC and how America's drilling and fracking will affect their production. At 1:00 you have Marland Butler assistant chief of the FBI."

"Couldn't it wait till the general staff meeting? What does he want? See if you can get me a heads up on this, George."

Fifteen minutes later, "I'm sorry to interrupts your sweet thoughts, Mr. President, but regarding Marland Butler, it's about an arms shipment the FBI knows about. He wouldn't say any more except that there is something you might want to know about before the staff meeting."

* * * *

At 12:46 PM, "Mr. President, Mr. Butler is here."

The President motioned for George to let Marland Butler into the oval office. “Come in Marland. What’s got you bothered so early in the week?”

“Sir, you remember the 17th of last month we intercepted a shipment of weapons that were supposed to go to a group of radical Muslim terrorists? Those weren’t M-16’s sir. They were Tivars. Tivars are the latest hand held tactical weapon the joint chiefs have approved. We have a large quantity of Tivars on order to the military but they haven’t been delivered yet. How can terrorists get them quicker than we do sir?”

“I see your point, Marland. Do you know where they came from?”

“Two of the terrorists have told us they are not sure but they think the Tivars were coming from New Mexico. We think the bunch we apprehended didn’t do the actual purchase. We’re looking for the ones who did but we haven’t caught them yet. From a different source, we’ve heard that the CIA actually paid top dollar for the 24 Tivars. Sir, To use the common vernacular, when General Richard Johnston hears about this, he is going to shit…sir.”

“Anything else I should know about this Marland?”

“That’s about all we know right now sir.”

“Marland, keep this under your hat till I get back to you. And thank you for bringing this to my attention, Marland.”

1 PM

“George, get Frank Fox in here.

A few minutes later, Fox, director of the FBI, steps into the oval office.

“Frank, I just finished talking with Marland. I want to compliment you on the progress you’ve made on that. We’ve got a very sensitive issue here and, as I said to Marland, it is important to keep this quiet until we know the whole story. Where these items came from, how they got them, etc. etc.”

“Mr. President, are you saying that you don’t want this brought up in the general meeting.”

“That’s exactly what I am saying.”

“I will do that sir but, you know, the press will find out about it sometime. And they’ll print it. They love stuff like this”

1:15 PM

“George, see if you can find Isabell Franks, and when you find her, get her in here as soon as you can. Reschedule my appointments as you need to fit her in.”

A few minutes later, Isabell Franks entered and stood at the President’s desk.

“Good afternoon Isabell, I just found out that Muslim Terrorists who live in the United States can buy the latest weapons from outside the United States and have them shipped inside the United States. And the terrorists got their shipment before our military got theirs. Jesus Christ Isabell!”

After their short conversation, Isabell Franks returned to her office. “This is Isabell Franks. I would like to speak to Lon Dove. I called his direct line and he didn’t answer. Can you reach him and ask him to call me please?”

“At this moment he’s out of the office and not available. He’ll be back in about three hours.”

"That won't be soon enough. Who, in your department, might have some information about interstate arms shipments?"

"You should talk with Doctor Make Caston. Caston knows Arms dealers. He is on special assignment for John Walker who works for Mr. Dove. But Walker's under the weather right now. Caston's in Arizona but I can probably reach him."

"Make Caston. I know that name. He's the one that got on the plane to nowhere isn't he? He was on the news the other evening."

"Yes mam. Would you like me to call him?"

"No. If you will just give me his number, I'd like to call him personally." She dialed through.

"This is Make Caston, Ms. Franks."

"Caston, what do you know about arms dealers in New Mexico?"

"Three things. One: his name is Thorp. He's the only one running arms in New Mexico. Two: what I hear is, he buys from and sells to anybody overseas and here in the US he mostly works with the military and the CIA. He sells new and used guns and he sells other military equipment. I think he sells stolen equipment too. It's my understanding that if you have the money, he can get you just about anything you want either foreign or domestic. And I'll bet he's not cheap. He has a home in Albuquerque. And the other thing I know about him is, he's the owner of a plane that I was in the other day. You may have heard about it. I don't know exactly what the connection is yet but I suspect he was trying to get rid of me and that plane. Except for that, I haven't had anything to do with him since I had that run-in with him two years ago. You may not have heard about it. I shot him. If you want more information, I know of somebody in the CIA that works with him."

"You shot him?"

"Yes mam."

"Is he still alive?"

"Yes mam. At least, he was the last time I saw him."

A pause, "Do whatever it takes to find out what he sells, who he sells to, who authorized the sales, and is he legal. Actually, I want to know everything about him and his business, and I need to know it quick. You call me directly. Don't talk to anyone else in my office about this. This is my direct line number…543-555-1212."

1:40 PM, Caston's home

"Could I speak with Mr. Level please? This is Make Caston."

"Level here. Who am I speaking to?"

"This is Make Caston sir. I'd like some information on a fellow named Thorp. I understand your organization does business with him occasionally."

"Who do you work for, Caston?"

"My Boss's name is John Walker but he's not available right now, sir."

"Well Caston, I don't know why you don't just ask your boss to call me when he gets available."

"I can tell you why sir. It's because sometime between immediately and tomorrow morning the fires of hell are going to rain down on you if you don't give me some information about Thorp."

"Are you threatening me, Caston?"

"Oh, no sir. The President is."

Make listened and then dialed. "Hello Ms. Franks. This is Make Caston. I have some information for you."

"Hold on a minute Make. I want to get this scrambled."

Fifteen second pass, "Ok, Make, what have you got?"

"Thorp has a contract with the military. He's agreed to supply 4200 new Tivars. A Tivar is the latest thing in hand-held combat weapons. They fire our standard seven point six two ammo, yet there's almost no kick to them. They're manufactured in Europe. The price for that order was four point four million dollars. It was signed for by General Richard Johnston. That's a legitimate contract approved by the Joint Chiefs"

"Jesus."

"The CIA has purchased twenty four Tivars for evaluation. I was not able to get the price of that order. Neither the CIA nor the military has received their order yet. I called Thorp's office but didn't get to talk to him. He was not available…Ms. Franks?"

"Yes."

"There is another thing I should tell you about. My boss's boss, Lon E. Dove, has suggested I look into other parts of Thorp's business. Thorp owns or controls a freighter. It's a good bet he gets materials in the country without going through customs. He may be bringing in explosives."

"Ok, when Dove gets back I'll tell him what you and I have talked about," Isabell said. "I want you to keep track of Thorp. He sounds like someone we should know a lot more about. If something comes up that you think I should know about, you call me immediately. I'm not saying leave Lon out of the loop. I just want make sure I'm in the loop."

"Yes mam."

Make sighed and hung up. He went in to the great room where Laura was reading, "I love this job. I think I have three bosses now. First it was only John Walker then Lon Dove came along with a little project and now Isabell Franks." He sat by the couch in his favorite soft chair. "Laura, you asked why Homeland Security picked me. There was a Vietnamese guy named Mal Thorp. He had spent a year in med school in Vietnam. Of course, he was not allowed to practice medicine here but he was allowed to work as a medical assistant in New York. He came to realize that lots of syringes and other medical equipment got thrown in the trash. He started collecting this stuff, cleaning it and trying to sell it back to doctors. No one would buy it. He was desperate for more money so he got into the Mexican drug business. He would buy saline and ringers down there and sell it up here. This was only marginally profitable so he started selling Mexican flu vaccines. This was making him a lot more money but there was a problem. The vaccine wasn't effective. CDC got involved after data showed there was a problem where doctors had gotten their vaccine from Thorp. CDC got the sheriff to pick up Thorp but they couldn't prosecute. Doctors wouldn't testify. There was no way to prove that Thorp was selling ineffective drugs. He just stopped selling and he got away with it." Laura sat aside her Sudoku, and Make continued, "Later CDC got suspicious of Thorp again. They thought he might be selling other prescription meds. This was even harder to get proof of, however. At that point CDC decided to try a different approach. They contacted Homeland Security. And that's why I was recruited. They needed someone with a medical background. I met with Thorp. I tried to appeal to his sense of compassion. There were five deaths that might be attributed to his activities. But he denied any responsibility. He told me to go fuck myself. I tried everything I could to get him to stop selling Mexican drugs in America. Nothing worked. I got so frustrated that, finally, I shot him in the foot."

"Make, my God, you said you had never killed anyone."

"I didn't kill him. I just shot his foot. But that worked. I told him he was killing people with his drugs and if he didn't stop right now I would shoot him again. I must have convinced him because he got out of the drug business for good."

"But Make, didn't they put you in jail? You can't just go around shooting people. Even guys like him. Jesus Christ, Make, I never heard of such a thing."

"I was in his house in his bedroom when it happened. While I'd been pleading with him to quit his crooked drug dealings I had been going around room by room nosing through all his stuff. He was following me. I was looking for drugs in his sock drawer when I found a small 25 caliber pistol. I picked it up using a couple of socks to keep my finger prints off of it. He didn't know I had it. I got behind him, reached around him with the gun held in front of him and fired a round into the wall ahead of him. Then I dropped the gun, went over near where the bullet had made a hole in his wall, pulled out my gun and shot his foot. While he was screaming around, I called 911 and got the sheriff and an ambulance headed that way. He claimed he hadn't fired the gun but he had GSR all over the front of him. And the sheriff had been trying to find a reason to arrest him for a couple of years, so I was home free."

"You crazy son of a bitch…My God, that was good."

"Anyway, that's how I got to know Thorp."

Chapter 18

Wednesday, 8: PM Scottsdale, (9 AM Yemen)

The Caston residence, Scottsdale, AZ

When the land line rang, Laura saw that caller ID said it was Make's secretary but she answered it because she didn't want Make to stop, "Hello"

"Hi. Are you Ms. Caston?"

"Yes, I certainly am."

"Ms. Caston, I'm Make's secretary. Could I speak to him please? It's very urgent."

"He's pretty busy right now."

"Laura, give me the phone. Make took the receiver, "I'm sorry hon. I've just got to take this. Hi Christy. Can you talk?"

"No."

"I'll see you soon." Make got up

"Jesus Christ, Make."

8:35 pm, Make's DHS office, old town Scottsdale

When Make dialed his Iridium phone number he heard a male voice, "Hello."

Make said, "Hello. You called this phone recently. Where did you get the phone you are using?"

"This phone belonged to Al-Absent. He gave it to me. He told me to use it when he is dead. He was my friend. I am so sorry. He was my friend."

"I'm sorry you lost your friend. What's your name please?"

The man sounded stressed, "I am Al-HAmi. I'm a doctor."

"Do you have other friends around where you live?"

"Yes, if they are not also killed."

"Who would be killing them? Why would someone want to kill people?"

"The Al-Asin people. They are mean people. They are angry people."

"Al-Asin, are they the ones that were making the explosives?"

"Al-Asin, yes. The leader was killed. My friend made him die."

"No, your friend didn't make him die," Make said.

"Yes, my friend told the Vizier of the bomb. The Vizier got men with weapons. They made the Al-Asin go. Then the Al-Asin killed Al-absent."

"Ah, so the Al-Asin killed your friend Al-absent because they thought he had turned them in to the authorities?"

"Yes, I am so sorry. The way he died. Bad Al-Asin. He was hung by his hands behind his back. They cut his pohak and he bled."

"Yes, I am sorry too. Where are you?"

“Yemen, I am in Yemen. I am in the mountains.”

”What part of Yemen? What mountains are you in?”

“I am in the Hadramaut Mountains. I’m east of Alabr village. I can see the lights at night.”

Make got his tablet up, “I’m looking at Google Earth. I found the Hadramaut Mountains.”

“My friend had a computer. The Al-Asin break his computer,” Said Al-HAmi.

“Have you traveled far? Did you walk?”

“No, you say, hitch hike.”

“That could be dangerous. Who did you hitch hike with?”

“The German ancient people. They are here. They are safe”

“Where is your home?”

“My living place is Rukob. It is near the sea,” Al-HAmi answered.

Pause, “I can’t find it on the map. What major city is it near?”

“I do not understand.”

“Your home location. Your place.”

“I am close to Epave. It is east. Al Mukalla is west.”

“Is that close to Mesoo Star?”

“Mesoo Star, yes. The bomb makers at Mesoo Star.”

“I would like to come to you. To visit you.”

“No, you cannot come. I must leave here now. They want to kill me. I must go.”

“Where will you go? Will you go to Sana’a?”

"Sana’a is far,” Al-HAmi said.

“I would like to meet you. Call me again when you are in a safe place.”

* * * *

Wednesday, 9:05 PM

“General Johnson, this is Make Caston. I met you a few days ago in Lon Dove’s office. I believe the location we talked about in that meeting is no longer occupied by anyone except tourists. I suggest that plans should be changed.”

“I assume you are certain of your facts.”

“No. I am not. A half hour ago I received a call on my confidential office phone. It was from a man who said he was a friend of my contact overseas. He sounded very distraught. He said that my contact was found hanging in front of his house with his hands bound behind his back. The rope he was hanging by was attached to his hands. His genitals had been cut off and he was bleeding to death. The man I was talking to had talked to his friend while his friend was hanging there. The caller is afraid he’ll be killed too. He said his friend had been killed because his friend, my contact, has caused the bomb makers in Mesoo Star to leave. The caller said that Asin, their leader had been killed. The caller had caught a ride with a group of German archeologists in order to get to a safe hiding place. Based on the conversation with the caller, I believe all of that was true. It’s possible that I will be able to confirm this in 5 days.”

The General asked, “Where did he say the organization had gone?”

“He didn’t know. He said he’s afraid he’ll be killed. He’s moving to a different location. He said he’ll call me.”

“Have you talked to Dove about this?”

“No I have not. I wasn’t able to reach him. Isabell Franks was also not available.”

“I am going to cancel the operation. You call me at this number as soon as you can either confirm or deny what we’ve talked about. Also, it would be a good idea to tell Lon Dove about our conversation as soon as you can reach him.

I don’t work for Lon. He’s John Walker’s boss. I work for John Walker and I’ve not seen him in a week. Where does he go? What does he do?

Chapter 19

Tuesday, late

LAPD

Lieutenant Watson asked, “Pizzametski, have you seen this report?”

“Yes. I’m the one who put it on your desk. What do you think about it?”

“That guy that was in the plane, he hadn’t been shot had he? Did he have any GSR on him?”

“A little on his shoe soles and his right sleeve. Nothing like the rest of the plane. He hadn’t been firing any weapons and he hadn’t been shot.”

“I’ve never seen anything like that. Even the tail section was covered with GSR.”

“I Know,” Pizz said.

“The report said they estimate “several thousand rounds” of military.”

“Yeah, I know. I don’t think the person who fired all that was Caston. He’s not the type. He might take out a twenty-two and shoot cans but not automatic weapons firing 7.62”.

“Keep at this. That’s too much ammo being fired to not be important. There is something going on here.” Watson said.

Pizzametski also thought there was something really scary going on. *I don’t think Caston was a part of it but he was in the plane. I gotta talk to that guy some more. Does he have any automatic weapons? Where would he get that much ammo? Has he ever shot anyone? Somebody wanted to get rid of that plane. Probably because it was used to do something that they didn't want anybody to know about. It was probably illegal. And two or three thousand rounds. Were they testing ammo or automatic weapons, or maybe it was just target practice. No, nobody needs to practice firing that much. Maybe it was two or three guys. But why was Caston in the plane? No, the right question is, how did he get in the plane? Somebody put him in there. I wish I had the tox screen back. It's obvious why he was in there, someone wanted him dead. What did he do to somebody to piss them off that much?*

Chapter 20

Monday, 8:30 AM

Office of the Deputy Secretary of Homeland Security

"Mr. Dove, this is Irene, Isabell Frank's secretary, Ms. Franks would like to see you. Could you drop by her office?"

"Absolutely. Do you know what this is about? What do I need to bring?"

"I'm not aware of anything you will need Mr. Dove."

"I can be there in 10 minutes." *Boy oh boy, this scares the hell out me.*

Lon Dove, Makes boss's boss was nearby and immediately went to Frank's office. "Isabell, how are you?

"I'm fine Lon, thank you. I just wanted to tell you about an incident that came up while you were away. Guns are being brought into the USA by an arms dealer named Thorp. Apparently some of them have been sold to Muslims who are suspected of being part of a terrorist cell. I talked to one of your people, Make Caston. He seemed very knowledgeable about it. This situation has to be resolved very quickly. I am interested in knowing more about Make Caston. I was told he has a doctor's degree. Do you know what his theses was about?"

"He is a medical doctor, an MD. He is a foot surgeon."

"Well how in the hell did he get in this business?"

"We recruited him. We had need of someone who knew details of the medical business. He owns a small outpatient facility and is, or was the chief surgeon there. He seemed to fit the profile.

And he's very competent. So far he's succeeded where others have failed"

"He said he shot this guy Thorp."

"It was self-defense. Thorp shot first," Dove said.

"Why would Thorp shoot at him, and why would Thorp miss?"

"I don't know. I just know he was cleared of any wrongdoing."

Chapter 21

Monday, 9:30 AM

Albuquerque, NM

Make caught a plane to Albuquerque. On board he wondered about the theft of Thorp's Cessna 172, why no claim was filed, what part did it play in this arms shipment and why, and when and how was he put in that plane. His first stop at Kirkland airport was the area where privately owned and corporate owned planes are kept, called the FBO.

The wide hanger door was open. Inside, at the front, near the door, Make saw a young man sitting at a small desk. Make said, "Hello, I'm Carl Knowles, Avemco Insurance. There was a Cessna 172 stolen from here a few weeks ago. I would like to get some information about that."

"Well, I don't think I can help you much. I'm new here. Mr. Thorp hired me because I have experience flying TBM 850's. That's his new one over there. Maybe you can insure it. The base price on that baby is over four million dollars. Oh, here comes Bill Jones. He's the manager of the corporate hanger area. He probably can help you better than I can. Bill, this is the insurance man. He wants to know about that 172 that was stolen."

"I'm surprised to see you here," Bill Jones said. "I understand Mr. Thorp didn't file a claim. I didn't think any insurance people would show up. But, anyway, if you can tell me what kind of information you want maybe I can help."

"The LAPD, FAA, and Homeland Security are about to run out of reasons to hold on to that plane. We are thinking they will release it sometime next week. We want to be assured that when that Cessna is returned it won't be stolen again. What I want to know is what kind of security setup you had, why did it fail, and what has been done to prevent future thefts." *I've got to check out the price of Mal's new airplane. How did he get enough money to pay for that thing?*

After Make strolled out onto the cement, apron away from the two men he had just talked to, he Googled 'TBM 850'. A minute later he called Isabell,

"Hello Make, what have you found out so far?"

"I'm at Kirkland airport in Albuquerque. That Cessna actually disappeared from this field four weeks ago but was only reported as stolen two weeks ago. And it was the manager of the corporate hanger area that reported it missing, not Thorp's people. Furthermore there has never been a claim filed with their insurance company. Also, Thorp has purchased a new turbo prop Daher-Socata. That's a serious airplane. It's a $4.2 million dollar plane and there's a five month waiting time when you buy one. We have been keeping track of Thorp's income. He lives well, but financially, he is usually right on the brink of going bust. So he must have come into some money between five and six months ago. No one seems to care about or want to talk about the Cessna. It was an old one with minimal avionics and it had been used hard and not maintained properly. I suspect they wanted to get rid of it for some reason and that's why it was headed out over the ocean. If I hadn't regained consciousness, that plane and I would be at the bottom of the Pacific about 200 miles west of San Diego."

Isabell had lots of questions, "What happened to the pilot?"

"I don't know. I believe the people I talked to in the hangar area don't know either. They said the pilot disappeared the same time the plane disappeared. He had no known relatives.

Albuquerque PD hasn't heard about a pilot being missing. No one has filed a missing persons report."

"Doesn't the FAA keep track of all the planes all the time?"

"Normally they do a good job of knowing where all planes are if you want them to know where you are. If you don't want anybody knowing where you are, you can fly all over the country and never be noticed. All you have to do is avoid class B air apace--stay low"

"Make, new subject. You and I need to talk. You really shot Mal Thorp Didn't you?"

"Yes,"

"Were you arrested?"

"No."

"Were you held, detained?"

"No."

"How the hell did you do that? You can't shoot someone then just walk away."

"Ms. Franks, I was told to do whatever it took to stop Thorp from selling drugs. I did that. If you want to know all the details I'll tell you. But I really believe you don't want to know. I mean, if you knew, you would wish you hadn't found out. I think you should not know any more than what you know right now, mam. But I'll tell you if you want me to."

Isabell paused for a moment, "Ok. Forget I asked. But, sometime later, I want to know. I would just like to know more about your M. O., that's all. I am not complaining about what you did, understand? I think you did very well. You accomplished what a lot of others, including CDC, tried to do and failed. I'm just curious."

* * * *

Monday, 2 PM

"Hi, Laura, it's me. I'm still in Albuquerque at the airport café".

"Oh Make, I'm so glad to hear from you. When are you comin' back?"

"I would have been back today but I hit a snag. Remember the guy Thorp that I was talking to you about? I spent most of yesterday trying to find him. This morning on the local news, I find that he's in jail. He tried to hire a two thousand dollar a night hooker who turned out to be a cop. It was a big sting operation. They also caught a priest."

"I thought those guys only liked altar boys."

"Be nice Laura. Anyway, I thought there was to be an arraignment hearing this afternoon before a judge but they let Thorp out before that with just a slap on the wrist. He never even had to go to the hearing."

"Hey, I've got confidence in you Make. You'll find him. When you find him are you going to shoot him again?"

"Laura, you sure are full of it today. What is going on with you?"

"I'm just lonesome, that's all. Sargent Pizzametski just left. I've been playing by myself. Sudoku that is."

"Pizzametski has been there for two days? What's he been doing there? What's going on?"

"Nothing's going on. He showed me around the campus. Did you know he graduated from the U of A? Besides, it was only a day and a half."

"Damn it."

"I'm just jerking you around a little. I miss you hon," She said.

* * * *

"Isabell Franks please. This is Make Caston."

"Hello Make, I was just getting ready to call you. Lon Dove is here with me and you're on speaker phone."

"Great, hi Lon."

"Make."

"Lon and I have reached a decision about John Walker. He has a chemical dependency problem and it's severe to the extent that he can no longer function. I have decided it would be better for our organization and for Walker if you report directly to Lon."

"That would be good for me. Sometimes John Walker is hard to find. So what's going to happen to him?"

"We'll put him in a good rehab program and see how it works out. If he recovers sufficiently he'll be transferred to another department. Ok. Let's consider that done. Make, this was really your call. What've you got?"

"I had one of my guys looking into Mal Thorp's history. Both of his parents are Vietnamese who came to the US after the war. My man found copies of two registered birth certificates, one for Mal Thorp and one for Ishe Thorp. Both were males born on the same day, about an hour apart. They were both born at home and both had the same parents. The only difference is the doctors. Doctor Baber signed Mal's certificate and Doctor Johnson signed Ishe's."

"So Baber and Johnson each attended a different birth. What does that mean?"

"Probably the first birth could have been attended by Baber who left the house not knowing another birth was on the way. I understand that can happen. When the parents realized what was happening they decided, for some reason, to keep one baby secret. After the second baby was born they called Doctor Johnson. They could have hid the first baby and only let Doctor Johnson see the second baby. He naturally signed thinking that there was only one child."

"So why would they do that? Why would you want to keep a baby a secret?" Isabell asked.

"I don't know why they did it. I know that when Mal was a kid, old enough to start med school, his parents sent him back to Vietnam to live with his grandparents. Maybe that has something to do with it. But there's more to this story. Almost everyone has had their fingerprints taken at least once. Pilot's license, food handler's permit, military service, there's a lot of things that require fingerprints. Mal's prints were easy to find. He has a pilot's license, a city permit to dump trash in the city land fill, a license to be a medical assistant. Each of those requires that you be finger printed. But we haven't found any for Ishe. His first income tax form was filled out when he was twenty five but he's never paid any taxes since then. So at this point, I can't know what's going on with Ishe or if he really exists Maybe Doctor Johnson was tricked somehow and there was really only one birth. Maybe Mal and Ishe are the same person. There's another thing I wanted to talk about. This is a new subject. I want to know where that Cessna that I was put in has been for the last seven weeks. If I knew that, I'd know a lot more about the arms shipments and the PETN shipments. I've talked to Frida in the LA office and asked her to make sure that plane stays in California till I tell her it's ok to release it. I'd like to get satellite recognition pictures taken of that plane. With that, the same algorism used in facial recognition can be used for plane recognition. A computer will go through all photo scans for the last seven weeks and maybe the plane was seen enough times to find out some of the places it has been. But I need a contact to talk to about the satellite information scanning. Do either of you know someone?"

Lon said, "I don't know how you find who runs satellites, Make."

Isabell said, "Make I'm not familiar with that whole process either, but I will find out and have that person call you."

A half hour later, Make's cell vibrated, "Hello. This is Lieutenant Colonel Wright. Are you Make Caston?"

"I am"

"Make, I'm with the National Reconnaissance Office. I was given to understand that you were interested in some airplane pictures. I may be able to help you with that."

"Thanks Colonel. I didn't expect to hear from someone so soon."

"I got the word from my boss, General Curtis, and I believe he got it from your boss, Isabell Franks, so tell me what you need."

"There's a plane parked on the tarmac, at the Compton/Woodley county airport. That is close to LAX. The "N" number is 913R. I'd like to know where that plane has been the last 7 weeks. I thought that you might be able to scan your existing photos and give me some locations."

"I can do that," The colonel said. "We've got reconnaissance satellites that are orbiting about 200 miles up, continually taking extremely high definition digital photographs. The satellite transmits the photos back to earth, and then they are electronically scanned, looking for whatever we're interested in. All we have to do is get a picture or your plane, enter that into our look-file and wait. The longest part of the process is waiting till our satellite gets over your plane. Hold on a minute Make…Ok Make. It looks like we are having good luck so for. We're going to get a picture of your plane in 116 minutes. Make, if you can get here this afternoon I can see you at about 5 PM. I'll make sure you can get in the front door, but that is all the further you can go. I'll meet you there at 5PM and we can go to an unsecured cafeteria on campus and talk. Does that sound good?"

"It sounds absolutely great. I'll be there."

* * * *

Monday afternoon at an outdoor café at NRO, Make was looking at a group of 8 x 10's pictures that had been laid before him. "Thanks for the pictures Colonel Wright. I'm just amazed at how little time it took. I had planned on having to get a programmer to write an algorithm to search for my particular plane."

"NRO has had a program like that in place for twenty years. The main time constraint would have been the satellite location. Fortunately, KH-12 is looking at our planet all the time and was approaching your airplane when we were talking. I was able to get its digital description to the HK's active and archive storage. I just looked at the last 7 weeks as you suggested. If you need to look farther back, give me a call."

Chapter 22

Late Tuesday evening

Scottsdale, AZ, Makes home

Back in Scottsdale Make threw his duffel in the car and immediately started dialing his crew. On such short notice, he was only able to get three of his locals, Brady, Marvin, and Mickey. Two hours later at a motel, “On your beds I’ve put satellite pictures of a Cessna 172. It’s believed to have been involved in illegal transportation of weapons and materials. The information at the bottom of the picture tells the date and time taken. The location of each picture is described in longitude and latitude. The elevation is shown in meters above sea level. Also, there’s a US map that shows longitude and latitude. Look them over. Use the magnifying glasses and lights if you need them. If you recognize anything let me know. I want to be able to plot the course that plane took. ”

“I’ve got one in my territory. Its picture number forty three, actually number forty three and forty four. The place looks like an old, WW2 landing strip. I’m looking on Google Earth at the coordinates shown. It looks like it’s south and a little east of Albuquerque.”

“Who’s talking?”

“Brady. That’s really out of the way. I didn’t know that landing strip was there. It’s like a million miles from nowhere. Anyway, number forty three shows four people standing around a box truck parked close to the plane. In the next pictures the truck and the people are gone and the plane is on a different part of the airstrip. Those were taken fifteen days ago about eighty seven minutes apart.”

"As we go through these pictures," Make said. "I want each of you to record the picture number, what time of what day it was taken, and where the plane is. Ok, who's next? By the way, that was good Brady."

"I'm Mickey and I've got several here. First..."

After the session was over Make collected all his equipment and the photos, and the information his people had written and put it all in his car Later, at home, he arranged the written data in chronological order based on the date on the pictures and marked the location of each sighting on a map of the US.

* * * *

Wednesday Make called Colonel Wright from home. "Hi Make. How did your photo project turn out?"

"Very good actually. But there are some parts of the project I think need more attention. I wonder if I could take a few minutes of your time to describe the problem I'm having."

"Sure Make, go ahead."

"I took a map of the US and marked in chronological order all the locations of those pictures. You gave me a few more pictures than I used because some were of the plane in the same place but from a slightly different angle. But, anyway, I put only twenty three in chronological order on my map and then drew what looked like the path that plane took. Fifty eight days ago it was tied down at his rental space at Kirkland airport."

Colonel Wright said, "Right."

"The next picture showed the plane headed east. That was taken fifty six days ago. Then the next two pictures were taken three days apart and the plane is sitting in the same place in both pictures. How do I find out what was going on there? That place is the Santa Rosa route 66 airport. I called there but couldn't find anyone that could help me. They just said planes frequently stop there. They thought the plane was there a total of four days."

"You mentioned you had two pictures of the same plane from different angles. Well we may have lots of pictures of the plane in the same place from different angles. We just gave you the first and last picture of that plane at that place. KH-12 takes a picture every five seconds. We may have half a dozen pictures of your plane in Santa Rosa."

"Every five seconds, that's a lot of pictures to look at."

"True, 10800 per fifteen hour day, but we have fast computers and lots of memory storage," Wright said. "Let me suggest that I get you all the pictures taken at that particular time and place and perhaps you can determine what that guy was doing there."

"Ok. Great. Now we have a couple more pictures of him going east, then he is parked at George Farm air strip in North Carolina. And he's there for at least five days. Then he goes back to New Mexico. Later he goes back to George Farm again. It's sort of a pattern for him. During the last eight weeks there are five other places that the plane is stopped at for more than one day. Colonel, I feel that I am imposing on you asking for all these pictures and using up so much of your time. It's just that it's really important that we know what this guy is up to."

"It's OK." Colonel Wright said. "We know how to do this. I've been told a little about your operation and I understand. What we've done here is the first part of what may turn out to be a longer task. I'm going to suggest that I mark a map just like you did on your map. Then I'll have all of the pictures that were taken at every place he stopped at and also I'll give you the appropriate pictures of the area surrounding the places he stopped at. If there's anything classified in there, I'll have to leave that out, of course. Also, this will turn out to be a lot of pixels, so I'll just supply you with the information on a blue ray disks. I'll send them to you, express mail. Blue rays can hold twenty five GB per side. I am assuming you can handle blue ray, right? I don't know what kind of computer you've got but this may take a half day to download. These are ultra-high resolution pictures. You could blow them up to as big as your wall and still have quality pictures. But since that's not practical I will also include a program that will allow you to download these as something less than ultra-high definition, but you can see any part of the picture in ultra by moving the magnifying glass to the part you want to see. It's a simple little program and it is easy to use. You'll like it. After you've analyzed all the material, you may have more questions. If so, don't hesitate. OK?"

* * * *

Wednesday morning

Make walked into their bedroom, "Hi Laura."

"Oh, hi Make. I didn't know you were home. When did you get here?" She threw her arms around him and kissed him.

"About 1 AM. Honey, I just slept in the spare bedroom because I didn't want to wake you up. Maybe I should have. Huh?"

"I'm glad you're home Make. I just got off the phone with Sargent Pizzametski. He is a delightful man. You just missed him. He called to talk to you but we ended up just gabbing for about an hour. He's coming here tomorrow to talk to you."

"Oh Christ. Honey I'm not going to be here tomorrow. I've got to be in the office or unavailable all day. What does he want anyway?"

"I don't know. He just said there were some things he didn't understand and he wanted to talk to you about them."

"Well, if he does show up, be mindful of what you tell him."

"Will you be back by tomorrow night?"

"I don't know. Probably not until after midnight or maybe not until Friday morning. I'll just have to see how it goes."

"Make, I get so lonesome. Can I call you if it gets late and you're still not here?"

"Sure. But honey, be careful around that guy, Pizzametski. I think he is hot for you."

I think he is too. Maybe I'll suggest that he just stay here till Make gets back. Oops. Now I've got to wash my mouth out.

Chapter 23

Thursday

Dove's office, Washington, DC

"Lon, I've got some things I'd like to show you. I've been working with NRO analyzing pictures they've supplied me. I've a good idea of where that plane went the last eight weeks and a suspicion of what Thorp is up to. Thorp's plane took off from Albuquerque heading east approximately fifty seven days ago. We've got him two days at George's Farm in North Carolina. There's a white box truck there and off shore there's the freighter, the *Golden Lie*. Thorp's plane made two trips back and forth across the country, hooked up with a freighter via that white box truck, both times. Stopped off once at Kansas City International, and eventually went to Phoenix. He sometimes goes to a remote air strip east of Albuquerque. I can track that plane right up to and including the day I got put into it. I know about the freighter too. She picked up two cases of Tivars, twenty four to the case from Calais, France, eight weeks ago then five days later she was at a dock in Yemen where she picked up two boxes of sweet pickles. I think Thorp's plane brought the Tivars back to Albuquerque then went back for the pickles. I know the CIA never got their twenty four Tivars. I want to know what he did with them."

Make has the feeling that Lon's mind is on something else, but he added, "Lon, it looks like the pickles went to that salt mine underground dry storage facility in Kansas City, Kansas. We are watching to make sure those pickles stay there; because I believe those pickles are PETN. I'm going to KC, to have a look at those sweet pickles."

"Make, I think you have a good handle on it. Go to Kansas City and do your thing."

Does he understand that PETN is an extremely powerful explosive?

Chapter 24

Thursday afternoon

Isabell Franks' office, DC

"Lon, could you come into my office please?"

"Sure, Isabell. What's up?"

"Lon, at your pay level you're entitled to take personal business off as you need it, but that privilege goes along with reasonableness. It seems you've been gone a lot lately. All I am saying is don't push it."

"Sure Isabell, I know I have been off a lot lately and it bothers me that I've have had to do that. It's just that my wife's brother, Jobi, has just gotten out of prison and he is kind of a lost soul. He wants to get into some kind of business but being a bookkeeper and being a felon makes getting a job pretty difficult. He wants me to go into business with him."

"What's that Lon? What kind of business?"

"He thinks, considering the kind of business I'm in, that we could make a killing, doing spy work. I have told him, of course, that I couldn't do that. I've got too good of a job here."

"Lon, are you telling me that your brother-in-law is a felon?"

"Yes. He got three years for abetting tax fraud. But he got out in 26 months for good behavior."

"And you've discussed your work with him?"

"Well, I didn't really discuss it with him, you know. It's just that, after a while, people seem to have an idea about what you do. I haven't told him any details."

“Was he in prison when you were hired?”

“Oh no. I’ve been here about four years.”

“Lon, do you remember the security classes you took when you first started working here?”

“Oh Sure.”

“Lon, I want you to go down to Human Resources right now and tell them what you’ve just told me. Now Lon.”

Isabell made a call, “Hello. Is this HR?” …“I have just sent Lon E. Dove down to HR. He is going to tell you about his brother in law…well, after he has told you, you’ll know why.”

One half hour later, “This is Isabell.”

“Ms. Franks, this is Robert in security. Lon E Dove will not be working for you anymore. Today was his last day. The next thing you should do is to talk to all his employees and find out if any of them have been the source of security leaks.”

As soon as she hung up she dialed Make, “Would you come into my office please?”

“I’m glad you called me. I have something too.”

“Close the door please. And sit down. Make, how well do you know Lon?”

“For the last couple of days he’s been my temporary boss. What do you mean?”

“Have you ever met his wife?”

“Yes. When I first hired in here, he and his wife took Laura and me out to dinner.”

"Do you know any of his relatives or any of his friends?"

"No. I don't think so. Why are you asking me about Lon? I don't know him very well."

"Do you know his brother-in-law?"

"No. I don't know his brother-in-law. I didn't know he had a brother-in- law. And I don't know any of his other relatives or friends. What's going on?"

"Has he done anything strange, unusual, or out of place?"

"He has never said anything out of line to me. I'm not aware of anything bad about him. Today, he didn't seem very interested in the information I have about where Thorp's plane has been, but other than that he seems OK. Isabell, you are my boss's boss, I like you, I think you are probably a good person, and I know for sure you are competent. Now, if you will tell me what the fuck is going on, I'll try to help you."

"Thank you for saying that, Make. Right now I need all the help I can get. Lon is no longer with us. Security has determined that he's a security risk. They'll probably want to question you. I'll tell them what you have just told me but don't be surprised if you get a call. No one has told me this but it looks bad for me right now because two ranking people in this section have left in the last two days, both under bad circumstances. Right now, you and I are the only two people on the payroll in this section. A screw up on our part, your part, either of our parts, that would normally go unnoticed, might be blown all out of proportion. *Capisci*"?

"What did he do?"

"Not much actually. His brother in law just got out of prison and asked Lon to go into business with him. The brother- in- law thought that, since Lon was in the spy business they could start their own spy business and go to work for us."

"Oh shit. Is that what he really said?"

"Pretty much."

"Oh, shit…Ok. Really, all we have to do, all we can do, is keep doing what we're supposed to do and not screw up. Right?"

Make reaches across the desk and put his hand on her hand, "Isabell, neither of us did anything wrong. It's going to be ok. *Capisci*"?

* * * *

Later that day in Isabell's office, Make said, "I've gone over the route Thorp's plane took the last few weeks. Isabell, I am convinced that those so called pickles are the first shipment of PETN. I think it is imperative that they're not given to the Muslims. I want to get them out of Thorp's underground storage locker and replace them with jars of look-a-likes. Does that sound right to you?"

"Off the top of my head I can't think of any way you can do it without alerting Thorp, but I think it has to be done some way."

"When I steal the pickles I will need a team to make dummy Pickles. I'd like to set that up before I leave. As soon as I get the pickles I'll take pictures of the boxes, the jars, and the individual pickles and send all the photos to the team. That way they can start making the substitutes. Are you good with this?"

"Make, I've got a lot of confidence in you. You get things done. That thing you did to get information from the CIA was something I, personally, would not have done that way but it worked out very well. I told the President about it."

"Shit. What did he say?"

“He chuckled and said it sounded like I’ve got someone who can get things done around here.”

Chapter 25

Thursday Evening

Make's house, Scottsdale, AZ

"Sargent, I'm surprised to see you here. What's going on?" Make asked as Pizzametski walked in.

Laura spoke up, "Make, remember, I told you Sargent Pizzametski wanted to talk to you. Well, here he is."

"Sargent, I am pretty tired so please make it short. OK?"

"Sure. Well first I wanted to tell you that I have some information on that plane you were in. It was at Kansas City international airport a few days ago."

"Is that right? I doubt that I was on it then. Thank you Sargent. I am going to go to bed now. I'm really tired."

"Another thing I wanted to talk to you about was the black stuff on the right side of the plane. Do you remember that?"

"Yes. I was told it was a mixture of engine oil and dust. They said that sometimes when a plane leaks a little oil and flies in a dusty area...Sargent, you're shaking your head. Tell me about the black stuff."

"It is gunshot residue. GSR covered the right side of the plane in a pattern from that torn up right window hole back to and including the right stabilizer. Somebody fired at least two thousand rounds of seven point six two military out of that plane while it was in flight. We determined the ammo was from lot number AAMR43 from Picatinny Arsenal. That lot of twenty thousand rounds was ordered by and shipped to the CIA a month ago. It never arrived."

That's why Mal wanted to get rid of that plane. He used that to promote the sale of those Tivars he had stolen. I'll bet he took a couple of terrorists for a plane ride and let them shoot out of the window while they were flying around. They probably shot up an old car or something out at some remote spot in the desert. Then he thought he could get rid of me and the evidence at the same time. That fucker.

"Pizzametski, that had to be an automatic weapon of some kind." Make said, *I wish I could tell him about Tivars*. "I've never fired an automatic weapon, if that's what you are getting at."

I checked. I know you don't have a license to own an automatic weapon, but I thought you might have bought one recently and hadn't got around to applying for the license yet."

"I'm going to bed now, Sargent."

"Oh, one more thing. I went looking for you and I stopped by your surgery. They said they hadn't seen you in a few days. Do you have another job or something? You've been real hard to find."

"I'm considering opening another surgery in another town. It's taken a lot of my time."

"Sounds like business is going good. What town is it going to be in?"

"Haven't decided yet. I've been going around to a lot of places."

"One more thing."

"Sorry Sargent. I've really got to say good night. Goodnight." *Shit…Well, I guess he's a good cop.*

The next morning, Make told Isabell, "Sargent Pizzametski LAPD, is getting to be a problem. He was at the house last night asking a lot of questions about my whereabouts. I may run out of answers pretty soon."

"That's really strange. Usually police departments don't have the money to send their cops out of their area. What's going on there?"

"He's been at the house a lot and Laura told me once that he was a "very interesting man so..."

"Hold the phone a minute, Make," Isabell said.

After she Googled LAPD's phone number, Isabell said, "Hello, this is Isabell Franks, Homeland Security. I'd like to talk to Sargent Pizzametski. Can you tell me which department he's in please... La Brea, thank you. Can you connect me please...? Hello, this is Isabell Franks, Homeland Security. I'd like to talk to Sargent Pizzametski... I see. Can you tell me when he will be back...Oh no, that won't be necessary. Thank you very much. Good bye...Make, He's on vacation. He has to be back in ten days."

"I'll talk to him." Make said. "But I want to tell you, his visit wasn't all bad for me. He told me where the CIA's missing Tivars were a few weeks ago. Remember the black stuff on the right side of that 172? It was GSR. He said more than two thousand rounds of 7.62 had been fired while in flight."

"So it's reasonable to think that Thorp somehow got hold of those guns and fired them out of that plane while the pilot was flying it around."

"Yes and the CIA is missing 20,000 rounds of 7.62 military too. Part of that lot of ammo was what was fired from that plane."

"Make. We've got to catch that guy."

"I know, but he may be into worse stuff than stealing guns. I am really worried about those pickles, Isabell. That PETN, if that's what they are, is really bad shit. It's probably the most powerful chemical explosive there is right now."

"Are they gaining on us? Do you need more help?"

"Not right now but I'll think about it. What about Sargent Pizzametski? He's a pain but that just means he's a good cop. I'll give it some thought. New subject. I needed a man in Kansas City to keep track of those jars of pickles that Thorp picked up off of the *Golden Lie*. We didn't have anyone available so I hired a KC investigator. He has a man watching the underground storage facility until I can get there tomorrow afternoon."

Chapter 26

Friday morning

On the triple seven to KC

After Make gets buckled in, he leaned over, “Sargent Pizzametski, what a surprise. I didn’t expect to see you on this plane.”

“Yeah, I’m surprised to see you here too.”

“That’s bullshit. Why are you following me, Sargent? I’d have thought you’d have been at my house screwing my wife.”

“Make, it sounds like it’s going to be a long flight. Why don’t we get a couple of those empty seats back in the back so we won’t disturb this lady?”

“Oh, please don’t leave”, she said, “I really, really want to see how this ends up.”

They both looked at the lady then resumed their discussion, “Here’s the thing, Sargent. You’re not working. You’re on vacation. What the fuck are you doing?”

“I’m working. I’m just working while I’m on vacation. Now what the fuck are you doing here? You’re never at work. You are never at home. You are hard to find. You have all the symptoms of a druggie but you’re not. Your financials look like you collect a nice salary in addition to the minimal income from your surgery. What are you doing, Make? And I am not screwing your wife, yet.”

* * * *

Friday noon in KC

"Isabell, Pizzametski was on the plane with me. He's following me. He's here with me now."

"What's he doing? Why is he following you?"

"He said it's because he suspects I'm up to something criminal, and he's a cop and it's his duty to find out what it is and arrest me and he is going to do it."

"I checked on him. He's got excellent reviews. He's studying to take the Lieutenant's exam. His boss thinks very highly of him. He has a master's degree in criminology from Stanford. He looks like the kind of guy we'd like to have."

"I can find a judge, get a cease and desist order on him but that would probably take two days."

"It might take longer just because he's a cop. Can he hear what we're saying?" Isabell asked.

"No, he is in the men's room. I haven't told him anything. I'd like to punch him out…but he seems like a nice guy. He's really sincere. He's just passionate about his work. And he said he's not fucking my wife yet."

"First, don't punch him out. Second, try to keep the wife fucking part of it separate from everything else. That's a completely different kind of problem to be solved in a completely different way. Make I don't know the answer right now. Do what you can. See if you can lose him, avoid him, talk him out of following you. I don't know. Have you tried begging? I'll get back with you."

"Sargent, won't you please, please stop following me. You are interfering with my life."

"Yeah I know. That's the way we treat felons."

“I am not a felon. Don’t you remember, “Innocent until proven?”

As they walked together toward the rental car lot, Make said, “Ok, pizz. I am going to tell you how it is. I am going to do this only because you are a policeman and a good policeman. You are very conscientious about your civic duty, and you have a good knowledge of guns and how to use them. I hope that part doesn’t come into play. It’s my belief that a person that I know of is trying to sell pickles that have not been properly inspected when they were brought into this country. It’s my intent to try to seize these pickles, have them tested and prove that they are not what they are supposed to be.”

“Boy that’s a shocker. Beyond a doubt, that’s the biggest load of bull shit I have ever had to contend with,” Pizz said, laughing.

“Believe what you will, but if you continue to follow me you will get involved in my business whether you like it or not. So you might as well get in the car and ride along. I believe if the situation arises where I need the aid of a policeman, you’ll step in and do your duty…Pizzametski, please get in the car.” They get in a blue Toyota Make has rented. Before he started, Make dialed his cell. Pizz said, “Are we going to just sit here or what?”

The call was picked up after one ring, ”Park here.” Make puts his cell on speaker, “Are you Don T Park?”

“Yes and I see by my caller ID that you are Mister Caston. Good afternoon sir.”

“Mr. Park, I am on my way to the storage facility now. I’d like you to call your man who has been watching the place and let him know that I’ll be there in a half hour.”

"No need Mr. Caston. Because of the serious nature of this job I have taken on this surveillance project myself and I'll be ready when you get here."

"Have you come up with a plan as to how we are going to get the pickles?"

Pizzametski spoke up, "Jesus H Christ, Caston, are you nuts? Are you really going to steal a jar of pickles to prove they are fakes?"

"Quiet Sargent. Pardon the interruption, Parks. What have you got?"

"Who's that with you?"

"He's my private police Sargent, and he's been told to stay out of this unless he's needed to protect us."

Pizzametski threw up his hands in an act of despair. *What the fuck is going on here? Are there two people that are equally nuts about pickles?*

Park continued, "Yes, I've obtained a truck exactly like the one the pickles were brought here in. Also, I have an authentic looking pick-up order from the owner of the pickles requesting they be removed from storage today. They lock their gates promptly at 4:30. If we get there about 4:15, they'll be in the process of shutting down their facility and will be less likely to check out our paper work too thoroughly."

"Sounds like a good plan. Where should we meet you?" Make asked.

"Make, stop the car right here," Pizzametski said, "I'm not going to be a part of this crazy scheme. Let me out."

"Sargent, just stay in the car. We are going to park a half block away and I'm going to get in the truck with Mr. Park. You can sit here and watch the whole process and not get involved at all. I'll leave the keys in the car. If anything goes wrong, all you have to do is leave the car at the rental agency, get a plane and go home."

* * * *

They drove north on 70th street in Kansas City, Kansas. The salt mine was on their left. They turned off 70th and drove down into the large parking area in front of the salt mine entrance. The long cement loading dock had steps in front of the tall doors. It was hot outside but when they pushed open one of the double doors and stepped in they felt the cool air immediately. Inside the small salt mine office, Make said, "We're here to pick up some pickles Mr. Thorp had delivered a few days ago."

"Le'me see that." Park handed him the pick-up order. "Oh yeah." The counter man picked up the mike, "Get me D822, two boxes of pickles." Ok, I see by the paper work Mr. Thorp has paid for a month's storage. Ok you are cleared there." To the man with the two boxes "Yeah, go ahead and put em in their truck. Ok, it looks like you two gentlemen are…Hold on a minute." The counter man looks at the original order. "This doesn't look like the same signature on the original order… Why don't you guys sit over there and I'll clear this up in just 'a few minutes."

Make and Park sit on a bench away from the door. Make whispered to Park, "I think he's going to call the cops."

"I think you're right. What can we do?" Park asked.

Make quickly called Pizzametski, "Pizz, go home. I think we're caught. Just turn the car in please. Oh, and tell Laura I'll call her."

A minute later Pizzametski came charging in. He grabbed both Make and Parks by the front of their coveralls and jerked them up to a standing position, "Ok you two birds. Just stay where you are. I got two guys outside just waiting for you to try something. You're both under arrest."

"What're you arresting us for?" Make said. "We're just making a pick-up"

"GTA for one thing. That's a stolen truck out there. And whatever you are planning to heist out of here." Turning to the counter man, with his fingers covering the "LAPD" part of the ID fastened around his neck, "What did they get?"

"Pickles. They got 24 jars of pickles. You sure got here fast."

"Not really. I've been sitting down the street watching these guys. I figured they were up to something. When the call came in I was ready. Pickles. That's the dumbest thing I ever heard of. That short one just got out a couple of weeks ago. Ok. The truck, you two, and the pickles are going downtown." Turning to the counter man, "Thank you sir. You did the city a service."

Make was actually surprised at how quick Sargent Pizzametski reacted. And his performance was flawless.

Pizzametski grabbed both Make and Park by the collar and shoved them out of the door. "Put these two birds in the car. I'll drive the truck."

Later, outside of Mann Laboratories in Kansas City, Make said, "Mr. Parks, I won't be needing your services any longer today. You did an outstanding job and I thank you very much. Now, as for you Pizzametski, you performed over and above and I thank you very much too. And, if you wait right here while I explain to the lab techs what I want them to do, I'll buy you a beer and a steak too."

I don't understand what is going on here. Pizzametski wondered. *Make Caston is obviously a sharp guy. And I can't imagine pickles being that dangerous. I'd like to know what's in those pickle jars.* "What do you have to explain about? They're just a bunch of Pickles. Why did you do all this in the first place?"

"Bear with me Sargent."

"Ok, I'll wait out here but you're going to have to do a lot of explaining."

Later, they ate in a Kansas City dinner. After the meal, "I have talked to my boss," Make said. "I told her what we did and how you performed. I told her that you saved this whole project. At this point, all I can tell you is that I work for Homeland Security. However, if you're interested in a different job… And you do not tell anybody about any of this. This is serious, Pizzametski. Do not write any report to your boss about this. Don't write anything about any of this anywhere, any time. verstehst du?" After a long period of silence, "Make, I'm just going home. You are a barrel of laughs but…I'll get back to you. And I won't tell. Actually, I'd be too embarrassed to tell." *Make, you sure do interesting things. I still can't imagine what the hell is going on.*

"Sorry Pizzametski, but you can't go home."

"Make, do you know what you're saying? I can go home any time I want and I'm going home tonight."

"Of course, you're right. You can go home if you want. But hear me out. I really need you here tomorrow and I'll tell you why."

"Oh, Christ. Here we go again."

"Those pickles are very dangerous pickles. I literally can't begin to tell you how really dangerous they are. You have to trust me on that. It's important, Ok?"

"Ok, I'll listen to you; it's not ok, that I'll stay until tomorrow." *I guess it wouldn't hurt to stay until tomorrow. I don't have to be back to work for another week. Maybe I'll stay in Phoenix for a while.*

"Sometime tomorrow," Make added, "some replacement pickles will arrive at Mann labs where they will be used as substitutes for the dangerous pickles. They will be put in the jars and the jars will be repacked in the boxes. Once the boxes are sealed you, Sargent Pizzametski of the Kansas City, Kansas, police department, should return the pickles to the storage facility. You might also say something to the effect that we, the Kansas City, Kansas, police department, no longer need them. And you might suggest that the fact that the counter man gave them to a couple of fugitives, need never be mentioned again."

"Make, I don't know what the hell is going on here but I believe you mean well. But I can't do that. I could lose my job if I did that."

He's right, Make thought. *He could lose his job and be barred from ever being a policeman again. Actually he could be imprisoned.* "Well, you wouldn't lose it for impersonating a police officer, you are one."

"Look, I already feel guilty for playing fast and loose with the law as much as I have. I don't want to compound that feeling. What you need to do is, find one of those sleaze bags like the ones I arrest frequently. Some of them could do that without batting an eye. I just won't do it and that's all there is to it."

The next day at the salt mine

Make waited in the car while Pizz returned the pickles.

The counter man said, “Thank you Sargent for returning them so quick. And if you say you haven’t told anybody about it, I won’t mention it either.”

“When I wrote my report, I just said that I observed the two felons in a stolen vehicle and I picked them up. It’s a lot simpler that way. You get your pickles back and I get a gold star for being proactive.” *God, I hope nobody finds out about this. I believe I could learn form Make Caston.*

Chapter 27

Saturday morning

On the triple seven back to PHX

"Pizzametski, you did very well. You are an innovative guy. Every time, when the situation required it, you did and said the right thing at the right time and you were convincing."

"You're right of course. That's why I have been invited to take the lieutenant's exam. The lower end of the lieutenant's pay scale is twelve percent higher than the high end of the sergeant's pay scale. I'll be rolling in clover."

I know what his salary is, and if he gets that twelve percent, and he probably will, he'll be making more than we pay newcomers. Also he likes California, but maybe he would like Phoenix too. I'll talk to Isabell; he shouldn't have to start at the bottom of the scale. He has experience. He must have been a cop for at least three years. "Twelve percent, that sounds great. Sargent, what do you do when you are not on duty? You got a girlfriend, you got a family in California, you take a sail boat to San Diego, what do you do?"

"Number one, I don't have a girlfriend, I have a cat. Two, my parents live in Needles and my brothers all live in California. Number three, I don't have a boat. Sometimes I run. Did you ever run in a marathon Make?"

Now there is something that might be of interest to Pizzametski, "No. I never did. I use to run though. But I was a miler, not a distance runner. So what was your time in the marathon?"

"I always run a half marathon," Pizzametski said, "I do it in about an hour and thirty minutes. What was your fastest mile?"

How can he run a marathon? He's a big guy. He's not over weight; he is just a big man. "You're not going to believe me. But that's ok because I didn't believe your hour and thirty minutes story either. I ran a four minute mile when I was nineteen years old. My dad had been running when he was in school too. About that time there was a guy, I think his name was Gunther Hague, who came close to the magic mile but he never did it. My dad really thought he might be the first one, but then in 1956 Roger Bannister ran a 3:59. My dad was sort of deflated. After that a whole bunch of people ran a four minute mile. So anyway, neither I nor my dad succeeded in being the first four minute miler."

* * * *

Saturday afternoon in Makes house

After Make had said hello to Laura and got Pizz a beer he called DHS, "Hello Isabell. The pickle operation is complete. The bad pickles have been replaced with nonreactive pickles and no one is the wiser. This bunch may have been a trial run to see if the whole process is doable. I think they had been planning to start large volume production and transport the pickles to the various parts of the world. They would do this by private boat to minimize inspection. I believe their plan was to detonate explosions all over the United States on July the fourth. Our pickle operation surely delayed that plan and maybe stopped it. By the way, this was all done, thanks to Sargent Pizzametski. He really did an outstanding job. He is very innovative. I talked to him about working for us. He would consider working for Homeland Security only if the salary was exorbitant.

* * * *

Later

"Hi Isabell. How's it going?"

"Fine Make. Why are you here?"

"I just got back from Kansas City and wanted to say hello. Were you ever able to hire Pizzametski?"

"Yes, he works for me now. He's your boss."

"What! But Isabell, you said I'd get that job."

"You weren't here."

"But I was in K.C. where you sent me, sort of. I think I got screwed."

"You should talk to your boss about that. That reminds me, he is screwing your wife too."

"My God, how can that be?"

"You weren't here."

"Isabell."

"Make! Make! Wake up or turn over or something. You're shaking the whole bed."

Chapter 28

11 AM

The oval office

The President keyed his intercom and said, "George, I'd like to talk to Isabell Franks. There is absolutely no rush. It should be at her convenience. Maybe we can get together for lunch or something."

DHS, the office of the Deputy Secretary, Isabell Franks, "Hello George. This is Irene, what can I do for you this morning?"

George said, "Good morning Irene. How is the day going for you?"

"Good George thanks. How can I help you?"

"Irene, the President would like to talk to Isabell. It's nothing pressing and it's very informal. He just wants to chat. Is there a chance she would be free for lunch sometime like today for example?"

Irene said, "I'll get back with you in ten minutes George."

"Isabel, George just called. The pres would like to have lunch with you today. You up for that?" Irene announced.

"You bet I am. Find out when and where. I've got a good suit here in my closet. I can be ready by eleven."

"He said it was very informal. And, besides, it's raining out. Maybe you shouldn't mess up a good outfit."

"Oh, ok then I can be ready any time."

George said, “Mr. President, Irene said Isabell would love to, and I told Irene you would send a car for Isabell at 11.40 and I believe I heard ’Hot zigiddy’ just I was hanging up, Sir.”

At noon George said, “Good morning Ms. Franks. It is nice to see you again. Here, let me take your raincoat.”

“Thank you George.”

“Go right on in Ms. Franks. He’s waiting for you.”

“Hello Isabell,” The President said. “I’m glad you could make it. Sit right there.”

“Thank you Mr. President.” Looking at the table setting she said, “This is very nice. Is there an occasion?”

“The occasion is you having lunch with me, Isabell. It’s nice to see you again. It really is.”

“Thank you sir. It is very nice for me too. I was delighted when I heard you had called.” Pause…“It looks like we’re having wine for lunch. Are you sure this is not an occasion?”

“Isabell, as I said, I am just happy that you could make it. Red or white?”

“Red, Mr. President. But I should limit it to one… sir.”

“Isabell, I’d like to be on a friendlier level than ‘Sir’ and ‘Mr. President: Would it bother you to call me ‘Fred’ instead?

Isabell said, “No Problem at all. Fredinsrtead.” The President thought this was funny. There was more chit chat as the meal went on. At some time during the conversation the President said, “I sure like your man Make Caston. Is he still making things happen?”

"Yes he is. And I can give you an example. Recently, he got two different pieces of information that lead him to believe that a certain shipments of pickles from Yemen were, in fact, a trial run of a terrorist plan to determine if a particular kind of very high explosive could be manufactured in a foreign company and shipped to the USA without being detected. These explosives were molded to the shape of pickles and were packaged just like real pickles would be packaged. They were shipped here, went through all the various incoming inspection process we use, and were transported to Kansas City and stored in a salt mine warehouse there. Make setup a team in Kansas City and a team here. Then, with the help of some other people he had enlisted, he went to the warehouse storage area in disguise and got the explosives. He then took them to the KC laboratory and had them photographed. While the KC lab tested them, Make sent the photos to his local team here. Overnight they manufactured, packaged, and shipped the dummy explosives back to KC. The next day he returned them to the storage warehouse in KC and, as far as I know, the owner still thinks he has a load of explosives."

"And were the pickles that the terrorist made really explosive?"

Isabell said, "Yes. They were PETN."

"PETN! Holy shit, I know about PETN."

"Did the President of the United States of America, the leader of the free world, just say 'holy shit'?"

"Yes Isabell, because your news is very disturbing. I mean the fact that they can get PETN here. I thought they had sniffers that would detect it."

"They do. But the terrorists coat each eight ounce piece with a sealant that emits acetic acid. The sniffers smell vinegar, not

PETN. And pickles are shipped in vinegar. Our tech's now say that they'll have a sniffer for coated PETN in 90 days"

The President said, "What has been done to stop the flow?"

"Right now we have satellite's tracking every move that the PETN shipper makes. So far, it is just one man and we're watching him very closely."

"Well, back to Mr. Make Caston," The President said. "Isabell, I wonder if it might be a good thing to start sort of grooming him for something bigger. Maybe he might sit in on a strategic planning meeting, get to meet some people, and get to know how things work at that level. Something like that. What do you think?"

"I think it's a good idea and I'll do that. I have to be careful though. Right now, I can't do that to the detriment of his work on the terrorist problem."

"I'm not in any way trying to tell you how to run your security section, Isabell. I was just remembering you telling me that one of your men, I think it's Caston's boss, has a drinking problem."

"Yes, it's John Walker, He was Make's boss. He is in rehab now. From what they tell me, I don't think he is going to make it. Right now Make has taken his place."

"Isabell, I like having lunch with you. Thanks for coming."

"I liked it too, Fred."

Chapter 29

In Yemen it is 7 PM, (8 AM Washington, DC.)

Sana'a, Yemen

Three MP's stood at the front entrance to the American embassy, two with M16's.

"Sir, may I come in your embassy?"

"Are you a United States Citizen?"

"No Sir. I am Sana'a citizen."

"No you cannot come in. Only U S Citizens are allowed inside the embassy."

"But Sir, I must get in. I am in danger."

"No. you can't get in. Only U S citizens can get in."

"Please Sir; I am friend of Al-Absnt. I have his telephone."

"How did you get his phone?"

"He is dead. I watched him die. He gave me his phone. Se…"

"Stop. Do not move." The two guards at the entrance pointed their weapons at the man, "Front guard. We need help. Do not move. Keep your hand in your clothes. Do not move your hand."

One rifle was pointed at the Arab's eye.

"Please sir. Do not kill me. I only want to return the telephone of Al- Absnt. Caston Make wants the phone of Al-

Absnt. Please sir. Do not kill me. I only want to return the telephone. Please sir, Al-Asiri people will kill me."

"Do not move your hand. Someone is coming. Do not move."

"What's the problem?" said the lieutenant of the guard.

"Do not move your hand. Lieutenant, this man said he is not a U S Citizen. He said he is in danger. He said he has to get in to the embassy. He either killed some guy or he watched someone else kill him. He wants to return a cell phone. When he reached for his gun, we stopped him."

Speaking Arabic, the Lieutenant asks, "Why do you put your hand in your thobe [Arab clothes]?"

"Please Sir; I only want to show you that I have Caston Make's telephone."

"Do you have a gun?"

"Oh no sir. I have a telephone only."

"Ok, do not move your hand till I get out of the way. Ok, now leave your telephone in your pocket and take your hand out very, very slowly. When you take your hand out your hand must be empty. If there is anything in your hand these men will shoot you. Do you understand? Your hand must be empty."

"Yes Sir. I understand. You do not want to see the telephone of Al- Absnt."

"That is correct, just your hand."

"Sir, I am afraid those men will shoot me if I take my hand out."

"No they will not shoot you. Take your handout very slowly."

”That’s good. All the way out. Very slowly. That’s good. Now walk over to this pillar. Ok, that’s good. Now put your hands straight out against the pillar. That’s good. Now take one step back with each foot and push on the pillar.”

“Are you going to shoot me, sir?”

“No, just keep pushing on the pillar. I am going to stand at your side and reach into your clothes and get your cell phone.”

* * * *

“I’m Make Caston, USA DHS. That’s Department of Homeland Security. I would like to speak with Mr. Tom Short, please.”

“I’m Short, Mr. Caston what can I do for you?”

“I believe you talked to my boss about my phone. It’s an Iridium.”

“Yes, a spectacular phone. I have it here and also the man who brought it.”

“Mr. Short, are you the ambassador?”

“No but right now I am the next best thing.”

“Sir I’m interested in the man who brought the phone to you. Is he there?”

“Yes, his name is Al-HAmi. He’s staying with us for the time being. He’s very fearful. He’s afraid he will be killed by the Al-Asin.”

“I would like to come to your embassy. I would like to get my phone and I would like to talk personally with Al-HAmi. . Can that be arranged?”

"Mr. Caston, we would be glad to have you visit us any time that it is convenient for you, sir."

Later

"Isabell, I want to go to Yemen."

"I thought you would. Go see Georgia. Lon's secretary. Tell her I said its ok."

"Hey Georgia, I want to go to Yemen. And when I get there I want to go to the American embassy and I want to see the US Ambassador to Yemen."

'You sure want a lot, don't you? What did you say your name was?"

"Georgia, you know who I am. Isabell said I should see you."

"I'll check with Ms. Franks."

"Georgia!"

"Just kidding, Make. Ms. Franks already called me. I've made travel arrangements–first class. There is an embassy there. I've arranged for an embassy car to pick you up at the airport. Make, Ms. Franks said for you to be sure you get in the embassy car. All cars but the embassy cars are bad cars. I believe, at this time, there is no ambassador there."

"Thanks Georgia. I'll check it out."

Chapter 30

Tuesday morning

Yemen Airport

"Hello, are you looking for someone from the embassy to pick you up?"

"Why are you asking me and who are you?"

"I'm Lieutenant Silvers. I'm from the American embassy and I am to pick up a fellow American."

"I'm your man. I'm Make Caston. It's nice to meet you Lieutenant Silvers."

"Mr. Caston, I don't mean to be telling you what to do but please get in the car. It's not a good idea to stand out here."

"Is it any safer in the car? Is the car bullet proof?"

"Yes sir, its bullet proof. I feel pretty safe from bullets."

"So why are you so anxious, Lieutenant? What is it you're not telling me?"

"I probably shouldn't tell you this, sir, but I don't think this car is RPG proof, and that's what makes me nervous, sir."

"Have you had any problems while driving this car?"

"No, sir. This is my first day. They used to have a regular driver and a different vehicle for this kind of duty."

At the American embassy in Sana'a, Yemen

"Ah, Mr. Caston. It's nice to meet you. I am Tom short. I'm the one who called your office in the states. By the way, that's the first time I had ever used an Iridium phone."

"It's nice to meet you Mr. Short. And I wanted to tell you how much I value your making the call. That phone and the man who brought it to you are both very important to me."

"Please have a chair, and by the way, you can call me Tom for short," He smiled. "And here is your phone and ancillary equipment. I was very impressed at how well it works." Short spoke on the intercom, "Would you get the Arab here please." To Make, "It may take a few minutes to get him here. He seems to sleep a lot. He was very anxious to have me call you. I believe he has confidential information for you. Mr. Caston, I understand you're a doctor. It seems very unusual to me for a doctor to have an Iridium phone."

"Yes, that is very unusual but not as unusual as it used to be. I understand you can buy older models on Amazon now. Tom, I don't understand. Why isn't there an ambassador here and what is your official capacity? What's going on in Yemen anyway? You have a bullet proof limo and the driver is afraid of RPGs."

"I can certainly understand your concerns," Short said. "At this time there's no ambassador here because he left. There have been demonstrations in the street in front of the embassy, and his name was mentioned and later an effigy with his name on it was burned. The ambassador was frightened and he told me, and I am using the common vernacular here, 'I'm going to get the fuck out of here' and he did. My capacity is that I'm the one that's left. The Marine guards and lieutenant Silvers and me anyway. And I'm still here because I believe it's very important to have an embassy in Yemen right now. Mr. Caston, I must tell you something about this area. There is north Yemen and there is south Yemen with no border in between. Some want a border between and some want to consolidate the country. If the country was organized enough to have a civil war right now, they would have another one. It is further complicated because, right now, Egypt acts as a protectorate of Yemen. There is also almost no border between Yemen and Egypt. That's why I feel it important to maintain relations between Yemen and the US."

"That is very noble of you to stay. I appreciate the fact that you're doing it. And I am sure others in the embassy business also appreciate it. And, regarding the phone and the Arab, I believe he would be more comfortable if he and I could talk together in private in another room. If you want to listen in that's ok. I just want him to not be afraid, that's all. And the only reason I have iridium is that I just need a phone that works anywhere."

"Ah, Mr. Caston here is your friend Al-HAmi. Al-HAmi, this is Mr. Make Caston. You two are welcome to use the room across the hall. If you need anything just come and find me or lieutenant Silvers."

"It's good to meet you Al-HAmi. I'm very glad you are safe and well."

"Mr. Caston Make, sir, it is my honor to meet you sir."

"Thank you very much for saving and returning my phone. I know that it was a difficult and dangerous thing for you to do."

"You are very welcome, sir. The embassy people have been well to me and have made me safe. For that I am thankful also. Mr. Caston, Sir, the embassy people here have told me that you are a doctor. I also am a doctor, sir"

"Yes, you told me that. Do you have a private practice near your home?"

"No, I am work with a hospital in Al- Mukalla. It is dangerous for doctors to be in the desert. Some people who live in the away kill doctors, sir."

"It must be difficult living here. Lieutenant Silvers is afraid of being killed at the airport and you tell me it's dangerous in the desert. How do you survive?"

"Sir, there are many different kinds of people, different religions, different areas, different tribes. And it is difficult to survive here. In my area, the Sunni kill many. There are thousands of years of hatred. Some of the police are Sunni. Sir, believe me please. In the away you are in danger."

"I must go," Make said. "I appreciate what you are saying about danger but I must go. And the reason I am going is I believe that we can make all the Al-Asiri people go aw…I believe we can eliminate the danger from the Al-Asiri people. Al- HAmi, I believe we can help each other. Will you help me? If you can tell me where the Al-Asiri people are I can make things better."

"I tell you with sorrow sir, I cannot tell you of them. I do not know them. Sir, you should go to Momar. I will take you to Momar, sir."

"I haven't heard of Momar. How far is it?"

"In the auto it is half hour, sir. I will take you to Momar, sir."

Chapter 31

Tuesday afternoon

Sana'a, Yemen

Al-HAmi and Make are in the car with lieutenant Silvers driving. "I'm sorry Doctor Caston." Lieutenant Silver said. "But I don't know where Momar is either. I've heard of it but I don't know how to get there."

"Ok Al-HAmi, which way to Momar?"

Pointing to the North West, Al-HAmi nodded. After two blocks, "turn as that" pointing to the left. Then another mile and, "Now."

"I think you should stop," Make said to Silvers. "I think we are in Momar." The car stopped.

"Is this Momar, Al-HAmi?"

Pointing to the market Al-HAmi said, "Momar is there."

Both Make and Lieutenant Silvers independently didn't understand how Momar could be on only one side of this street. It was just a market place, markets on both sides of the street.

"Lieutenant, are you armed?" asked Make.

"Yes sir. And I brought one for you too." He handed Make a Glock.

Opening the car door, "Ok Al-HAmi, lead us to Momar," Make said.

They walked into the market. Different vegetables were displayed on open tables. The odor was almost overwhelming. In the meat section there were a few pieces of cut meat, but most of the selection consisted of skinned animal carcasses hanging in the open. The flies were everywhere and although the smell was different it was still very bad. Past the meat they stopped in front of a well-dressed man sitting at a computer. The man looked up, speaking in Arabic, “Al-HAmi, it is good to see you. But it is dangerous for you to be here. Are you well my friend?”

“I am well, Momar, Thank you. I do not fear danger at this time because I have brought my friends. Momar, I would like to show you to Mr. Caston Make and Lieutenant driver.”

Lieutenant silvers interpreted the conversation for Make.

Shaking hands first with Make then with the Lieutenant, in English Momar said, “How do you do Mr. Make? It’s nice to meet you. And you too Mr. Driver. I’m Momar Al- Bami, at your service, sirs.”

In Arabic, Al-HAmi said, “Momar, I have good news. Mr. Caston Make and Mr. Lieutenant Driver are going to kill the Al-Asiri.”

“That is very good news, but why did you bring them here? The Al-Asiri are on the boat at Nishtun.”

“They are at Nishtun, on a boat?”

“Yes, and I believe they will be at work again soon. They have bought supplies and they have carpenters building inside the boat. I spoke with one of the workmen a month ago. He told me the carpentry would be completed within a week.” The Lieutenant interpreted.

When Make heard this he felt elated to finally get some positive information about where the manufacture of PETN may be. However, there was a strong feeling of apprehension. *I’ve never heard of Nishtun and don’t know how to get there. And, I don’t know what I will find when I get there or how I will deal with it. Also, so far, everyone I have talked to has told me that it is a very dangerous to go into the desert. This is going to take a lot of planning and I am going to feel a lot more comfortable if I can get some help.*

Back at the embassy

Mr. Short, I am interested in Al-HAmi as a possible operative here in Yemen," Make said. "He said he's in danger if he is living on the street and he can't return to his home in Rukob because his opponents are watching his neighborhood. Would it be possible to supply him a safe place to stay, and have a way for me to get in touch with him through you?"

"Yes. That sort of thing has been done before and can be done again. I will see that he is properly cared for and you will be able to reach him by calling me. How long do you think he'll need protection?"

"I'll probably be able to let you know in a week."

Chapter 32

Thursday afternoon

The harbor, Nishtun, Yemen

The workers that the chemist had hired had just finished compounding and molding the cargo, twelve hundred pieces of PETN, weighed and hand molded to the shape of pickles. Darkness was approaching and he was satisfied. If nothing went wrong during the coating and packing, the scheduled meeting with the Muslims would be on time. This would be the first of several shipments and timeliness would be very significant. Any delays might jeopardize future orders.

Ishe thought, *this whole project had been Mal's idea. I suspect there is mayhem involved, just because Mal is involved. Mal seems to almost never do anything strictly legal. And, with everything he does, he usually try's to cheat someone somehow. Because of some of the things I've heard, I suspect that sometime, in Mal's dealings, he may have murdered someone or had it done. He's my brother. What can I do? I really can't prove that he is guilty of anything. And if I told the police, they probably couldn't arrest him. And that would just make Mal hate me. Maybe he hates me now. Sometimes, I think he does. It always seems like, when he is doing something for me it always ends up really being for some scheme of his. I wish I could get away from him but I don't know how.*

The chemist that Mal hired was running the operation. Ishe didn't know much about chemistry, cleanroom conditions, or manufacturing, yet Mal stressed the importance of his job. Mal had made it clear to Ishe at the start of the operation. He, Ishe, and no one else was responsible for such a valuable cargo.

There had been only one failure in the manufacturing procedure. They had neglected to obtain a sufficient amount of the

RTV to coat the PETN that had been formed into the shape or pickles. Now, most of the pickles, about 934 actually, lay naked on waxed tables. In this condition they were vulnerable to many things. The chemist had contacted Mal with this information and Mal had, at first, been furious then consoling. Now the units had to lay undisturbed, awaiting the arrival of the RTV. Delivery was expected tomorrow.

The entire manufacturing area was covered with sheets of plastic to keep the pickles clean. The corrosive effects of the sea salt made them porous and structurally unsound. Gloved hands had to make sure none rolled together. Once separated, additional sheets of plastic had been placed on top of the pickles to maintain cleanliness and keep them separated. If the pickles touched they tended to stick to each other thus losing their *"pickle"* shape. If the ship rocked enough that any pickles fell to the floor, they were examined carefully for contamination and if any was found, that pickle had to be thrown into the sea where it would soon disintegrate. Fortunately, Ishe had been able to tie up to the land side of the dock. There had been almost no rocking of the ship.

The *Golden Lie* had been good to Ishe. Although she was old, the engine was still strong and would propel them along at eighteen knots. Once he had gotten too close to shore and had scraped the starboard side near the bow. Thankfully, no leaks had occurred.

They had been docked forty eight hours when the Harbormaster came aboard. "You must leave. The storm is approaching. All ships must leave now." Ishe had seen no indication of bad weather earlier. He said, "I can't leave. They have important supplies arriving tomorrow." But he knew he must leave. He had been here before.

"Go now. You can come back tomorrow. The storm will be gone by midday."

Unfortunately, the *Golden Lie* was not equipped with modern weather radar. The infrequent storms always came from the hills to the south west of Nishtun, and when they came it seemed as though everything was completely calm one minute and a gale the next. The wind blew mostly dust and rarely a little moisture. The problem was the sea. The wind whipped the sea into frenzy. Huge swells pounded the rock lined ocean side of the dock, occasionally slopping over the rocks and across the cement dock. However, that wasn't the worst of the situation. The bay was an oval shaped area, and before the dock was built, the swells that were frequent during storms were of little consequence. But with the dock protruding across 25% of the width of the bay, it hindered 25% of the water pouring in the bay on the northeast side. However, that part of the water surge was diverted so that it came in on the southwest side causing the water to swirl around the beach and pile up on the back side of the dock where they were tied. In the past, some of the ships that had failed to heed the Harbormaster had been washed over the cement expanse to the ocean side. They were then at the mercy of the sea and were pounded against the rocks along the ocean side of the dock.

Other ships were leaving in what seemed like confused frenzy. While the lines were being pulled aboard, the *Golden Lie* backed alongside the dock until the bow cleared the farthest point of cement structure, "All stop. Rudder hard to port." Ishe commanded. As she slowed, the stern swung around toward the back of the bay. Then, "Rudder hard to starboard, come to one hundred twenty degrees."

Then, "ahead standard." Dusk was upon them. As the *Golden Lie* glided past the end of the dock, Ishe could see the running lights of two of the three other ships that had been his neighbors at the dock today. *Where was the third?* All three had departed ahead of the *Golden* Lie. Well, the third was out there somewhere.

The anchor chain on the *Golden Lie* had never been long enough to anchor in very deep water. In similar storms, Ishe had gone out past the eastern most point of land then swung around to the left. There the rocky coast ran about 315 degrees to the Northwest and the bottom was shallow enough for him to anchor. By lying parallel to the shore the incoming swells would hit him head on. It was the best way for him to wait out the storm.

As he approached the spot he had used in previous storms he swung away from the land. Then, once he had gone due north for a while, he called for port rudder so that he would swing around to the left until he was parallel to the shore and about 100 yards out. He could anchor there.

When he was two thirds through his turn, Ishe heard, “Ship dead ahead.” He could see nothing ahead. No lights pierced the darkness. Now the lookout was running toward the stern where Ishe was. The lookout was screaming something unintelligible. The captain commanded, “Hard starboard rudder, engine astern flank.” The engine responded quickly. However, a third of the propeller was out of the water and it was cavitating. It was pounding the sea and throwing up a huge spray. Their forward momentum propelled the *Golden* Lie ever closer toward the shore as she gradually swung around toward the right. She continued to slow but when she was about forty yards from shore and headed straight toward it, there was a thump sound and the bow seemed to jump up out of the water then crash down again. There was more and louder grinding and scraping sounds before the forward motion stopped. Now the ship began to move back. Ishe cried, “No, no, stop, stop.” And finally they did.

Ishe had always been cool headed with the ship. His twin brother, Mal, was the hothead, the adventurer. But now Ishe was near panic. Everything was at stake. He thought the front of his ship was rapidly sinking. Probably the front compartment was flooding and possibly the second. For the first time in his sailing career, Ishe didn't know what to do. Thankfully low tide was two hours away. And the ship would not sink as long as they stayed on the rocks. Now the main concerns were the swells and the pounding waves. The anchorage he had planned for would have protected him, but now the surf pounded on the side of his ship and the bow was on the rocks....the thought was terrifying. *Would the stern swing around toward shore and pull them off the rocks? Was there enough damage to sink the Golden Lie in the open sea? If they swung around would the bow be broken off or would the hull be damaged more?*

"Get the Zodiac in the water. I am going to have a look," Ishe called out.

Ishe steered the boat while the engineer and the chemist hung on to the rope that was attached to the Zodiac's sides.

The port side of the ship was not accessible because of the wind and the pounding sea. The zodiac was a powerful boat, capable of maneuvering in rough water, but it was put to task even on the starboard side. The sound of the wind was ear shattering. It blew the tops off of the waves and drove the spray at them so hard it stung their faces.

As they maneuvered close to the bow the damage became obvious. With the lights they had brought they could see there was a massive rock sometimes protruding above the surface when a swell moved out. The front of the keel of the ship was resting on it. The *Golden Lie* had been riding high in the sea because the front three holes (holds) had been completely void of any of the materials that the ship had been designed to transport. Now, there was a gaping hole next to the keel on the starboard side. The gap was ten feet wide and it extended from the first bulkhead aft ten or fifteen feet. It was hard to tell but it looked like the torn metal had been pushed back and wadded up. Part of the wad was up inside the hold and part protruded below the keel. Water was surging in with the swells. This could only be seen when the swell was out. The sea water then ran back out.

The *Golden Lie* had its beginning in Japan. She had been designed to haul both raw materials like grain, cotton, coconut hulls and crude oil. It was called a combination hull design. Hold numbers two; the oil storage hold, had no hatch covers. Instead, there were eight inch diameter pipes used to transfer oil in and out of hold number two. The pumps, filters and valves used to handle the oil were also on the deck above hold number two.

She was 243 feet long with the bridge, crew quarters, and engine room at the stern. The bridge, crew quarters, and office were located in a superstructure above deck. The front compartment was never used because of its small size. The first bulkhead was only eight feet from the bow. The rest of the ship was divided into three forty five foot long compartments, and the one compartment that was 96 foot long, was used for the crude oil storage. The dry storage holes (holds) had great massive covers that could be hydraulically opened to the sky or closed and sealed air tight. The metal floor in these holds was only two feet above the keel.

All compartments were connected with water tight doors. For this project, carpenters and pipe fitters had built an additional wooden floor in hold number three, the one next to the engine room. This made the work place and the worker's quarter have fifteen foot ceilings, one above the other. The bottom floor was used to manufacture the pickles. It contained some expensive equipment, a printer that would make labels, shipping documents etc., a box cutting machine that was state of the art, the compounding equipment necessary to mix the chemicals for the pickles, and various tables and storage racks. There was a stairway built from the manufacturing area up to the quarters where there were beds for thirty, a dining area, and a separate room for showers and toilets. All the air-conditioning was in the lower half of hold number three. The sleeping quarters above could be miserably hot.

The last forty five feet of the ship, the forth section, was used exclusively for operating the ship. The bridge was high above the covers for the holes and afforded the captain and crew a 360 degree view. Below that were the crew's quarters that were about the same as those for the pickle manufacturing group, except the ship's crew quarters were much older. Below that was the office and below that, cavernous engine room. It contained the diesel engine with its gear drive, the fuel storage tank, the ruder mechanism, the auxiliary generator, the engine exhaust pump and the bilge water pump. Ancillary equipment included an air compressor, a water pump for fire emergencies, and the air conditioning system.

As they watched from the Zodiac, there was a groaning sound, then the bow dropped five feet. They were unprepared for this and were almost capsized. They had been lying parallel to the ship in the Zodiac. When the bow of the *Golden Lie* slid off the rock it had been settling on, a huge wave lifted them up even with the deck then almost rolled them over. Fortunately none of them were thrown into the sea. Now the deck at the bow was about twelve feet above the water and was covered when the swell came….and it was low tide.

Back on board, Ishe called, "Lower the anchor." *If we stay in this location during the coming high tide I believe we may save her. But, if we drift out to sea…*

The chemist, who was in charge of the pickle manufacturing process, came wearily up the stairs to the Bridge, “Captain, nearly all of our product has been lost. Two of the drying tables collapsed, throwing molded product all over. Three men have been injured. The Banbury mixer has fallen on one of the men. His leg is very bad. The men have applied a tourniquet but I fear he will bleed to death if we don’t get him to the hospital. And the salt water spray has covered everything.”

“Salt water spray, what salt water spray? Is section 3 leaking too? Where is the spray coming from?”

“I am not sure, Captain. Perhaps from the side of the ship. May we use the rubber boat to get the injured man to the hospital in Nishtun?”

“Yes, no, wait, you would capsize and you would all be lost. Wait here. No. Come with me. I must see where the salt spray is coming from. And see to the injured man.” They proceeded down the stairs to the engine room, thru the water tight door to the manufacturing area, “Oh, my God what has happened?” The beautiful room that was once antiseptic now looked like a junkyard. Pickles were smashed all over the floor; there were broken racks, blood here and there, and the injured man with a compound fracture. Eighteen men were standing near the far wall, looking at the box-cutting machine on its side against the forward bulkhead. The expression on their faces was one of apprehension. “Get someone to help you get the injured man up on deck. I will ready the Zodiac. As soon as it begins to get light, the three of us will get him to the hospital. The rest of you clean up this mess. You know how to dispose of the product. Wait. I forgot about the sea water spray. Where is the spray coming in from?”

The manufacturing area was in such disarray that Ishe had failed to notice the spray. He quickly discovered that it was a leak in the output pipe from the bilge pump. It was designed to keep water out of the engine room and pump it out above the water line. "Wrap a rag or something around that pipe. It won't stop the leak but it will keep it from spraying all over the place." *My God is there a leak in the engine room too. I'll inspect that when I get back.*

Chapter 33

Thursday

American Embassy, Sana'a, Yemen

Back in the Embassy, Make said, "Mr. Short, I need to get to Nishtun. I would like to get a vehicle and a driver who knows the territory. What do you suggest?"

"I don't think you should trust any of the locals to drive. I guess I'll have to lend you the services of Lieutenant Silver. He's as familiar with that area as anybody I know. As for vehicles, there's a problem. I know our limo would not make it. The road is paved most of the way but there are parts of it that are frequently covered with sand. To go over those, you need at the very least a four wheel drive vehicle. We used to have the perfect car for that but, unfortunately, now we don't."

"What happened to it? Was it wrecked?"

"Oh no, it was stolen."

"How did someone get it out of the compound?"

"It's embarrassing. When the Ambassador left, the regular driver took him to the airport. They both got out of the car and into the plane. They left the car at the airport. Now it is sitting a quarter mile down the road. It's at Sazar's Bazar. You might go down there and talk to him about renting it."

"That's crap. Did you go to the police about it?"

"Oh no. The police chief and Sazar are business partners."

* * * *

After lunch, Make caught up with Silvers, “Lieutenant, how do we get back the vehicle that was stolen from the embassy? Mr. Short didn’t have any good suggestions.”

“The first thing we should do is talk to the police chief. That car was abandoned at the airport and it has no Yemen papers–no Yemen Title or License. I doubt if they will just return it. Even if you could produce enough cash to buy a license, it would take days, maybe weeks, to actually get possession. Maybe, if you can throw your weight around, you might be able to make some kind of a deal with the Chief.”

Make asks, “Is he a real police Chief or just a master thief?”

“Oh, he’s a policeman all right. He goes after bad guys but he’s just a business-man. And I think that’s just the way business is done around here. There is another possibility. You could try to buy the car from Salzar, or maybe you might rent the car. But you would really be wasting your time. Just go see the police chief.”

* * * *

Inside the police department Make was asked to sit while the Police Chief was summoned. Shortly a six foot tall, 180 pound man with a red mustache appeared. He looked pretty healthy and he had a welcome smile. Make decided he was in his late forties. In perfect English the man said, “I was given to understand that you wanted to see me.”

“Good afternoon sir. Are you the chief of police?”

“That I am sir. I am Captain John Standard, and I assume you are an American who wants something.”

”Yes sir, you are correct on both assumptions. My name is Make Caston and I’m from the United States Department of Homeland Security. And sir, you seem to have a British accent and a name that sounds Scottish. Considering that you don’t particularly look British, I assume you must have lived there in your youth. You went to school there. Correct?"

The Police Chief was impressed with the accuracy of Make's assessment, "That is right. I have many fond memories to those times. But actually I am Irish. It is nice, that in just a few sentences, we each know something about the other. I like that. Of course, the main thing I do not know about you is what you want."

Make said, "I'm only here to catch the bad guys. But since I have no jurisdiction here, I need your help." He was enjoying Standard's crisp speech Patterns.

"I was not aware that there are any bad guys in this town sir."

"You are very astute. The bad guys I am referring to are not in town. I have reason to believe they're on a boat docked at the town of Nishtun."

"And you want me to go to Nishtun and catch them?"

"No sir. That would be asking too much. I plan to go catch them myself. But that will be extremely difficult for me since I am completely unfamiliar with the territory and the local laws. I don't even know where Nishtun is."

Standard was beginning to like Make already. He asked, "And if you could find Nishtun, how would you catch them?"

"I haven't worked that out yet. However, I am resourceful and I'm confident I could do it."

"Tell me, why you think these bad guys are bad. What have they done?"

"They know a chemical formula for a kind of explosive that is very powerful yet undetectable by all known sensing equipment. They plan to manufacture that material and distribute it to terrorists all over the world. They plan on killing a large number of people. Perhaps you and me."

Now John was intrigued. "Good Lord, how did they get that kind of technology?"

"I don't know, but that is one of the things we need to find out."

"If we go there and find them, do you plan on killing them?"

"I can't answer that. It's not something I would normally do. Probably there are some of them that should be killed and some that shouldn't be killed. I don't think I could just kill somebody. My God, I wish you hadn't asked me that. Except it's probably something I should think about now. Captain, I noticed that you used 'we'. Does that mean you are considering helping me?"

"Tell me more about this. Who is in charge? What do they do with this explosive once they have made it? Is there a chance it will blow up and kill us all?"

"Initially there was a man named Al-Asin. He had a group of followers. He was killed and the group seemed to fall apart. Without his leadership and knowledge they were helpless. I don't know if this new group in Nishtun is the remnants of the previous group or if this is an entirely new group of people. And I don't know who's in charge. More recently, there was a group in Mesoo Star. They made their first small batch of the explosives and were successful in getting it into a salt mine storage facility in the United States. Perhaps it was a test to see if the whole procedure was practical. I was able to neutralize that batch."

"You neutralized it–the batch of high explosives?"

"Yes."

*　　*　　*　　*

On the way to Nishtun the driver seemed completely fearless. There were places where the sand had blown across the road in two-foot deep piles that were twenty yards across. The Humvee hit these at fifty and sixty miles an hour throwing sand up in front of them so the road was obscured momentarily. For a brief time, the entire vehicle must have been covered with sand. There was a large truck behind them that contained twelve of Sazar's men. It seemed like Sazar was Chief Standard's lieutenant, yet neither he nor his men had any police identification or uniforms. Make was not able to see how they got through the sand but they seemed to be keeping up. Both vehicles must have been recently in Afghanistan. They were definitely U S military. In the truck behind them, Sazar's men each had a model1911 and an M-16. The truck also had a turret mounted, 30 Cal. Machine gun just behind the cab. As the saying goes, 'he was loaded for bear'.

Sazar sat in the Humvee next to the driver. They both seemed calm and accustomed to this kind of traveling. Chief Standard and Make sat just behind them. The whole trip was hypnotic to Make. It was so bright outside the Humvee that the sand almost looked white. Then, when they hit the miniature dunes there was a sudden darkness.

Prior to their departure, Make had told the Chief the details of the theft of the pickles from the underground salt mine storage in Kansas City. The Chief was impressed and amused. He said he would like to meet Pizzametski. "Pizzametski sounds like my kind of man, a man for all seasons".

During the trip it had been pointless to talk. No one could hear. But now the Humvee slowed. The road ahead gradually turned to the right and slopped gently down toward the sea. But there was something else looming ahead. The sun was bright behind them, but ahead, the sky was dark and threatening. As the sun got lower in the west the dark clouds ahead took on a dark orange color. “Red sky at night, sailor’s delight” did not seem appropriate.

There was discussion between Sazar and the driver. Make later learned that they were considering turning back. Sometimes the storm lingered over the harbor for a half day then went on out to sea. But sometimes it lingered for two days and sometimes it came back.

Now they slowed to about thirty. They were approaching the back side of the storm. And the sky ahead was a swirling, rolling mass that seemed to gain size and strength as it approached the sea. What a half hour ago had been a serene view of the eastern horizon, was now a darkness that obscured everything ahead. And they seemed to be getting closer. They had to look almost straight up to see the tops of the storm clouds.

They stopped. Standard interpreted what Sazar said: “It looks like the storm has some water in it. Lucky for us it is going away from us. If we were at the shore we would see what looked like a wall of sand coming toward us and when it got there the sky would turn black, and it would blow us over, trucks and all.”

* * * *

That evening, before they reached Nishtun, they pulled off on the right side of the road onto an area that had a stone fence along one side. Make asked, “Chief Standard, how does the justice system work in Yemen? Please don’t get me wrong. I’m really glad you’re here but I don’t exactly understand how you can justify being this far out of your jurisdiction with all these men and equipment.”

"We have a justice system in place in Yemen. You are considered innocent until proven guilty, etc. But there can be variations to that. There are lots of tribes in Yemen, and tribal leaders are very powerful. For example, recently a young man drove his car on the sidewalk in Sana'a and injured a mother and child. The young man was arrested but before he went to trial, his father, who was a tribal chief in the North, got the trial moved to his area. The young man was not punished. I know for a certainty that there was a vigilante group in one tribe and they have dealt out their own form of justice." John was standing with all his weight on one foot while leveling out a small patch of sand with the other. "The government in Sana'a, the Yemen government, is in complete control. At the last election, President, Abdel Rabbo Mansour Hadi won by getting nearly one hundred percent of the vote. So he sometimes influences justice. I could be reprimanded, or fired, or even put in jail for being here. I also may get a commendation for being here. You should keep in mind that this is a very old country with a new government. The first records of Yemen date back to 1000 BC. The Romans conquered it in 100 AD. In 1962; Egypt said the northern part of Yemen was theirs. The southern port of Aden, which is where it all began 3000 years ago, was colonized by Britain from 1839 until 1937. There have been revolutionaries supported by the USSR, Arab mergers, civil wars, different dynasties, different sects, protectorates; it's no wonder no one knows where the borders are. Anyway, it all makes this policeman's job more difficult."

Make asked, "With all of that having been said, what are you going to do when and if we catch up to these twenty of so people who I have told you are terrorists and are making explosives so they can kill people all over the world?"

"If I find that they are who you say they are, doing what you say they are doing, I will arrest them. I will gather up the evidence necessary to prosecute them and take them and the evidence back to Sana'a. That is my job."

"And what will happen to them?"

"Ah, that question has many answers. They could all be put to death, which I doubt, or they could all be found innocent or anything between. If the government wanted to gain favors from America, and if it was thought that it was America's wish that they be killed, then they would be killed. But if the government wanted to defy America, they might free the group. That's probably not what you want to hear but that is the way it is. The only really good part of the system is that here, justice is swift. Whatever is to happen will probably happen within ten days."

In his mind, Make knew what had to be done. *This must end here. My God, I can hardly think about this. They have to be killed. All of them and now. I've never been put in this position before–never even thought about this kind of thing before. What can I do? How can I live with myself? What will Laura say?*

John Standard interrupted Make's thoughts, "I know what I have told you has caused you trouble but what can I do?"

"It does cause me trouble, more trouble than you can even imagine. Let me ask you about some details. What if they all tried to escape? Started running off in the desert. What would you do?"

"I would send my men after them to try to catch them."

After a long pause, Make said, "I don't know what we should do but I know what I have to do."

"I know one thing we should do sir. First off, we have known each other for about seven hours now. I think it is time we started using first names. How would it suit you if I called you Make and you called me John?"

"Good idea, John. What are some of the other things we should do?"

"The most important thing for right now is we bed down for the night. That storm is at the coast by now and it will probably hover there till tomorrow. It will be dark soon. We have provisions for all of us for three days if we are not able to find lodging in Nishtun. I will order food prepared and our bedding laid out."

Fires were started and soon Make was offered a metal plate with food. He did not recognize some of the things on his plate but tried it all. "I recognize the beef stew, and it is delicious. But what is this fluffy stuff? It has a flavor that I have never had before."

"First off, that 'beef stew' is, I guess you could call it our national dish, is called 'marag', which is chicken and lamb with some local vegetables. And the 'fluffy stuff' is fenugreek, the leaves from a local plant and some tomatoes and garlic. I'm glad you can tolerate it because that is all we brought to eat. However we may be able to get a variety of foods in Nishtun."

After dinner, Make was shown his bed. It consisted of a blanket laid on the sand and some netting. "I haven't done this since I was a kid. Boy this is great."

"It will cool very quickly now. You should be under the blanket, not on it."

Standard gave Make a lesson on how to bed down in the desert. "First, in picking a spot, always pick the windy side of the dune. If you get on the lee side you will be covered in sand by morning. Secondly, in the winter we use sleeping bags but now, when it is warm, we use blankets. Open up the blanket, grab it by one end and shake it vigorously until your arms are tired. If it's winter, shake the bag the same way. Third, if it is winter, immediately get in the bag and zip the bag up completely. Now that you have a blanket, as I have said, get under it, put the netting over your head and tuck it down all around."

The slight cool breeze felt good at first, but by the time it was dark it became cold and then really cold. Fortunately the wind died down. For a short time Salazar's men were talking then all was quiet.

This was a harsh country, blinding light that can burn your skin during the day and cold air at night. Now there was no sound. As Make lay there his hearing became more sensitive. When everyone was quiet, he could hear the sounds of insects flying and crawling. His ears became more sensitive as the sound level diminished just as his eyes became more sensitive in the darkness.

But the night sky was something that city people can't imagine. It was like having a telescope. Everything was so clear one might think it a different sky.

Make was awakened by someone gently pulling on his blanket. John was standing close by. When Make sat up he could see the sun, low in the east, but the light was defused by the storm. "What a beautiful sight. But I see that the storm is still there." The black vicious-looking storm of yesterday afternoon had tamed down. The remnants were like tendrils of darkness interwoven with the morning sunlight. When he got up the sand was cold on his bare feet. *I bet that won't last very long.*

"Have you thought about a way to resolve your problem?" John said. "What are you going to do if you find the bad guys?"

"No. I doubt that there is a way. Let's just proceed and hope something will come to mind later on."

Chapter 34

Friday morning

The Arabian Sea, Yemen

Aboard ship they had all bedded down for the night, however there had been little sleep. The ship continually moved. When the sea surged toward the rocky beach the ship moved farther ahead, only to retreat moments later. All of this was accompanied by a lot of grinding and scraping, and all on board were concerned that the ship might move out into the sea and sink while they were sleeping. Actually, if she drifted out into the calm sea she would not sink. So long as the ship was not moving and the hatch covers remained air tight they were safe. As was customary with vessels capable of hauling oil or gasoline, when that compartment was empty, the engine exhaust gas was pumped in as a safety measure-to minimize the possibility of an explosion. This slight pressure tended to minimize the amount of sea water in the oil compartment.

Of the men who had been working with the explosive materials, a few never laid down, afraid that this might be their last dry night. The captain, Ishe, Mal's twin, was afraid of them. When the chemist had found that most of them were armed, some with guns and some with knives, he warned them that any gunshot anywhere in the room would detonate all of the explosive. He hoped that he had deterred them from any such action.

Three months ago, while the ship had been in dry dock, Ishe had been contacted by the leader of the group of Muslims. They said it had become necessary to move their assembly process to a different location.

The Muslims seemed surly to Ishe. He didn't trust them. They seemed so mean he was afraid of them and was reluctant to do business with them. But when he contacted his brother Mal, he was told that this was a great opportunity and that he, Mal, would negotiate the terms with them and would act as an intermediary. That way, Ishe wouldn't have to deal with them directly. Mal told the Muslims that it seemed like the ship might just be the right kind of place. When docked in a harbor secured to the dock, it would be quite stable. Also, it was not apt to be recognized as a manufacturing facility. No one would suspect what they were doing. And, on the off chance that someone might complain, they could simply cast off the lines and move to a different location.

Mal arranged for the plumbers, carpenters, and electricians necessary to build the wooden flooring that was needed for production. The production machinery and everything was paid for by Mal. Ishe was promised a nice percentage. Ishe knew that Mal had gotten a lot of 'up front' money from the Muslims.

The man with the compound fracture of his right femur had died. He had bled out.

The men who worked in the engine room came up to the sleeping room just below the ship's bridge. Ishe had his bed in the captain's suite on that level. He enjoyed the privacy of his own bathroom. These men had been on the ship for several months, since before the *Golden Lie* had gone back to sea. At first, Ishe felt comfortable with them, but now, after the ship was on the rocks, he had heard one of them say that they could do belter without him.

The *Golden Lie* had had rudder problems for some time. She could turn to starboard much better than to port. But when the underside became visible in dry dock, it was obvious that the propeller had been damaged too. Fortunately for Ishe, Aden was the major docking facility for Yemen and there were repair people there who could fix bent propellers and loose rudders. Money had always been tight for Ishe but Mal was financing this project and he seemed to have come into some ready cash. Ishe had only to place a call and the needed funds would soon arrive.

Now that it began to get light it was obvious how the sea was moving the ship. Ishe told the men that the anchor was what was keeping them safe.

About mid-morning, Ishe decided to go ashore and call Mal. He knew what Mal would say and how he would say it but he could delay no longer. There was a deadline. The first major delivery of the product was schedule for five weeks hence. If there had not been a storm they might have made it. Now Ishe knew that there was no chance. He dreaded the coming conversation. That's why he asked the chemist to come with him when they went ashore. He was going to rely on the chemist for backup. The chemist had confidence that the product they had been making was good.

The chemist would have gone with Ishe even if he hadn't been asked. It was in his best interest to get things rolling for he was the one who would have to come face to face with the terrorists. It had been agreed that before the shipment was made, a technical representative of the group would come aboard and inspect the product. Pickles would only be shipped if he gave his approval. The chemist knew that Ishe was not a technical person. And the chemist thought of Ishe as a weak person. He knew that, during the coming phone call he would have to speak to Mal in order to adequately explain what was needed.

The sea was not calm but the waves were much easier to negotiate than last night. Ishe steered from the back while the chemist held on to the middle seat. They had to proceed slowly. When Ishe had tried opening the throttle, it had been very difficult to stay in the boat because of the roughness of the sea.

THE GOLDEN LIE

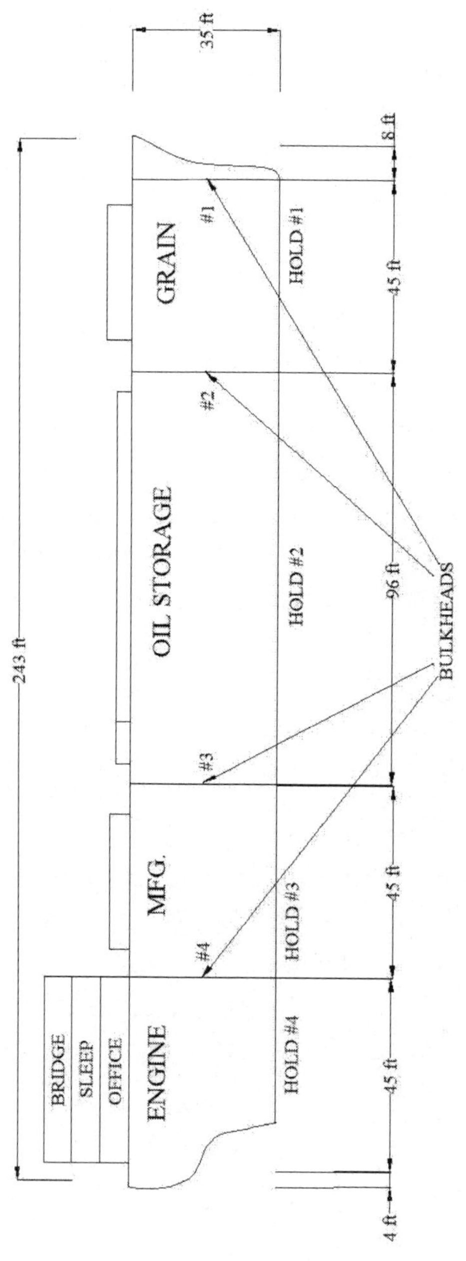

Chapter 35

Friday morning

The Harbor Master's building, Nishtun, Yemen

When Standard and Make arrived in the parking area at the Harbor Master's building, Make said, “Let's just talk a minute, OK?”

The Police Chief said, “All right, talk.”

“When we find that ship, will you help me kill the occupants, all of them?”

“No. We talked about that. I cannot just shoot a group of people. Make, I have rid the earth of two people in the line of duty because they were really vicious men. You do not even know if these men are guilty of anything. And for that matter, you can't shoot them either. It's just not the right thing to do.”

“Well then why don't you tell me what the right thing to do is? You know that it's a bad thing to make hundreds of pounds of explosive material that will be used to kill people all over the world. And you know that there are a bunch of terrorists doing that very thing in some ship around here somewhere, right now. Oh, and another part of that equation is that this material is undetectable at airports or any place else and there are terrorist cells all over the world who will use that material in a heartbeat.”

“I know that there are terrorist groups all over the world but the rest of the things you just said are unproven. Make, I think you are an honorable man and I think you believe all the things you just told me. But even if you are exactly right and if it was legal, I still don't know if I could just massacre forty people. And I don't think you can either. You're a doctor for God sakes. How did you get in this position anyway?”

"I volunteered. And besides that it's only about twenty five people. And, I don't think I can kill them either. I was hoping you would."

"Marvelous. So now, Doctor Caston. What do you think we should do?"

"SIDK."

"What?"

"SIDK, 'Shit, I Don't Know'. It's a technical term."

A long pause then suddenly, Make points to a couple of men coming up from the beach, one heavy set and muscular and one smaller. "Look. That guy in front, the little guy. That must be Mal Thorp's brother. They're twins. I've never seen this twin before but the faces are the same. This one is slightly smaller than his brother but there are lots of similarities. I know his brother well. I shot him. I've never seen that other guy but I know the smaller one is Mal's brother. I think he is called Ishe."

"I thought you said you hadn't ever killed anyone."

"Who, Mal Thorp? I didn't kill him. I just shot his foot. Come on. They are going in that building. I want us to be in there too. He won't recognize me. He's never seen me before"

Running, John said, "That's the Harbor Master's building."

They entered just behind Ishe and the chemist. The Harbor Master was standing behind a wooden desk. He was a young man dressed in a uniform that Make was not familiar with. Make said to Ishe and the chemist, "You were here first."

Both men turned to look momentarily at Make and the police Captain then Ishe turned to the Harbor Master, "I am Ishe, Captain of the *Golden Lie.* We have hit a rock and are in danger of sinking. I must use your phone to get assistance."

The young man spoke in Arabic saying, "I don't understand that language. What are you saying?"

Ishe turned to the chemist, "What's he saying? I can't understand him. Tell him what I said."

Speaking Farsi, the muscular man said to the man behind the desk, "My boat is aground and might sink. He is Captain Ishe Thorp. He wants to use your phone."

"But where is your ship? How did you get here? The Harbor Master told me you were missing. No one heard your distress signal. We have resources here and at Aden that will help you."

The chemist relayed what the young man said.

"Just tell him I need to make a long distance call," Ishe said. And again, the chemist interpreted.

The assistant Harbor Master said, "You are going to call long distance because your boat is sinking here. That makes no sense."

"What did he say?" Ishe asked. "I can't understand a word he said."

The chemist turned to Ishe, "Put your hand on your pistol."

The police Chief tensed.

Ishe said, "What?"

"Just put your hand on your pistol. Don't pull it out of your pants. Just put your hand on it." Turning back to the assistant Harbor Master, the Chemist said, "He wants to use your phone now."

The young man quickly handed the corded phone to the Chemist who hands it to Ishe.

Ishe yelled, "I can't use this! It has a cord on it! Doesn't he have a cell phone? This conversation is supposed to be private."

"Just make the damned call. These guys won't listen."

Make said, "No. We won't listen." All turned to look at Make.

Ishe didn't know how to operate the phone. It was a 1940's model with a receiver separate from the mouthpiece but attached with a cord. The Chemist took it from him, jiggled the hook and waited. In a few seconds, speaking in Arabic, "We would like to make a long distance call to the United States of America. We'll pay the charges to the Harbor Master."

Everyone in the room waited in silence for a minute then the chemist said to Ishe, "What's the number?" The chemist translated the number Ishe had given him into Farsi for the phone operator.

There was more waiting then the chemist handed the phone to Ishe. Ishe said, "Hi Mal" then immediately burst into tears. He was crying so hard that he couldn't speak for a short time. Finally he picked up the conversation, "Mal, there was a big storm and it drove the ship on the rocks and it wrecked everything and...What! No. Everything we made is in a big pile in a big metal trash container except some of the material is smashed on the floor. Some of the workers stepped on some of the pieces and tracked it around but most of it is in that metal trash can. We had it all made and completed. We were ready to send it. I am so sorry Mal...Mal, it wasn't my fault. It was a terrible storm and I didn't know what to do...I wasn't in the harbor." Pause. "They wouldn't let us stay in the harbor." Ishe started sobbing again as he listened to Mal, then, "No, Yes he is right here".

Ishe handed the phone to the Chemist, “He wants to talk to you”

The chemist said, “Well, partly. There was a storm and the entire product that we had made has been destroyed. Also the raw material we hadn’t processed has been contaminated. We’ll have to get all new materials… The Banbury fell but fortunately it hit one of the workers so it didn’t break… Oh, he is dead…All the stainless shelving is damaged but I believe that’s all. The box cutter and the printer were not damaged…It’s anchored about a mile north of here. It has a hole in the bottom just back of the bow. The first compartment is ok…Only the oil storage…I don’t think it’ll sink. But we’ll have to go very slow. With this kind of damage, if we run very fast, water is rammed into the hole with sufficient pressure to blow out the next bulkhead. That would be catastrophic for us. We would lose the ship…I don’t know. Maybe we could go backwards faster. Maybe Ishe knows. I know that big oil transport vessels have strain gauges all over the front and they continually monitor pressure on the bow…Ok, we’ll call you when we reach Aden. Do you want to talk to Ishe…?” The Chemist hung up the phone and returned it to the Harbor Master’s desk.

* * * *

Make and John moved to the edge of the mesa to watch Ishe and the chemist go down to the dock, start the Zodiac, and leave. “Now I know where the PETN is being made,” Make said.

John said, “I know of a road that runs northwest. It is up high along this ridge but it follows the shoreline. It’s a rather good road. We can probably beat them to their ship.”

* * * *

The police chief drove the Humvee.

"I thought you said this was a good road. It's a terrible road."

"It was good the last time I was on it."

"When was that?"

"About five years ago".

"Great. About how far have we gone?"

"A half mile. Maybe we ought to stop and take a look." Pointing ahead to the right, "That's a good place."

'I'll bring the binoculars."

The remains of the storm had gone farther out to sea now and the sky was clear for several miles. They looked up and down the coast as far out as they could see. "There is one small sailing vessel up near the shore but I am certain that is not the one'" John Said. "They were talking about an iron ship with a motor."

"Well he said a mile. Let's keep going. I want to at least see what kind of ship it is. If we can find it, maybe I can get the navy to torpedo it."

"Make, you've got to let this go! I hope you're joking but sometimes you worry me greatly."

At another stop farther along the road they had the same results except, there were no ships at all. Then, after another half mile had gone by, Make said, "Stop. I think I see them. It looks like a Zodiac"

When the Humvee stopped, cautiously they both went to the edge of the cliff. There was a small craft moving fast. It was a half mile out but it seems to be heading toward the shore.

"Looks like there is only one person in it," Standard said.

"I think we should get in the Hummer and go a little farther up the road. From the direction he's headed I'll bet the ship is just around that point."

Another quarter mile in the Humvee, they looked over the edge. A small freighter was below them. John said, "That's the '*Golden Lie*'. I can read the marking. And here comes the Zodiac."

"But there's only one guy in it."

"No, there are two. Here take the binoculars."

"Oh yeah, I can see. He's lying down. He is hanging over the seat with his legs on one side and his body on the other."

Lying on their bellies they continued to watch as the Zodiac came up to the port side of the *Golden Lie.* John took the binoculars back, "That's the other guy running the boat. Ishe must be the one laying in the bottom of the boat. The one running the boat has his leg over the other one's body. That's why it's so hard to tell what's going on. I think the guy in the bottom of the boat is dead."

"No shit. Why would you say that Sherlock? Just because a guy has been lying with his belly across the seat in the bottom of a boat for the last half mile and he has had his head hanging face down on the bottom of the boat in about a half inch of water and he is in the hot sun and he hasn't moved. Is that why you think he's dead?"

"Make, I think you might be making light of this because you think they should all be killed, and to you that is just one down and twenty four to go."

"Well, what are you going to do, go down and arrest them?

"No, I am going to stay here and watch. And so are you."

A narrow iron ladder had been hung down the side of the *Golden Lie.* After the Zodiac operator tied the boat to the ladder he climbed up to the deck and went in the office door.

A couple of minutes later two men came out and dragged the body from the Zodiac up to the deck and lay it face up on the deck walkway, just in front of hatch number two.

Make said, “That’s Ishe. And he is certainly dead. I wonder how that guy killed him--if that guy killed him.”

Chapter 36

Friday noon

On the Arabian Sea

Asif Kahn, the forty year old chemist, was born in Madras India. His parents, Menaka & Farhan Kahn, wanted him to be an architect like his father. At that time, as was customary among Indian parents, he was sent to England for his education. He did well in school. During his first year at Worchester College of Technology he attended a seminar on 'principles of physical design'. The speaker was an engineer by the name of Osama Ben Laden. He became interested in the speaker and his philosophy and they became friends. Although he never saw Ben laden after that, they continued to correspond. Kahn subsequently attended the University on Kansas in the USA where he got his master's degree in polymer chemistry. And it was during that time that he realized that his personal beliefs and those of the conservative Bible belt, USA, were so much in conflict that he would have to choose between the two--and his choice was clear. However, it wasn't until Osama Ben Laden was hunted down and killed that he decided that he could no longer stand by doing nothing. Once his Master's program was complete, he left the USA for Yemen.

* * * *

The chemist entered the manufacturing area, "Your attention please," He commanded. "Captain Ishe has made arrangements to get the ship repaired at the dry-dock in Aden. The repair should take ten days. During that time you will be at liberty to enjoy yourselves on shore. On the way to Aden, however, we will clean up the manufacturing area. Once underway you will collect any product you find that is in perfect condition and bring it to me. I will store it in the refrigerator in the engine room. That way, you will be able to keep all food supplies in our refrigerator. Any and all defective or damaged materials will be thrown overboard. As for the tables, trays etc. we will keep them if they are usable with a minimum of repair. I will make those decisions. Anything that is obviously beyond repair will also be thrown overboard. While you are doing that, the mechanic from the engine room will repair the leak in the bilge pipe. That should be finished tomorrow. Once all of that is completed, the manufacturing area must be cleaned and scrubbed completely. All of the old material is considered a source of contamination and must be removed before we start production anew. Ishe has also ordered all new raw materials. They will be delivered in seven days. We should be in Aden by then. Our trip to Aden should take five days. Because of the condition of the ship we will have to travel at a very conservative rate."

Then in the engine room, "Gentlemen, there is every indication that the ship will not sink. I suggest you raise the anchor. When we tell you, 'full astern', you should react quickly. With luck, we will get off the rocks without any further damage. We will then proceed to Aden for repairs. Because of the hole in the bow, we must go very slowly so as to not damage the bulkhead. When we start going forward we must start at four knots. When that speed is reached Ishe will check the bulkhead and see if we can increase the speed. So I want you to make sure we don't exceed four knots when we first start."

The Chemist picked two of his men and sent them to stand by the bulkhead with the handheld radio and told them to feel for vibrations and listen for creaking sounds.

As the *Golden Lie* started backing, the propeller threw so much water it looked as if it was raining at the aft end of the ship. Immediately, Kahn got a signal from the two men in the bow, "lots of vibrations."

With an empty vessel that was slightly down by the bow, forty percent of the propeller was out of the water. Even at this RPM, vibration was inevitable and there would be cavitation until they approach four knots.

As soon as he thought they were clear of the rocks, Kahn signaled, “All stop, left rudder, come to one hundred ten degrees”. On the handheld radio, “Do you still get lots of vibration?”

“No. It’s stopped. No vibrations.”

“That’s alright. It was a vibration from the propeller. Remember that vibration. It’s not the kind of vibration we are worried about. That vibration was when the whole ship vibrated. We are concerned about the bulkhead vibrating. What you are looking for is vibration caused by water pounding on the bulkhead.”

As the ship slowed it gently drifted around to the south-south east heading. “Ahead. Make eighteen revolutions,” Kahn shouted. Now the ship started moving forward, very slowly at first.

In the first hole, as the ship began to move forward, water piled up against the wad of steel at the end of the tear in the hull. Some spilled inside of hold number one. The two men the chemist had sent had been standing on the opposite side of the keel next to bulkhead number one – the wrong bulkhead. They held on to the door dogs.

On the handheld radio, Kahn asked, “Do you hear any sound like metal bending?”

“No.”

“Is there any indication that the bulkhead is bending in any way?”

“No. And no vibrations”

Now, as speed approached four knots, the bow entered a swell. The torn part of the hull was pushed back by the force of the water and the hull tore down more, forming a ten foot wide scoop extending a foot below the original contour of the hull. As water rushed in, most of it went up the ramp like scoop toward bulkhead number two, but some went sidewise knocking the two men down. They were terrified and tried to use the handheld radio, but the water, now like a whirl pool, overcame them.

"Good. I am going to gradually increase speed. If you feel any vibration on the bulkhead, call me immediately." To the engine room, Kahn said, "Give me forty eight revolutions"

To the hand held, "Do you understand? If you feel any vibration, any at all, you call me. Ok?"

As the speed approached eight knots, water shot across hold number one hitting bulkhead number two in the middle. The two men tried to keep from drowning.

"Do you hear me?"...Kahn kept trying…"Hello, answer me…" then, "These damned radios never work." To the helmsman, "I've got to go down there and see what's going on. Watch the speed. Don't let it get very much over eight knots."

Kahn went down through the crew's quarters, then down into the engine room and stepped through the door in bulkhead number four into hold number three. The manufacturing crew was making a show of cleaning up, but at this point, their morale was down and they were accomplishing very little. Kahn was both angry and disappointed. *How will I ever get thing operational again. It was difficult to get this bunch of people to work the first time. I may have to get all new workers next. At least I will not have to pay this group.* Kahn said nothing and continued through the door in bulkhead number three.

Had the helmsman in the bridge been paying close attention to the height of the bow above the water he would have seen that the bow was sometimes awash and the ship was heading for the bottom of the sea. With the momentum it now had, *the Golden Lie* would continue to plow down through the water at an ever steepening pitch. The propeller was now more than half out of the water. At this point, the path of the *Golden Lie* was not reversible.

There was a groaning sound as Kahn entered hold number two. Then another screeching sound and water began coming through the door seal. Water was coming in, both below and above the locked dog in bulkhead number two. At first Asif didn't notice the condition of the door. He didn't realize that hold number one was quickly filling with water. Because of the carbon monoxide his vision was blurred and he had some dizziness and a headache, but he knew it would go away as soon as he got out of the hold and in to the fresh air. Where were the two men he had sent down here? Now he felt some nausea and his vision was diminished even more. When he was ten feet from bulkhead number two, what he saw made him paralyzed with fear. The door in bulkhead number two was held shut with only one dog. As he watched, he could see that the door was pried open both below and above the dog and water was coming through. He knew that, on the other side of the door, water was at least as high as the top of the door. And he knew that one dog alone could not hold back all of that pressure.

The top deck at the base of hatch cover number one was nearly awash. Just then, the water level inside hold number one reached the hatch covers thirty five feet above the ship's bottom. And, as that happened, the pressure on bulkhead number two spiked like a giant hammer had hit it.

Just for an instant, Kahn saw that about two feet of the bulkhead steel just above the doorsill had parted. Then, with a terrific rending sound the sides of the *Golden Lie* sprang apart about a foot. The number two bulkhead weld-seam split from the top deck down to the door and the two sides of the steel next to the rip splayed outward toward the aft end of the ship. The one door dog lost its purchase and the door was flung open. In the instant before he was killed Kahn knew there was nothing he could do. "*I can't stop the ship in time. I c...*"

The surging water slammed Kahn against the steel wall behind him knocking him unconscious. At first his lifeless body was floating on the surface of the sea water in the cavern-like hold. Number two hold had twice the volume of number one. And there were no hatch covers to allow the air to escape. Kahn had secured the door in bulkhead number three. As the water level rose, the air above it was compressed, and so was the air in Kahn's lungs. He sank.

Normally, hold number two contained about two hundred thousand cubic feet of smelly air and carbon monoxide. This part of the ship provided a buoyancy of twenty tons. Now, instead of buoying the ship up, hold number two contained over eight hundred tons of water

When the sides of the ship at bulkhead number two had sprung apart that caused considerable stress at bulkhead number three and there was a domino effect. With the water level just twenty feet below the top deck, and the air compressed above it, the sides of the *Golden Lie* at the middle of bulkhead number three pulled away. The bulkhead remained attached at the top but pulled away along the bottom and sides. The tremendous force of the water caused bulkhead number three to bend back up toward the aft end if the ship. Because of the compressed air in hold number two, water shot into the manufacturing area with a terrific force. The wooden floor that the carpenters had built was crushed. And wood timbers, metal beds, cutlery, lamps, mattresses, factory workers, and steel lockers all swirled around together in the hold number three.

As water rushed through the open door to the engine room there was no place for the engineer and his assistants to go. They were swept toward the aft end of the ship. One of the men, the apprentice engineer, was able to surface and tried to swim but the current and the thrashing debris were too much for him. All were dead by the time the water reached the top of the stairs. The diesel engine continued to run under water until a wooden beam broke the engine's air induction pipe. Enough water got in the cylinders to cause the engine to seize; however the momentum of the eleven foot diameter propeller continued to turn the propeller shaft. The transmission shattered and the propeller shaft with part of the transmission still attached, continued to thrash around under water for a few revolutions. The propeller was now out of the water as the ship nosed farther down.

The man in the pilot house saw what was happening and ran down the stairs. But by the time he got half way down his feet were in water, and water was surging in through the open door. As he turned to go back up the stairs he saw Ishe's body rush past the window nearest him.

Chapter 37

Friday

On shore

Make and John were lying on the edge of the cliff as the *Golden Lie* backed away from shore, and then swung around to the left. She slowed and stopped when she was parallel to the shore. Then she started moving forward, headed south east.

John said, “I feel badly. I’ve stopped you from doing what you came here for. You’re a warrior and I have taken your sword.”

“That’s just so much poetic bullshit. I came here without a plan, and if you hadn’t been here the end results would have been about the same. I don’t have either the balls to kill off twenty five men or any idea how to destroy that ship.” After a brief pause, “I do, however, have the equipment.” Make pulled out the model 1911 from its holster. From the prone position he aimed high knowing the round would probably not go far. He cocked the hammer and fired repeatedly, empting the magazine. “Well that was a waste of ammo but at least I can say I did all I could and I fired the last shot.” The *Golden Lie* was now about in front of them and slowly gaining speed. “She’s really a nice looking vessel.”

“Yes, she is, but she’s sinking.”

“What! Let me see.” Make sat upright, “My God, you’re right. The bow is getting lower in the water. The waterline painted on the ship should have been above the water, now it’s under water.”

They watched in awe. It was like seeing a submarine submerge. It was horrible to think of the men inside. Now the propeller was half out of the water throwing a spray in all directions but the *Golden Lie* continued to increase speed while the bow pitched down farther and farther. Not long after she was awash at mid ship, water was at the base of the superstructure. Then the propeller stopped turning. It was completely out of the water.

In a half of a minute the *Golden Lie* had completely disappeared, but there was lots of debris on the water. Among all that was the Zodiac. Its bow was down, but other than that it appeared to be intact. Possibly, one of the front compartments had a hole in it. As Make scanned the area with the binoculars, "My God. That's Ishe. Come on. We've got to get him."

"What are you saying?" John asked. "All that stuff is a quarter of a mile out to sea. We can't get out there."

"Yes we can".

"How? You can't swim that far."

"Actually, I can swim that far. Maybe. Let's go down there and see"

The cliff they were on was about fifty feet above the sea. The area on top where they had been lying was sandy, but the face of the cliff was covered with rock and cactus. They descended as quickly as they could without falling but three minutes went by before they reached the rocky beach. To their right was an indented place in the beach, a place where floating things had gathered. It was strewn with foam cups, a plastic milk bottle and a few pieces of furniture. "How in the world did that stuff get out here?" John asked.

"Beats me. That's progress I guess. Anyway, I'm grabbing that bottle."

"You think it will keep you afloat?"

"Maybe. Where's the boat?"

Neither of them could see the Zodiac. Then, "There it is, way up to the left." The boat had moved closer to the shore but was now two hundred yards farther north. The two men started running up the beach. One was carrying a plastic, one-gallon milk bottle. They stopped only for a moment because they could see that the Zodiac was moving rapidly northwest. They had to run farther. Finally, stopping where they thought was the best place, Make stripped to his shorts. Putting his clothes in a pile, he tossed the empty 45 on top of the pile. He grabbed his milk carton and waded into the surf. "Why is the water so cold? The sand was so hot I couldn't stand to walk on it."

"The water really isn't cold. It's just a shock because everything else is so hot," John shouted.

By now Make was swimming while holding the milk bottle in his right hand as a float. It didn't work at all so he abandoned it and continued swimming. He was a strong swimmer and rapidly closed on the zodiac, which was being blown toward him. In less than five minutes, he was along the side of the boat, too tired to climb aboard. Then he worked his way around to the bow which was low in the water. There he was able to climb in.

Make shouted, "Boy, I'm out of shape. Hey, it doesn't have a leak. That metal ladder is hanging on the end of the tie-down." He was finally able to pull the ladder up enough to get it loose from the Zodiac. He then used the paddle to maneuver the Zodiac to where Ishe's body was. Most of the body was submerged just below the surface but his knees, face and forehead were above the surface. Pulling Ishe's head up out of the water, Make saw that Ishe had a floatation device around his neck and shoulder area. "No wonder he didn't sink."

Make held on to Ishe's left shoulder and dragged him into the bottom of the boat. By now, the Zodiac was fifty feet from the shore. Make paddled the rest of the way with the help of the wind.

Working together, John and Make dragged the front of the boat up on the rocks far enough that it wouldn't float away. Make tied it up to a piece of driftwood then put on his pants as John stared at Ishe.

In Arabic, "Who are you and why are you here?"

* * * *

Startled, Make and John turned and saw three men dressed in Yemen Thaub standing about forty feet away. Make quickly picked up the 45 and held it to his side but it was held so the three could see it. Two of the men were of average height but the third was a giant. He came toward them. At twenty feet Make kept the gun to his side but thumbed the hammer back. It sounded menacing. The man stopped.

Showing his ID, and speaking Farcie, "I am John Standard, Chief of police. We have been watching the boat that has sunk. We have searched for survivors. Who are you and what are you doing here?"

"I am Al- kabob and this is my area. We have been watching you." John interprets, "You shouldn't move that gun at me. I think you're bluffing. I think it 'Rub' al Khali'- I think that means empty chamber."

Make doesn't understand the language but he moves the model 1911 slightly forward. "I am not pointing it at you and there is one sure way you can find out if it's empty. Just step right up." John translated for Make.

In flawed English Al- kabob said, "No, I am not to want to find out. I said I think it empty. I did not know it empty." Then he smiled a toothy grin. "I see you are successful in finding a survivor."

Make said, "No, just a dead body."

"He's right Make." John said.

"What?"

"Ishe is alive. I saw him breathing a minute ago"

"Holy shit." Make turned to see Ishe, "He is alive! He's a very lucky man." Turning back to the Arabs, Make added, "I've noticed that you are a size bigger than your associates. Do you like doc-"

John interrupted, "Let me interpret for you."

In Arabic, Al-kabob asked, "What is it you said I am bigger than?"

John replied in Arabic, "Associates are the people you are with."

"Ah, very good. A new English word. And what is he associates?" pointing to Make.

"He is Make Caston; I think he must be an Olympic swimmer."

"Ah, I understand Olympics. We like Olympics. We see Olympics. We did well in shooting and snowboarding."

Laughing, Make asked, "You did well in snowboarding? How can you practice snowboarding in Yemen?"

After a brief pause Al-Kabob said, "Yes. Thank you very much."

Pause, then Make suggested, "John, why don't you use your Arabic to discover more about these gentlemen while I checkout Ishe's condition a little more?"

John continued to talk to the trio. He learned that two of the men were natives. They were born nearby and had lived all their lives in Yemen. Al- kabob however, was born in Ireland to two catholic missionaries. He had been brought to Yemen as an eight month old baby only to become an orphan before his first birthday. The two men he was with were his brothers. At least he felt that way because their parents raised him as their own. His natural parents died of an unknown illness soon after they arrived. They never got to achieve their goal of establishing a Catholic church in Yemen. And al-Kabob was not interested.

Make listened to Ishe's heart rate. It seemed slow but regular. He opened Ishe's eyes and his pupils seemed normal. The only indication of trauma was a puncture wound in his neck. The location seemed similar to the one found in Make's neck when the police doctor examined him. "John, I suggest that, since you and Al-Kabob are both Irish, they should do us a favor by toting Ishe up to the Humvee and, in return we'll give them our Zodiac."

"Our Zodiac?"

"Yeah, there it is. Our Zodiac."

"Make, when we get back to Sana'a, I may have to arrest you." John turns to the Arabs. In Arabic, he said, "Gentlemen. Are you interested in making a trade?"

"What do you have to trade and what do you want in return?"

"We are not asking for much. We would merely ask that you carry the injured man up the hill and put him in our vehicle."

"I understand your problem. This is a task that is too much effort for you and we are your only means of getting him up there. Because the cliff is nearly vertical, it would be a difficult task even for the three of us."

"Oh, we could get him up there but not quite as quickly as if the three of you did it. We are suggesting this only because we would like to get underway quickly."

"Yes, I can see that it is imperative that you leave quickly. But I can't imagine that you have sufficient goods to be equal to the task you have asked us to do."

"I am prepared to offer you four Yemeni Rial."

"Surly, you must be joking. Four Yemeni Rial; that is only a fraction of what we would require to accomplish the task you have ask us to accomplish."

"You are asking a lot, but since we are interested in your generous assistance, I can offer you five Yemeni Rial. That is all the money I have."

"Ah, Sir, I am sorry for your poverty but that is not adequate for the work we would have to do, climbing the steep cliffs and carrying the injured man. We would have to use great care not to cause him more injury. I do feel sympathy for the dire position you are in. Only because I am a compassionate man, I would, however, be able to take your boat for trade, assuming, of course, that it is not worn so much as to be unserviceable."

"I could not give up our vessel for just carrying our man up the hill. Our boat is in nearly new condition. It has only been operated for a short time."

"When we first arrived, I saw your boat in the water. It looked as if the front was low in the water. Perhaps it has a leak."

"Oh no, it is in perfect condition. It is my belief that the offer that you have made is not of equal value. Our vessel is worth much more than you three carrying the injured man to our car; however, if you will wait here I will ask my associate what he thinks of your offer."

John walked to where Make was examining Ishe and said, “Make, say ’no.”

“What?”

In a quiet voice John said, “Don’t ask questions. Just say ‘no’ loud enough that our Arab friends can hear you.”

“No.”

“Good. Now say ‘absolutely no’ just a little bit louder.”

“Absolutely no!”

“Ok. You did very well. I think we have a deal.”

John walked back to the three Arabs, “My associate is very reluctant to lose the vessel but in desperation he left the final decision up to me. So, as difficult as it is for me, I accept your offer. If you will very gently carry the injured man up the hill and place him in our vehicle, our ship will be yours.”

Ten minutes later Ishe was in the Humvee and they were headed back to Nishtun.

John drove, Ishe was in the center, and Make was on the left side. Sazar and all the troops had returned the day before.

“What’s that guy’s condition?” John asked.” Is he going to make it?”

“I don’t think he’s got any water in him at all. I put my ear against his back and I could hear pretty well. His lungs seem to be clear. He had that float collar on him and I think it kept him from drowning. But we do need to get him to a hospital and have him checked out. I’d be very interested in finding what drugs are in him. He seems like he’s almost awake.”

“Make, do you realize how strange this is? You came here to kill those guys and you found that you could not do it; now you are looking for a hospital to help this guy.”

“No, I’m not trying to help him. I just want to find what kind of drugs are in him. He has some of the same symptoms I had when I was on my plane trip that I told you about. And he and I both had needle marks about the same place in our necks. That’s all.”

“If that’s all, how is it that you swam a hundred yards through shark infested water to rescue him?”

“You didn’t tell me about the sharks. Anyway, I guess you’re right. It must be the doctor in me. This is all new to me. You’ve been in the bad guy business for a long time. You have probably seen lots of killings, lots of really bad stuff, mayhem I mean. I haven’t. Maybe I can’t do this kind of thing at all. It worries me that I like all of this activity. It’s probably because of the adventure and excitement involved. But, what if I have to go back to doctoring because I can’t finish things? Because I can’t kill people that should be killed, I mean. My God that’s even difficult for me to say.”

* * * *

Later, as they approached Nishtun, bouncing along in the Humvee, Make said, “John, I assume you have plans for Ishe. You’ll fix him up then let him go, right?”

“That’s not exactly how it will go but the results will probably be about the same. There will be a hearing and I will be asked to tell what I know. I will tell them that I heard one side of a phone conversation made by Ishe and his assistant. I believe they were talking to Ishe’s twin brother in the United States of America. Keep in mind Make, the words explosive and terrorist weren’t mentioned. I will tell them of the boat sinking and of your heroic rescue of Ishe.

After I have said all of that they will discuss it for a few minutes. Then they will turn him loose."

"That's terrible. There is no justice in that."

"Make, if this had happened in my jurisdiction, I would send a dive team to look at the wreck. They might or might not find explosives. But it is not in my jurisdiction. I work in Sana'a," Pause.

Make said, "Turn around."

"What?"

"Turn around Standard. This is not your jurisdiction this is Al-kabob's jurisdiction."

John stopped the Humvee. "Make, you can't be serious. We'll not be able to find them. We don't know where Al-kabob lives."

"John, you said yourself, this is not your jurisdiction. This is Al-kabob's jurisdiction."

"You are correct. It is my duty to turn Ishe over to Al-kabob." John began turning the Humvee around, "But he will be very difficult to find."

Up ahead they saw someone or something coming toward them fast. John pulled to the side of the road to let them pass. The three quads stopped right in front of them, in Arabic, Al-Kabob said. "It won't start."

They followed the three Arabs back. When they arrived at the ridge with the Zodiac tied below, Make said, "I'll go down and work on the boat. You get Al-kabob to agree that it's his problem, not yours."

Speaking Arabic, John said, "Al-kabob, do you trust me?"

"Oh, yes, of course I trust you. I know who you are and what you do. Actually, I have seen you on the TV. I believe you to be honest and fair and you make good decisions."

Make made his way down the steep path to the Zodiac. He saw that it was still tried to a piece of driftwood partially buried in the sand, just like he had left it.

"Do you trust my companion, the one who swam out to save the man, Ishe?"

"Oh, no. He is a doctor. You can't trust doctors. When doctors come people die. No I don't trust doctors"

Make waded in the water and checked the outside of the boat. Next he inspected the mountings to see if the engine was secure. Then he climbed into the boat and looked over the controls. Everything seemed OK.

"Al-kabob, I am going to tell you what I believe to be true." John continued. "I am telling you this because I believe you are a fair and honest man too. I believe the man, Ishe, who was saved from the sea, is the owner of the ship that you saw sink. People were making explosives on that ship. That is what was happening on that ship that you witnessed sinking. They were going to sell the explosives to terrorists all over the world. They were going to kill many people."

Make pressurized the fuel system then turned on the ignition switch. He shifted the gears into the neutral position and pushed the start button.

Up on the ridge, John said to Al-kabob, "Right now, Ishe is my prisoner but I think he should be yours. You are the authority here. I want you to take possession of him."

"Yes, he was in my area. He is..."

The engine on the Zodiac started running smoothly. Al-kabob and his two brothers turned and started running down the steep slope, jumping from bolder to bolder. John heard, "The doctor fixed it! He is a good mechanic."

Make untied the Zodiac and backed it away from shore. He then shifted to forward and opened the throttle momentarily. The engine responded immediately and the bow of the Zodiac came up out of the water. Al-kabob and his two companions stood and watch approvingly. Make cut the wheel sharply and opened the throttle again. The Arabs cheered. After he turned first right then left, Make returned the boat to the shore. All three Arabs ran through the surf out to the back of the boat where Make sat. They patted him on the shoulders and, Make assumed, congratulated him. They were still patting his arm when John showed up. With John doing the interpreting, Make told them all he knew about operating the Zodiac. He stressed the part about the importance of having the gears in neutral when starting the motor.

Speaking in his best English, Al-kabob said, "Much thanks is you. You are master doctor ship man."

Once the operating instructions were complete and John, Al-kabob and Make had a chance to talk, John picked up where they left off when the Zodiac's engine started. "Al- kabob, will you take charge of this man, Ishe?"

"Yes, I will question him and others who might have information and decide what to do with him. As of now he is my responsibility. Is that what you want, John?"

"Yes, that is what Make and I think is the right thing to do. When you interview the young man who was in the Harbor Master's office when we were there, you might get more information. He overheard a conversation that is significant."

Al-kabob told John, "Yes, I will speak to the Harbor Master, his assistant and all others who might have knowledge of the ship and its activities."

On the way back to Sana'a, Make complimented John on his Arabic communication skills. John said, "Thank you. By the way, when I asked him if he trusted you, he said no, you were a doctor. He didn't trust doctors"

"How did he know I was a doctor? I never mentioned that."

"You started to and I interrupted you. I think he got that. Besides when I first saw you I thought, 'what is a doctor doing out here'? Then, as all of us watched you examine Ishe, that was proof. You are a doctor through and through."

"See, John, that's what I was talking about a while ago. I was trained as a doctor. And I think I'm a good doctor. But I'm in a dilemma. I would much rather do the stuff I do for Homeland Security and I'm not good at it. What a mess."

"Perhaps it's the newness of it. After a while, this work may become more commonplace and you won't be as thrilled about it. Or, maybe you will become capable of killing someone then you will feel that you are capable of 'finishing things', as you put it."

"No, I will never kill anyone. I have learned that much about myself right here in Yemen. It's in my bones. I'm just not capable of killing."

* * * *

FIELD REPORT

NAME: Make Caston DATE FILED: 04/24/ 2015

TASK DESCRIPTION: Stop the manufacture of PTEN in Yemen.

ACTIVITY: I went to Yemen, found who was making the explosive, who was their leader and how many people were involved. I found their location, went there. All the people involved and all their capital equipment and supplies have been destroyed.

ANTICIPATED AFFECT: They won't be making any PETN in Yemen for a while.

COLATERAL DAMAGE: None

EXPENSES:

TRAVEL	$2400
LODGING:	None
FOOD:	None
ANCILLARY:	$36.00 US (1 box .45 ACP)

Chapter 38

5 PM Nishtun (9 AM Washington DC)

Nishtun, Yemen

Isabell answered. “Hi Make, Where are you?”

“I’m a couple of miles from Nishtun, Yemen. “I’m headed to the Harbor Master’s shack in Nishtun to charge up my phone, but I just wanted to tell you that the problem I came here to solve has been taken care of. I am saying that there is no longer a problem. I’ll try to write you a complete report on the way back. I’m going to call General Johnson as soon as the phone is charged. He had asked me to keep him informed.”

“Make, what’s he have to do with this?”

“I had sat in on a meeting of his where he was going to take care of the problem but I later found that the people involved had moved on so I informed him and he canceled the strike based on what I had told him. He just wants a f --- ow-up that’s all.”

“Make, th-t is -- od to kee --- im --- ormed. -ou s --- d --ow – at he ----.

“Isa - ell. - y -- one - s --- d”.

A half hour later, after his phone was charged, Make called General Johnson, “Good morning, this is Make Caston. Could I speak to the general please?”

“Mister Caston, he’s in a meeting right now but I know he would like to hear from you. He has mentioned your name recently. Can you hold on for a few minutes? I’ll see if he can break away.”

“Good morning Make,” General Johnson said, “Good to hear from you. What’s going on?”

“Sir, when we spoke last I had suggested we cancel a project that we had talked about at the meeting in Ft. Huachuca.”

“Yes, I know what you’re referring to.”

“I can now confirm that the problem we talked about no longer exists. I know that the threat level of that problem is now zero.”

“Make, I am interested in getting some more details. Could you come by my office later today?”

“I am out of town right now but I could probably see you in four days.”

“Four days, you must be way out of town.”

“I’m in Nishtun Sir. It’s a one day trip back to the airport. There is only one plane out of there per day and if I miss that that I’ll have to wait another day for the next plane. Then it’s a day and a half return trip sir.”

“Yes, I know Nishtun. I’ve never had the pleasure but I know it. Make, when you get back, Please call me at your convenience.”

Make said, “I will do that sir. It was nice talking to you General. Good bye.”

Chapter 39

Monday afternoon, 2:41 PM

On a 747

Make rested in a 747 headed for home. *I love this old plane, lots of good memories. I can still remember details of the champagne party they had on the 747's inaugural flight from LA to New York.* "Ah, I wish I was young again." He muttered.

The lady setting next to him said, "Young again, my ass. You don't even know 'young again'. You're still young. How old are you, thirty five?"

"Oh, I'm sorry mam. Did I say that out loud? I was just remembering a party we had on the first transcontinental 747 flight."

"Yeah, I know. I like to reminisce about stuff like that too. My name's Lois and I'm sixty-two. I'll be sixty-three years old the 2nd of next month."

"Well you don't look it, but I suppose everyone has memories."

"This is the captain speaking. We've started to let down now. We should be on the ground in about twenty five minutes. The temperature in Phoenix is ninety six degrees, the humidity is six percent and the wind is four miles an hour out of the southwest."

A flight attendant approaches, "Excuse me sir, are you Mr. Caston?"

"Yes."

"You have a phone call up front. If you'll follow me, I'll show you where it is."

"Pardon me, Lois." Make follows the attendant down the stairway. "What's this about?"

"You've got a phone call. That's all I know."

Past the forward restrooms they stopped at a spot next to the door to the captain's cabin. Another female passenger was standing there also. The flight attendant handed Make the phone, stepped back and closed the curtain. Now Make and the other passenger were alone behind the curtain. Make held the corded phone to his head, "Hello, this is Mr. Caston."

"Do you recognize my voice?"

Make knew it was Isabell Franks, his boss, but he didn't know why all the secrecy. "Yes."

"Who is there with you?"

"One other passenger, Pardon me miss. What's your name please?"

"Air Martial Halt."

Isabell heard the Air Marshal, "Yes. There's a serious event that will take place on the plane after you land. It might be dangerous. It involves you and agent Halt working together. You do not have to do this. It is strictly voluntary. Except for the Air Marshal, you are the only person on the plane qualified to do this kind of activity."

"Of course I'll do it. What do you want me to do?"

"Assist agent Halt. She has a plan. Thanks Make. Make?"

"What."

"Don't shoot him in the foot."

"Why'd you say that?"

"We need you, and the way it is shaping up, you get to shoot someone in the foot only one time in your life and not go to jail. *verstehst du?"*

"Yes." Make hung up the phone. Shaking her hand he said, "Nice to meet you agent Halt. What's going on?"

"There's been a Savings and Loan robbery in Scottsdale. The perp took a hostage. He's demanded a car to the airport and air transportation to Brazil. This is the plane he'll get on. He'll probably drag the hostage with him. This plane will never leave the ground with him in it. I want to make certain the hostage is not harmed, and I want to take the perp alive if possible. However, he has a gun, so if we have to shoot, it's ok. The plane will be moved to a cleared area. If we do shoot, no civilians will get hurt, and if this plane is seriously damaged they will probably just retire it. It is a bucket of bolts anyway. And if you shoot, try not to kill him. Just shoot him in the foot or someplace, ok?"

How can I do this? I can't kill anybody. Christ. "Ok."

"So, you got any ideas?"

"Agent Halt, I just got here."

"I know and I have a plan. But I want to hear what you think. It is always good to have plan B."

"We don't know what kind of a guy he is so we don't know if he will search the plane when he first gets here or maybe he has never been in a 747 before and will go upstairs first just to see what it looks like. We don't know what he's going to do so it seems to me we should hide, one of us forward of the door and one of us to the rear of the plane. Then, as he comes through the door, we both appear at the same time. If he points a gun at one of us, that one can duck and the other will shoot him. If we do it that way, it's important that we both confront him at the same time."

"Yeah, it's important that we don't shoot each other too."

"Right, so what was your plan?"

"I don't have one any better than that. I was faking it."

"Ok, as soon as he steps in the door we both come out of our hiding places. He will see one of us first. The other one of us should shout, 'don't move' or whatever seems appropriate."

Agent Halt said "Sounds good. If he has a knife instead of a gun and says he will cut the hostage if we don't drop our guns, shoot the elbow of the hand holding the knife. Probably that will pretty much end the knife business, momentarily at least. It will be up to us to get to him quickly. If it looks like that didn't work, shoot him in the head. Are you good with this?"

"Yes. I'm good." *I hope it doesn't come to that.*

"Hey, I wasn't kidding about us shooting one another. Always make sure you're not in the line of fire."

"The one flaw I see in this plan is, I don't have a gun."

"Yeah, makes you kind of nervous doesn't it? Have no fear; I have this one which is just right for you." The Air Marshal handed Make a gun. "It's a Ruger model 40 with an extended barrel. I'm probably a better shot than you because I practice all the time. The longer barrel will help your aim. I'm using my Glock."

"We need to find hiding places," Make said. "I can get slouched down in one of the seats farther back. You might want to get in one of the front lavatories."

"No, I'm going to hide in a food storage pantry. They've made room for me there. If I was hiding in the lavatory and he opened it that might be a bad thing for one of us"

The senior flight attendant announced, "Please return to your seats. We'll be landing in a few minutes."

Make returned to his seat. "Boy, you sure had a long conversation." Lois said.

Joking, Make said, "The stewardess said it was a long distance call."

"Funny boy. Do you practice a lot or is that just natural for you?"

"Neither, I've just got a lot of talent."

The plane touched down in Phoenix. Make said, "Nice talking to you Lois."

The plane has stopped and people stood, retrieving their luggage and waiting for the doors to open.

"What line of work are you in Mr. Gaston?"

"It's Caston with a 'C'. I'm foot a surgeon. We have an office here in Scottsdale. Look us up, 'Hand and Foot Medicine'." With that, Make left, pushing his way through the crowd as fast as he could without making himself obvious. He wanted to get hidden, away from Lois. He didn't want her to know he'd be staying on the plane. He got in the lavatory.

A few minutes later Make heard a tap on the lavatory door and the flight attendant said, "The passengers are all out and I'm leaving. Good luck."

Soon agent Halt showed up, "The plane is going to be towed to a remote spot. We should sit down."

After the plane had been moved, the Air Marshal put her left sleeve to her mouth, “How’s it going Frank?”

“It’s going. Are you about ready? If you are we will be there in five minutes.”

“We’re ready.”

“Good luck. We’ll be listening.”

“Wow, you’ve got great communications.”

“Yeah. Oh I forgot. Here, put this in your pocket and that in your good ear. Or the other way around if you so desire.”

“Funny. I’m ready to hide and try out my new walkie talkie.”

They both left their seats, air marshal Halt went up front and disappeared in the food storage pantry. She was thinking*, I like him. He seems very professional and quite capable*. Make went aft so he was about the same distance from the door as agent Halt was. *She is clever, nice, professional, has a very pretty face and a great body. Nice tiny waist.*

Make, slouched down in a side aisle seat, “My God, this seems like a long five minutes.”

Make heard, “Yes, it certainly does seem like a long five minutes, Frank.”

On the communicator, Make heard Frank say, “They’ll be coming in momentarily.”

A minute later a girl came in and glanced around. She was very young, maybe sixteen. She looked in Make’s direction but didn’t see him. It was bright outside and dark inside the plane. All the blinds had been closed. Then she looked back outside, “Come on. Nobody’s here. Come on.”

"Make, what do you see?" Halt asked.

"An overweight, sixteen year old girl. She doesn't seem like a hostage to me." Pause. "Now there is a man sticking his head in. Now he's gone. Now she's standing in the door. She's talking but I can't understand her." Make whispers, "I think she is telling him to get in here. She's yelling something at him but her head is outside the plane..."

"I can see her," Halt whispered, "Now it looks like she's pulling him in to the plane."

"Come on in Billy," the girl said, "It's goin'a be fine. We got the money, we got th ride. We're going to Brazil and we are goin'a fuck our brains out all the way. Whooe!. I got the money. Where's your gun?"

"It's in the car I'll go get it."

The girl, "No, no, no, it's all right. We won't need it in Brazil."

Billy said, "We could get in that car and be a long ways from here in a couple hours. It's got a full tank. And it's a real good car."

The girl, "Naw, come on in here Billy n make yourself comfortable. You don't want'a drive all night. See how all these arms fold up out'ah the way? It's just like a regular bed. Come on Billy. Lay down right here."

"I don't think so. I don't think I can do it. I don't feel right."

"Billy, you take your pants off and lay down right now. I am goin ta make you very, very comfortable."

Halt whispered, "You ready Make?"

"No let's wait. I want to see just how comfortable she can make him."

“Voyeur, voyeur, pants on fire. Can you see what’s going on?”

“No, all I see is the back of the seats and her head going up and down. I don’t know what they are doing.”

A voice echoed, “Come on Billy. You can do it.”

“Na, I cain’t. I cain’t do it”

Then Halt said, “Make, let’s go! It sounds like the only dangerous thing he has is an erection and I don’t think it’s working.”

“Ok, on three, 1, 2, 3.”

“Stay where you are. Don’t move. She’s coming your way, Make. Down the other aisle. I’ve got this guy.”

Make crossed the center section. At the aisle he ducked down and swung the heavy barrel of the pistol toward the girl’s shins, hoping to trip her. The gun went off. The girl sank down screaming.

Marshal Halt arrived with a flashlight. The girl was lying on her back holding her foot and crying.

“Good shot. You must have hit her left foot.”

A voice shouted, “Halt, speak to me. What has happened? Are they secured?”

“Yes, Frank. We’ve got them.”

Make said, “Oh crap. I didn’t mean to shoot at her. I swung the gun trying to trip her and I couldn’t see very well and I smashed my trigger finger on the bottom edge of the seat and the gun went off. This is going to be bad.”

“What do you mean, ‘bad’? Say it was a trick shot or say it seemed like the right thing to do. You didn’t want to kill her. Actually, I told you to shoot her in the foot.”

Two big guys showed up behind Marshal Halt, ”Where is she hit. Medical is on the way.”

Agent Halt said, “I didn’t shoot her. Make did. Make, this is Marshal Dixon and Lieutenant Frank. Make Caston, my assistant. As it turns out Make’s an excellent shot. She was running like hell and…”

Frank examined the girl’s foot. “I don’t think she’s hit. She just struck her little toe on the seat support. She should have worn real shoes, not thongs”

To the girl Frank said, “Get up. Put your hands behind your back. Halt, you know the drill. Go somewhere and write this up while it’s still fresh. We’ve got this covered. Go.”

Make asked Marshal Halt, “Do you need me? Maybe I should just go.”

“Of course I need you. You’re the one who shot the hostage.”

“I didn’t shoot anyone. No one was shot. The gun went off accidentally.”

“I know that. I’m just trying to illustrate how important you are in the capture of these two notorious killers. Come on. I’ve got a car in the lot. We can go to my place and write it up.”

* * * *

Halt drove to a neighborhood near ASU. Make asked, "You live around here? I thought most of these houses would be rented to students."

"Yes I live around here. Right there, as a matter fact." She parked in front of the house. "And most of them are rented to students. I own two houses in the neighborhood, this one and the one next door, there."

"A landlord. I'm impressed."

The house was old. Probably built in the fifties. It was getting dark and Make couldn't see details of the outside of the house but he could see that it was a bungalow style home. Inside, however, he could see that it had been renovated. The windows had been replaced and the walls, woodwork, and flooring looked to be three or four years old at the most. "This is very nice."

Marshal Halt said, "Thanks. I hired a couple of architectural students to do it.

After looking around Make said, "How do you want to do this report? What's your MO?"

"I've done a lot of report writing. I think its best if each of us writes, just briefly, what went down as we saw it. Then we get the two versions together so we each know what the other saw. Then we each make our final report. What do you think and do you want a beer?"

"Sounds good to me, I'll get the beers."

"My computer's in the bed room, the beer is in the fridge, and my tablet is where ever you want to use it. I don't know what's best for you. Can you write with an IPad?"

Make found the kitchen and the fridge. "Bud or Bud lite?"

"Bud lite."

Make got two beers then took the iPad. Halt went into the bedroom to her computer.

Later, "Hey Make, how are you coming? Do you want another beer?"

"I'm finished."

Make took two more beer into the bedroom. "Jesus Christ, you're writing a novel. Mine's only a few lines."

"I've finished now. You can sit here and read all of mine. You'll have to scroll up. I think I wrote three pages. I'll sit over there and look at what you put on the IPad."

After reading Make's report, Halt said, "Let me see your finger. It sounds like you really smashed it. I was caught up in the moment and didn't really think you were hurt. Let me see. Oh, that's going to be black tomorrow. I'll bet that hurts." She holds Makes finger to her lips and gently kisses it. "There that will make it all better."

"I hurt my lip too."

FIELD REPORT

NAME: Make Caston DATE FILED: 07/20/ 2014

TASK DESCRIPTION: Capture a Savings and Loan thief and save his hostage

ACTIVITY: While in a 747 on final approach into PHX, I volunteered to assist a TSA operative, Air Marshal Halt. The thief had demanded a flight to Brazil for him and his hostage. After we had landed and all other passengers deplaned, the 747 was taken to a remote location and the hostages entered the plane. Agent Halt and I were hiding in the aircraft. Agent Halt was near the cabin and I was in the rear of the aircraft.

The two people that entered the plane were young and it was immediately obvious that this was not a hostage situation. They were partners and lovers. Agent Halt and I waited until they were having sex in the center section then we subdued them. Other TSA agents came in the plane and took them away.

ANTICIPATED AFFECT: They won't be robbing any more Savings and Loans for a while.

COLATERAL DAMAGE: I shot a hole in the aircraft but it was scheduled for the bone yard in Tucson anyway so the damage was classed insignificant.

EXPENSES:

TRAVEL	None
LODGING:	None
FOOD:	None
ANCILLARY:	None

Chapter 40

Monday morning

The office of Isabell Franks, Deputy Secretary, Homeland Security

"Make. Good. Come in, close the door, and sit down. I assume you just got back from Yemen and have lots of things to tell me. I'm glad you're back safe and sound, and I don't mean to sound calloused but I've got things to tell you and I have a meeting in fifteen minutes that's going to occupy me the rest of the day so I am going to talk and then you are going to write me a report. Ok?"

"Yes. And it sounds serious. What's going on?"

"You and I have talked about my organization before. We were top-heavy and consequently, communications were difficult for all of us. I really had trouble knowing what was going on in this section. We have a fix for all of that. As of now you work directly for me. This is a temporary position for you only because I'm not allowed to move anyone up two levels at once. So your new pay level is sixteen. That's where Johnnie Walker was. In six months, if I'm still here, and you haven't screwed up, you will become a seventeen. *verstehst du*?"

"*Ja.* I mean yes."

"*Gut.* Then it's done. Congratulations on your promotion. Now go to work. You use Dove's office in this building. His secretary will be your secretary. His budget will not be your budget. John Walker's budget will be yours."

"Thank you very much."

"Another thing, now that you have your own budget, if you want to do something within your budget don't come to me. Don't come to me unless you have something significant to tell me. If you want to travel I want to know that you'll be away and for how long but the funding is on your shoulders, not mine. You tell your secretary where you want to go, she makes your travel arrangements and advises this office of your plans. If I want to discuss it, I will call you. If you want to discuss it with me, you call me. What I'm saying is, I don't want to know about the day to day stuff. On the other hand I don't want to be embarrassed because I'm not aware of some significant thing that has happened. Do you understand what I'm saying?"

"Isabell, I can do this. But I need to talk to you tomorrow."

Make went to his new office and said to the secretary, Georgia, "As of about five minutes ago, this is my office. Are you good with that?"

"What did you say your name was?"

"Georgia!"

With a grin on her face, "Of course, Mr. Caston. I'm yours to command."

"Good. First command. Quit jerking me around."

Georgia had always been attracted to Make. She knew that he would be a fun guy to know and to be around. She hoped he would be in the office a lot but she knew enough about him and the way he worked that she thought there was little chanced of that. He was always on the go. Always in a hurry. *It's too bad he lives in Phoenix. On the other hand maybe not. When he's here he will need a place to stay.*

"Georgia, I need to talk to Isabell tomorrow and I need a place to stay tonight. Could you get me a place that's close?

Hallelujah. "Sure, it'll probably take me 15 or 20 minutes"

Make went into his new office and looked around. It had been cleaned so there wasn't much to look at. On Lon's desk there was a list of things that were Lon's 'to do' list for tomorrow. It was dated six days ago.

Make reviewed the budget he had inherited then wrote his report. He clicked on 'enter' and went back to Georgia's desk. "How are you doing?"

"Ok, I got some places. How about the Renaissance, DC Downtowner, $550, it's on 9th street."

"Too much money. I just want to lie down. I don't want to buy the place."

"Ok, how about the Merrifield, Marriott Residence Inn $325."

"No I don't want to go all the way out to Merrifield. And that costs too much too. Isn't there something close in that's not and arm and a leg?"

"Make, the closer you get to the Pentagon, the more it costs. And when you start this late in the day you aren't going to have a lot of choices."

"Christ."

"Ok, here's a bed and breakfast. Do you like B & B's?"

"No."

"It's on Wilson Blvd., $200. That's closer and that's cheap."

"I don't know what to do. I'd probably wake up people in the next room. I don't like B & B's anyway."

"Ok. You've got two more choices. One, you can stay at my place. I have a guest room with a bathroom next to it. It's in the front of the house. I sleep in the back bedroom so you wouldn't bother me. Or, number two, go to the Inner Agency Motor Pool and check out a car. You can sleep in that."

* * * *

The next morning on the drive back to DHS, Make said, "Georgia, thanks for letting me use your bed room. That was a nice thing to do."

"Yes, it was very nice."

"Georgia, it was just for fun. It was very nice for me too, but we can't do that again. I'm married."

"Yes, I understand. You've been out of town for a long time and my husband is gone. I was just lonesome. That's all it was."

* * * *

Tuesday 9 AM Isabell's office

"Isabell, when I went to Yemen, in the back of my mind, I knew I had to kill off all the people involved with making PETN. I thought I would work out the details when it came time to do it. My conscience, or something, wouldn't let me do it. Wouldn't let me kill anyone. But that is what I am supposed to do and it would have been the right thing to do." Make got out of his chair and walked to the window, "All those people should have been destroyed. Of course, in the end, I didn't have to do it. They did it to themselves. But my point is, I really failed that mission. If they hadn't sunk themselves, they would have gotten away. My conscience wouldn't let me do what I thought was my job. Isabell, I want you to know this because I think it's important that you know all about what I can do and what I can't do. And I want you to tell me that...I want you to tell me what I should do about all of this, if anything."

“Well that’s pretty easy. I want you to go see our resident shrink and tell all of this crap to her.”

“That’s it? You think that will solve this entire problem?”

“No, I think the only problem is that you think it’s a problem. You’re no different than anyone else that I know. I would expect anyone that works for me directly to not be able to kill a bunch of people. I know I couldn’t do it. Look, there are people that can do that sort of thing. And, right now we’re not like that. Maybe you’ll change. I don’t know, but right now you seem perfectly normal to me. Someone in Doctor Kansee’s office will call you to make an appointment.”

“Gee, thanks.”

“By the way, what has happened to the twin brother? And, while we’re on the subject, I want a real report. Not that bullshit field report you sent me. I want to know what happened while you were there.”

“OK. Tomorrow, ok?”

“Yes, tomorrow is fine.”

* * * *

10:45 AM, Tuesday

Laura called, “Make, honey, I miss you. You’ve been gone so long. How long are you going to be in DC? I thought you’d be gone just three or four days. Are you ok? Is everything ok?”

“Sure, I’m fine; I’m just tired that’s all. I got into Washington about noon yesterday then I had to wait until today to get to tell Isabell about my trip. How about you, is everything ok with you? You seem different. What’s going on?”

"Ah…well…I've just got to tell you. Pizz came by Thursday asking about you. He was all happy about school He had finished some part of his doctorate program and he was so glad that it was over and he just wanted to tell someone about it. Next he is going to have to write a dissertation on international terrorism. Anyway he spent a lot of time telling me about the doctorate program and what all he has to do and then we went down to the park had a little picnic and…oh hell I slept with Pizz."

"Jesus Christ, Laura! Is that what you wanted to do? He didn't force himself on you did he?" Make jumped up and started pacing.

"No, of course not. Make, he is a long away from home and he hasn't had time for much social life and he was lonely and so was I and..."

"Laure stop." His voice got louder, "You're rambling. So you fucked Pizz. Is it just a one night stand or what?" Make stopped pacing.

"I guess not because he stayed Friday night too. Make, Make honey, I don't mean to sound flip about all this. I love you and I want you. I want to keep you and to love you… but I like Pizz too. He's a nice guy. He's different from you, but he's ok. And he likes you too. Honey, it did just start out as a one night stand. Actually it just got late and I thought it would be nice so I suggested he might stay but I never thought about anything except the moment. I never thought ahead. And I don't love him. I only love you Make. Honey, I was just lonely, that's all. Can you understand that?"

"Of course I can understand that. I get lonely too sometimes but I don't fuck around." *Oh boy.* Make started pacing again.

“I don’t fuck around either. This is the first time. I’ve never done this before.”

“Hold on a minute… ‘Georgia, get me on a flight back to Phoenix as quick as I can. Ok, I’m back honey. Now, what do you want to do?”

“I just want to go to bed. I want to be with you. Maybe have sex with you. Maybe just be with you, just touch you and talk to you. Tell me about your trip. Can’t we just talk?”

“Mr. Caston,” Georgia said, “I’ve got you on a Southwest flite1076, leaves here at 1:44, arrives PHX at 3:05”

“Good Georgia, get me a boarding pass please.”

“Laura, I don’t know what to say, what to do. I’ll be home about four this afternoon and we can talk. I want the same things. When I get there, let’s just go to bed. I’ll talk to Pizz tomorrow. I don’t know how that will go… Georgia, please call Doctor Kansee’s office and cancel my appointment for today.”

Chapter 41

4:30 Tuesday

Make, Laura, Pizz

"So, what do we do? Laura asked.

"So what we do is you and Pizz break it off. No more sex with Pizz. Actually, you and Pizz stay away from each other. When he comes to town he stays in a hotel, not with you. Not at our house"

"Make, he lives here in the valley. He goes to ASU. He's a student here."

"Yeah, I knew that. I'm just all screwed up that's all."

"Ok, ok, I got it. I won't sleep with Pizz anymore."

"Good. Then that is settled. Now I've got to go see Pizz. Laura do we have his address around here somewhere?"

"It's 345 north 74th street in old town Scottsdale, honey."

"Christ, have you been in his house?"

"No, I have not been in his house. We just drove by it once. He wanted me to see where he lived, that's all."

Make went to 345 north 74th street, a rental. It was a well-kept neighborhood of houses built in the fifties. Some houses had carports that had been converted into rooms.

When Pizz opened the door, the expression on Make's face caused him to suspect Make's reason for being here. Pizz asked Make to come in. "Have a chair Make, how have you been?"

Make ignored both the question and the chair, “Pizz, you’ve been fucking my wife. Are you trying to take her away from me or something? What the hell are you doing?”

“No. I just like being with her and sometimes things like that just happen, that’s all.”

“I don’t know what my feelings are. I like you Pizz, but I am in love with Laura and you are not. You are just fooling around.” They looked at each other, no antagonism, only concern.

Finally, “Yeah, I know. But isn’t that what you were doing when you first met Laura?”

“Yes but she wasn’t married then. It led to us getting married. You can’t marry Laura. She’s married to me.”

“Laura doesn’t want to marry me. At least, I don’t think she does. I don’t want to marry her. I just like being with her.”

“This is difficult for me. I really don’t want to talk about it right now.” Make headed toward the door then turned.

“Let me ask you something,” Pizz said. “Did you know I was sleeping with Laura when you were in Yemen?”

“No, of course not.”

“So it didn’t bother you.”

“Of course it didn’t bother me. I didn’t know about it.”

“So if you don’t know about it, it doesn’t bother you.”

“But I do know about it!”

“Ok. Here is how it is. I am not going to sleep with Laura anymore.”

“That’s bullshit. I’ll always think you are.”

"Well, you'll be wrong. Don't you understand that? I won't sleep with Laura again."

"I can't talk about this anymore. I'm leaving."

* * * *

Later, at home, they stood in the kitchen, holding hands. Make told Laura of his talk with Pizz. "Laura do you want to have sex with Pizz?"

"Sometimes yes, sometimes no. It was nice. But I like having sex with you too. I love you Make."

"I was hoping you would simplify things, but you haven't. Pizz said he would never have sex with you again."

"Ok. Then what's your problem?"

"One of my problems is, I don't believe him. Another problem is, if I'm not around and I don't know about it, it would be ok with me. That sounds really dumb doesn't it?" Make pulled out a kitchen stool and sat down.

"Yeah, but I think I understand what I think you're trying to say. Look, if you want me to stop with Pizz, I will."

"That sounds great except, I don't believe you either. I just thought of something else. If this ever got at out that you were sleeping with Pizz, I would be fired and Pizz would never be hired by DHS."

"What the hell does our sex life have to do with your employment?"

"Their position would be that they think you might be liable to be blackmailed because you don't want me to find out. The blackmailer might get you to tell DHS secrets. That is, he would say that he would tell me about you and Pizz unless you told him DHS secrets."

"But I don't know any DHS secrets."

"Sure you do. You know that I only pretend to be a drunk to cover up all the intel things that I do. You know about the Hardware Review group."

"Yeah, I guess. So, what do we do?"

"So what we do is you stop fucking Pizz"

"Ok, ok, I got it. I told you, I really won't sleep with Pizz anymore."

"Good. You tell Pizz that and I'll tell him that too."

"Ok. Agreed. Look, I don't have to sleep with Pizz anyway. I've got you."

"Laura, I'm so glad to hear you say that."

Chapter 42

Wednesday 4:00 PM

Doctor Kansee, shrink

"Hello doctor, I'm Make Caston."

Doctor Kansee was a tall woman with a narrow face and straight, black hair. He thought she might be African American, but he wasn't sure. "Yeah I know. Why am I seeing you?"

"Because my boss told me to. She probably told you why I'm here, didn't she?"

"Yeah, she said you were fucked up."

"I don't understand. You and Isabell talk like this is nothing. Like there is no problem at all. Well it is a problem for me. This is important to me."

"Ah, now you're talkin. I'll put on my shrink hat."

"Fuck you doctor." Make walked out the door then turned around and came back. He closed the door. "You work for Homeland Security, right?"

"Yes, part time, like right now."

"Is what I tell you really confidential or will you report it all to Isabell?"

"I will tell Isabell that the problem she asked me to talk to you about has been solved. I will not tell her anything about what you are going to tell me next."

Pause. "A good friend of mine has been fucking my wife. I like him and I love my wife. They each tell me that they are not in love with each other; they just like to be together. It seems to me that I should get all upset and punch him out but I really don't feel that way. And that seems like an abnormal thing. When I'm away, out of town, as long as he doesn't mess up my life, it's ok with me. I don't think he and Laura are going to run away together. It is just that I think I should be really angry and I'm not."

"Actually there are a very large group of people that think it's better to fool around. It makes their lives fuller. There are swinger clubs all over. Also, in Europe and Asia it's common for a man to have both and a wife and mistress. You see, there are all kinds of relationships. If you look at the big picture, the whole world, there isn't anything that's abnormal. There are guys whose wives are sleeping with someone else, who are really angry. They are so mad they might kill someone. Now that is serious. Your problem is not that serious. There is one part of the equation that you haven't mentioned and maybe don't know about. Contrary to what your wife and her lover, your friend, have both told you, they may change. They may fall in love. They may run away together. Would that bother you?"

"Yes, I love my wife. I don't want her to go away. We have a history together. I would be seriously pissed. Maybe that's why I'm here."

"Do you think you would want to kill somebody?"

"No. It turns out I can't kill anybody."

"If, at some time in the future, you get the feeling that your wife and your friend are getting serious, you talk to me. It sounds like that's not the situation now. It's ok to feel the way you feel, it is not uncommon to me. It is a thing that is not on the surface because most guys think they have to be macho. I think you're very insightful. You are ok. Is there anything else you want to talk about?"

"No."

"Then we are done for now. If anything changes or if you want to talk about anything, call me. "

"Ok."

"And I will not mention any of this to anyone including Isabell or anyone at DHS."

"Fine. But I do want to talk some more about this. What if I tell Laura that if she sleeps with Pizz, I don't want to hear about it and I don't want to come home and find them together? That would be an embarrassing situation for the three of us."

"I don't think you know what you want. When you tell Laura that you don't want to hear about it, you are telling her that it's alright for her to sleep with him. Is that what you want her to think?"

"I don't know."

"Make, all you have to do is decide what you are comfortable with, tell Laura and Pizz, and then come back here and tell me how it's working out."

"Thanks."

* * * *

Wednesday evening late

Make's home, Scottsdale, Arizona

Later that evening, after Make's returned from DC, there's a knock on the door. "I suppose that's Pizz."

"No, Make, Pizz doesn't knock. He just comes right in."

“Christ.” Make checked the peep hole. “My God, it’s Mal Thorp.”

Laura shouted, “Is that the guy you shot? Don’t let him in. Get away from the door. He may have a gun. Make, get away from the fucking door!”

Make opened the door a crack, “Sorry, we just sold the last one.” He shut the door.

“Caston, open this God damned door. I want to know what you did to my brother.”

Make opened the door and stepped out to face Mal, “Hi there, Thorp. How’s your foot? I see you’re limping a little.”

“Fuck you Caston. You stay away from me. I just want to know what you did with my brother.”

“Thorp, I’m just concerned about our relationship, that’s all.”

“Did you kill him? What did you do to him?” Make stepped closer to Thorp who said, “Get away from me.”

“How is your business doing? Have you got any new products? Is there anything new in the export/import business?” Make gave Mal a shove.

“You stay away from me. Keep your hands off of me, God damn it.” Mal shouted. “Tell me about Ishe. Is he dead or what?”

“He was alive the last time I saw him.”

“Caston, tell me what happened. Damn it, you owe me that, you son of a bitch.”

Make grabbed Mal’s ear, “I don’t owe you anything you little shit.” Make let go of Mal and pushed him back again.

"Ok, ok." Mal paused to compose himself, "Please tell me about my brother, Ishe. I know you were in Yemen and I'll bet you were after Ishe. I just want to know if he's alright."

"What makes you think I was in Yemen? Where did you get that idea?"

"Lon Dove's brother, Jobi, knows where you were. He told me."

"Ok. I'll tell you. Your brother and another, muscular guy were in a motorboat heading north. I was on the land watching them. They were out of my sight for a few minutes. Then, when I saw them again, it looked like Ishe was dead and the other guy drove the outboard to a ship, the *Golden Lie.* Ishe's body was laid on a wooden walkway on the deck of the ship."

"Oh my God,"

"Let me finish. I thought the *Golden Lie* was stuck on the rocks but then it backed off, turned southeast and then started forward. It was sinking right in front of me, and it just drove itself right down to the bottom. I saw Ishe floating around in a bunch of debris and I swam out and got him. He had a float collar on which kept his head out of the water. By the time I got him back to shore, he was beginning to come to. He had a needle mark in his neck just like I had when they got me out of your airplane. You fucker, you tried to kill me didn't you."

"No, I didn't. What happened to Ishe?"

"The local authorities saw the whole thing too and they took him. I don't know what happened after that."

"I want to know what happened to him."

"I've told you the truth, which is more that you deserve."

"Fuck you. You tell me what happened to Ishe or I'll shoot you right now." Mal pulled a short barreled revolver from his jacket pocket and pointed it at Make's middle.

Make held his hands out in a defensive position as another snub nosed revolver emerged from around the door sill. It was held by a very feminine hand and was pointed at Mal's left testicle. Her finger was on the trigger. No one said anything for a few seconds, and then Mal turned and ran down the front walk to a waiting car. As he ran he yelled, "Fuck you Caston."

Make said, "Thanks honey. You probably saved my life. I think you have just witnessed an 'intermittent explosive disorder'. That's a serious psychological problem. Mal may have killed people before…Now tell me how I get ahold of Pizz. I don't know his number."

"No problem honey. I'll call him for you. I've got him on speed dial."

"Christ."

* * * *

The next day, Pizz and Make sat in the living room. Make explained what Jobi had done. "This guy, Lon Dove's brother or brother-in-law, has some association with Mal Thorp. At least, that's what Thorp said and it's probably true. How could that happen? There are four million people in the greater Phoenix area. What are the chances that those two would meet? There is some connection that we need to find out about. Did Thorp and Jobi have a history? Thorp's a real bad guy and Lon's brother-in law is probably not bad clear through like Mal but he's talking too much. He needs to be convinced to keep quiet. I don't know how to do all that. Do you?"

"Yes, I do." Pizz said. "But first we need to find out a lot more about him, how bad he is, what he has done and what he's doing. What do we think he is going to do, and how those two guys are connected?"

"I can follow him around, see where he's going and what he's up to. I can also Google him. I can look into his work history; maybe look at his income tax reports."

"Looking at his tax returns would be a good thing for you to do. You're in a position to do that and we need that info. Following him around is not your thing. I know of a guy; he's in my doctorate program, who has a PI license and a PI business. He can do the following around much better than you. I know you have a budget for hiring independent contractors. We'll get him to check out Jobi. You may be surprised what a good PI can accomplish. I'll get you his name and number; you call him and set it up. I'd help you but I'm pretty busy right now; I'm writing my comps. You call him, and he'll take it from there."

* * * *

Make dialed the number. He heard, "We catch em, you cook em, how can I help you?

"This is Make Caston. Who am I talking to?"

"I'm Miss Leana Anna Loyd. I'm Dow Loyd's daughter. Dad's in school right now. Isn't that a shove? I'm sixteen and I'm home working and he is thirty four and he's in school. Sounds ass backwards doesn't it?"

What have I gotten in to? "Ask him to call me, will you please? I'm Make Caston at 480-555-1212.

"Yes, I have all that. Is there anything I can help you with?"

"Probably not, I just want to get some information about a person."

"We can do that. To follow a person around for twenty four hours costs between $1400 and $1600. That will get you appropriate pictures. Looking up records and checking documents usually cost $550 for an eight-hour day. There is a one thousand dollar retainer fee to be paid up front. We are licensed and experienced and all of our snoops have formal training in our kind of work. If you are interested you should come in and give us the particulars about what you want accomplished. Our office is open from nine to five. If you come in today, I can get things started today. Bring all the information you have. Anything that saves us work saves you money."

"Sounds impressive. I'll be there in an hour."

"We're at 345 Indiana. There's a parking lot in the back. If you park on the street, they'll steal your car."

Chapter 43

Wednesday Afternoon

The PI's office, old town Scottsdale

A half hour later, "Hello Mr. Caston. I'm glad you came in. Tell me what you need." Miss Leana seemed more matured than what Make had first thought.

"There is a man named Lon Dove. He has a brother in law named Jobi. Jobi is a felon and a recent resident of the penitentiary. There is another man, a con man named Mal Thorp. Mal Thorp is a bad guy. He lives in Albuquerque. He has a twin brother named Ishe. Ishe may be a bad guy. Lon Dove worked at DHS. He was my boss. He was fired recently because it was decided he was a security risk. Last night, Mal came to my door wanting to know where his brother, Ishe, was. Mal said that Jobi had told him I knew where his brother was. The last time I saw Ishe was a week or so ago in Yemen. He'd been turned over to the tribal chief just north of Nishtun, Yemen. I would like to know what those four people are doing and how they are associated with each other, if at all. I want to know how Jobi knew I'd been in Yemen. I'd like to know what they are planning. Leanne, what do you think you can do about all of this? Can you find out what I have asked you to do and, if so, how long will it take?"

"Ok, yes we can find out what you want to know, definitely. Right now I can't tell you how long it will take but I'll call you late tomorrow afternoon and will give you an estimate."

At about 3 PM the following day the phone rang in Make's office. "Hello Dr. Make Caston, co-owner of 'Hand and Foot Medicine', chief surgeon. How are you?"

"Hi Leanne I'm fine, thanks. What have you found out?"

"First off, as a matter of protocol, I have to tell you that my name is Leana Anna, L-E-A-N-A A-N-N-A. However, it would please me if you would continue to call me 'Leanne'. I like that better that than Leana Anna."

"OK, Leanne it is."

"Two weeks ago Lon leased a store front at 345 Tennessee with a PI sign on the front. They have been advertising on the internet and on a local radio station. Since they were competitors, we decided to keep watch on them for a few days. Luckily for you we've been watching for about a week. Some days Lon works there but most days Jobi runs the place. Mal Thorp must have seen their advertisement because four days ago he went into their store. He stayed twenty three minutes. The next morning Lon's brother-in-law, Jobi, came to us and asked if we could find out what you were working on at DHS and the organizational structure of DHS. I told him we couldn't do that because if we did we would have to tell his parole officer and that would put him back in the pokie. Actually, I just didn't want to deal with him. I can tell you all this because we didn't do any work for him." Leanne could see some concern in Make's face. "The next morning, three Days ago, Mal came back to their store. Lon was working that day. Mal only stayed ten minutes. Then two days later, yesterday at 3:42, Mal went back to Lon and Jobi's place again. Jobi was working then. Mal was in the building a short time, and when he came out, he seemed angry. Lon followed him out and talked to him on the sidewalk then Mal left."

"Do you know what they talked about?"

"Our snoop heard Mal say, and I am quoting here, 'go fuck yourself'. That's all we know for sure. As for the rest of it, I have been assuming that it was about you since that's what the brother-in law asked us about. Pause...So what do you want me to do?

"So Mal's been in their store three times in the last four days."

"Yes, so what do you want us to do?"

"Put a bug in their office. Can you do that?"

"Sure, the equipment costs you $2200 and part or all of it may or may not be refunded, Ok?"

"Ok."

When Make's phone rang Monday, morning, it was Leanne. "What's happening now?"

"Mal Went to Jobi's office again. He said 'the other guy said Caston was in Yemen'. I assume Mal meant Lon when the said 'the other guy'. Mal wanted to know how long you were in Yemen and what you did with his brother. Jobi said they told him where you live and he owes $2000 and they won't tell him any more until he pays them the $2000 for the work they have done so far. Mal said he wouldn't pay that much and he left."

"Christ. Ok Leanne, pull the plug and send me a bill. About how much have I spent so far?"

"Thirty two hundred forty six dollars."

"I want a tape of their conversation. Do you have that?"

"Sure and stills and DVD's too. You get all that. It'll show up at your place tomorrow"

The next day, the delivery brought a package to Make's house. He opened it, looked at the stills and, "Shit, that's not Mal, that's Ishe! This is wrong. Mal was just looking for Ishe." Make dialed 602-555-1212 again. "Hello Leanne, this is Make again. Do you have any more video footage of Mal?"

"No, sorry. We sent everything we had to you. What's the problem?"

"Look at the DVD. I guess you have it on your camera. I want to locate the last guy on my DVD that came in Lon's place."

"You're saying that's a different guy?"

"The first guy on the DVD, he has a scar on his left ear and he walks with a slight limp. The other guy…"

"Wait, wait, wait. I don't have a DVD. I sent it all to you."

"I'll be there as quick as I can. There's more work to do."

When Make arrived at Leanne's office they looked at Make's DVD. "See this first guy? He's walking with a slight limp. I shot him. See here and, and here, there he goes again. See how he walks here. Back it up. It's hard to see."

"You shot him?"

"Yes, I shot him in the foot. See how he walks. You have to watch close. And watch when he turns, There, you see the nick in the top of his ear."

"Do you shoot many people?"

"No, not many. Now run to near the end of the DVD. Back up, back up. Here, let me do it. There. See this guy. Right there. See, there is no nick in his left ear. And watch him walk. See?"

"Make, forget the walk. I don't see any limp in his walk any time but I do see that there is no nick. So the second one is a different guy. He must be a twin."

"Right. He's Ishe, Mal's twin brother. So that's how Mal found out that I was in Yemen. Ishe came to their store the next day after mal was there and mentioned that he had been in Yemen.

And Lon must have thought Ishe was Mal and told Jobi that 'Make Caston' was in Yemen last week.' That's why Mal came to my house wanting to know what happened to Ishe. So he doesn't know Ishe's in town. I didn't know he was in town either. And, obviously, Ishe doesn't want Mal to know. I want you to find Ishe without Mal knowing about it and arrange for Ishe and I to meet."

"So you can shoot him?"

"No. I am not going to shoot him. And, actually, you may need to convince him of that before he'll agree to meet with me. I saved his life. He may not know it but I did."

Chapter 44

Tuesday

North Scottsdale

Make was in his office at home when Pizz showed up. "Pizz, the PI you referred me to worked out well," Make reported. "As it turned out, Lon Dove and his brother-in-law had opened a PI business only four blocks from our PI and our PI had been watching them, just to see what the competition was like. Sooo, they already had a leg up when I walked into their office. And the interesting part is, they found Ishe."

"You mean, Ishe is here?"

"Yep. Leanne's people are going to contact Ishe and try to get him to talk to me."

"Do you know how Ishe got here so quick? It's only been ten days since you turned him over to that cop, Right?"

"Right. And I don't know how he got here. We may not get to see him right away. He may think that I want to throw him in jail. And maybe he should be put in jail but whatever he may have been guilty of happened in the Arabian Sea off the coast of Yemen. It's out of our jurisdiction. Anyway I'm certainly going to give him the benefit of a doubt. Until I find out otherwise, I am going to treat him just as a regular person. I asked Leanne, at the PI's office to find out the connection between those four people. A few days ago, Mal went to Lon's new PI office and asked them to find out what I was working on at DHS and also he wanted to know the organizational structure of DHS. The next day Ishe went to the same PI office, wanting to know about me. That's how we came to find Ishe and that's how they knew I had been in Yemen. Ishe told them. So I don't think there's a security leak at DHS. DHS is ok."

"Pizz, when and if I get to talk to Ishe I would like your take on what kind of guy you think he is. But, if he sees you, he may get scared and run. You look like a cop. I was thinking, if I make an appointment to meet with him, maybe we could make it in a restaurant or someplace open and you could be there too. I'd just like to know what you think about him."

"Sure, I can do that. When you make the appointment with him, make it a few hours ahead of time so that I have time to get there."

Make emailed Isabell saying there was no leak and explained how Mal knew that Make was in Yemen.

* * * *

Two days later, Thursday, Make's home office

Make's phone rings, "Hi Leanne. What have you got?"

"Ishe."

"What? You've got Ishe? Where is he?"

"He's right here. He's sitting next to me."

"I want to talk to him. Will he talk to me?"

Make heard, "Here he is" then, "Hello Mr. Caston. This is Ishe Thorp."

"Hello Ishe, how are you? Are you ok?"

"Yes, I'm fine thank you."

"Ishe, I'd like to talk to you. I'd just like to find out how things are with you and what you're going to do. Would you like to have lunch with me? I think you and Leanne could meet me somewhere and we could just talk."

"Thank you Mr. Caston. But I am afraid Mal might see me. I think he's mad at me and I am afraid of what he might do."

"Ishe, I live about fifteen miles north east of where you are now. If you and Leanne would come out here to my house, I can guarantee that your brother won't find you. My house is way up in the hills. And I know that my wife, Laura, would like to meet you. She's a good cook. What do you think of that?"

"I would like that Mr. Caston. Should I ask Leanne?"

"Yes, ask her if she will drive you out here. Tell her she is invited to stay for lunch."

Pause, "Yes Mr. Caston, she said she will drive us. She said she would love to see your house."

"Great, Ishe. I know Laura will like to meet you and Leanne."

Next Make called Pizz, "Pizz, change of plans. Leanne is driving Ishe out here, and we're going to have lunch. You'll have to meet Ishe later. If he seems ok I'm going to suggest he stay here tonight. He's afraid of Mal. I told him he'd be safe out here."

"It sounds like you've got things going ok. Call me tomorrow and let me know what's happening."

Chapter 45

Tuesday

The Caston residence, North Scottsdale, AZ

"This is a beautiful place. Look at that view!" Leanne said.

Ishe said, "Yes it is beautiful. Thank you for inviting us Mr. and Ms. Caston."

"Sit down and make yourselves comfortable," Laura said. "I'm making sandwiches and I have some tomato bisque soup. After lunch, if you like, we will show you around the house." Make had suggested this thinking that Ishe might be more comfortable if he could get an idea of what their house was like.

It was hot outside, so they decided to eat indoors with the glass wall on the west side of the house closed. "So, Ishe. Where are you staying?" Laura asked.

"I don't have a very nice place to stay. I got a room on north Scottsdale road. It's an ok place but it is old. I just got into town five days ago and I don't know Phoenix. It was just lucky that Leanne's friend found me. I've wanted to see you Mr. Caston but I have been trying to not be seen by my brother, Mal. He is mad at me because of the boat."

"What did you want to see me about, Ishe?"

"I was told that you saved my life. I just wanted to thank you. I don't remember any of that last part, the part when the ship sank."

"What do you remember?"

"I remember that there was a storm and my ship, the *Golden Lie*, got stuck on the rocks. It had a hole in the bottom near the bow. All the work they had done below was lost. That man that

Mal hired was a Chemist. He and I were going to go ashore and call Mal. But I don't remember if we got there or not. Do you know what happened, Mr. Caston?"

"Well Ishe, I can tell you what I saw but, of course, I was on the shore so there was a lot I don't know about."

"Please tell me what you know Mr. Caston."

"Yeah. This sounds good. I'd like to hear too." Leanne said.

Laura said, "Yes Make, I'd like to hear too. All I've gotten to hear of your adventure is the abbreviated version. Tell us the whole thing."

"Ok. John Standard and I had been told that there was a ship at Nishtun and they were making explosives on board that ship. We didn't know the name of the ship. We didn't know about the coming storm, of course, and we didn't know what we would do if we found it."

"So you were unprepared. What happened next?" Leanne asked.

"The storm was moving ahead of us. We had to wait a day and a half for it to subside. Finally, we got into Nishtun. The whole town was deserted so, we decided to go the Harbor Master's office. We saw you and a muscular man go into the Harbor Master's shack and we followed you two inside. You made a phone call to, I assume, your brother Mal, and told him the ship had been wrecked. Then the man with you talked on the phone for a while. After that, the two of you got back into your Zodiac and headed north." Make finished his soup and pushed the bowl back. "We drove along the ridge that followed the shore. It was forty or fifty feet above the water. For a while we couldn't see you because of the terrain. But, when you did come into view again, Ishe, you were laying across the center seat. We thought you were dead. Anyway, the man running the Zodiac tied up to a ladder on the side of your ship and went inside the super structure. Next, two other men came out and dragged you up on deck and left you there. The ship then backed off the rocks and headed south east. It kept going faster and faster, and the bow kept going deeper into the water. And it just plowed right down to the bottom of the Arabian Sea." Make scooted his chair back. "You and the Zodiac and a lot other stuff floated. I swam out to the Zodiac, got in it and paddled over to you. I pulled you into the boat and paddled to shore. I examined you, and your lungs were clear, but there was a needle mark on your neck. I assumed you'd been drugged because you were pretty much out of it. A group of Arabs came along and we talked to them. One said he was the chief of that area. He said he would take care of you so we left. Ishe, that's the whole story as I know it."

"Thanks again for saving my life, Mr. Caston. I don't know how I can ever repay you."

"Ishe, you don't need to repay me. We're good. Ok?"

"Thank you, Mr. Caston."

"Ishe, why don't you stay with us for a while?" Laura said. "Make is gone a lot and I get lonesome. I'd sure like to have man around the house. I would feel a lot better if you could stay here. Besides, you said you were just staying in an old hotel in Scottsdale. It's probably pretty hot down there. The weather is kind of nice up here in the mountains." Laura noticed Ishe's appearance. His cloths all seemed to be new but they looked very inexpensive. And, he wore well-worn shoes.

"Thank you Ms. Caston. That is very generous of you. Are you sure I wouldn't be in your way? I certainly wouldn't want to put you out."

“Ishe, I would like you to stay. We have lots of room. Down at the end of the hall there’s a nice bedroom with a TV, and it has an attached bathroom. I’m sure you would like it. ”

After Leanne left, Make stepped into his office to check his email.

“Hello Make. John Standard here. I have two things to wire you about:

1 A fellow called me from the states who said his name was Mal Thorp. He said he knew you and that you had told him to call me regarding the where-a-bouts of his brother Ishe. I naturally assumed that this was the villainous, Mal Thorp that you had told me about. I advised him of our adventure and how you had so gallantly swum out a quarter of a mile into the chilling sea to rescue his brother. He seemed surprised at this so I assured him of the truth of the matter saying I had witnessed the whole event myself. I also advised him that he might contact the Harbor Master at Nishtun in order to get more up to date information about his brother. He indicated to me that he had his own private plane and that he would fly to Nishtun in an attempt to retrieve his brother. He said he could not make this trip until six weeks from now however, because of pressing business elsewhere.

2 I just wanted to say again what a pleasant time I had while you were visiting. I felt we worked well together and I, for one, had a marvelous time at it. I feel we developed a true friendship while you were here.

I am in the early stages of planning to visit the place of my birth in the UK. The exact time has yet to be established however it will be soon. I was wondering if, while I was at it, I might just pop over to the states. I have been to the continent before but never the USA so it would be an adventure for me just to see your country. While there, if it is convenient for you, might we get together, as they say, just for a pint or two. I would like to at least take you and your wife Laura to dinner. In any event, I hope you have the opportunity and inclination to meet with me while I am there. I would consider it a great pleasure.

Your friend, John Standard"

Make clicked on 'REPLY'

John, we would love to see you. Tell me when you will arrive and where. Don't get a hotel room. You are staying with Laura and me. We have plenty of room.

We will show you around. Make

Laura reached for the keyboard:

John, I am so glad you are coming. Make has told me so much about your adventure. I look forward to meeting you. Laura

'SEND'

Chapter 46

Night time

Charleston, SC

Lester Cox, of Arab descent, was born in Sangar, Afghanistan 21 years ago. Sangar is a town in Ghazni Province. It is the center of Ajristan district and is located at an altitude of 2,623 M (8600 ft.) in the narrow valley formed by the Jikhai River. The winter snows were heavy, usually a meter deep. During the winter, goods or materials were frequently moved by walking on the snow and pulling a sled. He had fond memories of the valley where he lived. In the summer and early fall all the fields were green. The fields and paths were lined with beautiful willow trees and the steep hills were thick with poplar and ash. Fall was the time for beating the trees. Long poles were used to knock the leaves to the ground. The bark, small limbs, and leaves were then stored for feed for the animals during the winter when grazing was impossible. Bigger limbs were cut for fire wood. Although property lines were not clearly marked, his father generally harvested from behind the house to the crest of the hill. In front of the house was the road then the river.

He was the youngest of eight children and, in his Muslim family he was the one chosen by his father. His skin had a lighter hue than his father and his brothers, a subject that his relatives had discussed among themselves and with Aliyah Abd al-Rahman, Osama's right hand man. It had never been mentioned in his family but some even thought he had some features they had seen in the Russian warriors that had invaded his country. Had anyone ever spoken of this, his wife would have been killed and another woman chosen to tend the children and the household duties.

The Taliban was a continual presents in their lives. But, although he never spoke of it, as early as six, it seemed strange to him. He didn't like it and didn't want to be involved but no one knew of his feelings. He said his prayers five times a day when he had time and attended religious and political meetings but he frequently thought of his sisters. They were destined to be subservient to all men for the rest of their lives. He didn't think this was fair. When his father came home all his sisters and his mother had their heads covered. They remained motionless with heads bowed and their hands clasped together below their chins, yet he and his brothers were greeted and touched by their father.

His name in Sangar had been Seeza Jhahrans. When he was twelve he had been put on a freighter and with scant luggage and a note describing his name, Lester Cox and his address, 345 Indiana, Charleston, SC. He was sea sick almost the whole thirteen days of the trip. Finally, one evening the ship stopped and dropped anchor. The sea was calm and he recovered quickly only to discover the heat. He had never known such air temperature. In Sangar, at the elevation of 8600 feet the humidity was usually very dry and the temperature rarely got above 27 degrees C. Here it was humid and hot: near 40 C and the humidity was eighty percent. After dusk he heard people talking and went to the side of the ship to see the activity only to be told to go back to his sleeping area and gather up all his belongings. When he returned he was introduced to his new parents, the Vanderbarks. He was not surprised at this. It had been explained to him in Sangar.

He climbed into a small motor boat and they went swiftly across a lot of water. After a while, with no more seasickness, he began to see lights up ahead. Soon there were lights on both sides of him and he assumed he was in a river. He was very tired and went to sleep until he was awakened by his new parents. The man steering the boat pulled it up next to a small wooden dock and tied the craft only by the front. His new parents set his belongings and him upon the dock then climbed up themselves. He watched the boat back away from the dock and vanished in the darkness. Then they entered a car like he had only seen in pictures. He could see by the reflection of some distant lights that it was clean. He had only seen a few four wheeled vehicles and they were all small dirty trucks. This was his first car. He was eager for first light so he could see it. And it was even clean inside.

Life here was very different than what it had been in Sangar. There, school had been in a class room but there were only five pupils and they were all boys of different ages. Here everyone spoke American, different from the 'English' he had been taught in Sangar. And no one spoke Farsi. When he first met his new parents that night on the ship, he had spoken to them in the language he always used and they had understood him. However, they answered him in American and told him he should never speak Farsi again.

Les quickly learned, and there was a lot to learn. It was all so different that at first he rarely thought of his other family back in Sangar. He was not used to bathing so often. He had to take a shower every morning winter and summer. He grew to like it all and wished he could tell his old family, particularly his older brothers about everything. Sometimes he wished he could return, not to stay but just for a visit so he could tell everyone about what he had seen. But it was not to be. A few months after he had started his new life with his new family he received a letter from Sangar. His older brother, Assad, had been killed when a bomb he had made exploded while he was burying it at night. The letter also reminded Les of his religious teachings and of his purpose in life. He was told of the rewards he would receive when he went to heaven.

By age fifteen Les was completely Americanized both outside and inside. He had received several letters from his father always reminding him of the real work he was to do, yet never telling him what it was. Father always reminded him of jihad and of his duty. But Les wasn't interested in that crap. As far as he was concerned all that was something that belonged to another world. He was very fond of his American parents but he felt that if he told them how he felt about jihad they would be concerned. It seemed that it was very important to his real father that he be aware of his past life. Les wanted to get on with his American life instead.

His American parents treated him well and seemed to love him, a concept he had not heard of in Afghanistan. His father in Sangar had always spoken of loyalty and frequently reminded him that there was a purpose in his life, and he would be told of it when the time was right. Sometimes, when he was alone with his mother, she had held him tight to her and rocked him gently, but never when his father was around. Looking back on his life in Sangar It seemed to Les that there was no love between his mother and his father. To his father she was just someone to raise the children and keep the house and grounds in order.

He graduated from high school at age eighteen. That's when the Cox family moved to Fort Lauderdale, Florida. They bought a nice older house with a big back yard. He wanted a car of his own and his father said he would help him get a job in the shipyards. He was living at home and enjoying life when his parents introduced him to Vaughn, a man who looked more like his brothers. One Saturday they had a cookout. His mother fixed potato salad and his dad cooked steaks on the grill. Les was in charge of the lemonade. It was a wonderful afternoon, and after the food and dishes were put away Les and his parents and Vaughn sat around and talked. During that conversation it was suggested that Les move in with Vaughn and Vaughn seemed ok with the idea. It was time he was on his own, his parents said. That very day he gathered up his things and put them in the back of Vaughn's car. His mother wept when he and Vaughn said goodbye, but Vaughn assured his parents that he would keep in touch.

Les was surprised to find that a shipyard job was waiting for him. At first his only duty was to check the 'delivery to' address stenciled on the side of the shipping container with the manifest. He never found an error, but if he had, he was to report it to his boss. Vaughn also worked at the shipyard and helped Les learn more about shipping than stenciling letters on the sides of containers. They talked about work and sometimes had a beer together, but they did not become buddies. What Les didn't know was that Vaughn was his handler.

*　　*　　*　　*

One Friday, during the half-hour lunch time, Vaughn came to Les, "You have lived in this country six years and you have had a nice life," Les nodded yes. Vaughn continued, "Yet you have always known that someday you would be told what your duty was and you would be blessed with the opportunity to do it." There was a look of concern on Les's face when heard these words. *What is Vaughn talking about? I'm doing my duty here at the shipyard.* "There are two containers that are incorrectly marked. You will change the markings. I will tell you which ones to change. *This is some kind of bullshit? He doesn't know how containers should be marked. He's a hoist operator.*

"Vaughn, I think you're wrong but I'll check the manifest again and when I find the ones that are wrong I'll fix them." Les said.

"No. There is no need to check your manifests." Handing Les a single sheet of paper, Vaughn said, "This is your duty. This is your jihad." Les looked at the paper, *my God; he wants me to switch these two.* Vaughn, I can't do this. You are taking about sending military stuff to someplace in Laramie, Kansas and cattle food to the military weapons pool. That'd get my ass fired and probably put in jail."

"No you must do this. This is your duty. You will do your duty. And you will be taken care of. There will be no retribution. It is all arranged. When you have done this you will have done nothing wrong. Monday morning you will come back to work knowing you have done your duty. It is for Allah. And you will continue your nice life as you have before. I have put the containers in G section, number forty four and forty five, both on the ground. I have made it easy for you. Someday, there may be other duties for you to do. They may be more difficult for you. But you will do them also." Without saying anything else, Vaughn left.

There seemed to be no threat in Vaughn's voice. It was like he was stating facts. Les was sure that this was the wrong thing to do for the dock workers union and the Ajax Company. But perhaps he was too much into the American way. Maybe he should remember his roots. He thought of his real father's teachings and of jihad. What would happen if he didn't do it? What would happen if he did? He had the feeling that somehow he might end up with the short straw. If, after work, he went to Vaughn's and slept there tonight, would he wake up tomorrow?

The containers had been through customs and were ready for shipment. Sometime tonight or early the next morning they would be loaded on trailers headed for their designated home. Not knowing what to do or even how to decide what to do, Les found his phonebook. They were rare now, but he had managed to keep a reasonably new addition in one of his cabinets. *Department of Homeland Security,* 1-800-555-1212, He heard a deep voice, "Hello, this is Darwin P. Kingston the third, how can I help you?"

"Is this Homeland Security?"

"Yes it is. You have the right number."

"I'm a designator, checker at the docks in Fort Lauderdale. I work for the Ajax Company. I've just been told to re-identify two containers so that the military stuff goes to Kansas, and the army storage depot gets a load of dehydrated cattle food that no way can they use."

As soon as the man on the other end of the line heard this, he keyed his computer which started an alert signal. Another person at Homeland Security picked up on the line and also listened. All calls were recorded and reviewed. "Am I correct in thinking that if you do this, someone else will get what the army was meant to get?"

"Yeah, I'm scared to do it and scared not to do it, and I wouldn't put it past them to kill me even if I do switch them."

"What's your name and how old are you?"

"I'm Lester Cox and I'm twenty one." At this point a search was started for information on Lester Cox. The IRS records were made available. The FBI had his fingerprints, date of birth etc. Within an hour DHS knew much more about Lester ox than his natural father did.

"I need time to come up with a plan. How long before you have to make the switch?"

"I'll have to make one new stencil and it's about a twenty minute job to repaint the containers, and I have a half hour's report writing, I suppose I'll have to start in about an hour and a half from now."

"Good. Call me back in an hour, Can you do that?"

"Sometimes someone comes in here but they won't stay long, so I may be five or ten minutes late or early. That's about the best I can do."

"That will be good. When you call back I'll need some details about the shipments. Also do you have any brothers or sisters?"

"No, none at all. Why'd you ask?"

"Are there people there who know a lot about you, if you have siblings or not?"

"I think someone here knows a lot about me. Yes."

"How do we identify you?"

"I'm six foot even, 175 pounds, dark completed, with black hair."

"Where did you go to school?"

"Ft Lauderdale Central High. I graduated a year ago last spring."

"When you leave work, which gate will you come out of?"

"South east Forty First Street."

"Good, we are going to get you out of this. I'll be awaiting your call."

Les tried not to show how nervous he was when, forty five minutes after his talk with D.H.S., Vaughn came in his shack. "OH, shit. Vaughn. You surprised me. What are you doing here? You're supposed to be workin. Somebody will see you."

"It's taken care of. Are you ready?"

"Yeah, I'm ready. I've got the stencil made. I thought I'd do it around four. Most everybody is thinking about going home about then. Nobody will notice."

"That is a good plan. That's the time I would have chosen. I'll walk out with you when we go home. Wait for me."

When Vaughn was out of range and Les couldn't see anyone else headed for his shack, he called D.H.S., "Ah, good you're right on time. We have a plan. You should switch the marking as you have been told to do. An old school friend of yours will see you when you come out of the gate. She will be a very beautiful girl named Victoria. You call her Vic. She'll come toward you and call out your name. Is there any problem with that?"

"Maybe. The guy that told me to make the switches will walk out with me. That's not unusual. I live at his house"

"Victoria is a blond with shoulder length hair. She will be wearing a light yellow dress with small white flowers on it. How are you dressed and what is your name and how were you called in high school?"

"Wow. My name is Lester Cox and they called me Les in school. As for clothes, I'm wearing dark blue shorts and a white T-shirt that says 'Nova Scotia' on the front. And I wear dorkey shoes. Everybody has to wear steel-toed shoes here."

"Victoria will see you at the gate. She will ask you to come with her. She has a car. Go with her. There'll be other people there if there's any trouble. Do you see any problems with any of what I have said?"

"The only thing I see is Vaughn. He is one big fucker. He's probably six two and two hundred thirty pounds and he's strong, and he's a street fighter. So you probably should avoid fighting with him. Other than that, it seems great."

"Good. We'll meet at about five twenty. My name is Darwin P. Kingston the third."

"Yeah, I got that. Is she really, really good looking?"

Les has an aluminum pushcart with two wheels and a box bed. He loaded it with two cans of white spray paint and two cans of black He's made new stencils for 'The Trucker House', '345 Harrison, 'Laramie, Kansas 23456' He already had stencils for the army depot. Lots of containers went there. He pushed the cart to number G forty four and sprayed white paint over the Kansas address. He then leaned the Military address stencil down against the container and walked the fifty feet to G forty five. He sprayed white paint over the Army Depot address and went back to G forty four. The Military address stencil was gone. *Christ, I haven't been gone five minutes. Who took that fucking stencil*? He looked up and down the aisle but there was no one with the stencil. Finally he saw it around the corner at the end of the container. Someone had moved it out of the aisle. The military stencil had magnets attached to it so it held on to the side of the container where he placed it. As soon as he sprayed the black paint, he headed back to G forty five. The new stencil did not have magnets but he had brought some in his pocket. He quickly placed the stencil and painted the Kansas address on the container of military equipment. It had taken him longer than he had planned but it was still only 4:40 PM when he got back his shack. He was surprised to see Vaughn waiting outside his shack.

"Come. We must go." Vaughn said.

"I can't go just yet. I have to write up my report. It'll just take about 15 minutes".

"Write for five minutes then we must to go!"

"Ok. You put the paint away over there and the stencils in that box there and I'll write my report. Vaughn, you said yourself; we want to do everything the way it's usually done. Why are you in such a hurry anyway? You said all this was taken care of."

"It is all taken care of but you're right, we should not do anything out of the usual way. Write your report. Just don't linger. That's all."

At 4:55 they started walking toward the exit gate. As they stepped out of the gate onto the main drive, "Les, Les." A beautiful girl came toward them with outstretched arms.

"My God. Is that Victoria? Hey Vic, what the hell are you doing here?" She threw her arms around him and kissed his cheek. It's good to see you Les."

"Yeah, it's good to see you too. You look great Vic. It's been a couple of years."

"Come on Les. I've got a car."

'Great. Where're we going?"

"Les, I'm sorry to interrupt," Vaughn said. "But it's important that we leave now."

"Oh, hey Vaughn, this is Victoria Nelson. We went to high school together."

Vaughn put his hand firmly on Les's arm, "No Les, we must go together now. It's is important that we are not late for your doctor's appointment."

Two men behind them have been arguing. Just then, the bigger of the two shoved the other man who, in turn, grabbed Vaughn as he tried unsuccessfully to keep from falling. He turned Vaughn halfway around and nearly pulled him over. Then the big man grabbed Vaughn by both shoulders and pulled him back, "get outta th way buddy. I'm gonna get that little son of a bitch."

"The smaller man, who was pushed, quickly got up and got behind Vaughn, using him as a shield. Vaughn, who had been rotated 180 degrees, was momentarily confused by all this. The hassle continued and by the time Vaughn got turned around Les was in Vic's car, driving away.

The girl was a very good driver. She got them on the Port Everglades Expressway and quickly put a lot of distance between them and the shipyard. Her real name was Xandra Hunter. She had volunteered to be a marine and had training at Quantico where she'd been graded 'superior' in every field problem. Because of the sudden loss of her parents, she was given an honorable discharge. She was the only family member left to care for her grandparents. Now, to make ends meet, she worked some for DHS.

Customs inspection procedures' for incoming material

Inspection of shipments from overseas

1. **Two Containers one from France and one from Argentina are Craned off the ship and loaded onto container chaises (trailer).**

2. **The containers are taken to the Customs building.**

3. **They back the container to the dock inside Customs.**

4. **After the containers are moved to the Custom's dock, the tractors leave and the Customs doors are locked.**

5. **A US Customs officer cuts seals and opens the container's doors.**

6. **The crates are unloaded out of the container by forklift.**

7. **Customs inspectors examine all of the crates from France and open them. There are twenty Tivars per box, 210 boxes. Each box weighs 185 pounds. There are 4200 Tivars in the container for a total weight of 38,850 pounds, net value is $4,400,000.**

8. **The US Customs Officer examines all crates from Argentina. There are twenty four bags of dehydrated**

cattle food per crate, 200 crates. Each crate weighs 185 pounds. There are 4800 bags in the container for a total weight of 37,000 pounds, net value is $24,000.

9. **Crates from Argentina are loaded back into the container then container is sealed.**

10. **US Customs Officer inspects all products from France then has them repackaged into crates. Crates are loaded into the container and container is sealed.**

11. **Both containers are transported to a secured storage yard by longshoreman truck drivers.**

12. **Hoist operator (Longshoreman) removes both containers from truck chaises and locates them in spaces G forty four and G forty five.**

13. **Senior Longshoreman checks containers against manifest and records storage location per policy.**

14. **Containers are reloaded onto chaises and picked up by an owner operated trucking company (Like US Logistics) and are driven to their destination.**

Chapter 47

Friday evening

The Department of Homeland Security, Ft Lauderdale, Florida

Les sat at the interview table. First they discussed the two shipments and almost immediately a decision was reached. They decided to properly mark the containers and make sure they were on the right truck headed to the right place. This was accomplished by having one of their men go to the Customs headquarters on the dock and tell them the situation. All Customs workers have a 'Q' clearance so it was felt that there would not be any part of a Muslim terrorist cell within the Customs organization. Customs was able to correct the marking and get the two containers on their way.

The next part of the problem, however, was more complicated. It was decided early in the discussion that, despite his heritage, Les was not a terrorist; he loved living in America and was interested in doing the right thing.

Les sat in on the next problem solving discussions. He didn't have much to say but it was interesting. Four men sat at their computers and wrote. What they wrote came up on a large wall screen. And then they all decided there were four major problems:

1 What was to become of the relationship between Les and Vaughn?

2 Where did Vaughn get his instructions?

3 Was Vaughn being blackmailed or otherwise forced to switch containers?

4 Was there a terrorist cell behind this and if so how to handle it?

"Les, we want you to keep working just as you have been doing. Would you be willing to do that?" Asked Darwin P Kingston.

"Sure, I like my job."

"There will be a little more to it. We will want to be in daily contact with you. Can you do that?"

"Sure."

"We'll be asking you what is going on in your area of the shipyard. We'll want to know about what Vaughn is doing and your relationship with him. It's sort of like spying. Would you feel comfortable with doing all that?"

"I guess so. We aren't good buddies or anything like that. We just live in the same house. He does try to control me a lot though. But I guess he is just trying to make sure I get to work on time. When we were leaving for work this morning he was really uptight. He practically pushed me into the car."

"Did he leave the house last night?"

"I don't know. I just went to bed."

"See, that's the kind of thing we might want to know."

"I understand. I might like being a spy, who knows?"

"Les, I think that's all for right now. We're going to put you up in a nice hotel for tonight. We'll pick you up tomorrow and feed you a nice breakfast. Then we'll bring you here for some more talk. After that you'll go back to your house. Victoria will drive you there, just as if you had spent the night with her."

"I've got an idea that could save you guys some money."

"Forget it, Les. She's not in our section; we just have her do jobs for us from time to time. I'm not sure but I think she's married and has two little kids."

* * * *

It was late when Les was driven to a very nice hotel in downtown Fort Lauderdale. It was the nicest room he had ever been in. He was told he could order anything he wanted. When the two agents said 'good night' Les lay on the bed and looked around at his surroundings. He was in awe. It was like when his new parents had first picked him up. That had been awesome too. *I'm a spy. I'm a government spy and I'm only twenty one years old.* Les looked all around the room to see if there were hidden cameras. Before he went to bed he even checked the mirror in the bathroom to see if someone was on the other side watching him.

His night was not uneventful. He had a spy dream. He had been given the job of finding a group of mafia drug runners but he could never find them. It was a constant frustration, and he suspected they were watching him. His computer had a big screen on the wall and he used that a lot in his search for the bad guys. Then he found out that the camera hidden in the screen was hooked up to the mafia's computer and they had been watching him watch them. This revelation was so disturbing that he woke up. It was 2:22 AM. It seemed like minutes later when he was awakened again. This time it was the phone near his bed. It was Saturday morning.

"Good morning Les. You up for some breakfast? We're in the lobby."

"I'm not even up. But I'll be down there in a few minutes."

On the way to the restaurant Les told Kingston and the other agent of his dream. He remembered every bit of it. "Les, this is not like 007. It's a temporary thing till we find out what's going to happen with Vaughn. We will just be asking you what's he doing and how you and he are getting along, that's all."

"What's 007?"

"Do you have a computer?"

"No, I have to get a car first, then the next buy will be a computer."

Kingston said to the other agent, "You know, I think some compensation is appropriate in this situation. Why don't we ask your secretary to check out a nice mini laptop for Les?"

Les spent part of the day with the DHS men. Then, to his delight, he was put in Victoria's car that evening and she headed toward Vaughn's house. "Vic, what's your real name? If we are going to get to know each better I should at least know who you are."

"Just from a work standpoint, I think it is important that we stick with Vic. If you knew my real name you might accidently slip up some time and say it. That would blow my cover and make me useless to DHS, and it would do the same for you. And besides, what makes you think we're going to get to know each other?"

"I know what you're thinking. You're thinking that neither of us knows anything about the other – and you're right. So what I know about you is that I think you are very nice and I like the way you drive a car. If we really had been classmates, I'd know more about you. I just think it would be more professional if we knew more about each other. I have an idea. Let's go somewhere and get something to eat. My treat."

"That's a nice offer Les, but not tonight."

"Ok, how about this? They gave me this new computer and I need some help getting it set up. Could you help with that?"

By now they had stopped in front of Vaughn's and Les's house, "Les, there isn't any 'set up' here. You don't have a router here do you?"

"I don't think so." Les could barely concentrate on the computers; he was so hot for her. He really didn't know what a router was but he would say anything to delay her leaving.

"What are you going to do tomorrow, Sunday? Do you go to church or something?" She asked.

"No, but even if I did I'd give it up to go out with you."

"My God Lester. Calm down. What I was going to say is, why don't I meet you at that Starbucks on the corner about nine tomorrow morning. We can get a donut and they have Wi-Fi. They don't mind if you set there all day if you buy a cup of coffee occasionally. We can practice your computer skills."

"I would really appreciate that. I need a lot of help, more than you know."

"Lester, I think I know, so just keep it in your pants, Ok? This is not some romantic interlude; we are just going to talk about your computer."

"Ok, I'll be there at nine."

* * * *

At 9 AM Sunday morning, Xandra walked into the Starbucks, "Hi Lester. How are you this morning?"

"I don't know. Something happened. Vaughn wasn't there this morning and his car is gone. Actually I don't know if he's gone or not. I just haven't seen him since Friday. I called to talk to Mr.

Kingston and got someone else. When I told him Vaughn was missing he seemed pretty concerned and told me to stay right here and not go back to the house. What do you think?"

"I think they're concerned for your safety, that's what. Lester, I've been doing this for a couple of years longer than you have. I think someone from DHS is going to come through that door pretty soon and take you away to a safer place."

"Vic, I had to tell them. I thought it was important. I thought he might have been killed."

"You did the right thing, Les. Don't worry about it."

Immediately, a black car double-parked right outside the door and three men got out. The first one stopped at the door, and Darwin and another man came in. The second man went into the other part of Starbucks, and Darwin came directly to their table. "Xandra, you're here. Good. Come on, both of you, we've got to go right now. You two walk straight to the car and get in the back. Go."

In the car Xandra started to say…Darwin held up his hand for silence. He was listening to a report. There was an ear bud in his right ear. When he lowered his hand, Darwin said, "Vaughn is not in the house or on the grounds anywhere. And there doesn't seem to be any suspicious person around either. We are sending a team to check it out."

"What's to check out if he's not there?"

"There was a cheap bug in his phone. Low output. That means that somewhere close by there's a repeater. If it's also the cheap kind, the type that has a memory chip, we may get lucky."

Les loved the excitement. He sat close to Xandra. Very close. Even closer than necessary. And she smiled.

Later Les and Xandra were put up in a different hotel than the one Les was in the previous evening. They were in separate, adjoining rooms and were told that it would be best if they strayed in their rooms. "Just order what you want." Later, when Les was in Xandra's room they sat next to each other with Les's laptop on the small table in front of them. Xandra tried to show Les something about the computer and Les kept putting his hand on Xandra's leg. Les didn't learn anything about computers and finally Xandra jumped up and turned out the light. She pulled him up in front of her, kissed him lightly and said, "If we are going to do this, we are going to do it right."

Chapter 48

Friday afternoon, August 10, l0 AM

Make's Scottsdale home

Laura was sitting on a gardening stool on the back patio planting several pallets of petunias. It's was 10 AM on a beautiful morning. Make was in the office writing when there was a knock on the front door sill. The door had been left open because of the wonderful weather. In the hills of north Scottsdale, when the temperature drops below about eighty five, the comfort level outside is perfect. *But who would be knocking? We're pretty remote out here.* Make didn't want to leave his work but the knocking persisted. Finally he left the office. Rounding the corner into the great room he saw Mal Thorp standing in front to the open doorway. He quickly back stepped to get out of Mal's view, hurried back into the office and retrieved his Glock. Stepping back just barely into the great room again, "Thorp, what the hell do you want?"

"I just want to talk to you that's all."

"Ok, talk."

"Where are you? I can't even see you. How can I talk to you if I can't see you?"

"Have you got a gun?"

"No, I haven't got a gun. This is just a friendly visit."

"That's bullshit. We're not friends. What do you want?" Make has looked Mal over and it appears that he is unarmed. *But you never can tell.*

"That's what I wanted to talk to you about. I want to talk to you about our relationship," Mal said.

"Ok, first I want you to know that I have a gun, and if you do anything suspicious I will shoot you. If you want to come in, knowing that, walk straight in about ten feet and stop. You can either do that or get off my property."

Mal started walking, "It's kind 'a dark in here. I can't even see where I am going." Mal was facing the rear of the great room which was all open to the outside. The bright glare of the sun, reflected off of the pool, was in his face.

"Stop right there. I'm about ten feet on your right. So if you have something to say that's important to me, start talking."

"Is this really it? I was thinking something like you asked me to come out on the veranda and you offer me some lemonade or something."

"Are you shitting me? You really thought that?"

"No of course not. It would be nice, that's all."

"I'll tell you what. Don't move. Don't even blink. I'll be back in a minute. Don't leave that spot. Do not move, do you understand that?"

"Yes, I understand. I won't move."

Make went through the room to the veranda where Laura was. "Honey, Mal Thorp is here. He said he wants to talk."

"I didn't hear any shots. Did you use a silencer? You can make those out of an empty beer can, you know."

"Funny. I want to hear what he has to say but I want him out here in the light where we can both see him. I want you to go get your gun and come out here and keep it hidden under your apron or someplace. I'll sit in front of him and you sit to the side of him. Will you do that?"

"I'll be back in one minute, gun under my apron or some place." She returned almost immediately.

"Ok, Thorp walk straight out here." Make said. "Good. Now you sit here. Laura, you remember Mr. Thorp. He wants to talk to us." Laura sat on Mal's left side and Make sat facing him. "Ok Thorp, talk."

"I want your support. Mal said. "I'm going to run for governor. You are a prominent doctor and several different people come into your office every day. If they have an opportunity to see my picture or my flyer in your office, maybe half of them will vote for me; provided of course, that they think you are going to vote for me."

"If that's all you've got, get out. That is really dumb. You must be completely nuts. And I would never vote for you,"

"It's not dumb. I will be the next governor of this state."

Laura said, "You can't be governor of Arizona. You don't even live here." She looked at Thorp—compared him to his twin, Ishe. The faces were the same but Ishe was slightly smaller.

Make said, "Besides that, you're a crook."

"Actually, I do live here. I've been a resident of this state for four days now. Also, I have a business here that's been in place for three years and I've been paying all associated taxes."

"But, you're a crook! Recently, you were picked up for soliciting a prostitute."

"I was never charged for that or brought before a judge. There is no record of that."

"But I know about it" Make said. "I was in Albuquerque that day, looking for you. There are probably a lot of other people who know about it too.

"That's one of the reasons I want your support. And besides that, look at my opponents, Joey Stiff was jailed for getting a blow job in the back seat of a taxi. When that comes out, he won't have a prayer. He'd have a better chance if he filed in Vegas. And Henderson, the state Attorney General. He's been in court more times trying to stay out of jail than he has been trying to put people in jail. And Melissa Jolie. She is the most radical person on border control anyone has ever seen. She said she's going to have the President of the United States arrested. She's a nut. And Marven Newman owes more back taxes than he can ever pay off. They are going to take his mansion and his Bentley. Soon he will be living in a trailer and driving a six year old Mustang."

"The FBI has been watching you."

"Maybe they have. What of it? They watch lots of people. They've never said anything to me about it."

"You were picked up for selling illegal drugs you brought up here from Mexico."

"I think maybe, yes I think I remember them talking to me about that, but I was never charged with anything. My opponent Henderson, on the other hand, has been brought before a Grand Jury and has been indited. Don't you see? I have better credentials than all of my opponents. Remember Teresa Snickers? She filed but was brought up on drug charges the next day. She never got out of the gate. I don't do drugs. I am going to be the next governor."

"You were involved in manufacturing explosives in Yemen. You were going to help terrorists who were going to kill people all over the world."

"Why do you say that? You don't know that."

"I know that because I know you, Thorp. You would not hesitate to get into any kind of business that would make you a nice profit."

"Not true. I paid for the remodeling and renovation of a ship off the coast of Yemen in international waters. That's all I did. Unfortunately it later sank. There is no indication of any explosives involved. If you have heard otherwise it's a misrepresentation. So you can see, there are no negative things in my past. And you haven't heard about my platform yet. I'm running on the Democratic ticket. I'm going to be in favor of abortions, very liberal on our existing gun laws, tough on illegal immigrants, but fair, and I'm going to do so in a manner that will get the blessing of the Democratic Party and maybe even the President."

Laura interrupts, "If you're a Democrat, you should never have filed. You wasted your money. This is Arizona. They don't have democratic governors in this state."

"What you say is true and it has mostly been true in the past. But right now, in this state, there are nearly as many Independents as there are either Democrats or Republicans. I can get fifty five percent of the Democrat's vote and thirty two percent of the Independent's vote. That's a majority. I'm going to be the next governor of the great state of Arizona."

"Mal, this is crazy. There is no way you are going to get to be governor. It just can't happen."

"Why can't it happen?"

"At this point I don't know, but I know it won't happen. Thorp, I don't like you but even if I did, even if I was your best friend, I would have to tell you it won't happen."

"Make, I know we've had our differences but those are petty in comparison to the gubernatorial race. This is important. It is important to the state and it is important to you and me. For the moment, I can see that I haven't convinced you but you should remember that it is good to get on the bandwagon early. Stragglers tend to get the hind tit, if you get my meaning."

"I suppose you are talking about bribes. I'm not interested."

"No I'm not talking about bribes. But you know as well as I do that there are a limited number of favors given out in any political situation. That's what I'm talking about."

"Go away Mal. I've got some important things to do. Laura and I are planting petunias in the back yard garden, and you are wasting our time."

"Ok, I'm leaving, but think it over. Watch the local news and you'll see. I'm going to be the governor of Arizona." Mal turned and walked out the front door. Make followed him far enough to be sure that he had indeed left the property.

After Mal had gone and Make had come back in the house, Laura asked, "What do you think? Is there any chance he will make it? He had pretty good comebacks for everything you brought up."

"Yeah, he did but I just can't imagine him getting to be governor. He's a crook. But he has a point. If you watch the six o'clock news, all the people running for that office have short commercials advertising themselves and their ads mostly consist of telling how their opponents are crooked. And they are mostly right. I think Mal came here because he doesn't know what I know about the ship-wreck in Yemen and he wanted to find out. He thinks I know more than I really do." Make puts his gun on 'safety'. "John Standard and I heard a long distance phone conversation initiated by Ishe. Mostly, Ishe was crying, but the gist of it was, Ishe was telling Mal the ship was wrecked, everything was lost, and he was sorry. The words 'terrorist' and 'explosive' were never mentioned so I really couldn't prove that they were making explosives for terrorist groups. And, I think that's why Ishe wanted to get in touch with me. He knows all about what they were doing on that ship which probably included making explosives. He may be worried about what Mal will do to him. I know Mal would want to make sure that there is no way Ishe could be made to testify about what was done on the *Golden Lie* and what connection Mal had with the ship, the manufacturing program, the people they were making explosives for and everything about the whole process. I wonder if Ishe will ever tell us all the details."

"I'm sure glad Ishe didn't come out of his room while Mal was here. That would have been a catastrophe all the way around." Make went to his land line phone and dialed. "Hello Isabell. Sorry to bother you but there is something you should know before your meeting tomorrow morning. Mal Thorp dropped by this morning to tell us he is running for the governor of Arizona."

Immediately, Make's cell rang, "Is he serious and do you think he might win?"

"I believe he is serious but the whole idea is unbelievable. I can hardly imagine him winning but, I have to admit, he sounded pretty good."

"Well what did he say?"

"It was a pretty long speech but here's what he said.

He said he's had a business in this state for three years and he's been paying all associated taxes on it. And he's been a resident for four days. I guess he bought a house someplace in Arizona. Laura and I mentioned the illegal things he has been involved in and, one by one, he disavowed each one. Either he was never charged with whatever we accused him of or somehow there is no record of it. As an example, I mentioned that he was picked up for soliciting a prostitute. They just let him go the next morning. Then Thorp mentioned Joey Stiff. It was in the papers and on the news. He was getting a blow job in a taxi and got in a fight with the cabbie. Stiff was put in jail. Anyway the conversation went on and on like that. And he listed, one by one, his opponents and described their offences. They are all blatant. They are or have recently been on the six o'clock news. Their offences are out there for everyone to see. Mal is a crook and maybe a worse crook than his opponents. But he is either a smarter crook than they are or a luckier crook than they are. All his opponents have been caught or have been accused of a crime and the press loves that. However, I believe there's another reason for his visit. I think he was trying to find out about what I know about what happened in Yemen, and I bet he's looking for Ishe. Unlike me, Ishe knows exactly what happened and his testifying would blow away Mal's chances of winning. A few words about explosives and terrorists and Mal wouldn't have a chance. Isabell, do you know how lucky we were that Ishe didn't come out of his room while Mal was here? I'm not going to tell Ishe that Mal was here and just hope Mal doesn't come back.

* * * *

It was an August Saturday, about 8:30 PM when the Castons welcomed John Standard. He told them of his travels to England and Scotland and the friends he had known there. There was lots of catching up to do. Make and Laura told him of the recent events with Mal, and reintroduced him to Ishe. Within a few days John Standard was completely acclimated.

* * * *

Tuesday, Make's land line rang, "Hello Georgia."

"Make, I think you should call Darwin P Kingston, Ft Lauderdale DHS. He just called and said it's urgent.

"Thanks Georgia." Make dialed, "Hello Mr. Kingston. This is Make Caston. What's happening?" He put the phone on speaker so John Standard could hear. "My friend, John Standard is here and can hear this conversation too."

Darwin said, "Lester Cox has been told to switch addresses on two different containers again."

"Do you know what's in the containers?"

"Yes, we checked the manifest. One contains 9600 aluminum lawn chairs to be shipped to the salt mine in Kansas City, Kansas. Their net weight twenty four ton. The other one contains 200 boxes of dill pickles. It's addressed to Cisco Foods in Walla, Walla, Washington."

"When are they scheduled to be shipped?"

"I checked on that. Scheduling said that containers are backed up worse than they've ever seen. Right now, cat.3 stuff, sealed food like pickles, is two and a half weeks to get to Customs. And furniture is cat. 5. That'll probably take five or six weeks to get to Customs. When and if they switch addresses, they effectively switch categories at the same time. They would've been better to switch with a container of fresh fish. We are trying to rush everything but there is just no way."

"So if they make the switch, we are looking at five weeks or more, right?"

"Yes, that's what Scheduling told me just a few minutes ago."

“Ok. Go ahead and switch addresses. Let’s see where they go. We have plenty of time to change our minds”

Kingston said, “Actually they won’t be able to get the containers in place to make the switch for two more days. The containers have to be at ground level before Les can repaint the addresses.”

"How are the pickles packaged? You said boxes.”

“Yeah there are 200 boxes in there. They are boxes of four jars per box and eight pickles per jar. That is thirty two pickles per box. The whole box weighs about thirty five pounds, PETN, jars, boxes and all. Make, that container holds 3 1/2 tons and half of it is PETN. That turns out to be 3200 pickles. Somebody must be planning on doing something big.”

John had heard Make’s end of the call. He said, “Someone else must have gotten the process perfected too. I believe you said this is the first big shipment that has gotten this far.”

“You’re right about that, John, and we have to find out what it is they plan to do before the pickles get to Walla, Walla…Darwin, has Vaughn ever been found?”

“There is no trace of him.”

“Who told Les to make the switch? Is it somebody that Les knows?”

“No. Les said he had never seen him before and from the description Les gave us, we think he doesn’t work in the shipyard. There’s a camera at each gate but we can’t find him on either one. Actually the shipyard’s not that secured. It would be pretty easy for someone to ride in on a container if the hoist man was so inclined.”

“Thanks for calling Darwin. Keep close to this and please call me if there’s any change.”

Chapter 49

Make's home

Pizz, John and Make were sitting at the breakfast table. They finished eating and were enjoying the morning. It was Sunday. Laura was on the other side of the breakfast island when Make said, "I'm going to call Isabell to wish her happy birthday." He dials, smiling.

Isabell's phone rings, "Make, it's Sunday."

Make said, 'I know but it's your birthday and I just wanted to wish you a happy one. "

"Oh thank you. That's nice. How are you doing?"

"Great. Laura and John Standard, Sargent Pizzametski and I are just sitting in the early morning sunshine. We finished breakfast and I was thinking about you and thought I'd call."

At this point, Laura, John, and Pizz all say 'happy birthday Isabell', more or less at the same time."

"Thank you all. That's very nice. And I have something interesting and nice to tell you. I have a date tonight. I've been asked to have dinner with the President. He is having a birthday party for me."

Isabell heard lots of oo's and ah's. Then Make said, "That's really great Isabell. Lucky you."

"What are you going to wear? Laura asked. "Did you go out and buy something?"

"You bet your ass I did. I spent half of yesterday shopping. I got a dress from Neiman Marcus that I saw a few days ago. I have wanted to buy it but I didn't really have a use for it. But now I do, so I just got it. It cost an arm and a leg of course. And I got a white jacket to go with it. That's another arm and a leg. But I figured I may never have this opportunity again so what the hell."

Laura said, "You did the right thing. That just great. I'd like to hear about it sometime. I've never been to anything even close to as fancy and important as that."

"Laura, I'll call you some time. We'll talk. So Make, back to business, what's happening?"

"Lester Cox, the kid that works at the dock at Ft. Lauderdale, has been told to switch addresses on a couple of containers again. One contains lawn chairs to be shipped to the salt mine and the other contains pickles to go to Cisco in Walla Walla Washington. Those pickles aren't dill. We've told him to go ahead and make the switch. I'm told, however, that there's such a backup at the dock that nothing will happen to either container for five weeks so I am going to have to wait on that. I want to see where they're going before I confiscate them. I have a man checking on the salt mine in Kansas City but so far, there's been nothing unusual going on there. Actually it is pretty quiet right now."

"Ok, thanks for the call guys. I'll let you know how my birthday party at the Whitehouse goes. Bye."

* * * *

The Kansas City Star

Make was in his office at home. It was Sunday, just before lunch, when he got a call form Don T. Park saying Make should pull up the Saturday, August 16th issue of the *Kansas City Star*. sas Ci is a brief article about the sale of the salt mine in KC Kansas. And there is a picture of Mal Thorp." Make wasted no time getting the business page of the *Star* on his tablet.

He stepped into the great room, “Laura, John, Pizz, look at this,” he said. “First here’s a picture of Mal shaking hands with a red headed man” Make held up his tablet for Laura, Pizz, and John to see. ”Listen to this, “Phoenix business man, Mal Thorp, has purchased the locally owned salt mine storage company for an undisclosed amount from Real estate developer, Dow Kohman. The mining of salt in the area was started around the late 1800’s and was operated as a producing salt mine until 1936 when the price of salt made further mining unprofitable. It remained unused until 1941 when the US Government purchased the rights to store documents in the mine and it was limited to use by the government until 1951 when it was returned to the original owners. Kohman purchased the mine in 1951 for fourteen hundred dollars and has operated it as a storage vault ever since. Thorp indicated that there will be no changes in the operation of the storage facility and there will be no changes in the employee’s duties or status. Mr. Thorp indicated that there is room for more storage in the facility and he intends to expand. “There is an unused portion that has, here to fore, been sealed off. This area will provide an additional sixty thousand square feet of storage area. We intend to add more lighting and an automated material locating and retrieval system.” When asked how he chose this particular business to invest in, Mr. Thorp indicated that he has been a frequent customer of the salt mine and always thought it had great potential. Thorp said he intends to get information about the valuable aspects of salt mine storage to the general public. He said most people just think of it as another store room. “But it’s more than that. The relative humidity and temperature inside the facility never varies. I can guarantee seventeen percent relative humidity and fifty two degrees year around.” When asked when the actual transaction would take place, Thorp said, “It’s a done deal.”

Make said, “Thorp is amazing. In this article, he is painted as a completely different person than he really is. He has almost never worked; he has done a lot of crooked deals and now this. Now he's a local Phoenix business man who can afford to buy a salt mine for an undisclosed amount. And besides that, he's going to run for governor."

John admitted, "Yes he does seem like a man of many talents."

"John, you don't know this guy, but I do. I know he's up to something. Most of his life he's been nearly broke. Now he buys a piece of property that's pretty valuable. I wonder if there's any connection between that purchase and the three and a half tons of high explosives. Mal's a crook, a con man. He's not a Muslim. How does he fit in? I'll bet he plans on making a fast buck on the salt mine some way."

* * * *

The next day, Make called Don Park back, "Don, is anything happening at the mine?"

"No, my man drives by several times a day. He said it looks like business as usual."

"Don, I'd like you to start a continuous watch on the salt mine. Is there ever anything happening at night?"

"Not that we have seen. Their summer schedule is from 6:30 AM till 5:30 PM. By 6 PM everything is locked up and they've all gone home."

"Ok, can you start continuous surveillance tomorrow morning?"

"Yes. I'll have a man there at 6 AM tomorrow."

"Don, one other thing, in the article, Mal Thorp is described as a business man. That's not what he is. That guy has never worked; he has done a lot of crooked deals and now this. Try to find out more about the sale. How much did he pay for it, where did he get the money? Can you do that?"

"I'll have the price of the sale tomorrow morning. I'll call you. It'll take longer to find where he got the money but I'll work on it."

* * * *

That evening, in their bedroom, Make and Laura were talking, "Make, you have changed. I heard part of that conversation with Park. You use to do all that kind of thing yourself. Now you are having someone else doing it. What's going on with you anyway?"

"Well, John's here and we are having a good time together. This morning we were up at five and took a walk. It's cool that time of day and the sun has not gotten to this side of the hill yet. We walked up to that old mine shaft. It was great. You should go with us. We are going to do it again tomorrow."

"Oh ok, I will if you'll wake me up. But back to what I asked about, is that it? Have you changed just because John is here?"

"No there is more than that, there is Ishe. I don't understand Ishe. He's been here a week now and I can't tell if he is a good guy and innocent like he seems or if he is just faking it. It's possible he's a high performance autistic. Right now, he's interesting. He just doesn't talk much except about a limited number of subjects. But he seems happy or, at least he's not unhappy. And he isn't afraid Mal will find him so he appears to be comfortable here."

"So you've changed because we've got two house guests?"

"No…Laura, I really failed in Yemen. If those guys on the Golden Lie hadn't sunk themselves, they'd have gotten away. I didn't do anything but watch. I like my job but I'm worried that I can't do it."

"You mean you're worried that you can't kill anybody."

"Yeah."

"Make, I love you. And I've got a lot of confidence in you. You saved Ishe's life. That's a major, major accomplishment. I think you did just right in Yemen."

Chapter 50

Near Thomson peak, North Scottsdale, Arizona

On Tuesday, at 6 AM, on a bright sunny day, Make, John and Laura are on a hike in the hills near the peak when Make's cell vibrated. Make announced, "Its Darwin P Kingston, Fort Lauderdale DHS" He put the phone on speaker and held it so everyone could hear. "Hello Darwin. What's up?"

"Bad news, Make. The pickles container is gone."

"What do you mean? Where did it go? How did it get through Customs?"

"I don't know, I don't know, and it didn't go through customs. We are checking every container in this whole docking facility, and, so far, there is no sign of it. It certainly isn't where it should be."

John and Laura each select rocks of the appropriate size and sit down.

"Can't you do an aerial survey and find it?"

"Make, we hadn't put a designator on it yet. We thought it would take at least five weeks before it got through customs. With a can of spray paint one could completely change its identity. The whole country is covered with containers. They are being hauled everywhere. Hell, people buy them for garages, there are even people living in containers."

"My God, how could they lose that thing?"

"Make, I don't know where the pickles are but I think it might be a good idea to check all the containers in Walla, Walla, and all the containers going to the salt mine."

"Jesus Christ...Open up the container that has lawn chairs in it. See if it has pickles in it. How many containers are there in Walla, Walla, anyway?"

"I don't know. Maybe a thousand, maybe five thousand. Oh, and the other thing is, Les Cox is gone. He was never seen after he checked out last night."

"Oh shit. He may have been kidnapped. Maybe they've locked him in the container. That's very bad... Darwin, thanks for keeping us posted"

"Guys, I'm going back to the house. I'm not sure why, but I think I should be there. You can keep walking if you want to."

John said, "I'll go back with you."

Then Laura said, "Sure, let's go back." They all started trudging back down the trail. It seemed as if it had clouded up. Then Makes cell vibrated again. Make said, "It's Colonel Wright. Hello Colonel.

"I wanted to tell you that Mal's plane has been pretty much on the ground for a while, but now it has made two round trips to Ft. Lauderdale and back in the last fifteen hours."

"Do you mean back to Albuquerque?"

"No, Kansas City International. Make, he's apparently been staying in KC for about a week now."

"That's very interesting. Are you able to get an idea of what he is up to?"

"No, not really, sorry Make. Both airports are so busy, cars and trucks are all over. We've looked but we haven't been able to see who's getting in or out of his plane anywhere. We did get one picture of a big white Dodge pickup with a blue tarp in back. It was pointed toward the hangar where Mel has kept his plane in Ft. Lauderdale, but we don't really know that it's going to go inside the hanger."

"Thanks Colonel, I appreciate the call. If you see any more activity please call me." *And Mal just bought an underground d storage facility.*

"You got it Make. Goodbye."

Two round trips from Lauderdale to KC and back. How much will his plane carry, I wonder. Make googled Mal's plane stats. "Thirty six hundred sixty pound payload. "John, look at this." In their heads they are all dividing 3 ½ tons in to two parts. Almost at the same time they say, "Three and a half tons! Mal could have taken three and a half tons of PETN from Ft Lauderdale to Kansas city in two trips."

"Then why did they steal the container?" John said. "That's where the PETN is. What is going on here?"

Chapter 51

Tuesday morning, 8:30 AM

Make's house

While Laura scrambled eggs Make said, "Guys, I have to call Isabell. I am going into my office."

"It's about ready."

"Go ahead. Don't wait on me. This will only take five minutes then I'll be right back"

A half-hour later, John and Laura had finished breakfast and Makes eggs were cold. "That was a long five minutes. Is everything ok?" Laura asked.

"Only marginally. Isabell spent a lot of time telling me that it was my job to take care of the Muslim problem in America. I told her what steps I had taken and she said that was good. Then she again told me that it was my problem to fix and I'd better do it."

"Well, you didn't get fired did you?"

"No, she's worried. That's all. Remember, she had to fire my two bosses about a month ago and Isabell is worried that her organization looks shaky to the President. If this thing would unravel she'd probably be asked to resign for 'health reasons'. I tried to comfort her by reminding her that Homeland Security is a relatively new and unusually powerful organization. It might be reasonable to expect some problems. She said she didn't want to hear that from me. But it's true. Since its inception, DHS security has done a lot and has accomplished a lot of good things. And another branch, TSA has had lots of bad press. I didn't remind her about that."

Before John could reply they heard a noise out front, then they heard the front door open. Make was on high alert, scrambling in the drawer for his Glock. But Laura said, "For Christ sakes Make. What's wrong with you? It's just Pizz. He said he was coming over. He has some news."

"Good morning everybody. Have you all noticed what a beautiful day it is?" Pizz and John had met earlier in the week. John said, "Good morning to you Sargent. You are correct, it is truly beautiful here".

"Make doesn't think it's a beautiful day." Laura said. "His boss just chewed him out."

Pizz said, "Oh, I'm sorry to hear that Make. Did you screw up?"

"No. That's the problem. I didn't screw up. I've done really well, actually. I've got a lot of people in place to take care of things as they unfold. It's a hectic situation right now and I have managed it so far. Isabell pisses me off. She was wrong to jump me and I am going to tell her right now."

As Make returned to the table three other hands reached for his cell phone. Laure was the quickest. She put it in her apron pocket, "No, you're not going to call Isabell."

Make looked shocked. John said, "Laura is right Make. At another time it might work well for you but, right now that would probably end your career as an agent."

"I agree Make. It sounds like Isabell's upset right now." Pizz said.

After a few moments of silence, Make said, "You guys are right. I certainly should not call her. Thank you for saving me. I guess I'm just frustrated because I'm playing catch up and that's no good. I need to get ahead of what's happening. And Pizz, the thing you haven't heard yet is that container of three and a half ton of PETN is gone. Kingston just called from Lauderdale. They can't find it, they have no idea as to how it got out of the container area, it's just gone and so is Lester Cox."

"That's really bad." Pizz said. "That's probably why your boss is all excited, right?"

"Well that is certainly part of it. Christ, I'm afraid Les has been locked up in a container. That could be really bad. And also, Colonel Right just called. Mal Thorp, just yesterday, made two round trips to Ft. Lauderdale and back to Kansas City. And his plane can carry 3660 pounds which is just a little more than half of that three and a half tons. In two trips Mal could have gotten that PETN to KC. But how did he get it out of the container, for Christ sake? Is the container headed northwest toward Walla Walla Washington on a truck? Is it in somebody's back yard? We don't know where it is."

Standard spoke up, "The answer is he didn't get it out of the container during the last two days. The truck with that container on it has been under constant surveillance up until yesterday when it left the hoist area. We know the PETN was in a container two days ago. Some time, while it was somewhere in the dock yard, either the PETN was moved out of that container or the container identity was somehow switched so it could be moved out of the yard."

Make agreed, "John's right. So if they switched containers they must have some place to do it out of sight. That would take a container hoist and some room and at least two bad guys inside the hoist area. And if they just took the PETN out of that container what could they do with it?"

John added, "Yes, they must have some place to put the PETN. There isn't any place for three and a half tons of material packaged in boxes just sitting around. That's a container yard. There isn't supposed to be anything but containers in there."

Pizz knew about container docks, "I've had some business in the container yard in LA. That's a really big place and the containers are stacked sometimes seven high and the only way to look inside one is to take it out of the stack and set it on the ground and open it up. There are so many containers and people and so much activity in that area that anything could be done in there and no one would be the wiser. And I bet Ft. Lauderdale is just as bad.

A few hours later Make's cell vibrated, "Hi Darwin."

"Good news for a change. I just got a call from one of my guys. He said, as Les was on the way home last night, he passed the truck gate and saw the container, the lost container, leaving. It's a twenty footer and there aren't many of those. It was on the back of a flatbed. Les recognized it and he followed it. About forty miles out of town the truck turned off onto a dirt road and stopped. Les went on by and stopped down the road a bit then walked back and watched. Somebody was doing a lot of planning on this job. What he saw was amazing. My man saw part of it too. Soon a big box-truck backed in on the dirt road and parked behind the container truck. This was when it was just getting dark. Les had called in when he first recognized the container. Anyway, the first thing they did was, start up an air compressor and paint the back end of the container and the back of the truck white. Once the whole back was painted they started hauling out big white panels. Les thought they were sheets of aluminum or maybe fiberboard. Tim showed up about this time. Anyway they were smooth and white and when they were all put together they spelled "Poor Guy's

Moving Company" on them in big letters. Tim and Les couldn't tell what it was until it was all assembled because different parts of the words were on different parts of the panels. They had ladders and air operated caulking guns with some kind of adhesive in them, and they put glue on the side of the container and glued the panels on. They made it look like a new, shiny white box truck."

"Darwin that is truly an amazing story. I'm not sure about a few things though. I am assuming that Tim was your man and he got there because Les had called you. And, when you said 'my man' you were talking about Tim. Is that right?"

"Right, and now Les is home, probably asleep, and I have lots of people set up to follow that semi all the way to Walla, Walla."

"Darwin thank you for that report. Very exciting. I think you're doing everything just right. Call me if anything happens and I'll do the same for you." *Good. I feel much better.* Oh, wait, Darwin. You've undoubtedly already thought about this, but that dock yard must have been invaded by bad guys. Maybe even the US Customs people."

"Yes, we have a plan in place to screen every employee. An arrest has already been made. One of the truck gate-guards has been arrested. Although he was not a Muslim terrorist, on two different times he had taken a bribe to let an unauthorized exit at his gate. Because of the nature of the crime, the FBI has gotten involved. They're following the truck now. They've agreed to keep me posted as to what happens but they said they won't let a truckload of explosives go across state lines."

"Great Job. Thanks again Darwin. Keep us posted."

Smiles all around, "He talked so fast I wasn't sure which "they" was good guys and which was bad."

Immediately Darwin called back, “And another thing I forgot to tell you, Les has gotten a promotion of sorts. He’s now in charge of knowing and tracking the flow of containers from the time they are set on the dock to the point where they go in to customs. This was partly because of my urging the Ajax Company management. I felt he’d done very good work for us and, in his new position; he’ll have a better overall view of container flow and may be able to spot other problems we have suspected they were having. The manager also agreed that Les had done an outstanding job and they were considering a promotion for him anyway. The zinger is that he still has to do his old job too. No more money, just more responsibility. They told me, confidentially however, that he would get a raise the next pay period.”

"Thanks for keeping us aware of all that’s going on, Darwin.”

Make turned to John, Laura and Pizz, “Right. Now, it appears that everything we talked about has changed again; for the better it seems. I’m, very relieved. I was so worried about Les. Now the PETN is not lost and Les is not lost. So what do we have left? Oh, wait a minute. We don’t know where the PETN is. Did Mal take it? Is it in the truck? Shit.”

* * * *

Wednesday, August 22

The next morning Make stood on the patio talking with Laura. John was in the kitchen getting some juice. Laura said, “Ok, so that…” when Makes cell vibrated he held up his hand for silence and put his phone to his ear. "Hello Don.”

“Something’s happening at the warehouse, the salt mine. A van just drove in there to store something in the mine and he was turned away. They told him they were full right now and would not be available until they got their additional space opened up. Now there’s a semi-trailer parked in front of the dock and they’re carrying stored materials out and putting them in the semi-trailer. They're empting out part of the salt mine warehouse. I'm getting this as it's happening, by the way. I have my man there on another phone."

"Thank you Don. I have another call coming in. I'll get back to you soon. Hello Isabell."

"Look Make, you're doing a good job. You really are. I shouldn't have ragged on you because of my problems. Keep up the good work, ok?"

"Thanks Isabell. Don't worry. This will be taken care of."

Make said, "That was Isabell. Guess what, she apologized. And I need to call Don back. But I'm going to wait a little while. I have got to put this all together first"

Pizz came through the great room and joined them on the patio.

Make tried to summarize the situation, "Ok, I need to identify what's going on and where we're at. In the last twenty four hours, Mal Thorp's plane has flown two round trips between Ft. Lauderdale and Kansas City. In those two trips he could carry three and a half tons of material. That could be the dangerous PETN pickles or not. We now know where the rogue truck is and the FBI is taking care of that. We don't know what's in it but it could be the pickles. The FBI will open it at the state line later today. And there's something happening at the salt mine in Kansas City, Kansas. We've had a continuous watch on it since Tuesday morning. Putting this all together, we don't know where three and a half tons of very high explosive is and there's a change in the status at the salt mine." Make turned to Laura, "I will probably have to go to Kansas City tomorrow. Oh, and Pizz, you should know, Isabell Apologized."

* * * *

4:30 PM

The next hour was spent discussing possible actions they might take. Should Make go to KC or Ft. Lauderdale? What else could they do?

Then Darwin called again. “Make, they opened the truck in Tallahassee. No explosives, no PETN. I think it was a ruse to throw us off. Right now, I don’t know where the hell that stuff is.”

“My God, how did they do that? The pickles were there just yesterday. Was there anything in the truck?”

“I think it was really two days ago that we checked that container. But I don’t know how they did it. And to answer your question, there was a stack of fifteen old container doors just lying in the container. I think we’ve been snookered.”

After the call from Darwin, Make told John and Pizz about the empty container.

Standard said, “It seems that we have been ‘left at the post’ as the saying goes. It has been my experience that, in times like this, it is best to sit down and take stock of our situation, then try to come up with a workable plan that will reposition us. Right now we’re behind the game. We must get ahead of it.”

“You’re right John.” Make said. “I have got to do that again.”

Pizz spoke up, “Make, you keep saying the ’I’ word. John and I have been thinking that it would be best if we went with you. You’re sure to need some help so we would like to go and help. Right John?”

“Absolutely. We will be glad to go and I am sure we can help.”

Again there is talk of the three men going to Kansas City. Make asked, "What would we do when we got there?"

Pizz said, "We could look at the salt mine. See what is going on."

Make, "We can call Don Park. He can tell us that."

"Yeah but maybe seeing the place might give us some fresh ideas." Pizz said. "Has anybody ever seen a salt mine?"

Both John and Make shook their heads, no. But no one had anything to say for a while. Then Pizz said, "Where's the problem? That's where we should be, where the problem is. Don said they were taking stored material out of the salt mine and hauling it off. That's not much but that's something."

Make said, "Is it worth going to KC to see them unload a warehouse?"

Pizz said, "Well there's a problem in Ft. Lauderdale but, between Darwin and the FBI, it seems like that's being taken care of."

"Damn, this is frustrating" Make said. "I know I should be doing something and I don't know what it is. You guys have come up with a lot of ideas but, so far, I don't think we've been able to get the right course of action. Guys, I feel whipped. I'm going to turn in. Tomorrow's Thursday. In the morning I'll have a bunch of fresh ideas."

* * * *

The next morning, Thursday, eight AM, Make got a call from Emery, one of his guys in Albuquerque, "Mal is dead. His throat's has been cut."

"My God. When did it happen and who knows about it?"

"First, I've got to tell you, about forty five minutes ago, four Arab looking guys left here in a Mercedes. Ed Salazar's following them. He'll call you as soon as he figures out where they're going. He called me to come here, take pictures, see what I can see and report to you. I've emailed you the pictures but I want to tell you what I see before the cops arrive. Mal is duct-taped to a chair, he has his shoes and sox off and his feet have been worked over with a hammer. A bloody hammer is laying here on the floor. There are some garden clippers here too. It's really ugly. His throat's been cut with a saw tooth knife - very ragged cut. He bled out. Oh, the cops just drove up. I'll probably be busy explaining this to them. So call me back any time. I'll probably need your help to stay out of this."

Immediately after Emery hung up, Ed Salazar called Make, "Make, have you talked to Emery?"

"Yes, I talked to him. The cops were driving up so he decided he'd best get off the phone. He told me what it looked like and sent me pictures which I haven't had time to look at yet. Tell me what's happened."

"It happened between eight PM last night and about an hour ago. I'm the one who called the cops. I go by Mal's house most evenings after work. I came by yesterday about 5:45 and there was a party going on. That's unusual. Most of the time, it looks like nobody's home. Last night there was some music and I heard lots of loud talk. All non-argumentative. Just loud conversations. I think there must have been a lot of drinking. I didn't hear any women's voices. It sounded to me like they were in the back yard having a celebration of some kind. Anyway, I stayed around till 8:00. No one came or went and the party was getting quieter so I went on home. This morning, when I came by, the front door was open and four Arab looking guys were leaving Mal's front yard walking east down the sidewalk. I parked past them and watched through the rear view mirror. They got in a Mercedes and headed south on San Mateo. I followed them to the airport. They left their car in long term parking and went to gate fourteen. That's where I am now. I called the cops and told them all about it. The next flight from this gate doesn't leave for about an hour, 10:16 to be exact. I can follow them if you like but I really should get to work. Can you get somebody to relieve me?"

"Yes, I think this falls under the jurisdiction of TSA. Hold on. Oh, and by the way, how can you be identified?"

'I'm wearing a white T-shirt that says Nova Scotia on the front of it."

Make handed his phone to Standard, "Here John, this is Ed Salazar on this phone. Keep talking to him while I get him some help. It's an emergency."

It took Make two phone calls before he reached the right person, "Hello this is Make Caston, Homeland Security. Who am I talking to please?"

"This is Bill Wilson. I'm in charge of TSA, Albuquerque. I assume you need something."

"There are four Arab looking men at gate fourteen. My man, Ed Salazar is there watching them. At this point we think they may be connected with a murder in Albuquerque. But possibly, more important, they may be involved in a terrorist plot targeting the United States. I would like them to be allowed to get on the plane if at all possible. I doubt they have any contraband of any kind. And I want them watched from now until they get off the plane at their final destination. Do you have someone who could relieve my man at gate fourteen then follow them on their plane?"

"Yes, we can do that. We have people in place both on the ground and in the air. Tell me how I can get in touch with you and then you can consider it done. One of my men will contact you as soon as he's made contact with your Ed Salazar. He'll hand off to the man on the plane as soon as the Arabs have boarded and that man will contact you. What does your man look like and how can we contact you?"

"Thank you sir. Ed Salazar is wearing a white T-shirt with the words, Nova Scotia on the front and I can be reached at 480-555-1212." Make then took the other phone back from John and said, "Sorry for the confusion, Ed. I just talked to TSA. Their man will get to you soon. He'll be looking for you. And that was John Standard you just talked to."

"Yes, I know. He introduced himself. Well the Arabs are still sitting in the same spot. I don't think they've said a word to each other since they sat down."

"What makes you think they're Arabs?"

"Their skin color and their facial hair. They just look like typical Arabs I've seen pictures of. That's all. By the way, this is the gate for three different flights. Hold on Make. I think the TSA guy is coming."

"I won't keep you." Make said. "And thank you. I appreciate you doing this. When you get to work I am going to call you and talk to your boss explaining what has happened and what a good job you've done."

Make's cell rang again, "Mr. Caston, I am Tim Hann with TSA. I'll be watching the four gentlemen until they board. If anything out of the ordinary happens I'll call you. If not, this will probably be the last time we talk. As soon as the plane's doors are closed, the Air Marshal will take over. He'll call you while they're still on the ground."

Make dialed Emery, his man inside Mal's house. There were seven rings before Emery picked up, "Hello Make. I'm glad you called. What's going on?"

"I'd like you to talk to Salazar, get the plate number of that Mercedes, find the car and lift all the prints from the outside and from the inside."

"I can probably do that tonight and have them for you tomorrow. How can I get them to you?"

"Don't know. I'll call you tomorrow."

Make turned to John Standard, who was sipping coffee, "John, you've heard half of the conversation. You probably figured out what has happened so let's look at some pictures." When Make retrieved his laptop and pulled up the pictures that Emery had sent, John said, "Look at his feet. I've never seen anything like that before." The pictures of Mal's mangled feet were almost too horrible to look at. Probably all the bones were broken, some were protruding through the skin and his two big toes had been cut in half. Right beside the feet, on the floor, were a pair of garden clippers and a claw hammer, both bloody. Blood had splashed on Mal's pant legs and on a table leg nearby and there was blood spatter on the floor two feet away. There was a bloody blanket on the floor too.

Laura walked out from behind the kitchen island. "Would you men like some breakfast?" Laura saw the expression on their faces, "What's the matter?" Make quickly closed the Laptop and John said, "Nothing much. We were just playing computer. What's for breakfast?"

"What's on the computer? I want to see."

"No Laura. You don't want to see," Make said. "Mal Thorp has been killed. I've got one more call to make then I'll be ready to eat. Why don't you start breakfast and I'll be ready in ten minutes. I'll tell you about it while we eat. John, would you go with Laura and fill her in on what has happened so far? I'll join you soon."

* * * *

Later that morning, Make had laid his cell phone on the table beside the lap top. Now it starts vibrating. "Hello Air Marshal Halt."

"Hello Mr. Caston, I'm calling to advise you that four Arab looking gentlemen in well-worn navy blue business suits are on Southwest Air flight 216 and we're turning onto the runway. They're sitting in different areas of the plane, none of them even close to the other. One is in first class, one in tourist and two in business and all is quiet."

"Thank you, I don't expect that they'll cause any trouble. I'm sure the last thing they want is attention. Would you tell me their names please?" Make uses his computer to record the identity of the four men. "Would you pronounce their names for me please?"

"Mr. Caston, wheels up. I have to go. Good bye."

"Christ, I can't pronounce them either." In the midst of all the things going on right now in Make's life, he suddenly thought about them on that old 747 when they apprehended those two dumb kids. *Air Marshal Halt, you're a fun girl. I wonder what they did with those two kids we caught.*

* * * *

Make seemed in deep thought, *I've got to tell Ishe about Mal but I have to be very careful. I think he has some depression. I hope this doesn't send him off of the deep end. Psychotic breaks can alter people's lives…but he has to know. He doesn't seem suicidal. I think he'll be ok. He'd find out sometime anyway.*

Someone has to tell him sometime and it might as be me this morning. "Laura, I have to tell Ishe. I think he'll be ok but I'm not sure. I don't think he'll go off the deep end. He's got to be told sometime."

"Make honey, why are you rationalizing? You're right; he has to be told so just do it. I'm going with you. When we get back I'll fix lunch. You can wait a few minutes can't you John?"

"Certainly I can wait. But Laura, I've rarely seen Ishe since I've been here. Why don't you invite him to eat with us? Possibly, he would feel better."

Laura explained to him, "John, I always suggest that but he always turns me down. He just seems to want to eat alone. But thanks for the suggestion. I'll try again"

"Yes, I know. In Yemen he always seemed morose. Well, do what has to be done." John said.

Make knocked lightly on the door of the guest suite. Ishe opened it and said, "Hello Mrs. Caston. Hello Mr. Caston. Come in."

"Hi Ishe, you're looking good." Laura said, "Did you sleep well?"

"Yeah, I always sleep good. I could sleep twelve or fifteen hours a day if I wanted to, but I just think I should be up and around some."

"Ishe, we have something to tell you."
Laura added. "I'm afraid its bad news Ishe but you've got to know. Sometime last night your brother, Mal, was killed. They don't know who did it but the FBI is working on it."

"Mal is dead?"

"Yes he's dead."

"Wow. Who killed him?"

"Some people who looked Arabic were seen leaving his house but we really don't know." Laura said.

"Oh...How was he killed?"

"His throat was cut. He probably died instantly."

"I didn't think he would die from old age."

"Ishe, are you going to be ok?" Make asked.

"Yeah, I'm fine. Actually, I'm better than fine. " Ishe recalled some of the people Mal had had serious quarrels with, "I always thought something like this would happen to him. He usually treated people like shit...I've never felt this way before. I've always been living under Mal. He always told me what to do and he always took care of me, sort of. So he's dead. That is, it seems so strange. For the first time I feel, I don't know, I can't explain it. I get to do things for myself. I've always had Mal to tell me what to do."

After a pause Ishe said, "Actually, I feel great. Boy, this is all new to me." He stared off into space for a few seconds then, "Make and Laura, I want to thank you for all this. You've saved me. You fed me; you did my laundry, you kept me safe, thank you, thank you, thank you." Ishe grabbed first Make then Laura and hugged them both. Then he put his hand on his chin. "He's really dead...I can't thank you enough."

"We're just looking out for you." Laura said. "I think you had a pretty tough time in Yemen."

"Yeah, I did. He told me he was going to kill me. Did you know that?"

"Why did he tell you that?"

"Because he said I sunk his boat, the *Golden Lie*. I didn't sink his damn boat. The storm did it. That bastard. Well he's gone now. Besides, it was my boat, not his."

"Ishe, would you like to eat lunch with Make and I and John Standard and Sargent Pizzametski."

"Yes thank you. I'd love to have lunch with you. You are my favorite people. Make, I love you, Laura I love you. When is lunch?"

"Say fifteen minutes. Ok?"

"Yeah, I'll be there before then."

They walked down the hall to the great room, Make thought, *I've never seen anyone change so much in five minutes. I think I should say wow. He's almost manic.*

"You guys sit down and talk while I fix us something to eat." Laura said. "Ishe said he would be here soon."

"Well Make, how did it go?" John asked.

"Certainly not like I had expected, he seemed to change right before our eyes."

Ishe came into the great room. "John Standard, good morning. How's it hangin, John?"

"Ah, good morning to you Ishe. I'm fine thank you.

As Make introduced Pizzametski he noticed Ishe had started to cry. "I don't know why I'm crying. I hated him. But he is my brother."

"Crying is understandable under these circumstances," John said. "So, changing the subject, what are your plans for the future?

You have a full life ahead of you, there are lots of things you can do."

"I don't know but I am going to have a good time. I am going to do whatever I want to do. That's what I am going to do."

Laura prepared lunch while the four men sat in the great room. Pizz said, "Well, you may not be able to have fun without first getting a job, getting some income."

"Oh, I have some money." Ishe said, "Mal always paid me for the work I did for him and he paid me well. And I was usually out of the country. I've saved every cent of that since I was twenty five. That was the only year I paid income tax."

"That's great for you." Make said. "I'm frankly surprised that he would do that."

"Well he did. And I've had the same Italian financial advisor for the last fifteen years and he's averaged about a 6 ½ percent annual increase."

"Six and a half percent. I'd like to have an advisor like that." Pizz said.

"Yeah, I guess he's pretty good." Then Ishe continued, "Make, you know, you've been very good to me. I owe you and Laura too."

"No you don't."

"I am going to repay you some way."

"Not necessary, Ishe."

Ishe said, "Well, if you ever need something that I can do to help, you just call me. I'll keep in touch. And you have my cell number. And as soon as I get situated, I'll call you."

Laura came in, “Lunch is served guys.” They moved to the west side of the great room, near the movable glass walls which were now open. Pizz marveled about the architecture of the house. *Somebody was a verry clever architect to design all this. I would like to have a house just like this one.*

John thought about the company they were in. *Here we are, a thousand feet above a beautiful valley in a million dollar house with a gracious hostess fixing food tor five people. One man has a mysterious past, there are two men a beautiful young woman is in love with, and me, an old misplaced policeman who will soon go back to a dreary existence in Yemen. Maybe I'll stay here in the states. I wonder if I could.*

Ishe thought, *beginning tomorrow I get to start a new life. I'm the luckiest person here.”*

Laura said, “So Ishe, what are your plans.”

“After a couple of days I'm going to get out of your hair.”

“What's the first thing you're going to do when you get into town?”

“Buy some clothes I guess. Then I'm going to find something to provide some income for me. I want to see what business opportunities there are here. I like this area. I'd like to stay around here.”

“What kind of work do you have in mind?”

“I've got some ideas about things to manufacture that might be good. I don't know. I've got time to just look around.”

Laura said, “I just wonder if you shouldn't take it easy for a while longer, you could give more thought to what you want to do and you would be welcomed to stay here some more if you like.

You had a strenuous adventure on the *Golden Lie*. You are a hero, you know."

"Yes, it was strenuous but I didn't survive because of my wit; I survived because Make swam out and rescued me. You know, that whole thing was such a fiasco. I didn't like those guys when they first showed up. I was really afraid of them. And then, when I called Mal, he thought they were a great business opportunity. He thought up that whole business right while he was on the phone with them. From then on, I really had no control over what went on. I was just a flunky ship captain. I'm so glad he's out of my life. All I wanted was to get my ship in dry dock and get some repairs. Then I lost my ship and almost lost my life."

"By the way, Ishe." Pizz asked, "Did you have insurance on your ship?"

"Yes, I had Marine insurance, vessel and cargo, but Mal probably got that changed so that he was the beneficiary. I'll have to check on that."

"What have you been doing for the last fifteen years? You alluded to being out of the country. What was your life like?"

"When I was twenty five years old, Mal got me that ship. He put it in my name. He told me he got it as part of some deal he had made. After that, he hired an old man to show me how to operate it. The most important thing I learned was dock fees. I learned where the cheap ones were. One day the old man never came back. Three days later his body washed up. That was at the Rosario Terminal, Tijuana, Mexico. There was a puncture wound in his neck. I think the Federalizes thought I did it. I think Mal did that. He was a doctor you know. He knew how to do stuff like that. When we were in the dry dock in Yemen, he hired that chemist and I heard Mal telling him how he had drugged some guy and put him on a plane and sent him off to die. If he really did that, he was a mean son of a bitch."

All eyes turned expectantly toward Make, but he said, "Well Ishe, it sounds like you've had a lot of adventures in your life."

"Yeah, I guess. But my adventures were never like what you guys do. I never did anything that ever benefitted anybody but Mal. You know, I'm very glad I know you guys. You all are real heroes."

Pizz thought, *I am no hero. I'm so fucking tired of school. I wish I could quit right now and never go back. But all I have to do is write for a month, maybe two, and then I'll have 'doctor' in front of my name. I'd like that. I guess I'd better do the writing…But If I thought I had another six months of this I'd quit right now. I'd like to get on with my life.*

* * * *

Later, Make's cell vibrated, "Make, this is Emery, I got the plate numbers on that Mercedes but I had a problem. The FBI is notified when anyone like me checks plate numbers. I had to tell them what's going on."

"It's ok Emery. That'll be one less thing for us to worry about. It's not a problem. Did you get the FBI guy's name?"

"Yeah, His name is G.C. Jiayi. He looks Chinese to me."

Later that day, Make's cell vibrated again, "Mr. Caston, this is Don T. Park. Flight 216 has touched down and will start deplaning in a few minutes. I have four additional men here in case they each go different ways. How should we identify them?"

"I was told that they were four Arab looking gentlemen in well-worn navy blue business suits. Their names are Dancer, Prancer, Donner, and Blitzen."

"Thank you Mr. Caston. That's a great help."

"Sorry Don. I couldn't even begin to pronounce their names. I'll email them to you right now."

Make ended the call and Laura said, "Make, honey, don't screw up. He is a good man and you've given him a very difficult task."

"Yeah, I know. I've got to cool it. I'm just concerned because so many things are going on all at once."

Make went to his laptop and mailed the names and identities of the four Arabs to Don.

Make announced to Laura and his guests, "I think I have to go to Kansas City. I hate to leave you guys but this really is a matter of national security. I don't know how those four Arab guys fit in, I don't know if the salt mine is a part of the equation, I'm sort of going blind here, but I feel like I have to go. And I'm not sure how long I'll be gone either. Feel free to stay here and be available for consultation. I'll call as soon as I arrive in KC."

Pizz said, "Wait a minute, Make we're going with you."

"Yes, we have talked about this before." John said. "I'll be glad to help you Make with whatever you need. But don't you think it would be better if we all three went?"

Pizz agreed, "I think John and I could be of service to you. We are both cops, you know. We understand some of what is going on here, don't we John?"

John said, "Right Make, We can and will help you."

"Look", Laura said. "Sitting at this table are three of the most highly trained, experienced, innovative, intelligent, I might add, lovable police people in the whole world. If you three put your heads together you can do this with one hand tied behind your back."

There was a two second pause, then, in unison they all agreed. Pizz pulled a tablet out of his pocket and started writing. John suggested they didn't really know what the Arabs were going to do. "So we have to be prepared by making a list of the possible things they might do. Put them in the order of likelihood and decide on a course of action for each different activity the Arabs might take."

"I agree. I've already started a list." Pizz said.

"Well, three people doing this would be better than one person doing it," Make said. "But have you two given much thought to what we are talking about here? This is the real deal, a big deal. If you go it will probably be dangerous for both of you. And it really is a matter of national security."

Pizz and John both nodded. John said, "We know what we're doing, Make, and we both say yes."

Make added, "What this means is, we three have to go to Kansas City <u>right now</u>. Are you guys' game for that?"

The 'right now' part of this was a new thought for both John and Pizz. There was the briefest pause then they both agreed.

Make asked Laura to arrange for tickets for them and then they started to determine what they had to do to get on the plane with sufficient degree of preparedness to accomplish the task that they might have to do. That's when Darwin Kingston, Ft. Lauderdale DHS, called.

"Hello, Make, this is Kingston. You mentioned yesterday that the docks might be infiltrated with terrorists, and I have given that considerable thought. This morning I brought in a crew of ten people, two to do camera surveillance capability check. They are going to see which places need additional cameras. Two more people are to retrieve all surveillance data from all the equipment they have all around the dock yard. And I have six more people here to review all surveillance information we are able to come up with. We've been working on all that for about five hours now and we've got something interesting. At 4:03PM last Friday a girl driving a new white Dodge Ram 3500HD came in through Truck gate 2. That truck is a heavy duty vehicle. It was equipped with dual rear wheels and heavy duty suspension. A truck, outfitted like it was, could carry more than a ton of material. She came back out forty four minutes later, at 4:47 and made a left turn heading north. The gate guard wrote down that she had three skids of 8 x 8 x 16 concrete blocks in the back of her truck when she went in and they were still in there when she came out. Under 'purpose of the visit' the guard had written, "to see her husband". She repeated that visit about two hours later at 7:10 PM then again at 7:51 AM then again at 9:30 AM. She made a total of four trips in and out during that night. She timed her trips so she wouldn't be recognized by the guards as a repeat visitor. We've interviewed the two guards on first shift, one of the second shift, and the two on the third shift. All but one of the guards said they remembered her. She was very attractive. There's a camera on the incoming side that got a good view of her face. She tried to come through the wrong way on first shift and the guard had her back up and come in the right way. All of the other times she came in the 'out' side of the guard house and out the 'in' side of the gate. I think she was trying to prevent us from getting a picture of her face. We were able to get her license number but we got no more views of her face. We were able to do facial recognition on her. She's Gail Frederickson, also known as Yiardi-Qabbani by her closest Syrian Friends. She's a graduate student at Florida State, majoring in foreign language. We haven't been able to contact her yet. We don't think she has a husband."

"So she had a vehicle that could carry out 3 ½ tons of material if it made 4 trips."

"Yes, easily."

"Is she a Muslim?"

"I assume she is but, at this point, I can't be sure. And, keep in mind Make, there are nearly a million Muslims in Florida, and they aren't all terrorists."

"What's her license number? Do you have that handy?"

"It's a Florida plate number 'ECW-345."

"Thanks. You're doing a great job. I may be able to follow that truck by using satellite photography."

* * * *

Later, "Hello colonel Right, this is Make Caston."

"What can I do for you?"

"How are you on license plate numbers?"

"Not good Make. We can't read license plates. We just look straight down. Because of the width of the field of view, there is a very slight angularity but not enough for license plates."

"Ok Colonel. Thanks anyway." *I should've thought of that.*

* * * *

Don Park, the KC PI, called at makes home, shortly after Kingston called.

"Hello Mr. Caston, I have some information for you. First, the four Arabs hung around the airport for a few minutes then each one took a separate cab to the downtown Marriott. They left at different times, about ten or twelve minutes apart and, of course, arrived at different times. They took separate rooms on different floors and in different parts of the hotel. Part of the hotel is a separate building from the other part and they are separated by a street intersection. They each went directly to their rooms and haven't come out. I assumed you wanted personal information about them so I checked their passports. Dasher, also called Edfu Rahal is fifty six years old and lives in Cairo Egypt. He is on a special Visa and can only be here for seven days. Actually all four of them are traveling on that same kind of seven day Visa. Mr. Rahal owns or manages a large storage company in Cairo. Mr. Toah is from Yemen where he is in the General People's Congress; it's the ruling political party in Yemen. He's also fifty six years old. Mr. Baz has no occupational listing. He's the muscular looking one. He's thirty two years old and lives in 6th of October City, a suburb of Cairo. Mr. Nazari is an artist. He's thirty six years old, from the United Arab Emirates. I suggest, Dasher and Prancer are people who know how to run a warehouse business and Donner and Blitzen are thugs."

"Don, that's outstanding information. How did you get all that so quickly?"

"Sir, I would like to defer giving you the lengthy explanation of that until a later date because I'm anxious to tell you the really good stuff."

"The really good stuff?"

“Yes sir, the really good stuff is that Mal Thorp did not buy the salt mine. He didn’t buy it, he doesn’t own it, he never has owned it, and it is now obvious that he never will.”

“Don, we’re all waiting to hear.”

“The Al-Ihirsnah Islamic Center, 7200 west Troost Street, Kansas City, Kansas, owns the salt mine.”

“Holy shit.”

“My thoughts exactly.”

“Don, has anything happened at the salt mine. Are there any Muslims around or any unusual activity?”

“Yes, there’s a lot of activity at the mine. My man and I have been watching with binoculars. A semitrailer has been parked at the dock. I’m in a position to see what they’re doing with that semitrailer. It’s been filled with materials taken from inside the mine. It seems to me they just took things at random. They didn’t take any particular kind of things. They may have been clearing out an area to make room for something else. That truck’s gone now and another truck has showed up. It looks like they’re moving electronic equipment in. Also some Middle Eastern looking people have been arriving.”

“I wish I knew where that semi went.”

“I know exactly where it went. When they had it filled up and started to lock it up, another guy came out of the mine and got in a car parked across the street. When the semi started out, the car followed it. My man followed them. They went to the Fairfax district. It’s an industrial area north of the river. It’s just one huge parking lot. It’s like one gigantic truck stop. The semi driver parked the semi, got out and got into the white car that had followed. They waited about ten minutes until a yellow bus came and unloaded eight men, all dark skinned with dark beards. They all helped unload the contents of the semi. They left it in a pile on the ground then they all climbed in the back of the semi and the semi driver got in and drove it back to the mine."

"Ok, Don, sometime tomorrow I'll arrive in Kansas City. I'll be accompanied by two friends. You probably remember Sargent Pizzametski from the pickle business. He'll be with me and also John Standard, a police captain from Yemen. Tomorrow we'd like to meet with you and discuss how we can be more proactive. As soon as I know when we'll be arriving I'll let you know. If there's any interesting activity before that time I'm sure you'll inform me. Do you have anything else Don?"

"No, not now. And I will call you if anything develops."

Make turned off his cell, "Here is what we've got so far. Mal has been tortured and killed, probably by a group of four men from the Egypt/Yemen area. They immediately flew from Albuquerque to Kansas City and apparently are trying to not appear to be associated with one another and trying not to be seen. Before his death, Mal told the press he had bought the salt mine. However he must have done that as a front for some Muslim group who now own it."

While Make talked, Pizz typed on his tablet. He stopped when Make stopped.

Make continued, "At this time the four Muslims are in their hotel rooms in Kansas City and apparently have not visited one another. But Don said there's lots of activity at the salt mine. I think that's where we should go first. I think we need to know what is happening inside that mine."

"I agree." Pizz said. "I feel that there is a connection between the murder, the four Muslims, the salt mine and something else we don't know about. There are pieces of this puzzle that are missing. I suggest that most of the pieces, the important pieces, are in Kansas City and the closer we are to KC, the more apt we are to find the missing pieces. And those two guys, Dancer and Prancer worry me. They're big guns. There's something big going to happen and we better be there to stop it."

John said to Make, "Once when we were in Yemen, you asked me what I would do about a bunch of terrorists who were making explosives and I told you I would hunt them down, and take them and the evidence to the prosecutor. I remember, you didn't like that and wanted me to be more aggressive. Now you are faced with the same situation. What are you going to do when you catch the bad guys?"

"Yeah, that's interesting. I know the shoe is on the other foot now. I guess I will do the same thing you would have done."

Laura came into the room; "Here are three boarding passes I've downloaded for American Airlines flight 1054 to Kansas City. I could only get two seats together. It leaves here at 4:11 and arrives, KC at 8:30. So you boys belter get crackin."

Pizz went home to his rental and packed shirts and underwear and his Glock. Make went in the bedroom closet and packed some shirts, pants and underwear and his Colt Python with the silencer. John grabbed all the shirts and underwear he brought with him and packed them in his bag, no gun. Make had a model 1911 from his father. He handed it to John who seemed familiar with it.

Then Make called TSA and made arrangements for them to transport weapons on the plane.

Chapter 52

Thursday, Aug 23rd.

Make's car

Make sat in front. Laura drove and John and Pizz sat in back. She said, "This Phoenix airport must be one of the worst in the country. The street signs that direct you to whichever terminal you want are wrong. If you spend more than a few seconds unloading you will get a cop there hassling you to move on. And the parking garage is a hundred miles from the terminal. You have to stand in line a half hour to get through security. And when you get inside it's another hundred miles to the gate. I hate doing this."

"Laura, honey, we are going to be all right." Make said. Stop Worrying. We all are very qualified. We'll work this all out safely. We've got the law on our side and we will have lots of people helping us. Really, it's going to be ok."

"Make's right Laura." Pizz said. "Stop worrying. We have so much support that it'll be a piece of cake."

"Piece of cake, my ass. You are going to a town you are not familiar with. You don't know what's there and you haven't a clue what you are going to do when you face the bad guys." Everyone is quiet for a moment then Laura added, "I'm sorry. I can't stop worrying."

John spoke up, "Laura, as the senior member of this group, I give you my solemn oath that I will let no harm come to any of us. So you can rest easy."

"Thank you, I love you guys and I just don't want you to get hurt. That's all. And I guess, it's not such a bad airport after all." Tears were running down Laura's cheeks.

* * * *

On the flight to Kansas City, John slept. Make and Pizz were seated together. Make said, “So you have successfully defended your dissertation. What’s next?”

“Yes, my defense was successful, but it was tough. I’ve gotta admit, the board’s interrogation was very difficult. I had to justify everything and they didn’t miss a point. From now on though, it is going to be a lot less stressful. I just have to finish the remaining chapters of my dissertation and I’ll be a PHD. As far as what’s next, I don’t know. I haven’t decided.”

“Pizz, I’m embarrassed to have to say it, but I don’t know what your dissertation is on.”

“International terrorism, what else? As the population explodes there is destined to be more and more disrupted, displaced, unhappy, starving people. That’s what my dissertation is about. I‘ll make projections about future food supplies, future import/export trade ratios, predicted population changes, things like that. Actually CDC already has a prediction about the coming of an as yet unknown super viruses and the effect that they will have on future populations. Based on all that and some other kinds of predictions I’ll be able to extrapolate the spread of crime and where it’ll take place. Using all that, I’ll be able to predict our anti-terrorism activities for tomorrow. I think those predictions will bring into focus, the issues we have today.”

“My God that sounds complicated. I didn’t realize the magnitude of what you have to do to get your PHD. As you’ve been talking, I’ve been remembering getting to be a doctor. You know, to be a medical doctor, all you have to do is remember a lot of things. I think being a surgeon is the easiest branch of medicine to be in. A fair part of it is mechanical. And, I suspect a lot of that will be replaced by robots in the near future. My dad was a surgeon too, you know. He was into robotics a lot, but, most of that was for show. I think the robot had to wait outside until the surgery was complete…I really like what I am doing now, better than doctoring. All things considered, I certainly do like this job. So far, I think I would like to do this for the rest of my life."

"Unlike you, I don't have a clue about what direction my life will go. I had thought about getting a government job of some kind, maybe working for the UN or perhaps the FBI or DHS. But generally, they don't pay very well because, despite my PHD, it seems like they all want me to start at the bottom of the pay scale. And that doesn't seem right. I've already got a job offer to be a teacher. It's from CCNY. The salary is much higher than what Isabell offered me. But, the cost of living in New York is much higher. Make, I just plain don't know what I'll do. It worries me and sometimes I wish someone would tell me what to do and I could quit bothering about it."

"You talk like you think I know where my life is headed. I always thought I wanted to be a doctor and now that I am a doctor, I want to do something else. I suspect that I may change directions several times. But it seems to me, you're the stable one. You have a PHD in the criminal field and whether it's teaching, writing or working for some organization, it'll always be in criminal justice."

* * * *

Upon arrival in KC, Make got a call, "I am George Wolf, FBI. Your man, Emery, gave me your number. We have talked to the four gentlemen who recently arrived in KC from Albuquerque. I want to tell you what information we have gathered so far. We believe they were sent to KC to head up a meeting that was to start tomorrow in the salt mine storage facility here in Kansas City, Kansas. After they killed Mr. Mal Thorp they were advised by phone that there was to be a takeover of that meeting by thirty to forty ISIL men. They believe that the ISIL Is looking for them and if they were caught, the ISIL would kill them. At this time most of the people in that salt mine are ISIL. We intend to not interfere with the meeting at this point. One of the Arabs has told us that nearly two hundred Arabs have made arrangements to attend the meeting. We believe that those Arabs will be converted to ISIL or will be killed. We think that when they are in there they will all convert. At this point, we're not sure what the intent of this meeting is. However we suspect that it has to do with organizing. Perhaps cell organization or location of cells in this country. None of the four Arabs have confessed to murdering Mr. Mal Thorp. However, I believe that confession is eminent. Also, I wanted to thank you for your help. Your Mr. Don T Park's summery of the identity on the four men was of great benefit to us and so was the licensed plate information supplied by your man, Emery. I've told you where we're at and what we're going to do which is continue our interrogation of the four Arab individuals and gather sufficient information to prosecute them. We'll be standing by the salt mine in an attempt to detain any suspicious persons. It's our intention to let anyone go in but watch for any Middle Eastern looking people going out. We'll follow them and take action as needed. I don't know what you're going to do. I believe you got here first and are in charge of what goes on inside. What I'm saying Mr. Caston is, the ball's in your court."

"I understand Mr. Wolf, and I appreciate all the info you've given me."

Later, after a dinner at the Downtowner hotel, Make suggested they go for a walk around the town to see the sights. During the walk he told them of his conversation with Mr. Wolf of the FBI, "I believe the four Arabs were afraid for their lives and that is why they were holed up in that hotel room and stayed separated from each other in the plane."

"If you Google 'ISIL'" Pizz said, "It'll say that ISIL claims to be an Islamic state and wants to get all Islamic people to agree to be a part of it. They want all the areas that are primarily Muslim to be under its political control. At this point ISIL is not generally recognized as a state. If they are trying to take over the meeting as Wolf said, they will probably succeed. A large percentage of Muslims want to be organized into a state. There's an interesting addition to all this; at one time we had this guy, Abu Bakdi al-Baghdar, as a prisoner at Guantanamo. But we let him go. He's the guy who is now the new leader of the ISIL."

"Why was it that we let him go?" Make asked, "Didn't we have enough evidence to prosecute?"

Pizz said, "I don't know Make. But I do know that there is lots of pressure on our government to close that place down. Make, are you aware that lots of people think that our criminal justice system is dead? The USA has more prisoners' per-capita than any other country and we have the largest prison population in the world."

Chapter 53

Friday Aug 24th

KC Hotel

At breakfast the next day in the KC hotel, Make said, "I've rented a car. I suggest we drive by the salt mine so we can get the feel of the place. See what's going on. My intent is to come up with a plan of action."

"Keep in mind Make" John Standard said, "We've come up with several plans already and every time we do, something changes. What do you think will change this time?"

"I think that we have to make a plan that will get us into the mine and back out again safely. We can go in, come back out, and then make a plan as what to do next. The trouble with the plans we've made before was we were planning so far ahead; there were lots of opportunities for other things to come up. The four Arabs flying across the country could have gone anywhere. That was a variable. The container that we thought held PETN was stolen and Les had gone missing. That was a variable. All that stuff changed our plans because there were so many things happening that we couldn't depend on the outcome. How can there be any variables that will affect just going in the mine and getting back out again? When we get to the mine I think it'll be obvious how to get inside. And once we get inside and get to look around, we'll know what to do next and it'll be easy to get back out again."

Pizz said, "Make that 'getting back out again' part better be a pretty damn fool proof plan because those ISIL guys are a bunch of mean bastards."

Make said, "I know that. If we don't come up with a plan, a safe plan, we don't go in. It's as simple as that."

John said, "I would say the ultimate goal is to prevent detonation of three and a half tons of high explosive and to capture the terrorist people who plan on doing us harm with it. Is that what the rest of us think?"

"Yes."

Pizz said, "Yes. That's well put John."

"Then, we must keep that in mind that we don't know that the terrorists have the explosive. We don't know where the PETN is."

"True, Make said. "But considering Mal's flights from Florida to KC, there's a possibility that it could be in the salt mine right now. Except, if it is in there, I don't know how the hell they did it...So is everybody ready to drive by the front of the salt mine?"

"Yep."

Make said, "*Gute. Wir gehen*. I had a semester of German as a technical elective."

"Do you know what he's talking about Pizz?"

"I haven't a clue but don't pay any attention to it. He's just bragging about being a doctor."

"Good. We're going."

* * * *

They got on the Kansas Turnpike then maneuvered around to the corner of 70th and Kansas Avenue. On the North West corner of that intersection, there was an industrial building with a conventional parking lot. Turning left on 70th street, a hundred and fifty yards north of the intersection, they went past the mine complex. In front of it on the east side of 70th street was a dug-out parking area large enough to accommodate several semis or dozens of cars. There were two semi-trailers, a white pickup with a ladder on a rack, and a small school bus parked there.

On the west side of 70th street, some of the earth had been removed so that there was a depressed area that slopes down toward the west for a little more than fifty yards. There was a six foot wall on the east side of it that formed the west edge of 70th street. There were driveways from 70th street on both the north and the south ends of this dug out area, providing easy access to and from 70th street. It was large enough for semi's to turn around, back up to the dock, etc. On the west side of that area was a long cement loading dock with ramps at either end. The front of the mine was a thirty foot high cement wall. The huge double door, the entrance to the mine, was near the center of that cement front wall.

The mine entrance was at the east end of a dirt mound that was studded with scrub oak trees. In the grassy areas around the mine there were patches of white. Salt was protruding through the earth's surface and grass was growing on it. A half mile back west from the mine entrance there was the beginning of a forest of small trees.

They drove past the mine at a normal speed, then turned onto Speaker road and stopped. "Well, what do you think?"

Pizz said, "I think the first thing we should do is drive back past it going in the other direction. That way we'll each have a look at the other side of the street."

They did it, then Make said, "Ok. Now what do you think?"

John said, "I saw a semi backed up to the dock and some people coming out the back and going into the entrance. I believe the lettering on the side of the Truck said 'BestWays Transfer'. I wonder if they're using semi-trailers as busses so no one can tell how many people have come here."

"There's a white truck in the parking lot across the street." Pizz said, "It's from the Advanced Communications Company, at 345 McGee St. That's only a few blocks from our hotel."

"Pizz, that is just amazing. I wouldn't know that much detail if I went by here a dozen times." Make said.

"That is understandable, Make." John said. "You are driving and paying attention to the road as you should be."

"Thanks, but I wasn't paying any attention to the road. So Pizz, I'm thinking that you're thinking we should go to the Advanced Communications Company and hire on. And I know that's what John was thinking too. Right John?"

"Yes, that is exactly what I was thinking."

Make speed dialed Don Park, the PI watching the mine. . "Hello Don. We just drove by the salt mine."

"Yes, we saw you. What did you think?"

"Wow, you are good. We didn't see you."

"Yes, I know. What did you think?"

"I think I would like to know how long that white pickup has been there."

"It just got there, maybe ten minutes ago."

Make said, "Don, do you know where that semi came from?"

"I don't know that. BestWays is a transport company based in Tulsa Oklahoma but their trucks are all over the country. This one's probably from the same place the first one came from. And when they return they'll have another busload of passengers like the first one had."

Make said, “So they really are using those semi’s to haul people in and to haul material out?”

“Yes I believe they are doing both. That’s what they did the last time. This will be the third load. Each time they repeat the same process. When it gets there, the men from the bus unload the semi and leave the materials on the dirt. Inside the trailers, there are hand-holding straps attached to the ceiling. The men get in the back of the trailer, the driver closes it up and twenty minutes later here they are, going into the mine. There are eight of them this time. Last time it was seven.”

“Don, as usual, you’re doing an excellent job. I suspect you’ll be hearing from us again soon.”

“Ok. Do you both agree, we go to the Advanced Communication, Company?”

“Yes.”

John spoke up, “Possibly they have some affiliation with the Muslim community. If necessary, I can convince them I am an Arab. I might even convince them I was a member of ISIL. If they are pro Muslim and either of you say or do something that seems wrong to them, they might not help us. All I am saying is, I am concerned that we may not use an adequate amount of caution.”

“John, I appreciate your concerns and I absolutely guarantee that I won’t do anything that you wouldn’t do. Ok?”

“Yes, ok, thank you Make.”

Make pushed the OnStar button then, on cue, Pizz recited the address of Advanced Communication Co. The voice recited…“Thank you for that. While your route is being downloaded to your vehicle, is there anything else I can help you with?”

“No, we’re good thanks.”

“Thank you for using OnStar.”

Chapter 54

Friday Aug 24th

KCMO

They entered the Advanced Communication, Company at 345 McGee St., Kansas City, Mo. Make said, “Good morning sir. Are you the manager?”

“Nope. The manager is out. I’m the owner. What do you need?”

“My name is Make Caston and I’m with Homeland Security. And this is Sargent Pizzametski and this is Police Chief John Standard. We need your assistance at the salt mine in Kansas City, Kansas. Your men are there doing some work.”

“How’d you know about us being out there?”

“We just drove by there a few minutes ago and, besides that, I have hired a private investigator and he has been watching the salt mine for us. He told me about seeing your truck there. We believe there’s some illegal activity being planned inside that mine and we need to get inside and see. I’d like your assistance in getting in the mine.”

“Look. I can’t do that. I don’t know you. You guys look ok but, you have to admit, that is a pretty wild story. If I came to you with that story would you buy it?”

“I would if you could show me a proper ID and prove you are the one on the ID.”

“Ok, that sounds about right. Show me your ID’s.”

John placed his badge on the counter, Make got his DHS security clearance card out of his pocket, and Pizz handed the manager his police ID card. The owner examine each one in turn, “You guys must be jokein. You are the police chief in Yemen? And well, LA. At least that‘s closer. No, the only one I would even consider is this one, DHS, Make Caston. How you gonna prove you’re the guy on this card?”

Make handed him his DC driver’s license. “Christ, don’t you guys ever stay at home? How am I going to know this is authentic?”

“Call my office in DC.”

“OK, what’s the number?”

“If I tell you the number, you make the call and get a satisfactory answer, then you’ll think I gave you some number I fixed up with my wife or someone who would pretend to be DHS. But if you find the number yourself, then when you talk to someone who confirms my ID, you’ll be satisfied.”

“How am I going to do that?”

“Google DHS or look in the phone book.”

“We don’t have a phone book but we got Google.” The owner quickly found the DHS number and dialed.

Make said, “Ask for the security branch. Tell them you want to confirm the identity on an agent.”

The owner puts the phone on speaker, “Hello. I’m Jay Olsen. I gotta guy here said his name is Make Caston. Does he really work for Homeland Security?

“Where do you work and where do you live and what is a number where I can reach you, Mr. Olsen?”

Make leans over the counter close to the phone, “For Christ sake Georgia, tell him who I am. We are in a hurry.”

"Hello Mr. Olsen. Are you still there? That is the real Make Caston. He's always in a hurry. In more ways than one."

"Christ."

"Ok. Come back here." The owner led the three around behind the front counter and through the door to the equipment room. He slid a door to the side, exposing white coveralls with the company logo. Some appeared to be new and unused, some were just washed and there were several dirty ones. "Pick a suit you like. Now what else do you need?"

"We've got a man outside. I told you about the PI. We want to be able to talk back and forth when we're inside."

Olsen handed Make an open box with two small aspirin-box-sized devices that had a loop of cord attached, two sets or head phones and ear buds. "Here take this, give your outside guy one. This is the com box. There's an on, off switch on the side and a plus and minus button on the front for louder or quieter. Put the cord around your neck and you can keep the com box under your shirt. Wear the headphones or the ear buds. You guys can talk to each other. That's the best there is. You guys need one too?" Pizz and John both nodded. The owner opened another box and divided the contents between Pizz and John. "So what else?"

"We need to hear what's being said in the office or where the action is. We haven't been in there yet."

"Well, I'll tell you what's in there. Near the front, they're goina have a whole bunch of chairs in a big semicircle and a desk out in front of them. We're puttin a mic at the desk's and some small speakers around behind the circle of chairs so anybody sitting in any chair can hear the man at the desk in front of him. There's gonna be three areas just like that and we are putting the same equipment at all three. That whole thing is spread out over an area that's about fifty yards long. Each of the three stations has their own mics, amps and speakers, and it's all wireless. There's a main receiver amp that picks up all the mics and records all the mics outputs separately at the same time."

"How far does the mic amp broadcast?"

"Each of the three will broadcast about twenty yards to the receiver. They're not much good after about twenty five yards. They claim it will work fifty yards, but I never seen it that good."

"How about the main receiver?"

"Same thing, about twenty yards."

"We're going to want to go way back out of sight and listen and record what is being said. Maybe a hundred yards, maybe two hundred."

"Ok. You'll need a wire for that. Otto's got plenty of wire in the truck. Hold on." The owner opened his cell and speed-dialed, "Otto, you got a spool of bx in the truck?" The owner tapped his pencil. "How much you think?" More pencil tapping. "Oh, that's plenty. You got a speed rec. in the truck?" Tapping. "That's ok I'm sending three guys out there. They're undercover cops. I'll send a speed recorder with em. How you coming" Pause, "Ok, you better stall like you usually do. It's going to take em a half hour to get there. And you keep track of the time you spend helpin them, ok?"

Olsen turned to Make, "Ok, which one of you guys are paying for all this." Make nodded. "You got three outfits. You got two com boxes, you got a speed recorder and you got some wire. I'll give you the wire. And I'm charging you an hour of Otto's time" The owner tallied up the bill and handed it to Make. "Swipe your card and sign right there."

Make quickly complied. "Ok, when you get there Otto will take care of you. He'll give you a spool of wire and show how to hook it to the Speed rec. You'll have to tell your outside man how to run his com box. It works just like yours. Ok?"

"Yeah. We're good. Thanks for your help."

"Ok, good luck. Catch all the crooks and don't get shot or nothin."

The owner was right. The drive took almost exactly a half hour. On the way Pizz drove while Make called Don and explained what they were doing. They first parked behind Don's car. Don was impressed with their outfits. "You guys look very authentic. How did you get them dirty so quick?"

Don seemed to already know how the com box equipment worked. They all put them on and tried them. They worked great outside. They all wondered if they would be this good inside. Make told Don, "Continue your surveillance out here. If you see something going awry, you should inform Mr. Wolf, of the FBI." Pointing to a man in a suit, Make said, "He's standing right there."

Leaving Don parked on 70th street, they got back in their car and drove into the yard next to Otto's truck. Immediately a small, dark-skinned man came out and said, "You guys can't park here. We got lots of cars coming here soon. Why don't you unload the stuff you need and put it over there by the wall then drive your vehicles out and park on the street? Then you can carry it in as you need it. No one will bother it out here."

Otto replied, "Yes sir. We will do that right now sir." To Make, John, and Pizz, Otto said, "Get your car out of here and park in the big lot on the far side of the street. I'll set the bx out right where he said and follow you and park right behind you. We can talk out here. You can bring the speed rec back with you."

When they were parked, Otto said, I'll show how you do this." He set the recorder down on the tailgate of his truck and leaned it against a tool box so the back side was up. "The bx is a small shielded pair of wires. Here's what you have to do." You put one wire in this terminal and lock it in like this. It doesn't matter which color of wire you put in which terminal. Just make sure they are both locked in and the shield is far back enough that it doesn't touch the terminals. You got it?"

All three nodded yes. "Here's what's going to happen when we get in there. You are going to carry the bx. It's pretty heavy. Its got a battery in it. When we get to the desk where the main receiver is, I am going to pull out a service loop of bx and wrap it around the desk leg or something solid. Then you guys take off wherever you are going. It's best if two people carry the bx. Each one of you hold onto one end of the pipe and just walk. The spool will unroll as you go. When you get to where you are going, set the spool down so you have this side up. Then you pull this end of the wire out like this and hook the wires to the terminal of the speed recorder like I showed you. I'll hook this end to the main receiver amp. Your speed recorder will broadcast to that little box around your necks. You will hear everything that is broadcast over the receiver amp; probably better than the people listening to the speakers. It's all digital. On the front or the recorder are six buttons. You only need the first three. By pushing one or the other you can listen to which ever channel you want. This is a solid state recorder. It will record forever, as long as the batteries last, but you can only hear the last twenty four hours. But the way this shindig is filling up it'll probably be over long before that. The recording is on a chip. It looks like a thumb drive. You can pull it out any time you want and it won't damage anything or you can leave it in there and push the play back button and listen to the whole thing if you want. You good so far?"

Eager to go, all three nodded yes.

"Good. Go for it."

Chapter 55

Friday Aug 24th

Inside the salt mine

As soon as they stepped through the door Pizz said, "Where's the office?" When Pizz and Make had stolen and replaced the pickles a few weeks ago there had been an office, now there was none. They could see by the markings on the floor where the office walls had been framed in. Now, when they stepped through the door they were on a well-lighted concrete slab that extended away from the front thirty five feet. All three were surprised at what they saw. None of the three had been in a salt mine before. They were in awe. Fifteen feet above them was a concrete ceiling of equal size. Beyond the slab there was salt. The salt floor looked dirty for a few yards back but beyond that the floor, the ceiling and the salt columns were all an off white color. Twenty yards into the mine they could see that on each side of the isle, spaced about forty feet apart, were gigantic round columns of salt. The columns were massive, probably twenty five feet in diameter in the middle but fanned out wider near the floor and the ceiling. There were parallel rows of columns to the right and to the left, forming parallel aisle.

And it was cool. The temperature was fifty two degrees according to a big circular thermometer on the wall where they came in. They were glad they were wearing the jump suits from Advanced Communications. Some of the Muslims up front wore suits and one had an overcoat. But some were in their shirt sleeves. Nearly all had their collars turned up or something around their necks.

Some men were carrying chairs to what seemed to be a staging area near the front door and others were starting to place chairs in a circular pattern. There seemed to be a continual argument going on. It was obvious there was some confusion about the correct placement of the furniture, and it seemed there was a lot of tension.

Looking back away from the door the forty foot wide aisle looked like it went forever. It was lit for more than a quarter of a mile back with very low wattage bulbs. They followed Otto to the left where there was a desk and a table. He sat his equipment down and took hold of the end of the bx wire from the spool that Pizz and John were holding. He gave it a jerk which unwound about ten feet from the spool. He quickly wound it around the table leg and motioned for them to go. When they had walked about eighty feet farther to the left, two rows of salt columns, it was much darker, but the light coming between the salt columns from the center corridor dimly lit the adjacent corridor. They turned right and started down toward the rear of the mine.

For the first hundred feet back from the first column there were pallets of material stored on skids, in an orderly fashion. Beyond that was stored more material but it was just piled as if someone wanted it out of the way in a hurry. These piles of loose storage material extended back another forty or fifty feet. *Whoever piled that stuff there must think no one will ever need to find it again. Why would they think they could get away with that? And why'd they get rid of the office? They must have just ripped it out of there.* Beyond that clutter the giant hallways were empty except for a random piece of furniture.

They stopped to look at one of the columns. There was a gargoyle like carving in the side of it. Another column had a different look. A full sized carving of a naked women leaning against a rock. They could see that some of the other columns up front had carving on them too. Make said, “Come on. We've got to go.”

As they walked, the noise from up front diminished until they could hear no sound at all. They had walked for five minutes in the dimly lit parallel corridor when it seemed that the light went out. They stopped and stood still, listening. Gradually their eyes and ears became more sensitive and they began to hear some faint shouting from the men up front. And they could dimly see the columns in front of them. Looking to the right they could see that they were beyond where the center corridor was lit. Make asked, "Where do you want to set up?"

"Let's go one more column back," John said, "Our eyes will become accustomed to what little light there is and we'll be able to set up the equipment. And no one coming this way will be able to see us."

Make said, "I'm going to scout around. I'll see if I can find some chairs." Soon he returned with a small table. They placed it beyond the next column. "There is a pile of chairs over there. Help me carry a couple." Once they had enough furniture, Make said, "You guys start recording. I'm going to look around near the front. I want to get up close and see what they're doing. I can find you by following the wire back. Keep in touch."

* * * *

Staying in the dark areas, Make went to his left, one aisle. Then he walked toward the front, but as he got closer to the lighted area he hid behind the stacked storage. He could see the desk and the backs of most of the chairs. There were two other speaking areas to the left and each one had a circle of chairs. Make wanted to get closer but he was concerned he would be seen so he moved slowly and stayed close to the pillars. As he got nearer to the cleared area, there was more stored furniture so it was easier to remain hidden. Finally he got to a place where he felt safe and could see the whole span.

Some of the chairs were occupied now and a steady stream of people were coming in. The massive wooden double doors were now both open. As Make watched, he could see that the people, all men, went to the desk on the right. They seemed to be presenting some kind of Identification to one of the three men behind the desk. Then they would sign in on one of the many clipboards that were either lying on the desk or being passed around from one to the other. Once they were signed in, the newcomers went to one of the chairs in the semicircle and waited. There was a man at the desk calling out names. When his name was called the man would go to the desk and get something, maybe a ticket or some kind of chit. After that, the man would go to Make's left and disappear from his view.

There was one thing that surprised Make. The newcomers were all smiles! There wasn't an unhappy face in the whole bunch. *I thought Muslim terrorists were generally a miserable unhappy group. That's why they were fighting all the time.*

Make moved back farther and then to another row of columns. Now he was one corridor south of the two doors. Between him and the front wall were two pallets with materials stacked about two feet high. He hadn't seen them before. They were at the edge of the center speaker's area.

He had to move to the left a little to get closer so he could see what the pallets contained. Then he moved forward, crouching behind first one skid of storage then another. The man with the mic was calling out names, apparently from a clip-board. When a name was called a man would go to the two pallets where one of the men near the pallets would hand him a small bag and something else. Make couldn't see what was being handed out. He moved a little closer. Make saw the same process continue for several times. Then the next man got a small bag and a much larger item.

Make had decided he might be too close and moved back six pillars. He immediately wished he hadn't. Now at the table up front was a man wearing a green coat. He was facing to Make's right and he seemed to be leaning on something. In front of him were two men who had their backs to Make. He couldn't see what they were doing. When the two stepped away it looked like the man in the green coat had a dolly with something brown and about two feet tall, on it. The man turned around and pushed the loaded dolly to Make's left. Another man followed him. Make watched in silence as the two men went out of Make's view. By the time they came back, Make had moved forward but not as close as he had been. Soon they both returned with the dolly empty and repeated the process. He saw that the two men were loading something onto the dolly. Boxes, they were stacking three boxes onto the dolly. *What's that guy got?* Make crept close enough to read the label, 'New York Gherkins', "My God, oh my God. It's pickles. It's PETN." They're all pickles. That one guy took six boxes of pickles. That's what those guys had been getting but they only got one pickle, this guy got 192. Then Make realized that he had spoken loud enough that someone might have heard him. He wished he hadn't.

The speaker, who had been calling out the names and passing out the chits, turned in Make's direction. A few others looked his way as well. Make felt they couldn't see him because he was in a relatively dark spot, but, moments later, three young men headed in his direction. Make quickly moved further back. He could see the three men. They looked around the area briefly then moved back toward the speaker. *Do they know that someone was back here somewhere? Will another, bigger search party come after me. Should I go back to where John and Pizz are?*

* * * *

Outside, the FBI had become concerned because of the steady flow of Muslims coming into the mine. Their count was 193.

Now the arrivals had stopped and all was quiet. But because of what Mr. Wolf knew of DHS's involvement and because so much time had elapsed since Make had entered the mine, they'd advised the KC, Kansas police of the situation. Soon there were numerous police cars, a SWAT team van, and a motor home in place.

* * * *

John and Pizz sat on the back side of a column and listened. John knew enough dialects of Farsi to be able to explain the gist of what was being said. He switched to the third channel, the one where the guests were being instructed on how to use the PETN. They said that destroying an American aircraft when it was over a major American city or possibly a national forest was the most productive use of the material. "The airline companies try to keep their planes as full as possible. You can be assured of killing at least 100 Americans and probably three or four hundred."

Then they were told how to actually detonate the explosive, "If you have been given one pickle, go to where you cannot be seen or interrupted. You can break the pickle in half, then hold the two halves together so that the exposed ends are up. Hold the cap of the bottle between your teeth and unscrew the lid. Just dump the contents of the bottle on the two halves and you will be in heaven."

Most of the men had said they had only one pickle and a bag containing a syringe and a tiny glass bottle. Then one man had a box containing four jars of pickles. He told the instructor he had been given six boxes and the rest were stacked near the door. He asked for instruction.

The instructor asked, "What is the target you have been assigned to?"

“The container dock In Los Angeles, California. They have made a place for me to drive my car so that it will destroy all of the containers and all of the docking facilities.”

“Ah, a good target. You should keep the pickles in the jars. When you are in place, unscrew the lid to one of the pickle jars and set the lid aside. It would be best if you break the end off of the center pickle so that the exposed end is up. Work the plunger of the syringe in and out a little to make sure it’s free to move. Incidentally, this is important for the rest of you, if you intend using the syringe. They have been sitting a considerable time and are sometimes stuck. Once the plunger moves freely, push the plunger down into the syringe all the way. Then unscrew the lid to the small bottle. You can insert the syringe into the bottle and retract the plunger, thus sucking the catalyst up into the syringe. You should hold the syringe so that the small opening is up and you don’t let the liquid drip out until you’re ready. When the time is right you should then push the body of the syringe down into the center pickle and push the plunger down. Then you will begin your life of glory.”

“What of the other jars? Do they have to be close?”

“Well, to guarantee their uniting in the explosion, they must be within three meters, but from what you have told me you will be in an automobile so any place in the vehicle will be adequate-- unless you are possibly in a stretch limo.” They all had a good laugh.

Then Pizz and John listened to channel one for a time. This was the first location the men came to when they entered the mine. At this station, the men were congratulated for joining ISIL and told what a wonderful thing it was to die killing Americans. Pizz interrupted John, “My God, do you realize what is going on here? All these Muslims are being converted. They are all willingly agreeing that ISIL will be the ruling state for them and their families."

"Yes but all of them are also agreeing to blow themselves up."

"True but not necessarily right away," Pizz said. "We don't know when all this is planned for. They may have plenty of time to tell their families and friends about their joining ISIL. It may be a great advertising campaign."

"Yes and, this is a means of confirming that each of the men and their friends are loyal. So far, no one has turned away. Apparently everyone knows about ISIL and readily agrees to join."

Then John said, "Oh, I hadn't heard this part before. I think one man did not want to convert. Now he is being threatened with death if he doesn't join ISIL. He is being told that if he is killed because he doesn't join, he won't go to heaven. My God, what a religion. The speaker is making the rules as he goes along."

Make moved from place to place getting more of a feel of the layout. The feeling of safety that he experienced suddenly evaporated because now he could hear some men close by. He moved so that there was always one pillar between him and the men. He had to be very careful that he didn't make a sound. Now, background noise was nearly nonexistent. Hitting his foot on any of the various loosely piled stacks of stored materials would certainly alert the Arabs.

He saw that they were walking down the aisle that he, John and Pizz had used. As they passed by, Make could see they had the wire that ran to Pizz and John! There were three of them. One was holding the wire, letting it run over his hand as he walked. Make felt helpless. He knew he must follow them. As he headed for the wire, *I have to warn John and Pizz.* Make grabbed hold of the communicator that was hanging around his neck and held it close to his mouth. He whispered, "Company is coming, three guys are coming your way. Watch out." He didn't get any indication his message was heard.

Unfortunately, Make's message did not get through. Pizz and John were too far away. They didn't hear Make's whispering.

Make moved to where the wire was and picked it up. He had to stay far enough back so as not to warn the three men that he was following them. Yet he had to get there in enough time, just in case the Arabs found John and Pizz. Make started walking faster as he realized the dangerous position that John and Pizz were in. Make was terrorized. *Of course they will find Pizz and John.* Now he could see the three Arabs ahead of him. They were silhouetted by the very dim light of the recording equipment. A bright light was turned on for only a few seconds, then there was a scuffle and the light went out. Make could tell by the loud aggressive tone that things were not good. Now that the light had gone out, he couldn't see at all but he kept going toward the shouting, hoping he would be able to tell the good guys from the bad.

Pizz and John had arranged their furniture and now they were sitting facing the recorder. The wire spool and recorder were placed on the small table beside one of the salt columns. John was busy translating and Pizz was listening intently. They didn't realize there was a problem until a very bright light was turned on. Three Arabs moved to face them. One carried a multi diode lamp. He set it on the carton next to the recorder.

"Who are you? Why are you here?" an Arab man shouted in Farsi.

At first, John was startled, then he said, "We are recording the meeting. We were asked to do it where we wouldn't disturb anyone."

Two men grabbed Pizz and the other shoved John back against the pillar knocking the recorder and the light off the carton. The light went out. "No. No recording is allowed." One of the two holding Pizz let go and felt around on the floor searching for the light.

Both Pizz and John carried pistols in their pants pockets inside their coveralls but, because of the suddenness of the confrontation, neither had an opportunity to retrieve their weapon.

John grabbed hold of his adversary's arms trying to break the man's hold. He was able to move the Arab around getting his opponent against the pillar, but the Arab was very strong.

John said, "Why are you attacking us? We were told to do this. This is our job."

Now the one Arab had found the light and was hitting it against his palm. Finally the light came on.

"No Recording." The speaker, John's assailant, hit John in the face, stunning him. Now the two holding Pizz found his handcuffs, and badge. They handcuffed his hands behind his back then one moved to where the third man could see the badge. "You are police. You are fucking American infidels. I will kill you now."

John grabbed for the knife arm but the Arab with the badge grabbed john and held his right arm. The man with the knife grabbed John's hair with his left hand and used it to pull John's head back. He grinned, "You will not like this. I will do it slowly." He held the point of the knife toward John's throat. "No you will not like this." John's left hand held the wrist of the terrorist's knife hand, but the man was too strong. John was terrified as the knife point came closer to his throat.

The other Arabs grinned too. The one holding on to the handcuffs on Pizz drew his index finger across his throat, signaling to his comrade to slit John's throat. At first no one understood why the man pointing the knife at John's Adam's apple threw his head back against the column so violently. They didn't see a small black hole just above his left eye, but when he dropped like a wet towel, they saw something alarming on the salt column behind him. There were little pieces of red and white material and some black hair and some of it was running down the face of the pillar. When the man holding John's right arm pushed him aside to see what had happened to his companion, his head also exploded. The third man, holding the handcuffs on Pizz, didn't understand how this could be happening and he was terrorized. He thought, *it looks as if they might have been shot but there has been no sound of gunfire, no muzzle flash. Why did their heads explode? What is to happen to me? Will my head also explode? Will I go to heaven?* He squatted behind Pizz trying to determine the source of the problem.

Make came into the light holding his silenced Colt Python. John said, "By God you are a welcomed sight."

"I was scared to death." Pizz said. "I thought I was going to die. I didn't know what was happening. I didn't hear a thing."

"Yes, I was very frightened too." John said. "I was only seconds away from being killed. I have never been in such a desperate position. My God. I am Thankful that I am alive. And I thank you, Make. You saved my life." John's whole body was shaking.

Make pointed to the man behind Pizz and asked, "John, do we need this guy for anything?"

"No, not that I can think of. What about you Pizz?" The shaking stopped.

"No. We've got it all on the recorder."

Now the squatting man stood quickly and grabbed pizz with his left hand.

When Make saw that the man's right hand was on the handle of his knife, Make shot him twice in the side. He was thrown sideways and the knife he pulled from his waistband flipped up in the air and then clattered against the base of the salt pillar. The man collapsed and fell to the floor. He lay on his back gurgling and twitching. When Make fired a round into his forehead the dying man gave a big sigh and the twitching stopped.

Make stood silent. He looked around to make sure there were no other threats. He quickly put the gun in his fanny while John got the cuff key out of Pizz's pocket and freed him. Make had feelings he had never experienced before. He shook all over. He felt elated that he had saved the lives of his two companions but he had done it by killing. *Oh my God, I have killed three people. Did I do the right thing?* .

* * * *

After Pizz retrieved his badge, he said, "We have to get out of here now. And I suggest we run." He started running toward the front, and when John found his metal badge, he quickly followed. Make was still shaking. He had acted automatically but now, as the viciousness of what he has just done sunk in, he was momentarily powerless. The killing scene ran over and over in his head. Finally reality set in and he grabbed the recorder and started running behind John and Pizz. He stepped on the wire still attached to the recorder and the reorder was nearly jerked out of his hands before the wires pulled loose, pulling Make's hands with it. He almost fell forward then quickly regained his footing. Of the three, Make was the strongest runner. He rapidly gained on Pizz and John. Ahead he saw three Arabs running toward them. The Arabs shouted and John shouted back. The Arabs stopped and John, Pizz and Make ran past them. John was still shouting. Now the Arabs were running too. They were very fast. Make could tell by the sound of their footsteps that they were nearly upon him. He quickly sidestepped hoping to avoid being tackled but they ran past him. Now they were shouting too. Soon the group was in the open area nearly to the front wall. Several of the Arabs in close proximity stared in silence. One held out his arms as if to grab Pizz, but Pizz stiff-armed the man knocking him back into the crowd of bystanders. Another small Arab man grabbed at Make and got hold of his clothing. Make knocked the Arab's hands away but lost his fanny pack in the process. Make kept going. Most of the Arabs, some distance away, were either not aware of the commotion or didn't understand its meaning. But there was more shouting among the group of bystanders.

The six men, Make, pizz, and John and the three Arabs, raced to get out the door. The door was a massive affair made of five inch thick lumber with a steel plate on the inside. It was actually a double door twelve feet high and seven feet wide. The perimeters of the two doors were also covered with steel. One door was locked and the other side was open. One of the three Arabs got out first then Pizz and Make before the other two Arabs. The last Arabs started closing the door but John was able to squeeze through. He spent a few seconds getting the outside latch in place. It was strong enough to keep the people inside from pushing it open.

Now John became aware of people yelling. *What the hell are they yelling about out here? There is no need to yell now that we have gotten out.* He turned away from the door to see Make, Pizz and the three Arabs lying face down on the loading dock. Six

SWAT team members had assault rifles pointed at them, primarily at John. He quickly complied.

One of the SWAT team men told one of the Arabs to, "stand up and put your hands high above your head." The Arab didn't understand a word of English and was confused and frightened. When the command was given again, even louder, John, who was lying on his belly and had been watching how the Arab performed, interpreted. The Arab immediately stood and raised his hand high above his head.

One of the SWAT team put his combat boot on John's neck and told him to, "shut the fuck up." John was advised to put his hands behind his head with his fingers clasped together. Once someone got a firm grip around John's interlocked fingers, the boot was removed. Two others men grabbed his arms and lifted him to a standing position. His fingers were held while his 'Advance Communication' coveralls were unzipped and his shirt jerked nearly off. The Colt 45 was found almost immediately then his pockets were turned wrong side out. The pistol, his badge and the other contents of his pockets were discussed and bagged. They led John to the SWAT team communication van and told him to get in the back and keep quiet.

The remaining five had learned from watching John's helpful interpreting and remained quiet during the rest of the searching process. Pizz was allowed to join John in the back of the Van and the three Arabs were each put in the back of a separate police car. Make, the only one of the three without a gun, was placed in the front of the communication van and questioned by one of the SWAT team members.

Inside the mine there was confusion near the door. A few of those nearest to the door heard their fellow Arabs scream, "It's going to explode." Also one of the audio technicians was yelling something about explosion. They all seemed very frantic to get out. The wire was attached to the sound equipment. Was there some kind of device inside that box that would make the pickles explode? Most of the Arabs knew there were other ways to detonate the explosive besides adding a catalyst but they didn't understand the use of wires. *How can a wire make the* pickles *explode?* Others were excited just because there'd been running and yelling. About 200 men were still in the mine and probably 160 of them hadn't heard anything unusual.

One of the policemen saw the doors being pushed from the inside. He drove his police car to the access ramp at the end of the dock then up the ramp to the door. He turned the car around so that it faced away from the door and genially put the back bumper against the door.

It was now obvious to those pushing on the inside of the door that something stronger was needed. One of the men drove the forklift up to the door and tried pushing it open. The drive wheels turned but they just made black marks on the cement. The door would not budge. In an effort to use the inertia of the forklift, he backed away about three feet then rammed the door. One of the forks made a slight dent in the steel sheeting, but the door remained closed. There was no seat belt. The impact threw the driver forward, but he was able to stay in place by holding tightly onto the steering wheel. Some thought the forks were a hindrance, so the forks were raised to the upright position. He tried again with the same results. He was urged to get back farther and hit the door with greater speed. The driver was afraid he wouldn't be able protect himself from the impact if he went much faster. So he turned the fork lift around and rammed the door in reverse. The forklift wouldn't go as fast in reverse. Others urged him to back up a long distance and really hit it hard. He got off the forklift saying something to the effect that if you want to hit it faster, you drive it.

Now another man got on the forklift and backed away from the door about six feet. Many of those standing around told him that was not nearly enough distance to break the door open. He put the machine in reverse then advised everybody to get out of the way. He pushed the pedal to the floor and went straight back. The left rear corner of the forklift hit the front corner of one of the two pallets holding pickles. Some of the men had shouted for him to stop but it was too late. Boxes and jars of pickles were knocked back violently. Several of the unpackaged pickle jars were thrown off onto the cement floor. Some broke, exposing the pickles. Some pickles were crushed.

The other corner of the forklift struck the right front edge of the pallet holding gallon cans of catalyst and 4 ounce glass bottles with screw caps. The glass bottles littered the floor but none broke. The men doling out the catalyst, Dibenziol peroxide, had left one of the cans open. They watched in horror as it and some of the other cans were knocked to the floor. One can was crushed under the rear wheel and the liquid contents squirted up against the underside of the forklift. The can that had been opened lay on its side, its contents also spilled out.

Some of the observers, realizing the potentially dangerous situation, tried to stem the flow of the catalyst, but they were afraid of what they had assumed were its corrosive effects on their hands and clothing. One of the men stepped on a pickle, crushing it. The liquid soon found a minute crack in the cement floor and ran to some PETN also smashed into the crack. The resulting, minor explosion was only a forerunner of bigger things to come. It killed four men and injured two dozen others.

Chapter 56

Friday August 24th

Outside the salt mine

Outside they heard the explosion and saw the doors move slightly. To Make, it wasn't nearly what he had expected. However, everyone quickly moved back. Some ran. The SWAT team interrogator continued questioning Make. Make explained to the man how the catalyst worked. He told him, "It was probably ju..."

The next blast was literally deafening and was the brightest light that anyone there had ever seen. And the light seemed to last for a second or two. Closing your eyes was not enough. Some turned away and some put their hands or arms over their eyes. They said they could see the bones in their hands and arms through their closed eyes. The whole area had been cordoned off and there were only a few people standing near the mine and none were close. Anyone within a hundred yards or so were knocked flat resulting in abrasions, ruptured eardrums, and some temporary eye damage but no broken bones. Those who were farther away and remained standing said the ground moved under their feet.

The police car that had been against the mine door ended up against the east wall in the turnaround in front of the loading dock. It was mangled and on fire. One of its taillights was flashing, indicating a left turn. The retaining wall on the east side of the turnaround stopped the police car but the car hit with so much force that the wall was pulverized and the pavement on 70th street was buckled up.

In anticipation of transporting a large number of prisoners, two buses had been commandeered and parked on 70th street in front of the mine. The high end motor home the KC, Kansas police brought to the mine had been obtained last year. It had been stopped because it appeared to be over loaded. They found it was being used to transport pot instead of tourists. It was parked in the middle of 70th street and north of the front door of the mine. Behind it were the two large yellow school buses sixty five yards in front of the mine entrance. After the blast the motor home was lying on its side in the ditch along the east edge of 70th street. Its underside now faced the mine. The two buses were more nearly in front of the mine, and their chassis remained upright but were jammed against the far side of the ditch. However their sides, tops and backs were gone and were lying in the parking lot east of 70th. The seats were burned black but were still attached to the chassis floors. The only fatality was the driver of the motor home. He had told the other drivers he was going to remain in the vehicle in order to avoid the hot sun.

. The SWAT van was an M1117 Armored Security Vehicle. Its outside shape had been designed to resist blast damage. It had been provided by the Department of Defense through a program that allowed police departments to acquire such machines. It was parked in the middle of the large parking lot on the east side of 70th street about eighty five yards in front of the door to the mine. The blast caused the front of it to be swung around about 20 degrees and all four wheels had left skid marks. It nearly rolled over as it was blown against the side of the ditch on the far eastern side of the lot. If it hadn't been for the five foot high embankment it would have been blown into the woods. The vehicle's front door had been slid open, and Make was sitting on the end of the seat. He was facing the mine. His feet were on the vehicle door threshold. The right side of his face was burned slightly. The next day it would look like sunburn on the right cheek. The SWAT team interrogator Make had been talking to had been facing Make, facing away from the blast. He was supporting himself with his right arm raised to hold onto the top doorsill of the vehicle. He was wearing a protective armored vest. He was thrown against Make, knocking Make flat against the seat. His body slid over Make's body and he hit his head on the far side of the vehicle. Make's right ear drum was ruptured as was the left ear drum of the other man. The right sleeve of the SWAT team man's jacket was blown off and both of his pant legs were in shreads. Both men were bruised and both had minor cuts on their heads and arms, and the SWAT Team man suffered a dislocated shoulder. Fortunately for everyone in the van, it was heavily padded inside just for such occasions. The only thing Make saw of the blast was a brilliant white light. For a second it seemed like it was ten times brighter than the sun.

Pizz and John were in the back in the SWAT van behind the inner wall. They were bruised but not burned, and their eardrums were not damaged.

A few of the fifty or so officers inside the barrier were also burned and some suffered minor cuts from flying debris. Seventy-six people reported to have ruptured ear drums. Six had permanent hearing loss, but the rest healed in two weeks.

Fourteen people suffered some temporary eye damage.

Otto, the Advanced Communication man, was not harmed. He had left earlier.

* * * *

A car being driven along 72nd street by the wife of a mine safety inspector was damaged when a foot-long piece of rebar came down on the hood. It penetrated the metal and damaged the passenger side air induction filter.

Houses as far back as three blocks suffered some broken windows, roof damage and cracked plaster. Most of the damaged houses were in back of the mine. Debris from the concrete ceiling and the dirt above it went in that direction.

The forklift, the only really massive thing in the mine, had been south of the PETN pallets. Parts of it were vaporized but pieces of it hit the south wall near the cement front and gouged out large chunks of salt but caused no serious structural damage to any of the columns. Some molten aluminum, part of the forklift engine, had put a thin layer of aluminum over parts of the salt wall.

It had been easy to locate the center of the blast. Inside the mine there was a twenty five foot diameter hole in the cement floor. This was about fifteen feet back from where the door had been. The rest of the floor was cracked and buckled. When standing at the edge of the hole and looking up, one could see the sky. A thirty foot wide piece of the ceiling and the earth above it was missing and some dirt had fallen down through the hole.

A twenty foot wide piece of the front wall was missing too. The two ends of the wall were still in place and near the ends of the wall the steel bolts attaching the ceiling to the wall were still holding. However, closer to the blast center the wall was fractured and bent out. Some parts of the cement had been melted and looked like gray glass. Protruding pieces of rebar were also melted. Parts of the ceiling and front wall had been vaporized, however much of the front wall had been blown over the two lowered turnarounds knocking the bodies off of the schools busses..

Dirt and salt kept falling onto the floor for a month after the blast. To everyone's surprise, the rest of the mine seemed intact. The front salt columns were burned black and had suffered many gouges and scrapes but none had been broken or moved.

Initially the entrance to the mine was formed and supported using wooden timbers. Then in the early fifties it had been refurbished. When constructed, footers were first poured for the front and ends of the loading dock and for the 90 foot long cement wall. Then the cement floor of the loading dock and the inside apron had been poured as one continuous slab. Once the floor had cured the thirty foot high front wall, with the doorway forms in place and the slab that was to be the ceiling were poured lying flat on the apron/dock floor. After three weeks they were tipped up and lifted into place and secured using bolts that went through cast in-place metal plates and brackets. This method of construction had been started in the early 50's. Initially, it was called 'house of cards construction' but, for obvious reasons, that connotation was soon abandoned in favor of 'poured flat construction'.

* * * *

The industrial building to the south was the only structure nearby. At first glance, it appeared the only damage was the north side windows that were broken out and some ceiling tiles that had fallen down. However, city building inspectors determined it was unsound and it was scrapped off and rebuilt.

All of the goldfish in the front lily pond were belly up by the time anyone got around to looking. Once construction was completed, the lily pond in front was cleaned out and restocked, this time with koi.

* * * *

Ambulances were quick to arrive and everyone was temporarily patched up. The SWAT Team man Make had been talking to was the only officer hospitalized. It was later determined that he had a concussion in addition to the head wound, burns, and the dislocated shoulder.

Two men inside the mine survived. They had been following the wire and were a quarter of a mile back in the mine. They both had concussions and permanent hearing loss. During questioning after they had recuperated it was determined that Amir al-Mu'minin Caliph Ibrahim, and Ayman al-Zawahiri, had been at the first speaking table. The recorder that Make had carried out had captured their voices encouraging the incoming Arabs to join ISIL. Their remains were never identified. From what little information that survived the blast, authorities believed that there were between 200 and 250 terrorist/ISIL converts killed. Except for the two survivors, there were no whole bodies.

Twenty-one bodies were found with severely burned heads and shoulders. All of them were apparently facing the explosion but were back far enough that their bodies were intact. They were probably aware of the commotion at the front door because of the sound of the forklift hitting the door. All their faces were burned off.

The bodies of the three terrorists that Make had shot were found. But no bullets were recovered and no gun was located.

Three other bodies were found inside the mine. It was determined that they had also been killed before the blast. Their throats had been cut and their bodies had been moved to the North-West part of the mine a half mile from the front door. Their bodies had been leaned against four pallets of PETN. Fortunately it was far enough away from the blast center that it didn't enter into the explosion

Months later the two who had initially survived the blast died from pressure extremes, a damage similar to what some military personnel had experienced in Iraq.

The three Arabs that got out when Make did were the only ISIL members in the US to survive. Those three are now being detained in Guantanamo. They gave DHS some locations of ISIL group headquarters in Syria. More importantly, they were able to give the FBI information on the location of Muslim terrorist cells in the US.

Make never got to see the inside of the mine again. After a brief period of recuperation he went back to work for DHS.

Chapter 57

Saturday, August 25th

Make's house, North Scottsdale

Isabell called Laura and asked, "Is Make ok?"

"Yes. He's fine. Would you like to talk to him?"

"I'd like to talk to you first. That was quite an ordeal from what I can gather. Is he really Ok?'"

"Isabell, his only physical problem aside from some cuts and scratches is deafness in one ear. His ear drum is ruptured but the doctor said it and all his other abrasions would be healed in a couple of weeks. I think he is going to be ok physically but right now he is different. Last night before I went to bed he was sitting in a chair, talking to himself. He has never done that before. And he's a lot quieter than he was before yesterday. I don't know. He is different. You knew that Police Chief John Standard and Sargent Pizzametski were involved with Make too, didn't you?"

"I surmised that from what I had heard. Did either of them have any physical damage?"

"Minor cuts and bruises. That's all. They were all lucky they were in that military vehicle. It was designed to survive explosions."

"I'd like to talk to Make now."

"Isabell wants to talk to you." Make came into the room, took the phone from Laura's hand and said, "Isabell who?"

"Ah, that's the kind of Make Caston I know. How are you doing Make?"

"I think I'm ok. I can't hear on one side and I didn't sleep much last night but other than that".

"Make, we need to hold a press conference. The FBI is pushing for it. They want a chance to say that they weren't involved in the salt mine business. Which is fine with me. I, on the other hand, want to toot our horn and pat ourselves on the back. Are you up for something like that?"

"Sure, tell me when."

"Tomorrow morning. Eight o'clock at your place is ten o'clock here. We're sending you a list of questions you may be asked. Try to have answers for those. If they ask you to describe what happened, be brief and as truthful as you can without giving up any secrets. Tomorrow at seven a camera crew will show up at your house and set up. You'll have to look at a monitor to see what's going on at this end. This is not a live broadcast. It will be edited by our publicity team after its taped. You can watch yourself on the 6 o'clock news.

"Bright and early Monday I want you on a plane to DC. It is a requirement that you see Doctor Kansee. You can get here by noon. Your appointment is for one PM."

"Isabell, I don't need a shrink."

Isabell said, "Make, it's required. Just go."

* * * *

The news conference began with Isabell's opening statement, "For the past four days members of the Department of Homeland Security have been involved in the prevention of the distribution and the destructive detonation of approximately 3 1/2 tons of extremely potent chemical explosives. This project was first brought to our attention a month ago in Yemen. Our agents were able to stop production of the explosive material there and prevent any further on-site manufacture of it. Four days ago, another shipment of explosives was detected in Ft. Lauderdale, Florida. In order to gather information about the location of terrorist cells in the United States, we allowed the material to be shipped to an underground storage facility in Kansas City, Kansas. Unfortunately, the explosives were accidently set off by the group who had intended to use them. Mr. Make Caston is with us in Scottsdale, Arizona. He is the agent in charge and will answer your questions. Make Caston."

"Thank you Isabell. But why did you talk so long? You told them the whole story. There is really nothing more for me to say. But I will answer questions. Who's first?"

"Breanna Lloyd, *Kansas City Star*. The explosion in the salt mine was so terrific that most of the people in Kansas City, heard it. How was it that you escaped being killed?"

"Breanna, two of my associates and I were back in the salt mine about a third of a mile. A recording device had been set up back there to gather evidence. One of the two men is fluent in various dialects of Farsi and was advising us what was being said. While I was away from the recording area I became aware of three of the terrorists making their way toward the recording station. It was decided that the best thing we could do was run like hell. Keep in mind this is about a four minute run. I was carrying the recording device. As we approached the three terrorists, our man who spoke Farsi started shouting. I couldn't tell what he said but we kept running and he kept shouting. We passed the three terrorists then they started running and shouting too. Actually the three of them ran so fast they got out of the door ahead of us. Of course, as soon we were outside, the authorities had all of us face down on the dock while they decided who was who. We had been put in a SWAT team van across the road by the time the explosion occurred.

On the screen, Make could see three other reporters raise their hands. Make said, “The girl with the blue jacket.”

“Darlene Evers, *Washington Post*. So who ignited the explosion?”

“No one knows. The door was closed and all of those inside were killed. However we do know that the explosive material could be set off by coming in contact with the catalyst and they had both of those two materials in close proximity. That’s a dumb move, by the way. People who handle explosives are supposed to know you never keep the caps in the same box with the dynamite, or in this case, the catalyst with the PETN. Who’s next?”

“Charley Brock, *St Louis Post Dispatch*. You said PETN and compared it to dynamite. What’s PETN?”

“PETN’s is 35 ½, Dynamite is 8.”

Pause, “Oh.” A short pause. “Oh. I see.“ then “Oh shit.”

Make said, “The man wearing the throb.”

“Do you feel bad that you killed two hundred Muslims?”

“I didn’t kill them. They killed themselves. They screwed up. But all the people in the salt mine were terrorists. They had three and one half tons of explosive materials that they were dolling it out to men who were willing to die in order to kill Americans. And they were being given instructions on how to be the most effective killers. I didn’t kill them but I’m glad they’re dead. I’m glad they didn’t live long enough to do what they were being trained to do. The red head.”

“Jardeean Blunt, *National Reporter*. Some people say you are a national hero and you should get a medal for killing off all those fuckers.”

"Jardeean, I don't know anything about that. I haven't heard anything about that. And I reiterate, I didn't have anything to do with their blowing themselves up. The sequence was, we sneaked in the salt mine. We recorded data. They found out about us. We ran like hell. They blew themselves up. There's nothing heroic there."

Jardeean said, "Caston, that's just so much bullshit and everybody knows it. You didn't just do this salt mine thing. Last month you sank a whole shipload of those Muslim terrorist fuckers and their explosives too. The whole thing is at the bottom of the Arabian Sea. Now you are being considered for the Presidential Medal of Freedom."

Some of the material in the interview was not used. However, the next day. '60 Minutes' bought the segment and ran it in its entirety with bleeps.

Chapter 58

August 26th

Make's patio

Sunday afternoon, Darwin Kingston III called Make, "Hey Make. I've got some interesting news. I just received a call from Mr. Wolf, FBI. He called to say they arrested twenty one people, five of whom were working at the Ft Lauderdale container dock. And there are another twenty people in the Ft Lauderdale area that the FBI considers persons of interest. The FBI thinks that they've eradicated the Muslim terrorist cell in Florida."

Later that day Make, John, Pizz, Laura, and Ishe sat on the veranda during a delightful August evening. They were discussing the recent events over wine, except Ishe who drank lemonade.

"Do you know how lucky we were to get out alive?" Pizz said. "What happened to our plan to get out safely? We just got out because we were fast runners. Our original plan evaporated somehow. It seemed like once we got the scent we forgot everything else. We just went for it."

Make said, "I know I did. I was so excited about what we would find in there."

John said "I was captivated by the size of it. I think the whole thing was awesome."

"Another reason we got out when we did was because John started yelling while he was running. Were you speaking Farsi?" Asked Make?

"Yes a dialect of it.

"What exactly did you say?"

"Laura, I don't normally say things like this but, if you will excuse my language, I said 'Let's get the fuck out of here. This whole damn place is going to blow up in about a minute."

"Well it certainly went well in the long run. You men deserve a medal. You did a great service to the United States and if the details of what happened ever come out, you will be national heroes."

* * * *

After Laura went inside, Make said, "You know, whoever masterminded the whole process of the pickle's distribution in the salt mine, had a very smart plan. They were going to switch addresses on the pickles and on lawn chairs so we would think there was no rush in following the pickles when they finally started to move. They had us thinking it would be five or six weeks. But they had a way to get them to the salt mine in a couple of days using the Muslim girl and her big pickup and Mal Thorp's and his plane. They could have had several days to instruct their volunteers on the usage of the PETN and had a smooth operation all around. But instead, ISIL came along and took over the whole scheme. They made a junk yard out of the inside of the salt mine in order to get the place ready in a hurry. But that part of threatening to cut their heads off if they didn't join ISIL may have gotten them a few people who weren't as loyal to ISIL as they would have been, had they not been threatened."

"Yes," Pizz said. "And that whole process of moving the container at night and all that business about parking it in the woods and putting false sides on that short container to make it look like a box truck, that was all a dumb move on their part. I think that was a real screw up."

"Yes, possibly, but, as it turned out, Make getting Don's men to the salt mine in force, caused us to be sufficiently alerted that we sprang into action, as it were." John said. "Once we heard that there was some activity at the mine our basic plan of going to the salt mine was set. Don Park played a very important part in our being as successful as we were. My God that still gives me chills when I think about how close I was to death. When those two smelly bastards were going to cut my throat I was really terrified, Make. I wish you could have just shot them in the leg or the foot or someplace instead of their heads. Some place so they would have still been aware of what was going on. I would have liked to have had the chance to cut their throats. I would like to have them experience the same terror I had."

"John, I'm so sorry I got you into all that mess." Make said, "You too Pizz. I know it was terrible for both of you."

"Make, you didn't get us into 'all that mess' as you say. We volunteered. Actually, as I remembered it, both Pizz and I had to beg to get involved."

Pizz said, "Yeah, it was twice we had to beg. We kept saying we wanted to help you, and you just kept saying you were going to Kansas City and you never included us. It was always 'I' not 'we.'"

"Well anyway, you know how much I value your help. You guys are both outstanding. But changing the subject, as you said John, Don Park did an excellent job through all of this. He and his man were each a block away from the blast and didn't know all the details. He called earlier to say he had seen the '60 Minutes' segment about our Salt mine adventure. And, of course, he hadn't been aware of the part about the sinking of the *Golden Lie* in the Sea if Arabia. He had a lot of questions about both events so, in the end, I invited him out for a visit. He said he'd be here day after tomorrow and would stay a couple of days. We'll be able to get his perspective on some of the things that occurred outside the salt mine that we didn't have the opportunity to see. And also, Laura has invited Isabell Franks, my boss. She'll be here over the weekend too. Sooo, this is going to be a two day celebration and you two gentlemen will have to stay, of course. I have another favor to ask of you two. I would like to be able to give my boss, Isabell a complete and accurate report on all the recent happenings regarding the salt mine, the PETN and everything. Could we three get together and sit down and write it? I've learned that if all participants work together, we get a much more thorough perspective." Make remembered when he got together with Air Marshal Halt to write a report. It made his injured finger tingle.

John said, "Of course Make. Whenever it is convenient for you, I will be happy to."

Pizz said, "Sure Make. Me too."

Chapter 59

Monday August 27th 1:00 PM

The Shrink's office, DC

Thanks for seeing me on such short notice."

Doctor Kansee said, "Last time you were here about a love triangle-sort of. What's going on now?"

"A different thing actually. What we talked about before was, Sargent Pizzametski, my good friend, screwing my wife, Laura. It turns out that's not a problem. What my boss sent me here for last time was my concern that my job might include my killing someone, and I knew, or at least I thought I knew, that I couldn't do that. This is still confidential. Right?"

"Yes. No one but you and I will hear what is said here now."

"Ok…I killed three people. I shot them. It made me shaky for a few minutes but I don't feel any remorse. They were bad guys and they were going to kill my two friends, and I shot them bang, bang, bang. Just like that. But I haven't told my wife or anybody and the two of my friends who were involved in the whole thing haven't told anybody either. I'm concerned, because I don't know how long the secret will stay a secret?"

"So?"

"What do you mean, 'so'?"

"Well, what about it? There are people shooting people all the time and they don't come in here. Are you proud, are you concerned, are you going crazy, are you hurt, what?"

"I'm not any of those. I don't know. I guess I'm concerned about telling Laura. I told her once that I didn't kill people. Now I have to tell her that I did."

"No you don't. Don't tell her that. Just don't tell her."

"But we don't keep secrets from one another."

"That's very noble but, considering you're an agent, it's probably not going to happen. Anyway, it sounds like we have to go back and start at the beginning. Are you here because you killed some people or because you are concerned that you have to tell your wife that you killed three people?"

"I'm not as concerned about killing those three bastards as I am about telling Laura. That's the problem."

"She knows what kind of business you're in, doesn't she? And she knows about your trip to Yemen, doesn't she? So what you tell her is that you want to protect her. And to do that, you cannot tell her what you do or have done. Because, if she's ever called to testify, she will have nothing to tell. Make, that's the way your business has to be. Not just you personally but all of your people that work for or with you have to have that kind of agreement with their wives, friends, etc. It's necessary. You tell her I said so. Now, about killing three people. You said you are not concerned very much about that."

"Yeah, I know. But I guess I really am concerned. I've never stopped thinking about it since it happened. I didn't sleep very much that first night either. It's such a big deal for me. I've never shot anybody before. Well, that's not exactly true but I never killed anybody before."

"So now am I hearing that you have shot someone before?"

"Yeah but that was different."

"Let's start at the beginning again. When did you kill your first guy? Was it a man or a woman?"

"I didn't kill him. I just shot his foot. Like I said, that was different. He was a bad guy and I told him that if he didn't quit bringing illegal drugs up from Mexico, I would shoot him again."

"Did that work? Did he stop bringing illegal drugs up from Mexico?"

"You bet. He never did it again."

With a smile, Doctor Kansee said, "Maybe you've discovered a new method of controlling the illegal drug traffic."

"I know you think that's funny, but it did work."

"No, I'm not making fun of it. It sounds like you did a good thing. Now, let's get back to business. So you shot three more men and you did kill them. Is that right?"

"Yes."

"So how does it make you feel now?"

"Well, I'm glad it's over. And I certainly feel different."

"Different how?"

"Well, for one thing. I know now that what I was worried about won't be a problem. I can kill people."

"Tell me the details. Why did you shoot them?"

"We were back in this salt mine recording evidence. I went off looking around. I saw these three terrorists heading toward my friends and I followed them. When I got there, one of the terrorists was holding on to one of my friends who they had handcuffed. The other two were holding my other friend and one was threatening him with a knife. They were speaking Farsi so I couldn't tell what they were saying but it was obvious they were going to kill him, cut his throat, probably cut his head off. I shot the guy with the knife. Then I shot the guy who had been helping him. I shot them in the head, both of them. Their heads almost exploded. The third guy, the one holding the handcuffed friend of mine, got behind my friend in attempt to hide. I think when I shot those two guys I didn't even think about it. I just shot bang, bang. It was almost a reflex action."

"Did you shoot the third man?"

"Yes."

"But you didn't shoot him right away?"

"No, I asked my two friends if we needed him for anything and they both said no, so I shot him twice. He went down but he didn't die. He was just lying there twitching on the floor, so I shot him in the head."

"What did you think when you did that. When you shot him in the head?"

"I thought it was best that I killed him. I guess I thought he was a mean SOB and he should be killed. He was just one of the terrorists. He was one of them. They were all killers. If he had had a knife he would have cut my friend's throat. Actually he did have a knife. That's when I shot him--when he pulled the knife."

Doctor Kansee said, "Did you think the first two men you shot were just about to kill your friend? I mean did you think they were going to kill him immediately?"

"I didn't think at all. I had to shoot fast or my friend would have been cut in the next second--in less than a second."

"I want to hear more about the third guy. At first you didn't mention the knife then when you were explaining some of the details you said he pulled a knife. Do you know for sure he pulled a knife?"

There was a long pause while Make gave this question some thought. "I thought he did. I thought he had a knife. But now I'm not sure. Wait, yes I am sure. He had a knife. I remember the bullet hit his arm and it caused the knife to flip up in the air."

Doctor Kansee said, "So you shot the first two men. Then you ask your friends if they thought they needed the third man. Right?"

"Yes."

"Then when they said they didn't need him, he pulled the knife. Then you shot him twice, but not in the head. Then you shot him once again when he was down. Is that the way it was?"

"Yes, I think it was like that. But somehow that doesn't sound right."

"Here's what I've got so far. The first man you shot, you shot him in the foot. That's not a problem. You didn't kill him, and it stopped him from bringing in more illegal drugs. Of course, it looks bad, shooting him in the foot and you being a foot surgeon. Also, since you didn't kill him, he may file a law suit against you."

"No he won't. He's dead."

Another long pause, "Jesus Christ, Make, I'm assuming that, at some time later, you did not shoot him dead. Right?"

"Right. I never shot him again. Other people killed him"

"Ok let's go on to the last three. What I'm hearing is that the first two were killed almost as a reflex action. You had to kill them quickly or they would have murdered your friends. If I was the prosecuting attorney I wouldn't touch that one. What you did was what most people would do under the same circumstances. I don't think you have much concern about them."

"You're right." Make looked out the window. He wished this was over. Just for the briefest of moments he completely forgot about the salt mine.

"But the last guy, he was down and you shot him while he was down. Do you think he might have survived if you hadn't shot him that third time?"

"Very unlikely. The second shot was high. Probably hit his heart. They were hollow points. The first shot hit his lower arm. If that round had hit either the ulna or the radius, it would have expanded before it got to his chest cavity. I don't see any way he could have lived more than five minutes.

"Did you shoot him to put him out of his misery?"

"I think that was part of it. But I believe it was partly because he was part of a bunch of terrorists. It's just that he was such a bad guy that he should have been shot. And I shot him. And I'm glad."

"Let's talk about the last guy you shot. You shot him first to put him out of action. He was a dangerous person. He was a threat to you and your two friends. You shot him to protect yourself and your friends. That's what you should have done. You have the right of self-protection. Now, when he was down, flat on his back, probably in pain, you shot him in the head. That stopped his pain and you are glad you did that because you didn't want him to suffer. You don't like to see anyone suffer."

"Right."

"Also, he was a man that you knew to be a person dedicated to killing Americans. And you're glad you shot him for that reason too. Is that right?"

"Right."

"What about the gun you shot him with? Do you still have it?"

"No. Just as I was about to go out the door, one of the terrorists grabbed at me, he got hold of my fanny pack and pulled it off of me. The gun was in that."

"So he may still have it?"

"No he was killed in the explosion."

"Might the gun have survived the explosion? Or maybe there was enough of it to be identified?"

"No doctor. It was a big explosion. He was close to the center of it." Pause, "No, that's not right. He was close to the location of the explosion when he grabbed at me and got the fanny pack, but there was probably five minutes after that before the explosion occurred. He could have gotten quite a distance in that time and survived behind a pillar" Pause, "But wait a minute. That didn't happen. They didn't find any whole bodies except the three I shot, a group of three that were back from the blast and the two that later died. And there was no gun found. I'm ok Doctor!"

"Make, I think we've covered everything. Every shooting was done for good reason. There is no reason you should feel any guilt about the shootings. And there can be no legal repercussions. You are practically a national hero, and no lawyer would consider prosecuting you. Also there is no evidence remaining that a relative could use in a civil suit. You did the right thing and you are in the clear."

*   *   *   *

Two days later at the Caston household, Make, Laura, John, and Pizz sat outside. The grounds keeper had been tending the lily pond. Laura said, "I've heard the story twice now but I still don't know how you three got away from the three Arabs."

"Laura honey, because of my job and the kinds of things that are involved, there will have to be an area of non-disclosure. The shrink said that I had to tell you that and you had to understand that is the way it has to be. All guys in my line or work have to have that understanding with their friends and associates. John and Pizz, I know you are hearing this for the first time. I haven't told you about my visit to the shrink but that is what she said."

Laura said, "Make, what are you saying? Why did she say that?"

"It's because, if you are called to testify, you can feel perfectly safe in answering their questions. If you are asked something that you don't know the answer to, you can just say you don't know. I guess I should just simplify this by saying that I have told you all that I can tell you."

John said, "Laura, if I may interrupt this conversation, this is a common thing in police business. Everyone from the police captain down to the beat cop has to understand this. It is not a new thing; it is the way it has to be".

Make thought, *I killed three people in probably ten seconds. I probably killed the first two in two seconds. I blew their heads all to pieces! Christ, I gotta stop thinking about it.*

Laura said, "Ok guys, you've convinced me. I'm never going to find out what happened in the salt mine; I'm going inside and tidy up.

The grounds keeper was just finishing up for the day. He walked up to where Make was sitting and said, "I read your article about your adventures. Boy, you do some exciting things. Weren't you afraid of sharks?"

Make could see that Manuel has a magazine in his hand and a grin on his face. "What are you talking about Manuel?"

Without another word Manuel handed Make the magazine. It was opened to a page that had a picture of Make's head and shoulders and a hand with the "thumbs up" sign. In the background, to his right, could be seen the stern of a sinking ship. The aft end was protruding out of the water. Below were the words, "SUPER SPY" in wavy letters. The story was by Jardeean Blunt.

Below the picture and on the adjoining page was the story. Make looked at the first couple of lines then decided to read the story aloud. "Doctor Make Caston, super spy, has done some heroic stuff. Only three weeks ago he was in Yemen when he discovered that a group of fifty five terrorists were making TNT in a ship called the Golden Lay. Make was unable to suppress a smile and stopped reading for a moment...Doctor Caston waited until dark then swam through shark infested waters to the ship which was about ¼ mile out. He was able to get on board without being noticed and while the captain and crew were asleep, he backed the ship into deeper waters and sank her by opening the sea cocks. Just as the ship was about to go under, he got into an inflatable boat, inflated it, started the engine, and drove back to shore. He was able to bring one of the crew back with him who later confessed to the FBI that they had made about 3 ½ tons of the explosive which is still there laying In the bottom of the Mariana Trench, thirty four miles down. All this he did with the help of Al-kabob, a local policeman.

But wait, there's more. Just this last week, Doctor Caston and two other operatives discovered another, much bigger group of terrorist making explosives. This was being done in a salt mine. Salt is one of the chemicals used in making the gunpowder. The doctor was able to set off the explosive by using a long fuse. He lit the end closest to the door, got out, and locked the door behind him. He lay in a ditch so he could make sure the powder went off. He didn't want to be hit by flying debris.

During a private interview with Doctor Caston, he indicated there had been a much larger group of terrorists killed three months ago but, because of the government involvement, he was not able to give out as much detail. He did say however, that the number killed exceeded three hundred."

Guys, can you believe this?" They all three start chuckling. Them Make called Laura, "Honey, you've been wanting to know about some of the things we have done." They are still grinning when Laura came into the room and they watched in anticipation as she read about their adventures. But Laura didn't think it was funny, "That woman must be stupid."

John said, "Yes it is a dumb story, but, looking at it from a different prospective, she was able to come up with a full two page story when she had almost no information. And her timing was perfect. This came out a few days after Make's press conference; just the right amount of time to answer the questions that were on people's minds after they had seen the abbreviated story on the television."

Chapter 60

Thursday, August 30th 11 AM

Make's house, North Scottsdale

Make took her small suitcase and temporarily set it in the hallway. "Good morning Isabell. I'm very glad you came." Make said.

Isabell said, "What a beautiful view. Does that…I mean, are those just big glass panels that slide open?"

Make said, "Yes. I'll show you." Then he reached through the food portal and pushed a remote button. The panel farthest to the right started moving left, then the next, and the next. "I'll close them in a couple of hours so it won't get too hot in here. Noon temperature will probably be in the ninety's and it may rain. Come on in the great room. Isabell, this is John Standard, Police Chief of Sana'a, Yemen."

"It's nice to meet you John. Make has told me of some of your exploits."

Without any warning John started crying. He was embarrassed but was not able to hide the tears. Then, "I'm so sorry Isabell. It is really very nice to meet you. It's just that I was so terrified in that salt mine that suddenly I remembered how near I was to a horrible death and I just couldn't control myself. Please forgive me for popping off like that."

"Oh, of course John. I'm very sorry that you had such trauma. I have not as yet heard the details of that adventure." Isabell glanced at Make with a look that said, 'When are you going to get me that fucking report'?

"Isabell, both John and Sargent Pizzametski narrowly escaped death. It was very traumatizing for both of them and me too. My report is finished, thanks to the help from both John and Pizz, and there is a copy on your bed. Probably you should wait until morning. It contains some real heavy stuff."

Laura, who had been watching from the kitchen area, came to the front hallway with her hand extended, "It's nice to meet you at last, Isabell."

Then Pizz shook hands with Isabell, "Nice to see you again Isabell."

"Make." Isabell said, "I met Air Marshal Halt. You remember, she's the one that you assisted in handling that couple of Savings and Loan bandits."

"Yes I remember her but I'm surprised she was on the same flight. I would have thought those marshals would have been rotated so that frequent flyers wouldn't recognize them."

"Well, she just looked like anyone else to me. Just before deplaning, one of the flight attendants said I had a phone call and that I should follow her. When we were near the cabin, she closed the curtain and left. Then Air Marshal Halt, who had been standing there, introduced herself. She'd seen my name on the passenger list. She thanked me for volunteering your services and said you were an exceptional man."

Christ. But, at least, she thought I was exceptional. Of course, maybe she thought I was exceptionally bad.

Laura said, "Isabell. Would you like something to drink? You just got off of a plane. Would you like to rest or freshen up?"

"I would like something to drink. What have you got? If that is lemonade that the Sargent is drinking, I'd like that."

“You got it.” As Laura poured a glass of ice cold lemonade for Isabell, she said, “So Isabell, tell us, how was your birthday party with the President. Was it exciting, dull, or what?”

“That’s interesting that you ask that question because it was a lot of things. It started out exciting, of course, because I’ve never had a birthday dinner in the White House before, but then it headed toward ‘dull’ because he wanted to talk business. He’s very goal directed. He has a lot of trouble letting go of his job. I finally suggested that since there was nothing critical happening, he could get all the details during the Monday morning report. Then, finally, he started getting quite friendly.”

At this part of her conversation, Make interrupted, “How friendly did he get Isabell?”

Laura said, “Make, stop it. Please continue Isabell.”

“It’s ok Laura. I value Make’s ‘telling it like it is’ approach because, as it turns out, that’s what I was going to say. I felt that it was a little too friendly for the first date. So I kind of tried to slow that down a bit. But he’s a nice man and we are both living alone so the way we left it was that we were going to do this again. Now it is up to him. We’ll see what happens.”

Later, Make said, “You will have to wait to meet Ishe, Mal Thorpe’s twin brother. He is in town right now shopping. He’s turned out to be a clothes horse. You’ll be impressed.”

Isabell said, “By that, I assume you’ve decided he’s innocent of any part of the manufacturing of the explosives in Yemen.”

After a pause, John said, “We’ve almost decided that. We have discussed it amongst ourselves and we have heard Ishe’s side of it too. If he isn’t completely innocent he is close to it. And I doubt that any prosecutor would go up against him. His brother Mal is dead and all the other evidence is at the bottom of the Arabian

Sea. The only problem I have with his story is, I just can't imagine him not knowing what they were making on that ship and what the intended purpose was. One thing in his favor was, Ishe doesn't speak Farsi. And there were only three people on his ship that Ishe could talk to; the chemist, the engineer, and the helmsman. Ishe did all his own navigation so any conversation he would have with the helmsman would be to give directions. Ishe said, the helmsman didn't speak Farsi. And Ishe said he never talked to the chemist. Ishe's certainly no chemist. And when he communicated with the engineer, it was by way of the ship's telegraph. So he didn't have much of an opportunity to get involved. Since Ishe doesn't speak the language, It is just possible that he didn't comprehend a thing that he heard during the whole time those men were aboard the *Golden Lie*. In any event he has seemed right to me. At least for the short time I've known him."

Laura said, "I think that's the way I feel about him too. When we told him that his brother, Mal, was dead, he showed a little surprise at first, then he said he wasn't surprised because Mal was so vicious, so crooked. Then he expressed a great deal of relief and said he felt like he could start life anew." As Laura returned to the kitchen she said, "Guys, sit down and relax. I am going to fix us a little lunch. Make, when do you think Don Park will be here?"

Don Park, the Kansas City PI, arrived about 4 PM. He had been driving around the valley, "Just looking at the sights."

It was after six when Ishe arrived. After the introductions, Ishe brought out his new wardrobe. There were lots of compliments. It was true; Ishe did have good taste in clothing. Remembering Ishe in Yemen, John and Make were surprised at how nice he looked He appeared to be a different man.

By 8:30 PM Ishe and Isabell had gone to bed, Laura was in the kitchen making dessert. She baked an angel food cake and later served it with crushed strawberries and real whipped cream. While she was cooking, John, Make, Don and Pizz were reliving the events in the salt mine for the fourth or fifth time. Don was very interested in what happened to Pizz, Make, and John inside the mine and how they got out. When Make told Don T Park what the shrink had said, it was old news to John and Pizz. But they all discussed it again for Don's benefit.

Later, after Don had retired, the whole thing was again relived. But John, Pizz, and Make could never agree whether or not the third terrorist had a knife.

Much later, after the shortcake, they finally reach a conclusion, "Hey, we're pretty good at this."

After lights out, Make and Laura were laying face to face. Laura was nearly asleep when Make said, "Laura…honey, there is something I should tell you."…

The end

Epilogue

John Standard liked the southwest so much that he became a US citizen. Because of the help he gave DHS in the salt mine and because his English was better than 82% of the US population, he was given some help with his citizenship program and became a US citizen in 10 months. He got a job with the Yuma PD as a detective and was made chief detective in 8 months.

Make was rewarded for his work with terrorism and given permanent status as head of the securities section of DHS, a job he liked best, even better than medicine. Besides, it looks bad, shooting people in the foot when you are a foot doctor.

Doctor Pizzametski, renowned, experienced authority on international terrorism is working on his book, some of which is based on his dissertation in his Doctorate program, but a lot more is based on his experience in the pickle business. He teaches a class on counter terrorism at Phoenix College and he frequently has sex with Laura Caston when Make is out of town.

Ishe was awarded $4.6 million from his Marine insurance for vessel and cargo loss. He hired an engineering student from UNM, Albuquerque, and together they designed a hospital bed that, with the push of a button, transformed into a wheel chair with the patient still in it. Ishe formed a manufacturing company and started making and selling them. After he went public, Google bought his company for $39.95 million. With the IPO's the engineering student had, he was able to donate one million dollars to UNM toward a new Biomechanical Engineering lab.

Now Ishe is working on a compressed gas ion storage battery that will be able to store more electrical energy than 700 NMH batteries yet weighs only 85 pounds. They are currently talking with Tesla.

Laura was a happy housewife taking care of her men--until she turned 36. That's when she found she was pregnant.

The salt mine was donated to Wyandotte County, Kansas by The Al-Ihirsnah Islamic Center thus defraying taxes on something they wish they had never been involved with. The county, always in need of money, shored up the entrance and converted the mine into a Muslim terrorism museum. They charge $8.00 plus tax admission.

"10-27-16"

Done "1-10-17"